THE MERRY MONARCH'S WIFE

THE MERRY
MONARCH'S WIFE

The Story of
CATHERINE *of* BRAGANZA

JEAN PLAIDY

Previously published as
THE PLEASURES OF LOVE

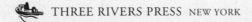 THREE RIVERS PRESS NEW YORK

Published in the United States by Three Rivers Press, an imprint of the Crown Publishing Group, a division of Random House, Inc., New York.

www.crownpublishing.com

Three Rivers Press and the Tugboat design are registered trademarks of Random House, Inc.

Originally published as *The Pleasures of Love: The Story of Catherine of Braganza* in hardcover in Great Britain by Robert Hale Limited, London, in 1991, and in the United States by G. P. Putnam's Sons, New York, in 1992.

Library of Congress Cataloging-in-Publication Data

Plaidy, Jean, 1906–1993.
[Pleasures of love]
The merry monarch's wife: the story of Catherine of Braganza / Jean Plaidy.
Previously published as The Pleasures of Love.
Includes bibliographical references.
1. Catherine, of Braganza, Queen, consort of Charles II, King of England, 1638–1705—Fiction. 2. Great Britain—History—Charles II, 1660–1685—Fiction.
3. Queens—Great Britain—Fiction. I. Title.
PR6015.I3P57 2008
823'.914—dc22   2007027959

ISBN 978-0-307-34617-9

Printed in the United States of America

Design by Karen Minster

10 9 8 7 6 5 4 3 2

First Three Rivers Press Paperback Edition

Contents

But when I consider the truth of her heart
Such an innocent passion, so kind, without art
I fear I have wronged her, and hope she may be
So full of true love to be jealous of me
O, then 'tis I think no joys are above
The pleasures of Love.

CHARLES II

THE MERRY
MONARCH'S WIFE

PRELUDE

MY LIFE WILL END WHERE IT BEGAN, FOR IN THE YEAR 1692 I left England where I had gone some thirty years before as a bride to the most romantic prince in Europe.

I smile now to consider how ill-equipped I was for such a position, and when I look back I say to myself, "If I had done this . . . ," "If I had not done that . . . how much happier my life would have been." But then, although I was not very young—I was twenty-four, which is a mature age for a princess to embark on marriage—I was quite innocent of the world and had hardly ever strayed from the walls of the convent where I had received my education, or the precincts of the royal palace. I had been brought up between the nuns and my mother with the strictest rules on moral rectitude, to be plunged into what was known as one of the most licentious courts in Europe. Naturally there was much which I could not understand and could not accept. I was lost and bewildered and desperately unhappy.

But when I came back to Portugal and my brother, Don Pedro, the King, gave me the Quinta de Alcantara, one of his summer palaces, where I lived in comfort, his wife, Queen Maria Sophia, became my good friend, and I was fêted by the people wherever I went. They could not forget that, by my alliance with England, I had helped to free them from the Spanish yoke.

Everywhere I went, I was assured of their gratitude and that was heart-warming.

When my health worsened, my brother sent me to the palace of Santa Martha and then to Belem where I have stayed. He and his Queen show great concern for me.

It was a great joy to visit the Villa Viçosa, called by some the Paradise of Portugal, where I was born and spent the first two years of my life in those idyllic surroundings. And as I wandered through those leafy glades, I thought of that day—my second birthday—which could be said to be the beginning of all that followed, for if my father had taken a different decision on that day, it is unlikely that I should have gone to England.

It is interesting to contemplate what my fate would have been; and there, in the Villa Viçosa, I decided to look back on it all, to ask myself how much my actions had played their part in that drama— which was sometimes a comedy, as I suppose all life is. I want to see it all clearly—the hopes, the dreams, the eager expectations and, after the bitter revelation, the joys, the pleasure, the pain and the passion: I want to live it all again in my thoughts.

There are days when I must take to my bed. I am plagued with illness and at such times my great solace is to escape into memory, to see again that glittering court; the elegant costumes of the men; the curled periwigs, the lace-edged breeches; the cloaks trimmed with gold cord; the feather hats; all proclaiming the joy to escape from Cromwellian puritan rule to royal splendour. And at the centre of it all, the King himself: merry, witty, gracious, rarely roused to anger and with a charm that exceeded handsome looks. It was small wonder that he fitted my dreams of him.

I had been quite young when I had heard that there was a possibility of his becoming my husband, and in the years that followed, in my thoughts, he became a romantic ideal. I wanted to hear all about him: his exile, his valiant attempts to regain the crown snatched from his murdered father. I loved him in the beginning, and for a time I believed he loved me too. He did in a way, but I had to learn that he was capable of loving many women at the same time. In fact, there were two deep abiding passions in his life: women, and, as I had heard him say, "never to go wandering again."

I was feeling emotional after my visit to the Villa Viçosa. Donna Inez Antonia de Tavora, one of my favorite ladies-in-waiting, was with me. She said I was tired and she would prepare me for my bed.

My thoughts were far away in the past and I did not speak for a moment.

"I am tired, yes," I said, "but not in the mood for sleep. I wish to amuse myself by writing. Bring my materials to me, Inez, please."

If she were surprised she gave no sign.

She did as I commanded and I began.

THE LONG BETROTHAL

I REMEMBER THE DAY CLEARLY, FOR IT WAS THE BEGINNING.
It was then that I realized that the dream which had haunted me so
long could come true.

We were working on an altar cloth—my ladies and I—and it was
a task which had occupied us for weeks; the work was detailed and
delicate and while we stitched one of us would play some musical in-
strument and we would sometimes sing together; at other times, one
of the party would read aloud from some holy book. A great deal of
our time was spent thus.

Presiding over us were those two ladies who were never far from
me, for they had been specially selected by my mother to guard me.
One was Donna Maria de Portugal, the Countess of Penalva; the
other Donna Elvira de Vilpena, the Countess of Pontevel. They were
much aware of their dignity and determined to do their duty by
watching over me.

I was often exasperated by this, but I was generally of a docile disposition. I had led a very sheltered life and had scarcely been outside
the palace walls or those of the convent where I had been educated;
and I was inclined to accept my fate with a certain placidity.

Donna Maria was the senior of the two. She was the sister of Don
Francisco de Mello, of whom my mother thought very highly. He was
not only my godfather but he held a very important post, Ambassador to England.

England had always been held in great respect by my mother, even
when the English murdered their King and set up a Commonwealth.
Strong-minded, practical woman though she was, she had a strange pre-
monition about that country, which was alien to her nature, for she was
in all other matters firmly realistic; but where England was concerned
she allowed her wishes to get the better of her usually logical reasoning.

As we sat there on that sunny afternoon, she came into the room. I knew at once that something important had happened. She rarely visited us unexpectedly. If she wished to speak to us she would send for us, and anything concerning us was generally of small consequence compared with matters of state with which she was usually concerned.

She was Regent of Portugal because my brother Alfonso was not suitable to be King. She had been in that position since my father's death four years before, and though Alfonso was no longer a boy—he must have been seventeen at this time—she still considered him unfit to take on the burden of state; and she continued to rule.

None in royal circles questioned my mother—not even my father had done that; she had always been actively involved in state matters, so we knew something of great moment must have brought her to us on this afternoon.

We all rose and curtsied as she entered, and my mother turned to the ladies, which was a sign that meant they were to leave us.

"Donna Maria, Donna Elvira, you may remain," she said.

A smile of satisfaction spread over Donna Maria's face. She was delighted when her special place in the household was acknowledged. She immediately placed her chair for my mother and took another herself.

My mother acknowledged the service with a nod and, sitting, said: "I have news. The best of news. Dispatches have arrived from England."

Donna Maria nodded her head to remind us all that they would have come from her shrewd and clever brother Don Francisco.

My mother's eyes were on me. "The King of England has been recalled to his country. I have had several account of the scenes there in the English capital. It would seem that they are a good augury for the future."

Donna Maria said: "I believe, Your Highness, the people there must have been heartily tired of the Puritan rule."

"It would appear so," said my mother, smiling. I, who knew her so well, could see that she was so delighted by the turn of events that she had dispensed with some of her dignity and was not averse to a little light conversation.

"My envoys tell me that the bells are ringing all over the capital and the people are in the streets dancing and making merry, as they did in the old days before Oliver Cromwell came to put a stop to their gaiety."

My mother paused. I could imagine she was thinking that that much merriment was not entirely to be praised, and that the people would be better engaged in attending church to give thanks to God for the return of the King.

"How glad they must be to have him back!" I said.

"Not more than he is to be there, I'll swear," said Donna Elvira.

"It is certain that the King is pleased to come back to his country," said my mother. "He is now a king not merely in name. England will return to its greatness."

"I wonder what all those Roundheads are thinking now," said Donna Elvira.

"There will be some to mourn and regret, I doubt not," replied my mother, "but there will be many to rejoice—and none more than the King!" She was looking at me. "This is a very important day for us. As you know, the English have been good friends to this country. I have always wanted to strengthen the alliance between us. I am re-calling Don Francisco. I have much to discuss with him."

Donna Maria was slowly nodding her head again.

"We must all watch events in England," went on my mother. "I believe this to be a time of great importance, not only to England but to Portugal."

"Amen," said Donna Maria.

"Great events could come out of the restoration of King Charles," continued my mother. She was smiling at me. "We must be prepared. As yet . . . perhaps it is early. But . . . we shall talk of this later."

I knew why she was recalling Don Francisco. Long ago, I had been suggested as a wife for Prince Charles—as he had been at that time. It was when I was not quite seven years old and he was fourteen. That had been the beginning of my dreams.

The matter had been set aside then. How could it have been oth-erwise with the country in turmoil? And then his father had been murdered, and he became an exile, wandering through Europe from court to court, wherever he could find some refuge. The years had passed and I was at this time twenty-two years of age. He was now thirty and it was time he married.

And through the years my mother had waited. She had some pre-monition and she had refused all offers for my hand. What she wanted was an alliance with England. She had waited all these years. It might have been too late for me to marry at all; it was getting near to that time now. But she had always believed that the King would re-cover his throne and, when he was safely there, she would set about pursuing her dream.

No wonder she was delighted; no wonder she forgot her royal dig-nity and came to the sewing room to chat with us.

This was a great day. It was the beginning.

So clearly I remember that day: the wonderment in Donna Elvira's face, the pride in Donna Maria's, because she believed her wonderful brother would play a big part in bringing this about. There was my mother's exultation, and my own excitement because the dream which had never really left me could now be coming true.

EVERYTHING THAT HAPPENED really began on that important day, some twenty years before, on the second anniversary of my birth.

I had heard so much of that occasion from Donna Maria and Donna Elvira—and not only those two—that I am not sure whether I remember or imagine I do. It was such an important day, for if my father had taken a different decision then, it is almost certain that I should never have gone to England.

When I visited the Villa Viçosa, I believed I remembered it, for it was so easy to visualize the idyllic life we led there. I know my father was very happy there, for he had often told me so; and I shall never forget the sadness, the nostalgia in his eyes when he spoke of it. He was so contented there . . . in obscurity . . . in that quiet paradise, with his beloved wife, whom he greatly revered, his two little boys and his two-year-old daughter. The little boys, alas, were to die before they grew up, but there was no shadow over his life at that time.

He died when I was eighteen, so I had time to know him well. He was a gentle and kindly man who valued peace and the life he shared with his family. I understand what his feelings were on that significant day.

Guests had gathered to celebrate my birthday. My arrival into the world had been greeted with great joy. There was none of that disappointment so often felt in royal circles because a child proves to be a girl and not a boy. Why should there have been? They already had their two boys. How were they to know then that they were going to lose them?

Donna Maria liked to tell me about it, so I heard often of the joy at the Villa Viçosa when I was born.

"There was rejoicing throughout the palace . . . the whole country, in fact . . . for although your father lived the life of a country gentleman, it was not forgotten that he was the Duke of Braganza, and it was hoped that one day he would be in his rightful place on the throne of Portugal, and our country would no longer be the vassal of the hated Spaniards. Only the best was good enough for the Duke's daughter, and, as you know, your godfather was the great nobleman Don Francisco de Mello, the Marquis of Ferreira."

"Who," I never forgot to say at this point, "is your brother."

"That is so, my child. We are a highly respected family, and have always been the good friends of the House of Braganza, which is one of the reasons why your mother has entrusted you to my care."

"I know, dear Donna Maria."

And she would go on: "As you were born on St. Catherine's Day, it seems right and proper that you should be named after the saint."

My first two years had been spent at the Villa Viçosa in the province of Alemtejo, and very happy they must have been until that fateful day.

According to Donna Maria, from all over the country, people had come to celebrate my birthday.

"It was not only that," added Donna Maria, anxious as ever that I should not grow up with an inflated idea of my importance. "The occasion was used to express the people's loyalty to the Duke of Braganza, and to remind him that they were aware that, although he was living as a country gentleman, they did not forget that he was the rightful King of Portugal."

Our country had been a vassal state of Spain for sixty years. The Portuguese had lived through troublous times since the death of Henry, the Cardinal King, who had died before he named his successor. Consequently there were several claimants to the throne. My great-grandmother, the Duchess of Braganza, was in the direct line and considered herself the rightful heiress, but she was a woman.

Philip of Spain laid claim to the throne. He was perhaps the most powerful ruler in Europe, and he was successful, which was a sad day for Portugal; and the people never ceased to chafe against the invader.

So . . . now my father, grandson of Donna Maria, Duchess of Braganza, was in truth the King of Portugal.

That was the state of affairs on that November day when the celebrations of my second birthday were in progress. There was great joy and merriment until Don Gaspar Cortigno arrived, with his special mission which was to change our lives.

Knowing my father as I did, I understood his feelings on that day. He would be enjoying the merry company, delighting in his family, revelling in the serenity and peace of the Villa Viçosa with his loved ones around him. He was not an ambitious man.

Gaspar Cortigno had been selected for this mission. He must have been an eloquent man and a fervent patriot. I could imagine his words. "The time has come for you to do your duty to your people, Your Highness. The throne could be yours for the taking. The country is behind you. We want you to leave this place and come to Lisbon. We have the men. We have the means. The time has come for Portugal to be free."

And my father's dismayed response, what had that been? At first, I was sure, he would have vehemently refused. Others had tried and failed. He wanted to cling to his pleasant life. He had large estates; he was wealthy; he did not seek to rule; he only wanted to live in peace with his family; he had little stomach for battle; blood would be shed, lives would be lost.

But there was my mother. She was different from her husband.

She was the daughter of the Duke of Medina Sidonia; she was proud; she had decided views of right and wrong; and she was ambitious for her family. She believed that my father's rightful place was on the throne.

Gaspar Cortigno's words made a deep impression on her. The people of Portugal were asking my father to rise against the Spaniards and they were ready to stand beside him.

I can imagine my father's dismay when she joined her pleas with those of Gaspar Cortigno.

"Your father said he could not do it," said Donna Maria. "He said it would plunge the country into war. It was better to let life go on as it was. But there was one thing which persuaded him to change his mind." She looked at me proudly. "It was because of you."

I was delighted to think that I was so important—at least had been on this occasion.

"There you were, in your birthday gown. You looked . . . er . . . very pleasant. Your mother took you by the hand, and she said to your father: 'Could you deny this child her due? Could she grow up the daughter of a mere duke when she is indeed the daughter of a king? It is your duty, if for no other reason than for the sake of this child . . . and your boys.' After that your father gave way. What could he do? If he would not act for himself, he must for his family."

I knew that Donna Maria's version was near the truth because I had heard the story from other sources, and I think I remember my father's serious look as he took me into his arms, holding me tightly and saying: "This must be."

And soon after that he left the Villa Viçosa and went to live in Lisbon, where my father was proclaimed King Juan IV of Portugal.

I WAS FIVE YEARS OLD when the next momentous event occurred. Both my little brothers were dead. I did remember the sorrowful atmosphere throughout the palace when it happened—one death following quickly on another.

My mother shut herself in her apartments and appeared rarely, and when she did her grief was apparent; but she was not of a nature to flaunt her sorrow and soon she was emerging to dominate us all.

I was delighted to see her with us again. I think she had a special fondness for me. She had loved her boys, but they had always been delicate and, although she had never failed in her tenderness toward them, she had a natural distaste for weakness of any kind. I was a healthy girl and she delighted in me.

I realized that something was happening when I heard Donna Maria and Donna Elvira whispering together.

"Can it be true?" murmured Elvira.

"What a blessing it would be . . . after the tragedy."

"Do not speak of that. It is too grievous . . . even now. But if this should be . . ."

"I shall pray for it."

"And so shall I."

I was not sure of what they were speaking, but I sensed there was some secrecy about it, so I refrained from asking my mother.

We had moved to the palace at Sintra and I saw little of my father. He was always away, driving the Spaniards out of Portugal, I supposed. He was known as King Don Juan, and my mother was very anxious that everyone should be aware of the family's rank.

She was angry because my father was not generally recognized as King outside Portugal. The Pope, terrified of the Spaniards, had refused to acknowledge the title. There were only two countries who did. France was one, England the other. Both of these countries had reason to hate the Spaniards.

I discovered that my mother did not always trust the French, but she did have special feelings of friendship toward the English.

I had heard a great deal of talk about the troubles in England. It would appear they were in a worse state than Portugal. Their King was fighting his own Parliamant and there was civil war in that land. We, at least, were only trying to free ourselves from the usurper, and the Portuguese nation stood firmly together, whereas Englishmen were fighting Englishmen.

Reluctant as my father had been to take up arms, he had had several successes. This was encouraging, but not decisive; there was great rejoicing throughout the country at every success and hopes were high.

"It is Donna Luiza who is behind the King," I heard Donna Maria say to Donna Elvira; and they nodded in agreement.

"The day will come," said Donna Maria prophetically, "when King Don Juan with Donna Luiza will free this country absolutely."

I wondered when that time would come and whether we should then go back to the Villa Viçosa.

Then the long-awaited event took place. My mother retired to her bedchamber and a hushed atmosphere pervaded the house. Everyone was waiting.

It had happened. There was rejoicing throughout the palace.

Later I was taken to see my new brother Alfonso in his cradle.

→>—<←

I WAS NEARLY SEVEN YEARS OLD when I first heard of Prince Charles.

My father's success had continued, and although to the Spaniards he was still the Duke of Braganza, to the English he was King Juan of Portugal, which was no longer the subject state it had been before that important day at Villa Viçosa.

My mother sent for me, and I could see at once from her demeanor that she was about to talk of a very serious matter.

She was gentle but tender toward me as always, which gave me a feeling of warm comfort, for she was inclined to be severe when dealing with most people.

"Catherine, come here," she said, and when I stood before her, she kissed me on both cheeks.

"You are growing up," she went on. "Have you ever thought that one day you might marry?"

"I do not want to leave you," I said in alarm.

She smiled. "Certainly you do not. But it will not be for some time. Your father and I have been talking of your future, and, as you know, it is the duty of us all to consider our country in every way."

I was beginning to feel uneasy. She saw that and went on quickly: "There is no need to be afraid. Your father and I have decided that you should know now what is happening, as it concerns you. We did not want you suddenly to be presented with a situation of this nature . . . as has happened to so many. You know something of the state of our country, and that we are trying to rid ourselves completely of Spanish tyranny. You know of the great work your father has done and that we are succeeding in our task. Your father is the rightful King of Portugal, and we are determined that soon every state shall recognize him as such. The English have always been good friends to us. They are a more powerful nation that we are . . . one of the most powerful in Europe. But the King is now engaged in a war with his Parliament, who are trying to impose their will on the people. They will not succeed. The King has a son—more than one—but it is the eldest in whom we are interested—Charles, Prince of Wales. It is your father's wish, and mine, that you shall marry him."

"Go to England?" I cried.

"It would not be for some time. I am just telling you that your father has sent our ambassador with a suggestion that this might be. They are a great nation, but at war. We are a small one in semi-captivity. These matters depend on negotiations. Your father is in a position to bestow a good dowry on you and the King of England will need money to conduct his war."

"So because of the money . . ."

"No, because you are the daughter of a king and young Charles is the son of one. We must accept these things as they are. It is the rulers who decide them. To marry a man who will one day be a king is a great destiny and one must be prepared for it."

"I should like to know something about this prince."

"He is fourteen years old—a charming boy, so I have heard."

"That seems very old," I ventured.

"You think so because you are younger. As you grow up, these seven years will seem nothing. It is better for a husband to be older than his wife. Charles is clever and charming, a loyal son and he will be a good husband." My mother drew me to her. "You must not be anxious," she went on. "It will not be for a long time, but I tell you now so that you will be prepared when the time comes. So far this is only a suggestion. With Oliver Cromwell at his heels, the King may have many matters with which to concern himself as well as the marriage of his son."

It proved to be that he had, for there was no enthusiastic response brought back by my father's ambassador. I learned from little scraps of gossip that my religion was a handicap. The King of England had had enough trouble through marrying a Catholic wife. He did not want his son to fall into the same trap.

That startled me. Our religion was of the utmost importance to us and I had always believed that anyone not of the Catholic faith was doomed.

I asked my mother about the King of England's objection to our religion.

"Where do you hear such things?" she demanded.

I did not way to betray anyone, so I said vaguely: "Oh, it must have been something I heard someone say . . ."

"Who has been talking?"

"Oh . . . several . . . Not talking to me but to each other. I cannot remember who . . . but there was a good deal of talk about the proposed marriage."

She was thoughtful for a moment, then she said: "The people of England have rejected the true faith. It happened a long time ago after Queen Mary died and Queen Elizabeth came to the throne. And after Elizabeth there came the Stuarts."

"But if they are not of the true faith . . ."

"First," she said, cutting me short, "we have to think of an alliance which would bring honour to you and to our country."

"But . . ."

"My dear child, you are too young to concern yourself with such matters which can safely be left to your father and to me."

"But if Prince Charles is a Protestant . . . a heretic . . ."

"The Prince of Wales must be brought up in the religion of the country he will one day rule."

"Then how . . . ?"

She smiled secretively and whispered: "Who knows? If he had the right wife . . ."

"But the King himself married a Catholic . . . and . . ."

Again I was interrupted. "How knowledgeable you have become! That pleases me. You must learn what is going on. King Charles of England married the daughter of the great King Henri of Navarre who became the fourth Henri of France. It was a match of great benefit to both France and England. King Henri was a Huguenot at one time and he became a Catholic. Sometimes these matters are necessary. Who knows what might happen?"

"Prince Charles's mother did not make his father a Catholic."

"Perhaps she was not clever enough. If the Prince married a good Catholic wife, who knows what influence she might have on him . . ."

"You mean, I might lead him to the Truth?"

"Hush, my child. You must not say such things. You must learn to keep such matters to yourself. What people in our position say is often repeated. We must be careful at all times . . . even little girls. It is different with humbler folk. We do not know what the future holds, but I believe that one day you are going to be Queen of England, and when you are, you will do your duty to God and your country."

"Oh yes," I said fervently, "I will."

I had a mission now. Not only was I going to marry Prince Charles, but I was going to save his soul.

I set about discovering all I could about him. It was not much. I did hear that he was taller than most boys of his age; he was dark and somewhat swarthy, not handsome, but of great charm. He bore a strong resemblance to his maternal grandfather, the great Henri, who had been known in France as the Evergreen Gallant because he had loved so many women.

I was constantly thinking of Charles.

Even when the overtures of our ambassador came to nothing, and there was no more talk of a possible marriage, he remained in my mind.

MY MOTHER WAS DETERMINED that I should have the best education possible, and that it should be presided over by herself; and I was sent to the convent of her choosing.

The Mother Superior of the chosen one received me very graciously and I was soon absorbed in the rules of the establishment.

It was a change from life in royal palaces. Lessons and prayers took up the greater part of my time. My actions were regulated by the bells which summoned us to our duties throughout the day. I joined the nuns in meals and religious duties and longed to be like them; it was a quiet and peaceful life if one obeyed the rules, and as I was of a docile nature I fitted in with comparative ease.

I learned a great deal about the saints, their endurance, their unshakeable faith and the sacrifices they made for their religion. I prayed with especial fervor for those who sinned against the Church, for I was thinking of Charles who, for no fault of his own, was in danger of losing his soul; and even greater than my desire to be a saint was my longing to save him.

I grew to love the hushed and holy atmosphere of the convent. I never strayed from its walls, but took exercise in the gardens which were tended by the nuns and in which was produced most of the food on which we lived.

It was a life of peace lived in the service of God. There was little excitement but I realized it had compensations for those who shared it. The nuns seemed content and at peace with the world. They believed that they were doing their duty on Earth and that they would in due course go to glory in Heaven.

I was different. I had a duty to perform. I had to marry for the good of my country and save Charles from eternal damnation. I had to think beyond the convent. But in the meantime I could enjoy the serene life.

I had a new brother. My parents were delighted and there had been great celebrations when Pedro was born. Alfonso was then five years old.

During my years at the convent I paid periodical visits to the royal palaces when my mother would question me closely about convent life. She was satisfied with my progress and the strong religious feelings which were being inspired in me.

I discovered that my elder brother Alfonso gave some cause for anxiety. He was a wayward child, given to tantrums, and he was not very pleased with the arrival of a brother.

It was during my visits to the palace that I was able to learn something of what was going on in the world. I was very eager to hear what was happening in England, and grieved to discover that the situation had not improved there. This news, because of our friendship with England, caused disquiet throughout Portugal.

Donna Maria and Donna Elvira knew of my interest in England, although they believed that those plans for my marriage to the Prince of Wales had long been set aside. It was just another of those suggested marriages between royal houses which came to nothing. It was happening all the time.

Donna Maria said one day: "It would seem as though this is the end of the monarchy in England."

"How can that be possible?" I cried.

"You have seen what can happen in your own country. Kings can be dethroned."

"Unless there is a miracle . . . this seems possible," said Donna Elvira.

"Then there must be a miracle," I said. "Or Prince Charles will not be King."

"I think his father will not be King for long," said Donna Maria. "Oliver Cromwell is going to see to that."

"I don't believe it," I said.

"You dream too much, my dear Catherine," said Donna Maria gently. "It was only a suggestion all those years ago that you should marry into England. It came to nothing, as so many such suggestions before. There will be many offers for you, and some of them may again come to nothing. It is the way with these proposed marriages. They are never certain until the marriage ceremony has been performed."

"This is different," I insisted. "The English have always been friends of Portugal."

"That does not mean that you will marry a king without a throne."

"How can you know?"

"I know from what I hear."

Donna Elvira and Donna Maria exchanged glances. Then Donna Maria said: There is no point in keeping it a secret. Soon everyone will be talking of it. The King is now a prisoner in the Isle of Wight and, having him in his keeping, it is hardly likely that Oliver Cromwell will let him go."

"And what will happen?"

"There is talk that he may lose his head."

"They dare not."

"Catherine, you must face the truth. It is never wise to delude yourself that it does not exist because it is unpleasant to you. The King is defeated. He is a prisoner. The Royalist army is routed. The Parliament is supreme. They will dare."

"And Charles . . . the Prince?"

"He has fought bravely."

"Is he their prisoner?"

"Not yet."

"What will they do to him?"

There was silence and another exchange of glances.

I knew that Donna Maria was deciding whether I should be told the truth or be kept in ignorance. Then she made up her mind that I must know the worst.

"The same thing as they do to his father," she said.

"You mean . . . they will kill him?"

"They will think he is a threat," said Donna Elvira.

"But I was going to . . ."

"It is in God's hands," said Donna Maria. "He is a brave young man. I have heard that he sent a blank paper to Cromwell—no, not entirely blank, because his signature was at the bottom of it. With it was a note saying that Cromwell could write his terms for saving the King's life. The Prince's signature meant he would accept them, whatever they were."

"He has in truth done that?"

"I have heard it from several sources," said Donna Elvira.

"I think we can vouch for its truth," added Donna Maria.

"What could they ask of him?"

"Perhaps that he take his father's place on the scaffold. They could ask anything."

"And he would do this to save his father's life? How noble he is! And yet he is a Protestant."

Donna Maria smiled affectionately.

"It is God's will," she said.

I was sad thinking of him and what he must be suffering now. He was in danger . . . acute danger. He could lose his life and die a heretic because there was no one to save his soul.

I was in the palace when the news came. It was a shock to us all even though we had known the King was the prisoner of his enemies.

They had taken him to London where his trial had lasted seven days; and at the end of it they took him to the scaffold in front of Whitehall and cut off his head.

There was no longer a King of England.

That should have been the end of my hopes of marrying the Prince of Wales; but they persisted and I could not stop them. His image was as strong as ever. He was noble and brave; he had offered his life for his father's. I believed that he would live forever in my mind.

I HAD LEFT THE CONVENT. I was eighteen years old and still unmarried. It was seven years since the English Parliament had murdered their King. The Prince had eluded them all those years; he was a wandering exile on the continent going from court to court, wherever he could find a friendly refuge. I often told myself that one day he would be successful and come back to rule the country of which he was undoubtedly King.

I was sure that my usually practical mother felt the same, for although there had been several offers for my hand her reception of them had been lukewarm.

This surprised my ladies, for I was no longer young. Most princesses were affianced at a very early age, as I should have been to Charles if our plans had gone as we hoped. I was not disturbed by the rejections, for the only bridegroom I wanted was living a nomadic life far from home.

He had found refuge in France, Holland and Jersey. His sister, the Princess of Orange, had been especially hospitable. I learned that he was liked by most and, in spite of his precarious position, he was far from being a tragic figure. He was said to be merry, amusing and witty and his company was sought, but that was poor compensation while his kingdom was in the hands of his enemies.

I had never forgotten him through the years and I had a strange feeling that it was right for me to wait and that one day some miracle would happen and all would be well.

I remember my father paying one of his rare visits to the palace.

I was shocked when I saw him: he had aged so much. He seemed fatigued but happy to have this respite with his family. I was gratified that he sought my company.

My mother was deeply immersed in state affairs, for she had taken over many duties which would have been my father's if he had not been away fighting. My brother Alfonso was a not very serious thirteen, and of little help. I believed his nature was causing my parents some concern. Pedro, of course, was very young. Perhaps that was why my father turned to me.

I asked about his health and he admitted to a certain exhaustion.

"Dear father," I said, "I believe you would be happy to return to the country. Do you remember when we were at the Villa Viçosa all those years ago?"

"Ah, Viçosa! Yes, I well remember those days."

"It was my second birthday."

"That was when it started."

"You must be proud of what you have done for your country."

"Perhaps. But although we have to some extent had our successes, we cannot rest there. They will be ready to strike again at the first opportunity. They do not give up easily. Your mother is a wonderful woman. She should have been the King."

"But you are the King, and she is happy to be of service to you."

"Without her it would have been so different."

Yes, I thought, we should be at the Villa Viçosa, living quietly, contentedly. But perhaps not. There would never have been a suggestion that I should marry the Prince of Wales. The daughter of a duke would not have been for him. And if my father was not recognized as a king by some countries, he was one in the eyes of the English.

"It was God's will," he said.

"And you have done your duty."

"Under God's will . . . that may be so."

And, I thought, you have worn yourself out in doing so.

"Dear father," I said, "you are unwell."

"No," he replied, "just tired. I cannot tell you how contented I am to sit here with you. You are a child no longer, Catherine."

"I am eighteen years old."

"It is an age of maturity. Do you regret that no marriage has been arranged for you?"

"No . . . I believe . . ."

"I know. You share your mother's belief. She has always wanted you to marry into England."

"It was talked of once."

"That was long ago. It must have been more than ten years ago. Of a surety that was no time for the King to think of the marriage of his son."

"No. It was a tragic time."

"With an even more tragic end. There have been approaches, you know, but your mother has rejected them all. She cannot rid herself of the belief that you are going to England . . . and for that reason she has rejected all offers for your hand. I cannot understand her. It is a kind of dream of hers. It is so unlike her to cling to fancies."

"I think I understand," I said.

"I have been the most fortunate of men in my marriage, and I trust when the time is ripe you will find a partner who is as good to you as she has been to me. My greatest regret has been that I have had to be away from you for so long. I have had too little of my family and too much of war."

"It has been a sadness for us all, dear father. But you are here now."

"For a short time. I confess to you, daughter, while we are alone, that I should have been a happier man if I had not been a king. Now let us talk of other matters. You are eighteen years old—as I said, an age of maturity and wisdom."

"I feel sure I fall short of the last."

"You are as I would have you, my daughter, and to show my love for you, I have gifts for you. I propose to put certain lands into your possession. First, there is the island of Madeira. It is a beautiful spot, fertile and temperate. The city of Lanego is also to be yours, with the town of Moura. There will be tributes from these which will come to you."

"But, father, it is too generous . . . I do not need . . ."

"My dear daughter, you are a child no longer. You need independence and security. So . . . they will be yours. But we must remember that they belong to Portugal and if you should marry out of the kingdom you would perforce relinquish these. On the other hand, if you married some Portuguese nobleman they would remain in your possession."

I saw that my father thought this would be my eventual fate . . . if I married at all; and he wanted to assure himself that I was in the possession of independent wealth.

It was good of him, but I, with my mother, shared the feeling that one day I should go to England. I was, though, deeply touched by his generosity and care for me.

I told him this.

"I want you to be happy," he said, "whatever may befall you."

It was only a few months after that when he died.

IT WAS MORE THAN the loss of a beloved parent. The court was thrown into turmoil. My brother, Alfonso, at thirteen, had few of the qualities necessary to a ruler. There was rejoicing in Spain, where they must have been assuring themselves that it would not be long before Portugal was once more their vassal.

They had reckoned without my mother.

She said firmly: "I shall complete the work my husband has begun."

Our people had always been aware of her strength and many of them knew of the part she had played in my father's successful campaigns. She was without hesitation proclaimed Regent and the Spaniards' jubilation was short-lived. Very soon they began to realize that they had little cause for rejoicing. Donna Luiza, Queen Regent, was not only a leader of resolution and dedication, she was a shrewd and skillful politician. My father had been right when he had said she should. And now she was the ruler.

She was more decisive than my father had been, less sentimental, more ruthless. Our armies were more successful under her direction and the government more secure.

Within two years of her dominance, Portuguese independence from Spain was established and there was growing prosperity throughout Portugal.

We now had some standing in Europe and Donna Luiza was one of its most respected sovereigns.

There were two offers for my hand which my mother feigned to examine with care, but nothing came of them. My worth had risen. Alfonso might not be recognized universally as king, but my mother could not be ignored; and her daughter was considered an important match.

And I was getting older.

"Is there never going to be a marriage for the Infanta?" my ladies were asking each other. "Is she going to spend her days as a spinster in Lisbon?"

I wondered, too. But the dream was still there, incongruous though it might seem. Charles, King of England in name only, was still wandering about the continent, flitting from court to court in search of hospitality. The Puritans still reigned in England. Charles was getting older, as I was—and we were still apart.

And then one day my mother sent for me and she said, with an excitement rare in her: "There is news from England. Oliver Cromwell is dead."

I stared at her in amazement. "Does that mean . . . ?"

"We shall see," she replied. "His son Richard will succeed him. Oliver Cromwell was a strong man."

"And Richard . . . ?"

"It is not easy to follow a strong man. People want change. Whatever they have they dream of something different. They believe that what they cannot get from one they will get from another. Then the disappointment comes and the desire for change."

"Do the English want change?"

"I am not sure. They are not a puritanical people by nature and are inclined to be pleasure-loving and irreligious. It surprises me that they have endured Puritan rule for so long. But Oliver Cromwell was such a strong man." There was a grudging admiration in her voice which she tried to suppress.

"We shall see, daughter, we shall see," she went on.

There were plans in her mind. I knew it. I wanted to talk to her but she would say no more. She was not given to speculation. She just wanted me to know that it would not altogether surprise her if the death of Oliver Cromwell was significant, and perhaps it would not be long before there were changes in England.

I was thinking of Charles more persistently than ever.

MY MOTHER HAD BEEN RIGHT when she said it was difficult to follow a strong man like Oliver Cromwell. He had died on the third of September of that year 1658, and less than two years after his death the King was restored to the throne.

Richard Cromwell, who followed his father, it appeared, was of a likeable nature. Perhaps the same could not have been said of his father, but Richard was pleasure-loving, fond of the sporting life and prone to extravagance, which led to trouble with his creditors. He was certainly no Oliver Cromwell.

The English were restive. Under Oliver Cromwell they had been kept under control. Now the resistance grew. The truth was that they were tired of Puritan rule, which was alien to them. It must soon have become clear that the majority of them wanted the return of the monarchy.

Charles was in Breda when an emissary was sent to him to discover whether he would come back to England and take the crown. With the offer came a gift of 50,000 pounds, that he might discharge any debts and equip himself for the journey.

I can imagine his joy. He was now asked to accept that for which he had fought and struggled for more than ten years.

He accepted with alacrity.

And what a welcome he received! I could picture it all so clearly when later he talked to me of that day. I know he never forgot it.

The people were exultant. I can picture his riding among them. He would have looked—all six feet of him—the perfect king. I knew how he could mingle that quality of regality with familiarity which enchanted all. I doubt whether there was ever a king of England so loved by his people.

He always called himself an ugly fellow, and when one considered his features that could be true, but his charm was overwhelming. There could never have been a more attractive man. I know that I loved him and one is apt to be unaware of the faults of the object of one's devotion, but I can vouch for it that I was not alone in my opinion.

He used to talk of the ringing of bells, the flowers strewn in his path, the women who threw kisses at him, the shouts of loyalty.

"Odds fish!" he said. It was a favorite oath of his. "They gave me such a welcome home that I thought it must have been my own fault that I had stayed away so long."

But he was home, and from that moment the excitement grew.

My mother was exultant. She had known, she said, that this must be. She had planned for it since my seventh birthday when the matter had first been raised. Keeping me from suitors, which had amazed so many, had proved to be right. She had not been fanciful, as so many had thought. She had been shrewd and realistic. She had one regret—that my father was not alive to see how she had been vindicated.

But we were not there yet. A king restored to his throne, fêted by his people, having learned the lesson of his father's downfall, being determined—in his own phrase—"never to go wandering again," seemed secure on the throne. He would need to be married, of course—and such a king was a very desirable *parti*.

My mother was very much aware of that. And, being herself, she immediately took action. Don Francisco de Mello was already in England.

She talked to me a good deal, for indeed I was at the very center of her plans. She watched me anxiously, wondering, I was sure, how well

I should play my part. She took me into her confidence as she never had before.

One day I said to her: "England is an important country. There will be many eager to marry the King."

"That is true," she replied. "The King of Spain will have his protégées. But I trust Don Francisco. He is an able man. He knows the importance of this match to us. I tell you, Catherine, we need this marriage. I wonder if you realize how much."

"I have always known that you wanted a union between our two countries."

"It does go deeper than my personal hopes for you, my daughter. At this time we have freed ourselves from the hated Spaniards, but our hold on freedom is frail. We must remember that they have the might. We have been fighting for our freedom which has given us great strength. That is good, but it is not everything. They are a mighty nation. We shall live in fear until we have strong allies to support us."

"You mean the English."

She nodded. "The nation the Spaniards fear most is the English. They do not forget, though it is some hundred years ago, the ignoble defeat of their so-called invincible armada. They still talk of El Draque—the Dragon—their name for Sir Francis Drake who drove them to disaster and destroyed their dreams of conquest. They will say it was the storm which defeated them, but they were defeated before the storm arose, and they know it was the English sailors and El Draque who beat their armada. If England were allied to us, they would not dare attack us. So, my dear daughter, you must marry the King of England to strengthen the alliance we already have with them. Your country needs this."

"Do you think I shall?"

She looked fierce. "Anything else is unthinkable. It would be the happiest day of my life if I could see you Queen of England."

"Countries always look for gain in marriages," I said.

"Our country would gain a good deal from this. I may tell you that the English will not be without gain. I have sent a good offer by Don Francisco. I believe it will be one which the impoverished King of England will not be able to refuse."

I waited and she seemed to be convincing herself that, as I was deeply involved, I should be told the facts.

She said: "Five hundred thousand pounds in ready money, the possession of Tangiers, which is on the African coast, and Bombay in India, shall be part of your dowry. We shall grant them the right to free trade in Brazil and the East Indies. Of course, the possession of Tangiers and Bombay will give the English immense opportunities for increasing their trade."

"Am I worth so much?"

"This alliance with England is worth everything we could reasonably give. In it lies the security of our nation and the final triumph over our enemy Spain."

"I see," I said slowly, "that it must succeed."

CHE CIME WAS PASSING. There were prolonged delays, for, in spite of my tempting dowry, there was hesitation.

My mother was watchful of the Spanish. The last thing they wanted was an alliance between Portugal and England and they were going to do everything in their power to stop it.

Vatteville, the Spanish ambassador at Charles's court, was spreading evil tales about me. I was deformed; I was ugly; I was barren. I did not know then of Charles's great admiration for female beauty, otherwise I might have been alarmed.

I was passably good-looking. My eyes were dark and large; my hair was abundant and chestnut brown. I had always disliked my teeth which protruded in the front—not a great deal, but too much for beauty. I was short in stature, which made me lack grace. But I was certainly not ugly, only just not handsome.

The delays must mean that our offer had not been entirely acceptable and my mother could not hide her anxiety.

Every day we had news that Spanish troops were massing on the border. They were waiting for the match to founder. Then they would attack. I began to wonder whether even my mother's optimism was beginning to wane.

Dispatches reached us from England. My mother was taking me more and more into her confidence because the matter so deeply concerned me.

"It is that villain Vatteville who is doing everything he can to stop the match. It shows clearly how much Spain is afraid of this alliance.

If it were to fail . . . but it will not . . . but if it were to, they would immediately attack us. We need more troops . . . we need ammunition. It must not be . . . It would be the end of all our endeavors. Oh, why is there this delay?"

I went to her one day and found her laughing.

"Vatteville is a fool," she said. "I think he has gone too far this time. Francisco writes of this. Until now I did not realize how very much those Spaniards are set on breaking this match. They are really alarmed. Did I not say they were still in awe of the English? Oh, Catherine, this must come to pass. How right I was to hold out. Listen to this. They can be arrogant, those Spaniards. It blinds them to the truth. They are powerful . . . very powerful . . . but not quite as powerful as they believe themselves to be. Vatteville had the temerity to tell Charles that if he went through with this marriage to a daughter of the rebel Duke of Braganza he, Vatteville, had been ordered by his master, the King of Spain, to withdraw from the court and war would be declared on England."

"Could that really be so?" I asked.

She snapped her fingers. "It was nonsense. He could have had no such orders. He was just a little too clever that time."

"And what did Charles say to that?"

"He replied that Vatteville might be gone as soon as he wished, for he, the King of England, did not receive orders from the King of Spain as to whom he might marry."

I clasped my hands and said: "He is so wise, so brave, so clever . . ."

"Well, of course, Vatteville realized he had gone too far. He immediately became ingratiating, and I am sure the King must have been amused. But that wretched Vatteville is still fighting hard to stop the marriage and the alliance between our countries. He dared to make a suggestion that the King should marry the Princess of Orange and that, if he did, the King of Spain would give her a marriage portion to equal that of a princess of Spain. She is reputed to be a beauty."

My heart sank. I pulled my lower lip over my teeth—a habit I had formed when I was conscious of my physical defect.

"And what said the King?" I faltered.

"There again Vatteville showed his folly. There had already been negotiations for a match between the King and the Princess of Orange some years before. The Dowager Princess, whose daughter she was, had stood firmly against the match. The King of England was a king in name only, she said, and she saw no sign that he would ever be anything else. Naturally the King's pride would not allow him to accept a princess who had scorned him in the past. So nothing came of that."

"But still there is this delay."

My mother frowned. "It must be decided soon. Don Francisco is hopeful. He is certain that all will be well in the end."

And still we waited.

The days seemed long. We watched for messengers from England. Meanwhile, the Spaniards were gathering on all fronts for the attack. My mother would not give up hope. She dared not. This was not only the marriage of her daughter, for which she had schemed for so many years; it was also the salvation of her country.

Then there came a glimmer of hope.

Louis XIV of France had seen an advantage in a marriage between England and Portugal. He realized that if the marriage did not take place, Portugal most likely would become a vassal state of Spain, increasing the power of that country. That was the last thing Louis wanted. Spain was too powerful already. Moreover, an alliance between England and Portugal would be to the detriment of Spain, so he advised Charles to marry me and declared his support for the match.

Another supporter was the King's mother, Henrietta Maria. Her reasons were different. She was an ardent Catholic and she wanted her son to marry a Catholic. And who better than the Infanta of Portugal?

Then came the day of triumph.

My mother summoned me to her, and when I came she forgot all formality and waved a paper at me.

She was between laughter and tears, and my delight to see her so was great.

"It is a letter from the King of England," she said. "He is eager that your marriage should take place as soon as possible."

She took me in her arms and held me tightly.

"The day is won," she said. "Let us get onto our knees and thank God."

This we did, and there was joy in my heart.

→>◄◄

DON FRANCISCO DE MELLO had returned to Lisbon where he received a warm welcome. He was given the title of the Conde da Ponte
for his services. His assiduous care and shrewd diplomacy had helped
to bring about this happy result, said my mother.

She was in his company constantly and the matter that now concerned them was that of religion.

There must be a clause in the treaty to give me freedom of worship. It was not easy to be a Catholic queen in a Protestant country;
and much as my mother desired this match, necessary as it was to preserve us from defeat at the hands of the Spaniards, duty to God must
come first in all things.

It seemed that no sooner had we overcome one obstacle than another one presented itself.

One of the most lovable facets of Charles's character—which I was
to discover later—was his lack of dogmatism and his tolerance of the
views of others. It was really due to the fact that he had an inherent
abhorrence of conflict; he hated trouble and difficulties were often
smoothed over in order to avoid it. He was lazy in a way; he liked life
to flow smoothly. He immediately confirmed that I should have freedom to worship and I might have my own chapel fitted up wherever
I lived.

My mother was immensely relieved.

But no sooner had that matter been settled than a more serious
one arose. It was from Donna Maria that I first heard of this.

"There will have to be a proxy marriage," she said. "You cannot
leave the country without it."

"Why not?" I asked. "I am going to marry Charles. Why should I
need a proxy?"

"The King cannot come here and you cannot go into a strange
country as an unmarried woman."

"What harm would it do?"

"My lady Infanta, you are very innocent of the world. Unpro-
tected virgins do not leave their homes unless chaperoned."

"I should be surrounded by attendants."

"How could we know what might happen to you?" she said
mysteriously.

"Well, there will have to be a proxy marriage, I suppose, but it seems unnecessary."

My mother was even more concerned than Donna Maria, but for a different reason.

"But why?" I cried. "You have the King's letter. He says he is sending the Earl of Sandwich to take me back to England."

"There should be a proxy marriage first," said my mother.

"Well, there will be a proxy marriage. Is that so difficult?"

"If everything were as it should be there would be no difficulty," she said. "But if you are married by proxy, it will be necessary to get a dispensation from the Pope because your husband is a Protestant."

"Does that mean waiting?"

"It is not that so much which makes me anxious. The Pope does not recognize you as the daughter and sister of kings. He will give the dispensation; he would not dare offend Charles by not doing so, but at the same time your name will appear on it as the daughter of the Duke of Braganza, and that is something I will not allow."

"What shall we do then?"

"There is only one thing we can do, and I do not like it overmuch."

"What is that?"

"You must go to England without having a proxy marriage first."

I smiled. "I think we need not worry about that," I said. "Charles has said he wants me to go to England to marry him."

She looked at me searchingly, and I thought she was about to tell me something; but she evidently decided not to. She merely nodded and said: "Well, there cannot be a proxy marriage."

I did not attach too much importance to this. I was going to England to marry Charles after this long delay, and I was very happy about that.

DISPATCHES ARRIVED FROM LONDON which made me realize more than ever how very important it was for me to marry Charles, apart from my own inclination.

There were riots in London. These had been inspired by none other than the villain Vatteville, who had circulated rumors that if the King married a Catholic there would be trouble in England. Had the people forgotten the days of that Queen whom they knew as Bloody Mary? Did they remember that the last queen had been a Catholic? They were ready to blame Henrietta Maria for what was beyond her control. But it served a good reason for objecting to me.

For Vatteville and his master to act in this way was certainly ironical. They themselves were ardent Catholics. Why did they campaign against me? The answer was obvious. What they wished to avoid above everything was an alliance between England and Portugal.

The King and his ministers acted promptly. They had long become weary of Vatteville's meddling. He was found to be in possession of subversive papers when his lodgings were searched, and was forthwith ordered to leave the country. Even then he tried to stay, to plea his cause, but Charles was tired of him, and refused to see him.

It was a great relief to know that Vatteville was no longer in England.

My mother said: "The fact that the Spaniards have shown themselves so eager to stop the match will make the English realize how important they think it. That is all to the good."

As for me, my joy was complete, for I had received a letter from Charles. It had had to be translated, for it was in English, and I shall always treasure it. I know it by heart.

It ran as follows:

My Lady and Wife,

Already, at my request, the Conde da Ponte has set off for Lisbon. For me the signing of the marriage has been a great happiness; and there is about to be dispatched at this time after him, one of my servants, charged with what would appear to be necessary; whereby may be declared on my part the inexpressible joy of this felicitous conclusion, which when received will hasten the coming of Your Majesty.

I am going to make a short progress into some of my provinces; in the meantime, whilst I go from my most sovereign good, yet I do not complain as to whither I go; seeking in vain tranquillity in my restlessness; hoping to see the beloved person of Your Majesty in these dominions, already your own; and that, with the same anxiety with which, after my long banishment, I desire to see myself within them;

and my subjects desiring also to behold me amongst them, having manifested their most ardent wishes for my return well known to the world.

The presence of your serenity is only wanting to unite us, under the protection of God, in the health and contentment I desire. I have recommended to the Queen, our lady and mother, the business of the Conde da Ponte who, I must here avow, has served me in what I regard as the greatest good in this world, which cannot be mine less than it is that of Your Majesty . . .

The very faithful husband of Your Majesty whose hand he kisses.

Charles Rex
London, the 2nd of July, 1661

It was the perfect love letter and I felt ecstatically happy.

I am glad I did not know then that after he had written this, he went off to spend the night with the woman who was to prove one of my greatest enemies.

CHE MARRIAGE CREACY had been ratified and it was my mother's wish that in our court I should be known as the Queen of England. I emerged from my sequestered life as an unmarried Infanta and had a place beside my mother, my brother King Alfonso, and the Infante Pedro.

"It would be well to leave before the winter comes," said my mother.

But the winter came and still the Earl of Sandwich had not arrived with his fleet which was to take me back to England.

It would be too late now to leave before the weather made the journey too hazardous. Christmas had come and gone and I was still waiting.

"It cannot be till spring now," said my mother. She was anxious. The Spaniards were augmenting their forces on the frontiers. There had been so many delays. People were beginning to say the match would never take place.

It was a time fraught with apprehension. I was glad I did not know to what ends my mother had to go to make sure we had had adequate defence against the enemy—but I was to learn of this later.

I remember well that joyous day.

It had been preceded by the deepest anxiety. Spring had come and Spanish ships were sighted off the coast. The attack was imminent.

I could see the despair in my mother's eyes. She had been so certain of her wisdom in keeping me as a wife for Charles as the means of saving my country; she had been so sure of success; and now it could be that, because of these delays, all her hopes were foundering. If the Spaniards attacked now we could not resist them. Would the King of England want to marry the daughter of a defeated country, a vassal to Spain? In any case, the King of Spain would not allow the match.

I knew she prayed for a miracle—and her prayers were answered.

Spanish ships were preparing to land when those of the English fleet, in the charge of the Earl of Sandwich, came to take me back to England.

It was a triumph for us and defeat for the Spaniards.

Those Spanish sailors remembered the stories of the little English ships which routed the mighty armada of Spain. Their grandfathers had told them of that misadventure. They had told of El Draque, who was no ordinary man—a giant, a dragon, possessed of unearthly powers. Only such could have destroyed the great armada.

The Spanish ships made off with all speed and the troops massed at the frontiers could not act without the supplies of ammunition they were bringing. They could only disperse—and we were safe.

Lisbon went wild with joy. Bells were ringing and crowds gathered on the shore to greet the English ships.

"Viva il rey di Gran Britannia!" cried the people.

My mother's relief was immense. The Earl of Sandwich must be given a royal welcome. Alfonso must send the Comptroller of the Household out to his ships; there must a twenty-seven-gun salute; the Earl must receive the warmest welcome possible from a grateful country.

There must be rejoicing. The finest apartments were prepared for him; there should be the grandest of banquets and the best bulls must be brought out for his entertainment. The anguish of uncertainty was over. The marriage could not fail to be celebrated now.

I did notice that after the first great relief my mother still seemed anxious. I wondered why this could be and, buoyed up by my newly acquired status—after all, I was styled Queen of England—I had the temerity to ask her what was wrong.

I waited until I could be alone with her, and I said: "I fear that you are not entirely happy, as I thought the arrival of the Earl of Sandwich would allow you to be."

She bit her lips and hesitated for a moment or so, then she said: "I will confess to there being a certain difficulty. You know full well how, over the last few months, we have lived in fear of an attack from our old enemy. I had to keep the borders guarded. That has been extremely costly. The fact is that the money which was set aside for your dowry has had to be used to maintain the army. I had promised that five hundred thousand pounds should be delivered and the Earl of Sandwich should take it back to England with him. During our dire need of the last few months, I have had to use some of that money . . . indeed a great deal of it."

I was horrified. "Which means you do not have the money which you promised?"

"That is so."

"But . . ."

"It is a delicate situation." She was looking at me anxiously. I knew her to be a woman who was never at a loss, even in the most desperate situation. She went on: "I have decided what I must do. I must throw myself on the mercy of this man. Tangiers is now in the hands of the English and he is here to take you back. Surely he will see that it is too late to abandon the mission for the sake of the money. I shall tell him that he shall have half of it and the other half shall be paid within a year."

"Will that be possible?"

"My dear daughter, I must make it possible."

"When will you explain this to the Earl of Sandwich?"

"You may trust me to find the appropriate moment."

I was uneasy. I hated this bartering. It spoiled my romantic dreams. It was as though the King were being paid to take me for his wife.

Of course, I should have faced the truth. He was. But that was how marriages were arranged in royal circles. The advantages to both sides were weighed in the balance, and if the result was good enough, the marriage took place.

I did not want to look at it in that way. For me, Charles had become a hero in my life . . . the perfect man, the only husband I could ever want, and I was as anxious as my mother was that all should go well. I had unpleasant thoughts of the Earl sailing off with his fleet . . . and of the Spaniards laughingly watching him do so and then coming to strike.

SO IT WAS WITH SOME QUALMS that I prepared for my meeting with the Earl of Sandwich. He was a good-looking man, in his late thirties, I imagined. He had a pleasant countenance and my spirits rose at the sight of him. There was something comforting about him.

I learned afterward that he was not a man of deep convictions, for he had served Oliver Cromwell with loyalty and had continued his duties under Richard Cromwell. Now the King had returned and the Earl's devotion was proved to be to whatever government was in power. He was a sailor; he worked for his country and whoever was head of the state; he remained in his post of Admiral.

He was delighted with the welcome he had received from the people of Lisbon. He had come just in time, and by his presence had saved our country; so naturally they were eager to show their gratitude.

If only the money had been there, I could have been happy. When he kissed my hand and declared how honored he was to do so, I could have been enchanted if I had not been haunted by thoughts of the missing dowry.

There came at length the time for confession. I knew what was happening, for my mother was closeted with the Earl and I had seen the apprehension in her face when she prepared for the meeting. There was resolution too. I had told myself that she would not fail; she had never done so yet. She was the most resourceful person I had ever known and this marriage had obsessed her for years. She would not let it fail now.

They were a long time together, and when the Earl left I hurried to her.

She was looking uneasy, and I forgot all formality. I think she did too. She was trembling slightly, which I had never seen her do before.

"I beg you . . . ," I cried. "Tell me . . ."

She was silent.

I said: "It is over then. He is going back without me?"

She shook her head. "He is naturally perplexed. The money is so important. The King is greatly impoverished. Richard Cromwell has been a disaster . . ."

"And so . . ."

"He needs time to think."

"You believe he may refuse . . . that everything will come to nothing?"

"No," she said fiercely. "He could not do that. He has already taken Tangiers. He could not relinquish that now. In the long term that is more important than the money."

"But it is only half of it he has to wait for. He can have half now and the rest in a year."

"Well, daughter, it is not quite like that. I have had to tell him the whole truth. You know the Jew Diego Silvas?"

"I have heard him spoken of."

"A man of great integrity . . . a business man . . . a loyal subject."

I had been surprised by my mother's admiration for him. As a fervent Catholic, she would be distrustful of the Jews. Under the Inquisition, they had been persecuted more than any other people. Diego Silvas was a wealthy man, an honest man, a businessman, and as such had been of great use to her. She respected him and made of him a friend. His religious beliefs were set aside for the benefits he could bring. But where was he concerned in this matter?

"I have called on him to help," she said. "I told the Earl that we could pay half of your dowry now and the rest at the end of the year. But the fact is I do not have the money even for part of the first half. So what I propose to do is to put on board the value of the money— the half we are speaking of—in goods, spices, sugar, such things, merchandise as we would export from our country. Diego Silvas will travel to England with the goods and when he arrives in England he will store them and see that they are sold to the merchants he knows in London, and when this is done the money will be delivered to the English treasury. She took a deep breath and spread her hands with a smile. "It was the only thing I could do."

I looked at her incredulously and thought how wonderful she was . . . how imaginative . . . how resourceful. She was the most remarkable person I had ever known.

I felt the tears in my eyes. For the first time I fully realized what my departure would mean to me, because after I had gone, I might never see her again.

She watched me, reading my thoughts.

She said: "I could think of no other way."

"And do you think it will be accepted?"

"I do not know. I can only pray. The Earl was astounded. He was not sure what he should do. He has gone away to ponder. I believe he must accept. How can he return without the bride? And what of Tangiers? After all, is the money so important beside Tangiers . . . and Bombay . . . and all the free trade which will come their way? And he is favorably impressed with you. I could see that. All will be well, daughter, I am sure of it."

It was agonizing to wait for the Earl's decision. There had been so many obstacles to the marriage that I began to fear that this one would be insurmountable.

How would the King feel? He was expecting money and would receive sugar and spices.

Only my mother could have thought of such a plan.

She came to me.

"He has agreed to accept," she said. "I knew he would. What else could he do? It has gone too far. He could not leave now."

"Has the King agreed?"

"My dear daughter, how could there be time for that? It has to be the Earl's decision. He is a worried man, but he sees the inevitability of this. There is only one course of action for him."

"It is a difficult decision for him to make."

"We all have difficult decisions to make, and he is a sensible man. How could he go back to England without the bride everyone is expecting? I have given him our bond that the rest of the money will be paid before the year is out."

"Can that be done?"

"It must be done. He knows that Diego Silvas, who has a reputation for honest dealing and shrewd bargaining, will see that the King gets his first installment as promised. So . . . we can forget our fears. In a short time you will be sailing for England."

THERE WAS A GREAT DEAL of interest in the English court among those surrounding me; and there must have been gossip about its nature. I often marvel at the successful manner in which this was kept from me. It must have been on my mother's orders, for both Donna Maria and Donna Elvira were fond of gossip.

She had chosen these two to be close to me and to accompany me to England. There would be other waiting women, of course, but these two were in command. They had grown in importance and had increased their care of me—somewhat ostentatiously, I must admit.

I soon realized they had something on their minds. If I asked them, they immediately became cautious, and it was almost as though they buttoned up their lips, because they were fearful that words would slip out.

One day I heard Donna Elvira say: "I think we should speak to Donna Luiza. It is only right that the Infanta should be prepared."

To that Donna Maria replied: "It is a thought which has been with me for some time. The poor child will be unready for what she must surely find."

I confronted them and asked to know what they thought I should find.

They blustered and said I must have misheard their words.

Shortly after that, when I was with my mother, I decided to tell what I had overheard, and I felt there was something which was being kept from me.

"They seemed quite anxious about it," I said.

She hesitated for a moment, as though she were making up her mind. "Tell me," she said at length, "what have you heard of the King?"

"The King? Charles? Oh, that he has been welcomed back . . . that the people are glad to have him . . . that he has made England merry again . . . that he fought valiantly and offered his life for his father's . . . and that it is wonderful that he is back where he belongs."

"All that is true, but there is more to know."

"It is my desire to know all I can about him and his country."

It may be that there are certain aspects which you might not like."

"I do not understand."

"My dear Catherine, you have lived what is called a sheltered life. You have hardly ever left the walls of the palace or those of the convent. Life can be rather different in certain places. You were very fond of your father. He was a wonderful man . . . devoted to his family . . . a good man in every aspect. He loved you children dearly and was a faithful husband to me."

"Yes, I know."

"Because you have seen so little of life, you might judge all men by him."

I was puzzled and wondered why she, who was usually so direct, should now be so hesitant.

"The King is thirty-two years of age. He is unmarried. He has led an adventurous life, wandering about the continent. Such is the nature of men that there will be women in their lives. Do you understand what I mean?"

"Mistresses?" I began.

She nodded. "You see, the King has never had a wife . . . well, you see . . . it is only natural."

"Yes . . . but when he is married, that will be over . . ."

"Of course. But . . . er . . ."

"Please tell me, my lady."

"There is talk that at this time he is enamored of a certain woman. . . ."

"Oh, but now I shall be his wife. You saw the letter he wrote to me."

"Yes, I saw it." She smiled brightly. "It is just that we think you should know that there has been this woman. By all accounts, she is handsome and . . . very demanding. If you should hear of her, you must ignore her. Do not let her come to court. You should treat her as though she does not exist."

"But of course I shall, and when I am married, she will certainly not be there. Who is this woman?"

"Her name is Barbara Palmer, Lady Castlemaine."

It was the first time I heard the name of that evil woman.

ON CHE CWENCY-CHIRD OF APRIL, St. George's Day, the time had come for my departure—and by a happy coincidence, St. George is the patron saint not only of England but also of Portugal. All I could think of was the parting with my mother and that this might be the last time I set eyes on her.

My two brothers were with me and they escorted me down to the hall where my mother was waiting for me. She looked at me with such affection that I almost burst into tears. I knew I must not do that. She must not be ashamed of me. She was restraining her emotions and so must I mine.

She held me tightly in her arms; and then it was over and my brothers were leading me to the coach. Surrounded by an array of the nobility, we went in procession to the cathedral. The bells were ringing and the guns were firing the salutes; there was music in the streets and the people cried: "Long live the Queen of England!"

When the cathedral service was over, we made our way to the sea.

I was surrounded by a great company led by my brothers. Don Francisco was present. He had recently been ennobled for the excellent work he had done in negotiating the marriage contract and had become the Marquis da Sande. That he was delighted in the manner in which everything had been resolved was evident.

Waiting for us was a splendid barge which was to take us to the Admiral's ship, the *Royal Charles*.

When I stepped aboard this magnificent vessel, the Earl of Sandwich was waiting to greet me, and my brother Alfonso formally handed me over to him. Donna Maria and Donna Elvira stood beside me, my protectors. The Admiral conducted me to the splendid cabin which had been prepared for me, and my brother said a sad farewell and departed.

I was on my way to England.

MARRIED BLISS

WE COULD NOT SAIL OUT OF THE BAY THEN AS THE WIND was too strong and I was told it might be some time before we could leave.

I settled into my cabin, which was truly magnificent. I marvelled at the amount of care which had gone into making it so; it was not only comfortable but luxurious. The walls had been lined with velvet; there were curtains of damask and taffeta; and there were rugs on the floor. I imagined Charles giving orders that all should be of the best for his Queen.

How miraculous it was that all our plans had worked out. I should be rejoicing, but I could not help thinking of my mother. I should never forget her face as it had been at that last moment when we embraced. There were no tears. How could she weep with so many watching her? But her grief had been none the less because of that.

"I shall never see her again," I kept saying to myself; and then waves of misery would sweep over me.

And yet our purpose—the dream that had been with us for years—was realized. It could not have been any other way. That was like life, I supposed. Nothing could be entirely perfect.

I had to stop thinking of my mother. I had to remember that I was going to my husband—the man of whom I had dreamed for so many years . . . ever since that day when I was seven and I had learned that there was a possibility of his being my husband.

The hours were passing and we still remained in the bay.

In the evening my brothers brought a group of noblemen from the court to serenade me. They sailed in their little boats round the *Royal Charles,* playing music and singing to me. It was very moving.

And when I awoke next morning, the sun was shining brilliantly. The wind was still strong but the Admiral decided that we would wait no longer. We would defy the weather and set sail. So, with Donna Maria and Donna Elvira, six maids of honor and their servants, with Don Francisco de Mello, who was to supervise my safe delivery into England, with Richard Russell, my almoner, who was an excellent interpreter, and others who were necessary to me, plus boxes of sugar and spices, I left my country for a new life in England.

It was a most hazardous journey. Some of my ladies were so ill that they wished for death; I myself suffered slightly less. We really believed that our last moments had come and we should never see England; and when some of the vessels were damaged by the storm, we were certain of this.

The wind roared and buffeted us and we were at one stage forced to take refuge in Mount Bay, off the coast of Cornwall.

We were heartened to receive a welcome from the people on shore. They knew that I was on board one of the ships and they were clearly determined to show their pleasure in my arrival. Bonfires were lighted along the coast and we could hear people singing; salutes were fired and there was a wonderful display of fireworks.

After that brief halt we were able to pursue our journey, and came to the Isle of Wight, where the Duke of York, the King's brother, was waiting with a squadron of frigates to greet us.

A message was sent to me. The Duke wanted permission to come aboard the *Royal Charles* that he might "kiss my hand."

There was excitement in the cabin. Donna Maria and Donna Elvira were shocked when I said I must greet the Duke of York in English dress. Clothes had been thoughtfully provided for such an occasion, and I ordered my women to dress me in a gown of white silk trimmed with lace.

Donna Maria covered her face with her hands when she saw me in it, and Donna Elvira held up her hands in horror.

"It is most unsuitable!" wailed Donna Maria.

"Quite immodest," agreed Donna Elvira.

"It is the English fashion," I told them.

"Then," retorted Donna Maria, "we had better turn back and go home."

"What!" I cried, mocking her. "Face the sea again? I heard you say that nothing on earth would make you sail again."

But Donna Maria was truly distressed since, having just emerged from one ordeal, she was confronted by me in a most unsuitable gown. It was too much for her.

I heard the arrival of the Duke. Don Francisco was on deck waiting to receive him and bring him to one. My heart was beating fast as he approached.

The Duke was tall, his features heavy, but his complexion was fair, whereas I had heard Charles's swarthiness referred to often. It had been said that he was more like a Spaniard than an Englishman, so therefore James's comparative fairness surprised me. He had a certain dignity, but there was a friendliness about him.

He started to kneel before me; but I thought that was too formal for one who was to be my brother-in-law. So I asked him not to do so and embraced him. His response was immediate.

He then spoke in English which I did not understand. Richard Russell translated for me. James was saying what a great pleasure it was to welcome me to England on his brother's behalf, but he included an earnest welcome from himself at the same time.

He asked me how the voyage had been and then suggested that, as he knew a little Spanish, it might be easier for us to converse in that language; and this we did.

He then told me that his brother was awaiting my arrival with the greatest eagerness, and how the whole country was jubilant.

The people were still celebrating the return of the King. Poor souls, they had suffered under Cromwell. He had made England a country without laughter. That was no country to live in. But at least it had made them appreciate the merry times the more.

He wanted me to know that he was determined to be my friend and if he could be of service to me at any time I must tell him, for nothing would delight him more than to help. I wanted him to sit beside me, but he said he could not do so because that was his brother's place. He would sit in a chair without a canopy.

I had not expected such rigid regard for etiquette in England and think, from what I gathered afterward, that it was just the Duke's way of showing he wanted to honor me.

When he left he brushed aside ceremony and remarked that I did not do justice to my rank, to which I replied that I acted out of affection, and I could see that this pleased him.

So my meeting with my brother-in-law was most satisfactory.

Before he left, he presented to me the Earl of Chesterfield and the Duke of Ormonde, with other gentlemen who had accompanied him. All were most effusive in their welcome and, with the horrors of the sea voyage behind me, my spirits were considerably lifted.

Shortly after the Duke had left, Donna Maria said she was feeling unwell. I insisted that she went to bed immediately, and to my surprise she did not protest. So I guessed that she was indeed ill, for nothing else would have induced her to leave my side at such a time.

When we reached Portsmouth she was so ill that she could not be with me, and I was left to Donna Elvira and my ladies-in-waiting.

I was taken to the King's house in Portsmouth where the Duchess of Suffolk, who was to be Mistress of the Stole, was waiting to be received by me. She appeared to be a very pleasant woman, although we could not understand each other very well.

Donna Maria was suffering from a feverish cold and was not seriously ill, which was comforting; and I settled down to await the coming of the King.

My only regret was that my mother was not here with me. How gratified she would have been by the welcome I had received! She would be thinking of me now, I knew. We were separated, but at least she had acheved her ambition; and in such circumstances it could not be otherwise. I was as good as married to the King of England and the Spanish would not dare attack Portugal now that England was brought closer to us by this alliance.

If only she could be with me now, what great happiness I should know!

There was consternation when, a few days after my arrival in Portsmouth, I caught Donna Maria's cold. I was sneezing and had a slight fever. The doctors were called and they said I must keep to my bed.

Several days had passed since my arrival and I had not yet seen the King. He was detained in London on urgent business, I was told. I was a little uneasy that he should be delayed so long. It might seem that he was not very eager to see me. I wondered what the business in London could be which was so urgent. Matters of state, of course.

It was five days after my arrival in Portsmouth when he came. I was in bed. The fever had subsided but the cold still persisted.

Donna Maria, now recovered, said: "You must not leave your bed, and one thing is certain, the King must not see you in it."

"He will expect to see me when he arrives."

"If he is a sensible and right-minded man, he will realize the impropriety of seeing you at such a time."

I wondered. I had already noticed that formality was not so rigidly insisted on here as it was in Portugal. It existed, of course, but the English had a habit of discarding certain things if they become inconvenient.

He arrived. I heard the commotion below. Donna Maria and Donna Elvira were standing at the door like two angels with flaming swords guarding Eden.

Then I heard a voice—the most musical I had ever heard. It was soft and caressing, though I could not understand the words which were spoken.

The Earl of Sandwich was there.

He said in Spanish that the King had arrived and wished to see the Queen.

Donna Maria replied that the Queen was indisposed.

"The King will see her," replied the Earl. "He has traveled from London for this."

Donna Maria was about to protest, but with a courtly gesture, the Earl led her to one side. And there was the King.

I felt myself flushing and trying to shrink below the bedclothes, fearful that, unadorned as I was, he should find me ill-favored.

He came to the bed. He had taken off his plumed hat and flung it onto a chair. He was smiling and he was all that I had dreamed him to be. One was immediately aware of his height, and his dark face with the heavy-lidded eyes. They sparkled with merriment and friendliness. Yet there was a certain gentleness about him. He was swarthy, yes, that was true enough. He was quite unlike the fair-skinned Englishmen whom I had met so far. In fact, he was different from anyone I had ever seen before. He may not have had perfect features, but he had something far more attractive. It was an excessive and indefinable charm. For so long I had created an image—now here was the embodiment of my ideal.

He sat on the bed and took my hand. He kissed it, looking up into my face as he did so.

He spoke in English and then, laughing, slipped into Spanish.

"The Spaniards have a use then," he said. "They gave us a language which we both understand. My little wife, how it delights me to see you! But I am sad that you should be indisposed. But you will be well soon. Your doctors have told me that. It is nothing much . . . just a little inconvenience. That makes me very happy."

"You are kind," I said.

"Kind?" He laughed. "And to whom should I be kind if not to my Queen? Life is going to be good. I can see that you and I will be of one mind. We shall be merry together. The sea was not good to you, they tell me. That grieved me much. And now you are here, all shall be well from now on. How I have longed to see you!"

It did not occur to me until later—such was the magic of his presence—that if he had so longed to see me, he need not have waited five days before doing so. But I was to discover that, while one was with Charles, he beguiled one into believing him. Or perhaps one did so because one wanted to.

"As soon as you are well, we shall be married," he said.

He saw the furrow in my brow and asked me in a tender voice if anything worried me.

With a certain apprehension, I broached the subject which was uppermost in my mind. Perhaps he was not the one to whom I should have spoken, but there was a kindliness in him and I sensed he would be tolerant and understand a point of view which might not be his own. I should certainly not have mentioned it on our first meeting, but I had already tried to speak of it to Don Francisco, who had brushed it aside.

I said: "There is something, Your Majesty."

He took my hand. "Charles . . ." he said reproachfully, and I immediately felt able to confide in him.

"It is the ceremony . . ."

"Oh, the ceremony! What fuss! For myself, I could happily dispense with such encumbrances."

"Your Majesty . . . Charles . . . I could not be happy if there was not a Catholic ceremony."

For a moment he dropped his bantering mood. Then he smiled and said: "You need have no fear. Our marriage will be regarded throughout the world as a true marriage."

"It would not be so to me," I said.

"Ah," he replied. "They have made an ardent papist of you, have they! Papists are so earnest." He laughed. "You remind me of my mother. You and she will be good friends when you meet, I'll swear. As for this Catholic ceremony . . . you see, my dear, you are Queen of this country and you must be married according to the religious observances of the place. But you say you will not be happy . . . and I cannot allow you to be unhappy. I will tell you how we will resolve this matter. There shall be a ceremony here in this bedchamber. It shall be as you wish, and the other one will take place as arranged on the same day. It means you will have to marry me twice. Could you bear that?"

I felt my lips tremble. I was going to weep because I was so touched, so happy.

"You are all that I hoped for . . . and all that I dreamed," I said emotionally.

He looked at me in mock dismay. "Do not have too good an opinion of me, I beg you. I fear you will find me a somewhat sinful fellow."

"Oh no. You are the kindest and best man in the world."

He leaned toward me and kissed my cheek. He was sober suddenly. He said: "You shame me." Then he was merry again. His gravity seemed always to be fleeting, as though his gaiety was waiting impatiently to break in on it.

"So," he went on, "that little matter is taken care of. There is nothing now for you to be anxious about. All you have to do is get well. I am impatient for these ceremonies to be over."

When he left me, I lay back in a daze of happiness.

Donna Maria came in and looked at me.

"I never heard of such," she was muttering. "I can guess what your mother would say if she knew that a man not yet your husband had visited you in your bedchamber . . . and you abed!"

I pulled the bedclothes up to hide my face and stifle my laughter. It was the laughter of happiness as much as amusement.

I RECOVERED ALMOST IMMEDIATELY and it was arranged that the ceremony should take place without delay.

There was a great deal of secrecy about the Catholic nuptials, and I realized what a concession it was that it should have been allowed to take place.

It was to be held in my bedchamber. The Lord Aubigny, an almoner of Queen Henrietta Maria, was to perform the ceremony. Francisco de Mello was to be there with three of his trusted servants, and Donnas Maria and Elvira. The only other witness was to be the Duke of York, and I was pleased to see him again. He had made me feel so welcome on my arrival and he had seemed sympathetic and to understand my urgent desire that it should take place.

Charles was as charming as ever. He was less earnest than I, and I felt more and more grateful that he should have granted my wish, which could not have been easy. If he had refused, I should have been most unhappy. He had understood this and was determined to please me. What a wonderful husband I should have!

After the ceremony Charles kissed me. He whispered: "Don't forget you have to go through all this again."

I replied that I should be very happy to do so.

Then the Duke of York kissed me and said most graciously how delighted he was that I had come to these shores to be his good sister.

I was so happy. My cold had disappeared and I was now ready for that other ceremony which would take place later that day.

Lady Suffolk helped to prepare me for it. Donna Maria clucked her disapproval and whispered with Donna Elvira, who shared it. They had been somewhat placated because of the earlier ceremony in my bedchamber. At least I was now Charles's wife and that set their minds at rest. It was a pity, said Donna Elvira, that we had to go through this heathen performance.

They did not approve of my wedding dress, which Lady Suffolk and I thought charming. It was cut according to the English fashion. "Disgraceful," murmured Donna Maria.

"Too low cut and showing too much of the shoulders," added Donna Elvira.

It was of the color of roses—a beautiful shade which would be becoming to my dark eyes, and there were little knots of ribbon all over it. I thought it was the most delightful dress I had ever seen.

Communication was not easy. I knew that I must learn the English language as quickly as I could, for I could see many difficulties ahead. I thought: I will ask Charles to teach me. Perhaps I shall teach him Portuguese.

"You must not get exhausted," warned Donna Elvira.

"Indeed not," added Donna Maria. "Do not forget that you have just arisen from a sick bed."

"Oh, Maria . . . it was nothing."

"You have to remember, my lady, how excitement upsets you."

I knew what she meant. Once or twice, when I had been overtired or became too excited, I had fainted, and this was accompanied by a tiresome bleeding of the nose. It had happened only a few times but that was enough for Donna Maria. She was continually reminding me of it. It had happened once in the convent and had alarmed the nuns. Donna Maria was now shaking her head prophetically.

"I shall be watchful," she said. "And if I see the signs, I shall *insist* on your returning to your bed—no matter who shall try to stop me. It was foolish to have two ceremonies on the same day. The morning's was necessary, I agree, but this other . . ."

"Dear Maria, this is the one people here think is important."

"I can only wish that we had come to a country of the Faith."

"I'm happy here, Maria."

Lady Suffolk fortunately could not understand this conversation, so perhaps there was some advantage in the language difficulty after all.

The ceremony was to take place in the great hall of this house, for which I was grateful. I was buoyed up by excitement, but I did feel a trembling of the knees, due no doubt to this excitement rather than my recent indisposition.

The grand hall, or the Presence Chamber, where Charles received visiting emissaries and ambassadors, was an impressive room, especially as it was fitted up for this occasion. Two thronelike seats had been set under a canopy, and a rail had been put across the room to partition off that section where the nuptials should take place, separating us from the rest of the company. The place was filled with nobles and those of high standing in all professions.

Charles led me to the seat under the canopy, and with us was the Bishop of London, who was to perform the ceremony, and Don Francisco with Sir Richard Fanshawe, whom I knew because of the part he had played in the negotiation of the marriage.

Charles took my hand and the ceremony began.

I could only nod my head when told to do so, for I was not able to say the words which were required of me.

I learned afterward that when the Bishop proclaimed us man and wife, what the people were shouting was: "Long may they live!"

There was to be a banquet and the King, holding me by the hand, took me to his apartment, the people following us.

There we stood side by side and many came to congratulate us and to wish us a long and happy life together. Charles explained this to me. He looked very happy—and so was I.

Lady Suffolk indicated that she would like one of the blue knots of ribbon on my dress. It would be a memento of this happy occasion which she would treasure all her life. I thought it was a charming suggestion, so I pulled one off and gave it to her.

People pressed round and I realized that they were all demanding a knot of blue ribbon.

"You cannot refuse them," said Charles. "You are going to be ribbonless before they will let you go."

It was all very merry and there was I, plucking off the knots of ribbon, which I knew later had been lightly tacked on so that they could easily be pulled off.

I looked down with dismay at my denuded dress.

"Do not regret the loss of the ribbons," said Charles. "It still looks delightful, as any dress would on you."

I noticed that only one knot had been left, and Charles plucked it off. "This one shall be mine," he said. He kissed it and held it to his heart. Everyone applauded.

I turned to him and smiled. I was so happy. There was only one regret. My mother was not here to see my contentment, and the successful culmination of the dream we had shared through the years.

Suddenly I felt almost faint and might have fallen if Charles had not put an arm about me.

"You are unwell, my dearest?" he said with concern.

"No, just a little tired."

Donna Maria, watching me intently, had seen what had happened. She was beside me, indignant and vociferous.

"I should think so. You have had enough. It is time you were in your bed. You will be ill. I have never heard the like . . . two weddings in one day."

I was glad few could understand her.

The Countess of Suffolk was talking to the King. He looked grave. Then he said to me: "They are saying you are overtired. This is too soon after your illness. The Countess thinks you should return to bed."

I said: "There is the banquet . . ."

"Your good health is more important than all the banquets in my kingdom. The ladies are right. You must go to your bedchamber at once. You must rest."

"But . . . ," I began.

"Yes," he said firmly. "It is best. There is the rest of our lives for us to be together."

Donna Maria was chattering about the folly of doing too much too soon. Elvira was with her. *They* knew, they were saying, what was best for me.

I said: "I shall miss the banquet . . . my wedding banquet . . . and I shall not be there."

"A plague on banquets," said Donna Maria. "Your health comes first."

The King came with me to my bedchamber. Donna Maria pursed her lips and I wanted to remind her that he was my husband now.

Lady Suffolk was there. She implied that she, with my ladies, would help me to disrobe.

I lay in my bed. Yes, I was exhausted and it was a relief to rest. But I could not stop myself thinking of the splendid banquet, the merry-making, and the King sitting there with an empty chair beside him, which made me feel a little dispirited, when the door was flung open suddenly, and two men appeared, carrying trays.

I thought: I do not want to eat. Oh, how I wished that I had been able to hide my weakness.

And then Charles was there. He gave an order to the men and one tray was set down on the bed. He seated himself on the other side of the tray, smiling at me.

"What . . . ?" I began in Spanish, and he answered in that language.

"I could not sup on my wedding day without my wife."

Oh, what a merry meal that was! How we laughed and how we talked! It was so amusing for us because we found our Spanish not always adequate and must resort to miming.

Charles said: "I wonder if you will share my view that this is far more agreeable than the grand banquet they are having downstairs."

"It is the most enjoyable meal I ever had," I told him.

We kissed over the tray, and I was happier than I had ever been before in the whole of my life.

I SPENT MY WEDDING NIGHT alone in my bed. Charles was so considerate that he realized I was too overcome by the excitement for anything else.

I scarcely slept. How rarely is the realization more delightful than the dream itself! That was what I believed had happened to me.

How charming he was! He had a nonchalant air, a carefree manner which implied that everything would be well if left to him. And above all, there was his kindness. I remembered how grim Don Francisco had become when I had told him I must have a Catholic marriage ceremony. How different from my dearest Charles! It was a delicate matter, I knew. I was asking something which had to be performed in private because the people here would not have wanted it to take place. But he had immediately understood how much it meant to me. He was wonderful. I must be the happiest woman in the world.

He was in the room early next morning asking me, with the utmost tenderness, how I was.

I told him I was completely well.

"We shall take care of you," he said.

Then he talked of our honeymoon which, he said, if I were agreeable, should be spent at his palace of Hampton Court.

I said that would be most agreeable.

"It is one of my favorite palaces," he told me. "You will enjoy it, as I shall. It is a place where a great deal has happened and I shall tell you of some of this. It was built many years ago . . . four hundred, I think, and much later it was bought by a man who is very well known in our history. He was called Cardinal Wolsey. He displeased the King, Henry VIII, who took the palace from him, and it has been royal property ever since."

"I want to see it very much."

"We shall dally there for a while. You will like the gardens. You will like the river which runs alongside, and you will not be afraid of the ghosts who haunt the palace, because I shall be there to protect you."

I told him I should not feel afraid of anything if he were there.

Now our relationship had deepened. I was young, innocent and ignorant. He, as I learned later, was as well versed in the art of love-making as anyone on the earth. And I was sure he must have been born with it. How charmingly and romantically he initiated me. And what an apt pupil I was. I believed I delighted him. I did not realize then that it was because of my innocence, which must have made me very different from most of the women he had known. Few would have lived such a sheltered life as I had.

I found life enchanting. We were together for most of the days and nights during the time we spent in Portsmouth; and we were to leave for Hampton Court as soon as enough carts could be found to take the court there.

Charles joked about the Portuguese costumes which my ladies had brought with them.

"It is fortunate that the ladies of England do not follow the same fashions. If they did, there would not be enough carts in England to carry them and their belongings from place to place."

It was about four days after our wedding when we left for Hampton Court.

What a welcome we received there! There were two reasons for rejoicing. It was the twenty-ninth of May, the King's thirty-second birthday, and the second anniversary of his restoration to the throne. The English loved excuses for holidays and pageants and making merry. Moreover, Charles told me, they were also celebrating his marriage and my arrival in England.

"So you see, my love, there is ample reason for rejoicing."

There were bonfires all along the route. People lined the roads to see the King and Queen. They shouted loyal greetings and threw garlands at us. We smiled and waved as we passed along.

They seemed pleased to see me. I had learned to recognize the shouts of "God save the Queen." Charles was always delighted by their recognition of me.

And thus we came to Hampton.

It has always been one of my favorite palaces. To me now it is the one place where I was most happy, where I had spent those magical days . . . childlike in my innocence. How happy I could have been if I had never lost that innocence! But one cannot go blindfold through life.

When we arrived at the palace, the guards were waiting to greet us. How I wished that we could have come there alone and have entered the palace without ceremony, but we had to pass through the lines of soldiery, followed by our retinue, and there must be presentations and kissing of hands. As the new Queen, there were important people whom I had to receive. It was so difficult because of the language. I could only nod and smile, for I was not at that stage ready to attempt those few words which Charles had taught me.

Hoy joyous that homecoming could have been if only we were alone!

my memories of those days at Hampton Court will remain with me forever. I was perfectly happy during them, or almost, the only flaw being that we were so rarely alone. But to be otherwise would be asking too much. Charles was, after all, the King and I the new Queen; and it was our duty to receive the many people who were eager to see us.

There were morning levees at which Charles must present the leading people of the court to me; and it seemed there was always some ceremony to perform. He would smile at me apologetically during these sessions, because I believed he too was wishing that we could be alone; and happily I would return his look with understanding.

It was only at night that we were free.

There was continual revelry. The Portuguese court had been much more formal. The English flung themselves into pleasure with an abandonment which at first astonished me. Then I reminded myself that they had only just escaped from Puritan rule, so perhaps in time they would grow a little more restrained.

There were banquets and balls, pageants on the river; plays were performed and there was much dancing. Charles was always at the center of these. He was noted for his wit and was as addicted to pleasure, light-hearted banter and laughter as the rest. He danced most

gracefully, and I always applauded him loudly, and during those hal-
cyon days he always looked at me and acknowledged my approval. It
was deeply touching, and I was more in love every day.

There were minor disappointments.

For instance, on the first day after our arrival, I was preparing to
go down to the levee where certain ladies were to be presented to me.
Six of my ladies-in-waiting came with me, dressed in the costumes of
our country. Their hair was frizzed to resemble a periwig, and in their
farthingales—I now noticed—they walked awkwardly.

Donna Maria looked at them with approval.

She said to me: "They look like ladies. I declare the loose fashions
of the English shock me. Indeed, they shock me deeply. I tremble to
think what your mother would say if she saw you in these unholy
English fashions. Come, let us dress you as a Portuguese queen should
be dressed. Let us give you back your dignity."

I wondered, after, that I allowed it. It was due to the mention of
my mother, perhaps. I knew that she would not have approved of the
English customs.

So I relented and sat there meekly while they dressed me. They
called in the hairdresser, whom we had brought with us from Portugal
and whose services I had not yet used because Charles had so admired
my hair that I had worn it loosely dressed most of the time.

So I went down to the reception with my attendants, in the costume of my native land.

There was a brief silence, which was eloquent enough. I saw one
or two of the ladies put their hands to their mouths, as though holding in their laughter.

Charles was looking at me. For a few seconds I saw his expression
of bewildered amazement. Was it horror? Or dismay? I glanced at the
ladies. The somber colors made their skins look darker. Or did they
seem so against the English skins, which for the most part were fair?

Charles took my hand. He was then smiling as blandly as ever.

I received the ladies, but I knew my appearance was causing a certain amount of amusement.

When the company had gone I said to Charles: "I think some of
the company were surprised to see me in the fashion of my country."

"I think they were indeed," he replied.

"And you?"

"I must confess I was a little taken aback."

"I think they were laughing at me. Were you?"

"I think you look enchanting, no matter what fashion you adopt." He smiled and added: "Even the Portuguese."

Then he laughed and I could not help laughing with him.

He touched my hair. "It is so beautiful," he said. "It is a pity to treat it so."

I said: "It is the fashion."

"I know it is the command of the dragons. Is that so? The fierce Donna Maria, the stern Donna Elvira?"

I nodded.

"They are good souls," he said. "They love you well and I love them for that. But they are not, I dare to say, the arbiters of fashion. Here we follow the French . . . and the French, as you know, have an understanding of these matters. I myself am half French, so I should know."

He pulled at my hair and released it from the pins. "Ah, now you look more like my fair Catherine. You are beautiful, and nothing can change that . . . not even . . ."

"My hideous costume?"

"I was going to say the ministrations of your hairdresser."

"I am not beautiful," I cried. "I am too small. Oh, how I wish I could grow a few more inches. You are so tall, and most of the ladies stand higher than I do."

"Nay," he said tenderly. "I would not have you otherwise. You are delicate and tiny . . . and that makes you doubly precious."

I said: "I shall not wear this costume again. I shall dress in the English fashion."

"I think you will find it more comfortable. It suits you well. You have such a pretty neck and shoulders. It is a sin to conceal them."

"You will make me vain. I am not beautiful." I added: "There are so many beautiful women at your court."

"In my eyes . . . none so as my Queen."

"I cannot believe you really mean that."

"My dearest, I swear I speak the truth."

"Look at my teeth."

"Delightful."

"They stand out."

"Of course they do. They are so pretty, they insist on showing themselves, and quite rightly."

"You are so comforting to me."

"From now on its is my mission in life to comfort you."

"I shall change my costume now."

"With my help."

"I think perhaps Lady Suffolk would be more proficient at the task."

"You disappoint me," he said in mock dismay.

That was typical of him, but I was determined not to let Maria and Elvira persuade me to wear the Portuguese costumes again, for I believe he thought them as hideous as the others did.

AMONG THE PEOPLE WHO were presented to me soon after my arrival at Hampton Court was my sister-in-law Anne Hyde, Duchess of York, wife of James, who had treated me so courteously on my arrival.

I had asked Charles about her when I knew I was to meet her.

"Ah, the Lady Anne," he had said. "Thereby hangs a tale. She is the daughter of my Chancellor Clarendon. You have already met that stern gentleman. He is a clever fellow and his daughter takes after him. I am fond of Anne. But I must tell you that her entry into our family was not easy for her, poor girl. My mother was fiercely against it, and my mother, as you will no doubt one day discover, can be a very formidable lady. She will love you though, for she is of your faith . . . most fervently so, and that will be a bond between you two. As for Anne . . . well, it was not easy for her."

"Tell me about her. It is good to know something of people before one meets them."

"It was during my wandering days. Anne was lady-in-waiting to my sister of Orange, who was very good to us. I have been blessed in my family. She gave us shelter at her court and it was there that my brother became enamored of Anne."

"And she became Duchess of York."

"She might so easily not have done so . . . in spite of the fact that she should have been." He smiled wryly and looked at me in an amused fashion.

I said: "Why do you smile at me?"

"I smile because you are so sweetly innocent and I am the luckiest man in the world. I was wondering if you will be just a little bit shocked by the story of my brother James and his wife. Please don't be. Don't judge them harshly—neither James nor Anne—because I am devilishly fond of them both."

"That is natural. They are your brother and sister."

"James is a young man who is very fond of the ladies. And it is only natural that the ladies like him. He is a little gauche at times, but he is the brother of the King and the Duke of York—titles which are not without their charm. He fell in love with Anne and she with him, which was delightful, but sometimes there are . . . results."

He paused and studied me with mock concern.

"You mean . . ." I stammered, "there was a child?".

He opened his eyes wide and nodded.

"How . . . ?" I began.

"Shocking, yes," he said. "Well, James married her."

"Oh, I am glad of that."

"It was thought to be something of a *mésalliance,* and you know how fierce some people can be about such matters."

"*You* were kind to them, I know."

"But of course, I understood. Not so Anne's father, Clarendon. He was enraged . . . or pretended to be. He ranted against the poor girl. Poor Anne, she had a trying time."

"I suppose he was very shocked."

"I think my Lord Chancellor protested too much. At heart he could not really be displeased to see his daughter marry into the royal family."

"And . . . the baby?"

"It was born close on the marriage."

"How dreadful for them!"

"But they were safely married. And the baby died."

"That was tragic."

"Anne has just given birth again—a girl this time. It was not many weeks ago. They will have more. Anne is a shrewd and clever girl. She may give herself airs, as people sometimes do when they are elevated beyond their expectations. Forget that. You could find a good friend in Anne Hyde. She is good for James. She holds him in check. James can be foolhardy at times. So I believe this to be a good match on the whole."

When I met her, I could believe this. She was by no means as handsome as some of the court ladies, but it was impossible not to be aware of her intelligence. She spoke Spanish, so we were able to talk together, and I told her of my desire to learn English as soon as possible.

I asked her about her child.

"A little girl," she replied. "She is called Mary. There was the usual disappointment because she was not a boy. She seems strong enough. She is beautiful and lively."

"She must make you very happy," I said, and I wondered when I should have a child. Perhaps already . . .

I could see from her shrewd eyes that she followed my thoughts. She said: "It is a great consolation for everything."

She was looking at me intently, as though there was some meaning behind her words.

I said: "The Duke was very kind to me when I arrived. I was feeling very uneasy and bewildered, as you can guess."

"Oh yes," she replied. "I am glad you found him helpful. He is like the King, his brother, in some ways."

Again that significant look.

"They are not much alike in appearance," I said.

"Oh, the King has a style of his own."

I nodded, smiling.

"I hope you are going to be very happy here," she went on earnestly.

"Everyone has been so kind, and the King . . . he is very good to me."

"He has great charm," she said.

"And the people are so delighted that he has come back."

"That's true. And no one in the country is more delighted than he is himself."

"He has told me more than once that this is so. You must have known the King before he was restored to the throne, when he was wandering on the continent."

"Yes, I did. He was often at his sister's court. He was very fond of her and she of him. They are a very devoted family."

"The King has told me that, too."

"There was great sadness when the Princess of Orange died, and in the same year his brother the Duke of Gloucester died. What a year that was! A year of tragedy and hope . . . and death . . . then the King's restoration to the throne. His favorite sister Henrietta was also near to death. Praise God, she recovered to marry the brother of the King of France. Of all the family, the King loved her the best, so he was spared that grief."

"I must hear more of these matters," I said.

"Indeed. You are of the family now."

"I hope to meet the King's mother."

Anne's face hardened for a moment. Then she smiled. "You will be in her favor."

"She very kindly wrote warmly to me."

"She approved of your marriage to the King, and is delighted that he has a wife who is of her faith. How different it was with my marriage!"

"I know that she opposed it."

"Opposed it! She did everything she could to prevent it. I do not look forward to her arrival. She is so emotional. She could not restrain her feelings if she tried . . . and of course she does not try. She will always resent me for marrying her favorite son. James is her favorite, you know. Charles understands her too well . . . and she knows it. And sometimes he does not attempt to hide his knowledge."

"There is so much for me to learn about this country and my new family, as well as the language."

She looked at me steadily. She said: "Yes, you will find much to learn."

And again I had that feeling that she was trying to warn me.

CHE HAPPY DAYS CONCINUED. Charles and I rode often together—unfortunately, never quite alone.

"Thus it is to be a king," he said ruefully.

Some little distance from us would ride my Master of Horse, a very earnest young man about my age, who had shown himself always eager to please me. He was Edward Montague, a relative of the Earl of Sandwich.

Charles told me that Edward Montague had been brought up as a Puritan and that accounted for his serious manner.

"He is a good fellow," he said, "and reliable. I daresay he deplores our gaiety at times, but we will forgive him that, for he certainly knows how to handle horses."

I had taken quite a liking to Edward Montague.

I loved those rides with Charles, but it did seem as though we were watched continually, and I often saw a glint of something I did not understand in the eyes of the watchers. They appeared to be amused . . . and I had the feeling that they were waiting for something.

Charles talked to me a good deal about the past. He made me see the days of his exile. They would have embittered some—not so Charles. He had an irrepressible spirit which gave him the power to laugh at life, however grim it might be, however seemingly hopeless. I could see that he had the power to attract people to him, for he could never be entirely sad, and in his presence people must share in his gaiety. He could usually see something to make him smile . . . in people . . . in situations . . . in life. . . . It was a most happy trait, and I knew that I was not the only one to feel stimulated and enchanted by his company.

Through his eyes I saw it all . . . those terrible days when it became clear that the Royalists would be defeated . . . when he heard that his father was Cromwell's prisoner . . . when he himself was wandering about the country, constantly in danger of being captured. Even then he could talk light-heartedly of it, finding humor in desperate situations.

"Picture me . . . hiding in Stonehenge, disguised as a serving man. My friends said they had never seen such a servingman in all the palaces in England. I could as easily have been mistaken for a Druid risen from the dead."

And so many times he had come near to being captured.

"I must have been singularly blessed," he said. "They could not catch me because, always at hand, there was someone to help."

He told me about Jane Lane, the girl who had risked her life for him, as many had before and after.

"It was September," he said, his eyes smiling as, a little dreamily, he looked back to the past. "It must have been more than ten years ago, as it was after Worcester. I knew I had to get out of the country or my fate would be that of my father. I came to Bently Hall.

"Jane Lane was there, visiting her brother before calling on a friend near Bristol. Her cousin, a man named Lascelles, was to travel with her, and she would take a manservant as well. I was to be that manservant, and we planned to go to a house near Sherborne where friends could get me to the coast and shipped to France. They dressed me as the servingman and I took the name of one of the family servants . . . William Jackson, I remember."

"I cannot believe that you could ever look like anyone's servant," I said.

"You have guessed correctly. I was a poor actor. They would never have accepted me in the King's Players."

"Please tell me about Jane Lane."

"A beautiful young woman." He smiled, remembering, and I felt a twinge of jealousy. I should have liked to have been the one who helped him to safety.

"I rode the mare and Jane rode pillion behind me. Jane's brother-in-law and sister rode with us. What a journey that was! They were terrified when we stopped at inns, certain that I would betray myself. I did encounter some strange looks, I can tell you. Jane eye's were on me, fiercely condemning when I committed such folly . . . but she forgave me. "It is hard to be a servingman when you should be a king," she said.

"I remember as we came into Stratford-upon-Avon we rode into a troop of Roundheads, and Jane's sister and her husband turned back at the sight of them. Jane was furious with them. She was afraid they would be seen leaving us and that suspicion would be aroused. "Ride on," she commanded. "Keep your head down. Don't look so regal. Look humble, for the love of God." So, for the love of God and Jane, I hung my head. The soldiers gave us a quick glance and decided that we were of no interest—and so we rode on.

"I remember putting up at an inn in Cirencester. We had some tricky moments there. I can tell you, Jane had reason to admonish me. 'Try to play the part with some reality,' she scolded me. And then she would blush enchantingly and murmur, 'Your Majesty.' She was delightful. You would have liked Jane. So resourceful. Do you know, in such situations I would give the palm to the ladies. They have more subtlety. They are more capable of deceit."

I protested.

"Not you, my love. You are a woman apart. Well, Jane saved my life. I owe much to Jane and many like her. Determined as she was that our plan should succeed, yet she could not forget that I was the King . . . a king without a kingdom assuredly, but nevertheless a king.

"When we reached Abbots Leigh we were to stay a night at an inn, and she asked for a private room for me, her servant, mark you . . . because I was suffering from the ague, she said. And, would you believe it? It was given to me. Oh, Jane Lane was a lady of great character."

"And what happened after that?"

"Jane took me to a colonel, Francis Wyndham, at Trent, which is a place near Sherborne. He was to take me over the sea and get me to France . . . which, God bless him, he did."

"And did you ever see Jane Lane again?"

"Indeed I did. Cromwell's spies were everywhere. The last thing he wanted was for me to escape to France. He would never be at peace while I was alive. Poor fellow, he must have had some uneasy years. The French were friendly to me. After all, I am half French . . . and any monarch knows that the fall of one king is a danger to all kings. So I could rely to a certain extent on the French. I had my sister Mary to help me to regain my throne. So there would be some consternation in Cromwell's camp. They had set a reward of a thousand pounds on my head, and I had left taking that head with me. There were rumors. There were some who remembered seeing a somewhat incongruous servingman who had accompanied Mistress Jane Lane on her journey toward the coast.

"So one day, when I was in Paris, a courier brought a message to me. Colonel Lane, Jane's brother, had brought her to Paris so that if there were inquiries about that journey she had made with me, she should not be there to answer their questions. She and the Colonel disguised themselves as peasants and made their way to Yarmouth, where they found a ship to get them out of the country."

"How very dangerous it all must have been!"

"We lived in dangerous times, Catherine. The days had become filled with hope and despair. No, not despair. I always knew in my heart that one day I would come back . . . and that hope was kept alive by all those good people who risked their lives for my sake."

"What happened to Jane Lane?"

"They had come to Paris and I went to meet them. I remember it well. My mother was in the party . . . and my brother Henry was alive then. They all wanted to thank Jane for what she had done. I was overjoyed to see her. I was eager to thank her. I kissed her cheek and called her my life . . . because it was true, I owed it to her."

"Did she stay long in France?"

"She was in Paris for some time where she was treated with great respect by the court there. They were very good to me. I owe much to Louis. Oh yes, I like to think that Jane was rewarded for what she did for me."

"I am sure she did not want payment."

"That's true. She was one of my most loyal and loving subjects. I was glad when she went to stay at my sister's court. Mary was in Cologne at the time and Jane went to join her household there. It was unsafe for her to go back to England after what she had done. Cromwell could be venomous against anyone who helped the monarchy. Now, I thank Heaven that all that is over."

I still wanted to hear more of Jane and I persisted, "Where is she now?"

"She married Sir Clement Fisher of Warwickshire, on my restoration. The government gave her a thousand pounds and from me there was a gold watch. I suggested she should keep it as a memento of her bravery and it should go from eldest daughter to every eldest daughter in the household to remind them of what their noble ancestor had done for the King of England."

"What a wonderful story!" I cried.

"With a happy ending. Would that all stories could have them. Without Jane I might not be sitting here at this moment. I am sure I should be mouldering in my grave . . . in two parts perhaps, head in one place, body in another."

"I pray you, do not mention such."

He touched his head lightly. "It is safe now," he said, "and I intend it shall remain on my shoulders for the rest of my life. I will do everything to prevent the parting."

"It is not a matter to joke about."

"My dearest, life is a matter to joke about. It is the only way to live it."

He went on to tell me of his stay in Scotland, where he was crowned at Scone.

He shrugged his shoulders. "It was no fun being King in Scotland, I can assure you. It was more like being a state prisoner. I must repent my sins, put away most of my friends, resist the merry way of life and change it for one of fasting and prayer. Odds bodikins, I'd as lief be a wandering exile far from home. At least there was some merriment in that! I was glad to leave Scotland behind and march into England. You know that they caught up with us near Worcester . . . and after that I wandered through England, west and south . . . on one occasion hiding in the branches of an oak tree in Boscabel while Cromwell's men searched for me, even coming under the tree, but the kindly leaves hid me from view—so that oak tree was yet another that saved my life.

"Two years in Cologne . . . three in the Low Countries . . . and three in France . . . an exile . . . waiting, waiting for the call. Then on that glorious day . . . it was the twenty-sixth of May . . . my thirtieth birthday approaching. What a birthday gift! Could ever a man have a better! They wanted me back. The country was weary of the Protectors. They wanted a king on the throne."

I clasped my hands together. "What a wonderful life you have had," I said. "How different from mine."

"My dear one has seen so little of the world . . . and I so much."

"Does that matter?" I asked anxiously.

"It will not . . . if we do not let it," he said, and I did not realize then that that was a somewhat cryptic remark. He had told me so much . . . and so little.

ONE OF OUR MOST DELIGHTFUL PASTIMES was teaching each other our languages. I said that it was far more important that I should learn his than he mine; and with this he agreed.

I said: "I find it very trying that I cannot hear what the English ladies are whispering about. There seems so much to amuse them."

"Perhaps it is better not to know," he said with a sudden smile which was half humorous, half serious.

"I want to know . . . all."

"Sometimes there is greater happiness in ignorance than knowledge."

"Never."

"Think of Adam and Eve and what happened to them. Thrown out of the Garden of Eden."

"Whatever there is to know . . . I want to know it."

He was unusually silent then, but a few seconds later he was laughing at the pronunciation of some word I had spoken.

I PERSISTED. I did so want to master his language. I was helped considerably by Lady Suffolk, of whom I was becoming quite fond. She had been so kind and helpful and took such pains to please me. She had made me see how unbecoming the Portuguese costume was, and I never thought of wearing it now. I could see how ill it became my women. Of course, Donnas Maria and Elvira deplored my adoption of the English fashions, but they were ready to disapprove of everything in my new country.

I was beginning to improve my knowledge of English sufficiently to enable me to carry on a somewhat halting conversation . . . lapsing now and then into Spanish or Portuguese. Charles was very encouraging and I often talked to him in English, with him helping me along.

Then suddenly the happy days were over. I had known we could not stay indefinitely at Hampton Court. We would return to Whitehall and perhaps make a progress through the country. There would be more presentations, more levees and more ceremonies generally to be attended.

It appeared that some dispatches had arrived for Charles and he had to leave at once. He assured me he would not be away for long.

"It is urgent business," he said.

I wanted to share everything and was disappointed that he did not tell me the nature of this urgent business.

So he went away and I felt very lonely, which was silly of me. He would soon be back, I assured myself. Perhaps that very day.

He did not return that day.

I noticed that there was a great deal of whispering and giggling among the ladies. I guessed something amusing, interesting—perhaps scandalous—was taking place at the court, and I felt shut out. How frustrating it was not to be able to interpret the words . . . to feel excluded.

I was preparing to retire that night and found myself alone with Lady Suffolk, and in faltering English I asked what had happened to amuse the ladies.

She hesitated and I thought she was going to say she did not understand, as I fancied she might do if she thought the subject was not for my ears.

Then suddenly she seemed to make up her mind. She said slowly and clearly, so that I understood most of what she said: "It is something which has happened to one of the ladies."

"Something . . . of scandal . . . is that the word?"

"It is the word, Your Majesty . . . and it fits the case perfectly."

"Tell me . . ."

She looked puzzled for a moment and then she said: "Oh, this lady has left her husband."

"And that is this . . . scandal?"

"In the circumstances, yes."

"What are this circumstances?"

"She has just given birth to a baby boy."

"And this?"

"Well . . . Your Majesty. Her husband is a Catholic, and the child has been baptized in the Catholic faith."

"And . . . and this is Protestant country."

"It is not that so much. The lady says that her husband has no right because the boy is not his. And she is leaving him . . . her husband, I mean."

"I do not understand."

"It is not easy to explain, Your Majesty."

"But she leave because the child is baptized in the Catholic faith?"

"Yes, she says he has no right. The child should not be baptized as a Catholic just because he is . . ."

I looked at her in puzzlement. "Because . . . why is because?"

"She says his father is a very important man and not a Catholic. So she has left her husband, packed up her jewels and possessions of value and taken the child away."

"And this . . . amuses?"

"Well, the lady does provide amusement."

"Because she is a woman who has a child . . . not her husband's?"

"That . . . and other things."

"So what will be now?"

"That is what everyone waits to see."

"She is one of the ladies of the court. Then I will know her?"

"Oh, no, Madam. She had been away from the court . . . having the baby, you see."

"Who is she? What her name?"

"She is Lady Castlemaine, Madam."

My heart began to beat fast. I heard my mother's voice. I remembered the grave look in her eyes. "If by chance you meet this woman—which you should not—you must treat her as though she does not exist. You must never allow her to come to court."

Lady Suffolk, herself overcome by embarrassment, was not looking at me.

I heard myself faintly: "I do not think I have met this lady."

I was shaken and wanted to be by myself.

THE NEXT MORNING I felt better. I must stop thinking about Lady Castlemaine. Just because she had once been a friend of the King did not mean that she was now. I had to cast off my conventional ideas. My mother had understood. A young man with Charles's gifts, his high position—even though at that time his rights were not acknowledged—would have many women to fawn on him. He was human. It was natural. And I was certain now that any amour of the past was over. We were married and he had shown well enough during the time we had been together that he loved me. He had said so many times.

I had to be worldly. I had to understand. The past was over. I must not look back. Soon he would be with me and I should be reassured.

Ignore her, my mother had said. Treat her as though she does not exist.

What sound advice she always gave.

I would forget what I had heard. There would no doubt be many stories about such a woman. It was no concern of mine that she had left her husband.

Charles returned. It was wonderful to see him. His eyes shone with joy at the sight of me. He put his arms round me and picked me up. I was so small and light that it was easy for him.

"Well," he said. "Have you missed me?"

"Very much," I answered.

"And I you . . . so much, my Catherine."

I felt wonderfully happy.

We talked together. He said my English had certainly improved.

"Lady Suffolk has become my tutor."

"*I* would be your tutor."

"But when the master is away should not another take his place?"

"No one must ever take my place with you, Catherine."

"Nor mine with you," I added.

"You are my wife. Does that not mean something?"

"It means everything to me."

It was wonderful to be together. When we were about to retire for the night he took a paper from his pocket and said carelessly: "Here is a list of the ladies I have agreed shall be in your household."

I was about to glance at it when he took it from me and put it into a drawer.

"Look at it tomorrow," he said. "There is time for that later." He was smiling. "We shall be leaving this place soon and you will need a household fitting for the Queen of England. I know these people well and you have yet to meet them so I can vouch for their suitability . . . and you know you can take my word. I want you to be well served, my love. So . . . leave it all to me."

I said I should be happy to do so.

It was not until the following morning when I was alone that I remembered the paper in the drawer. I took it out and studied it.

I felt faint, for the name at the top of the list was that of Lady Castlemaine.

My hands were trembling. What could this mean? He had chosen this woman, who had been his mistress, and was now involved in some scandal, as one of my ladies-in-waiting!

I could not understand what it meant. "Ignore her. Do not have her near you," my mother had said.

I would not. I took up my pen and scratched out her name.

I sent for my secretary, Sir Richard Bellings, and said to him in Spanish, "Sir Richard, this is the suggested list of the ladies of my household. I have amended it. You will know where to take it."

"Yes, Your Majesty," he said and took the paper from me.

I sat down. I felt dizziness coming over me and I thought I was going to faint.

I sat there trembling, wondering what this could mean.

CHARLES CAME TO ME. He dismissed the women who were with me and I knew what he wanted to talk about before he began.

He said: "I see you have scratched out the name of Lady Castlemaine on the list I left for you."

"Oh yes," I said, speaking in Spanish. I was too emotional to think in English. "I could not have her in my household."

"I have selected her," he said coolly. "I have promised her the place."

"How could you do such a thing?"

"My dear Catherine, I am choosing those whom I think would serve you best."

Like most docile people, I am aroused to temper rarely, but when it is released it is apt to be more fierce than tempers which are allowed to show themselves more often. I felt angry now, and my anger was the greater because of the sadness behind it. He had chosen her. There could be only one reason. Because he wanted her here. She had been his mistress. She had borne a child. Whose child? She had left her husband, implying that he had no claim on the child. Then who . . . ? It was becoming clear to me. The urgent business which had taken him away from Hampton Court had been to go to her. I had been deceived. I had been innocent . . . ignorant . . . and he had used my innocence to betray me.

I said: "Are you sure you do not mean she would serve *you* best?"

"What does that mean?" he demanded.

"It means that I know she has been your mistress in the past. The indication to me is that she still occupies that dubious position."

He was angry; he was disturbed; but even so he managed to be amused. I felt then that he would be amused by any situation, no matter what pain it caused to others.

"What amuses you?" I could not help asking.

"Your solemnity, my dear. This is nothing . . . a bagatelle. We can arrange this."

"I have already done so by crossing her name off the list."

"But I wish her to have the post."

"Why?"

"Because she is the most suitable for it. I know these ladies."

"Very well, it would seem."

"Catherine, you are so different. Where is my sweet little wife?"

"You cannot expect sweetness from her when she is asked to accept your mistress into her household."

"I admit to a liaison in the past. There were . . . others, you know. It is natural enough. I was never meant to be a monk. All that is changed now. I swear I have not been with Barbara since our marriage."

"Barbara!"

"Barbara Palmer, Lady Castlemaine."

"And you are now proposing to resume the relationship?"

"Catherine! What has happened to you?"

"I should have thought that would have been clear."

"This jealousy . . . this unreasonableness . . . it is so unlike you."

"I saw no reason for jealousy before this."

"There is none now. Catherine, you are the Queen. You must behave like one."

"And tolerate the presence of my husband's mistress in my bedchamber?"

"She is not my mistress now."

"She was."

"I have never denied it. Listen to me. I will vouch for her. She will serve you well. Do you think I would not insist on that? Never think for a moment that she should be allowed to presume on her past relationship with me. If there were any sign of that, she would be dismissed. I promise you that."

He held out his arms to me and smiled apologetically.

But I kept hearing my mother's words. "Do not receive her. Do not have her in your court."

I turned away. I thought: my heart is broken. Whatever he says, he wants her here. I have been deceived by him. So much charm . . . so many assurances of devotion . . . they did not go very deeply.

I said in a cold voice: "Charles, I will not have that woman in my household."

His manner changed. I had never seen him look like that before. His face had darkened. He looked saturnine.

But he said nothing. He turned away and walked out of the room.

THE AWAKENING

MY DREAM WAS OVER. FROM BEING THE HAPPIEST WOMAN in England I had become the most miserable.

I had not seen Charles since that scene. He was really angry with me, and that could only mean one thing: the appointment of Lady Castlemaine was of the utmost importance to him. And why? It could only be for one reason.

But he must know that I would never have Lady Castlemaine in my household. He must understand. Surely anyone would see the reason for it. He was certainly aware of it, but he was angry because he greatly desired the woman to be there. She had asked for the appointment and he had promised it.

So he must have seen her. His urgent business was to be with her. She had just left her husband because he had had her child baptized as a Catholic . . . and the child was not her husband's.

Whose child was it? Why was she so incensed that it had had a Catholic baptism? The inference was obvious. Oh no! I could not believe it. But I must not shut my mind to the obvious. Charles had been so loving to me, so charming, because he was indeed practiced in these matters. I had been one of the many . . . albeit that I was his wife.

No wonder Maria and Elvira had looked so grave; no wonder Maria had talked to my mother, who had sought to prepare me for Lady Castlemaine.

I was seeing it all clearly now. I had been duped during those weeks at Hampton Court. And how easy it had been to deceive me! No wonder I had so often seen amusement in his eyes. He must have been laughing at the simplicity of the task.

I wanted to go home . . . back to my mother . . . back to her palace . . . back to the convent where I could live with my dreams.

It was several days since I had seen him. At times the longing to do so was so great that I was on the point of sending a message to him. "Please come back to me. I will do as you wish. I will accept her in my household." Then I would say to myself: Never. Never will I have her near me.

And so I did not see him.

I had to make a pretence that nothing unusual was happening. I did my best, but it was not easy. Maria and Elvira noticed the change in me.

"Are you well? Is anything wrong?" asked Maria.

"I am well, thank you."

"You are overtired," said Elvira.

"Perhaps you should see the physician," added Maria.

"Please . . . please do not fret. I am quite well."

They looked at each other skeptically. Their disapproval of English ways as well as their manners of dress had not diminished.

Then came that day which I was to remember as one of the most unhappy of my life.

I was in the Presence Room and some of the ladies of the court were being presented to me. Maria and Elvira had taken their stand on either side of me as they always did, like a pair of dragons guarding me, which mever failed to cause some amusement in the company.

I was trying to behave normally when I heard Charles's voice. My heart leaped with pleasure. He had come then! He had decided to end this trouble between us. He had realized, of course, that I had only behaved as a wife naturally would. He had accepted my decision. All would be well between us.

He had caught my eyes across the room and was smiling at me.

I felt my features relax. Happiness filled me. It was over. All was well between us.

He was coming toward me, holding the hand of one of the ladies as he always did when he presented them to me.

One could not help noticing her. She was tall and one of the most beautiful women I had ever seen. Yet, statuesque as she was, Charles still towered above her. They looked splendid together. I often thought that his height made me look smaller than I actually was, and I was very conscious of that and felt a certain envy of tall women. This one's hair was bronze in color, falling in luxuriant curls over her bare shoulders; her eyes were large and sparkling; she held herself proudly, arrogantly, one might say: she gave an impression of complete assurance. I supposed one would have that, with such looks. She was the sort of woman who would be noticed immediately whenever she appeared.

Charles presented her to me. She smiled and lowered her eyes as she bent to kiss my hand. The King murmured something I could not catch.

She turned away, Charles with her.

Maria bent toward me. "Do you know who that was?" she demanded.

"I could not catch the name."

"He intended you should not. He did not pronounce it clearly for that reason. Can you not guess?"

I looked at her blankly.

Elvira whispered: "It is Lady Castlemaine."

Now I understood why there was tension in the room, why there was a lull in the conversation.

How could he? I thought. How dare he!

I felt the dizziness overcome me; then something warm was spreading over my face, for the blood was gushing from my nose. I saw the stain on my gown and fell fainting to the floor.

I CAN IMAGINE the consternation, although I was unaware of it. What a spectacle it must have been! The Lady—as I learned later they called her—sauntering away with the King, and the Queen lying on the floor in a faint, her face and gown covered in blood.

There could never have been anything like it in the court of England.

I can picture Maria and Elvira fussing over me, giving directions, implying that no one must dare touch me but themselves. Charles would know what had brought this on. Did he find it amusing, I wondered. That was unfair. He would be distressed. He *was* fond of me. He could not have deceived me as blatantly as that. If I would be the complaisant Queen, accepting his mistress, I could still have a small place in his affections.

I lay in my bed, and with consciousness came back the memory of

that Presence Chamber and Maria and Elvira telling me who it was
who had kissed my hand.

I never wanted to live through such a moment again in the whole
of my life.

And there I was, in my bed with the physicians standing by, and
Elvira and Maria hovering over me, determined to protect me from
whatever disaster should come to me next.

I think the physicians understood that there had been such attacks
before and that seemed a matter for relief. I must rest, they said.
They would give me some physic. I must remain quiet and not excite
myself.

So I lay in my bed, going over it all. I longed for my mother. She
would know what I should do. I believed there was one thing she
would be certain of: I should never have that brazen woman in my
household.

A day passed. I left my bed. I sat about miserably, hoping that the
King would come. Surely he must understand my reason for refusing
to have Lady Castlemaine in my household. He was usually so ready
to understand the problems of others; he was always so sympathetic.
But perhaps that was only when they did not inconvenience himself.

Maria came to tell me that I had a visitor. My heart leaped. I was
sure it must be the King. But it was not. It was Lord Clarendon.

He was brought in and came to me and kissed my hand. He was
neither tall nor short and had a ruddy complexion, inclined to be fat,
and he walked with difficulty. He had a clever face, but I did not need
this to tell me that he was one of the most able men in the kingdom.

I was amazed that he should come to see me.

He immediately asked after my health and I asked after his.

"It is this accursed gout, Your Majesty," he said. "It makes a slave
of me."

"Then pray be seated and tell me your business," I said. We were
able to speak in Spanish, which was convenient.

He was a man of great insight, much traveled, as I knew; he had
remained loyal to the Royalist cause throughout its darkest days; he
had traveled on the continent with Charles and was his most trusted
adviser; he had shared hardships with him, sometimes, as he had written, "with neither clothes nor fire to preserve him from the sharpness
of the season and not three sous in the world to buy a faggot."

"Your Majesty," he said, "I come on behalf of His Majesty the King."

I said: "Why does not the King come himself?"

"Madam," he went on, "he is uncertain of your mood and it seems, on this occasion, that an intermediary is advisable."

"That is not so," I retorted sharply. "If the King wishes to speak to me, it is for him to do so."

Clarendon looked excessively uncomfortable. He shifted painfully in his seat.

"This little misunderstanding between Your Majesty and the King is deeply to be deplored."

"None deplore it more deeply than I."

"Then I am sure we can smooth it out."

He then began to talk at some length of the King's dilemma, and I gathered from his tone that I had been a little hasty and not as understanding as I might have been.

I was hurt and angry because it seemed that he believed I was the one who was in the wrong and that it was really rather foolish of me to make such trouble about an insignificant matter.

I looked at him steadily and said: "I do not think, my lord, that you and I see this matter in the same light. I will not have Lady Castlemaine in my household."

My face was flushed and my heart was beating very fast. He was aware of my agitation and he rose quickly, saying he did not wish to distress me and would call again at a time more convenient to me.

I did not seek to detain him, and he left.

I tried to calm myself. I must not become so agitated at the sound of that woman's name. All I had to do was refuse to see her. After all, was I not the Queen?

The next day Lord Clarendon called again. I felt much calmer and ready to talk to him.

"Pray be seated, my lord," I said. "I am sorry for my reception of you yesterday. I was unprepared. I fancied that you believed the blame to be mine and I found that insupportable. I cannot see it in that light. I had looked upon you as my friend. I know you came on the King's behalf and you have always been his most loyal servant. He has spoken to me of your fidelity to him at all times, but you must understand that I have suffered great anguish over this matter, which has made me a very unhappy woman."

He replied earnestly that his great desire was to be of service to me. He would be very unhappy if, in explaining the effect my conduct had had on the King and how it would be wise to put matters right between us, he had appeared to be ungracious to me.

I replied that I was not averse to hearing if I had committed some fault.

He said: "Oh, Your Majesty, everything that has happened is very understandable. Your Majesty has had a restricted upbringing, if you will forgive my saying so. There are certain imperfections in mankind that have to be accepted, lamentable though they may be. I would point out, Madam, that these little failings are not only to be met with in this country." He smiled wryly. "It has come to my knowledge that they exist in your own land in no small measure. But you have been sheltered. *Your* ears have never been sullied with these . . . er . . . little follies which are common to all mankind."

"It is all so unexpected . . ."

"Your Majesty, you will agree with me that, had we sent an English princess to Portugal, she would not have found a court completely virtuous."

"I cannot say . . ."

"Then I can assure Your Majesty that it would be so. The King has been devoted to you. Anything that happened before your marriage ought not to concern you, nor should you attempt to discover it."

"I have not inquired into the past. I merely refuse to accept this woman into my household and she is being forced upon me. I do not want her. She is not a virtuous woman and therefore my ladies should not be expected to associate with her."

"Madam, if the King insists . . ."

"If he insists, he exposes me to the contempt of the courts of Europe and shows he has no love for me."

"I must warn Your Majesty that you should not provoke the King too far."

"But it is he who is provoking me."

"Accept this . . . as others have before you. The great Catherine de' Medici accepted her husband's affection for the Lady Diane de

Poitiers, and she held her position at court. In fact, it was strength-
ened. It is all part of the duties of a Queen."

"I wish to please the King, but I cannot accept that woman in my
household."

He gave up in despair, but he was not as despairing as I was.

I was deep in misery.

THAT NIGHT CHARLES CAME. I had never before seen him look as
he did then. The tenderness was missing and he looked displeased.

"I hear you remain stubborn," he said. "And I see that you have no
true love for me."

"Charles! It is because I love you! That is why I cannot bear to
have this woman here."

"I tell you, I have given her my word that she shall come."

"That means that she will come . . . no matter what I want."

"All I ask is that you receive her."

I murmured: "To bring her here as you did . . . without warning.
I cannot forget that you did that to me."

"You should have controlled your venom against her. Instead of . . ."

"I know, I know. It was a distressing scene, but I had no control
over it. Charles, it was due to my overwhelming grief, grief that I had
been so deceived."

"It is a great deal of fuss about a matter of no great importance."

"If it is of no great importance, why do you insist that she comes?"

"I mean of no great importance to you. I can only marvel that you
can behave so."

I shouted at him: "Not so much as I marvel at your behavior."

"You are completely unworldly. You reason like a child."

"I reason like a wife who is ready to love and please her husband
and has now been so ill-treated that her heart is broken. I wish I had
never come here. I will go home. I will go back to Portugal."

"It would be well for you to discover first whether your mother
would receive you. I shall begin by sending back your servants. I have
a notion that they maintain you in this stubborn attitude."

We had both raised our voices and I thought afterward of how
many people would be listening to us and how soon the news that the
King and Queen were quarrelling over Lady Castlemaine would be

spread round the court. It would reach her ears, and I was sure she would be gratified.

"You have not kept to your vows," I cried.

"Can you upbraid me for that? What of your family? Did they honour our terms? Did they carry out the obligations of the treaty? What of the portion which was promised and was not there when the time came? What of the spice and sugar that has yet to be transformed into cash? If I were you, I should not talk too much of honouring vows."

This was unkind. It was no fault of mine that the money which had been waiting had had to be used in our conflict against the Spaniards.

"Oh, I should never have come," I said. "I want to go home."

I saw the expression cross his face. He was shocked that, in spite of all this, I should want to leave him. And did I? I was not sure. I was too bitterly wounded to know what I wanted.

He seemed suddenly to decide he would hear no more. He left me in my misery.

CLARENDON CAME NEXT DAY. I think he was sorry for me, but at the same time he was determined to see this through the King's eyes. I suppose that was his duty.

"Your Majesty, this has become a grievous matter indeed," he said.

"The King was here last night. He was most ill-tempered."

"I understand Your Majesty's temper matched his. I have come this day hoping to persuade you to take the course which will be most advantageous to your happiness."

"That must surely be to insist on not having that woman near me."

"Will Your Majesty have the patience to listen to me if I try to explain how it appears to me . . . and to others? No wife should refuse to accept a servant who is esteemed and recommended by her husband."

"How could such a woman be esteemed and respected by him?"

"If Your Majesty will forgive me, she is esteemed and recommended by the King, and if you refuse to receive her, what I ask you to remember is this: this thing will be done with or without your consent."

I was silent.

He went on: "The whole court has been aware of the King's devotion to you in the first weeks since your marriage. He sought no company but that of Your Majesty. Do you not see that you are charming enough to lure him from others? Have you such a low opinion of your attractions that you do not realize you can do this?"

I stared at him. I should have understood, of course. He was trying to help me. He was telling me that whether or not I agreed to Lady Castlemaine's coming, she would do so because it was the King's wish that she should. He would insist, since he had promised the lady. I did not know then, of course, of the power she had over him. I could not have understood then the depth of her sensuality, which matched his own. Temporarily I had had the appeal of innocence—unworldliness in a worldly court. I had had an initial advantage because I was so different from other women he had known. I did not know then that he would never have been faithful to me, but if I had been compliant, sweetly forgiving, I could have kept some hold on his affections. He was a man who hated trouble, and I was now causing him a great deal of it.

But I did not understand then. I could think only of what was right, and I firmly believed that to give my consent to that woman's coming into my household must surely be wrong—and I determined to stand against it.

Clarendon was looking at me appealingly. But I did not understand.

I said: "The King will doubtless do as he wishes, but I shall never give my consent to that woman's coming into my household."

Clarendon shrugged his shoulders. He had done his best.

THOSE WERE VERY UNHAPPY DAYS. Charles and I scarcely spoke, and then only when absolutely necessary. He was not by nature a vindictive man. When he had returned to England and the Royalists had dug up the bodies of Roundheads and exposed them in public places, he had been the one to call a halt to the practice.

I think it was because of his deep disappointment in me that he acted as he did. He had believed I adored him—as indeed I had—and therefore would accept anything for his sake. It was a bitter disappointment to him that I was adamant on this matter which meant so much to him. It was not, I knew, entirely his devotion to Lady

Castlemaine which made him act as he did, but his dislike of the storms she created, which she was prone to do vociferously and sometimes in public.

How could I be expected to understand such things at that time? His reference to the unpaid dowry had shocked me profoundly. He was slighting to Don Francisco; Diego Silvas was sent to prison for failing to make the arrangements for the sale of those goods which were meant to be part of my dowry; and there were preparations to send my Portuguese attendants back to Portugal.

I was shocked and bewildered. Everything had changed so suddenly. I had been too happy. I should have known it could not last.

Then something happened which at least temporarily lifted me out of my gloom.

I was dressing one morning with my ladies around me when Charles appeared. I started in amazement. Lady Stanhope dropped a deep curtsey, so did the others, with the exception of Donna Maria whose sight was failing so that she did not immediately recognize him.

He had changed. He looked more like the man I had known in the beginning. He was smiling at me, and I was suddenly happy.

"I would speak with the Queen," he said, and in a few seconds they all had gone.

"I have news," he said to me. "My mother is coming here. She will be leaving Calais shortly. We must give her a warm welcome."

The words thrilled me. I desperately wanted us to be back where we had been.

It was characteristic of Charles that he should behave as though there was no rift between us—as though it had never been. I should have to be beside him to greet his mother, and we should have to pretend that all was well between us. Even pretence would be better than this prolonged indifference.

"She will go to Greenwich," he said. "Later, I think, Somerset House would be more fitting . . . but while that is being made ready . . . it will be Greenwich."

"And we must go to see her there?"

He was smiling. "We must let her see how glad we are that she is here. I wonder what you will think of my mother, Catherine?"

"I long to meet her."

"And she to meet you. She has said that is the reason she is making the journey."

"I hope she is pleased by our marriage."

"Indeed she is. How could she not be? Poor James will get something of a drubbing, I do not doubt. And I am sorry for Anne. I hope she will be able to defend herself. But I am of the opinion that she will do that very well."

He was laughing, and I thought how foolish I had been. I had missed so much, I should have given way; then I could have been with him all this time. If he could not be entirely mine, in that moment, I would have been prepared to give way and accept what I could get.

Our relationship had changed again. I was in his company more as we prepared to go to Greenwich to meet Queen Henrietta Maria. He talked to me about his mother.

"You must not allow her to bully you," he said. "She is overpowering and will certainly try. She likes her own way. Who does not? But Mam thinks it is only right that she should have hers. She and I never got on as well as the others. Perhaps I liked my own way, too. I disappointed her in some ways. I was never her favorite. James shared that position with my youngest sister Henrietta, until his marriage. She has never forgiven him for that."

When we went to meet her it had to be in royal style.

"My mother will be very much aware of that. She would not like to think that the very best had not been given to her. Poor Mam! She has had a tragic life. She did not enjoy those years in exile, and then . . . what they did to my father would have broken a woman of lesser spirit. She came through, but she has suffered a great deal through her husband and those children whom she lost. Elizabeth . . . Henry . . . Mary . . . all gone. Hers has been a tragic life."

"I shall do everything I can to please her."

"I know you will. I have a notion that you and she will be good friends. You have a good start. You are of the same religion and that counts for much with her."

I was lifted out of my misery. It was amazing, but Charles seemed to have forgotten that there was any trouble between us. It is true that talk was all about the preparations for his mother's arrival and comfort; but it was wonderful to have something to keep him with me.

In due course we set out, accompanied by our splendid company. We sailed along the river to Greenwich, and there were loyal shouts to greet us. I stood side by side with Charles to acknowledge the cheers; and I was almost happy.

At Greenwich Queen Henrietta Maria was waiting for us.

She was tiny. I was pleased to see that she was shorter than I, for I continued to deplore my lack of inches. She had been beautiful; that was still obvious, although her face was ravaged with the suffering of the years. But she was animated; her dark eyes were alert, darting everywhere; and although she was so small, she held herself proudly, as though to remind everyone that she was the daughter of a king and the wife of one: there could be no doubt that she was a woman of strong opinions and of a nature to force them on others.

I saw a flicker of pride in her eyes when they rested on Charles. Of course she would be proud of him. He looked so truly a king. His height set him above others; and those heavy features which on most men would be ugly, with him exuded an inimitable charm. I was proud of him; so must she be.

She had turned to me, her eyes taking in every detail of my appearance. Her face relaxed into a smile.

I made to kneel but she quickly put her arms round me and drew me to her.

"No . . . no, no," she said. "You are my daughter now." She kissed me. "You and I must know each other." She spoke rapidly, half in English, half in French, which somehow I managed to interpret. "It is to see you I have made this long and tiresome journey. Oh that wicked . . . wicked sea! How I hate him. But I must come to see my new daughter . . . so we will not kneel and kiss hands . . . that is for others. Not for us . . . eh, my daughter?"

There could not have been a warmer welcome.

I stammered my appreciation of it.

"I have said I will never come here again. I shall never face that sea. It is always worse when I am on it. It likes me not, no more than I like it." She lifted her shoulders in a gesture which I later learned was characteristic of her. "But I must come; to see my daughter . . . and to serve her as the Queen."

I was so overcome by these words, which touched me the deeper because of the slights and humiliations I had suffered of late, that I burst out: "Your Majesty must not speak of serving me! I know I shall love you. Not the King, nor any of your children, can love you more than I shall."

I think we were both overwrought. I certainly was. As I came to know her, I realized that her return to England had brought back a mingling of memories: her happy life with the King, her husband, and the terrible tragedy which overtook them both.

She was a highly emotional woman; she loved fiercely and hated in the same manner. There were no half measures for Queen Henrietta Maria.

I knew that when she looked at me she was thinking of herself as a young bride just come to England. She understood my feelings. I wondered how much she knew of the rift between Charles and me. But if she knew, she would understand. She would be my ally.

She walked back to the palace—Charles on one side of her, I on the other. James, with Anne, walked a little behind. I had noticed her chilly reception of these two. I was amazed how she could change in a matter of seconds. Anne held her head high. She was the Duchess of York and nothing Queen Henrietta Maria could do would alter that.

Henrietta Maria kept me beside her.

The conversation was conventional, as it must be on such occasions, but even so Henrietta Maria was determined that all should know how she felt towards certain members of the company. There was a great show of warmth towards me, a vague criticism of Charles, a reproach to James and disapproval of Anne.

Charles showed his amusement by a somewhat light-hearted bantering manner toward his mother; James was inclined to be sullen; while Anne assumed an air of indifference. So it was pleasant for me to bask in the Queen's approval and to feel that she was more pleased with me than with any member of her own family.

We remained at Greenwich for four hours and at the end of that time said farewell to the Queen. We were to meet again, for she was to join us at Hampton.

She whispered to me: "There you and I will talk together . . . alone." And there was an air of conspiracy about her which I found exciting and reassuring.

We returned to Hampton Court and that night supped in the great hall. I sat beside the King and the people came in to watch us, according to the custom. I knew they marvelled to see me with the King. It was the first time we had supped together for some weeks.

But I think they were pleased. Charles appeared to be, too. But of course I could not be entirely sure of that.

Oh, certainly I felt a great deal better than I had for some time.

AFTER THE ARRIVAL of the Queen Mother, my relationship with Charles had taken a new turn. It was not possible, after being together so affably during the Greenwich visit, to continue aloof. There were matters to discuss. My entry into the capital could not long be delayed. The people wanted to see me, and a King and Queen who were not on speaking terms would not please them.

Charles, as I knew, had a habit of shrugging off unpleasant situations. One could not be long in his company without realizing that. He behaved as though there had been no trouble between us. True, I had refused to receive Lady Castlemaine, but she came to court and Charles was often in her company. At least she had not been forced into my bedchamber, but he made no attempt to disguise his friendship with her. But it was obviously his wish that no more should be said about the matter.

Of course I had lost the lover of my honeymoon days, but there was no doubt that the presence of the Queen Mother in the country had wrought a change.

I would sit at my window, watching Charles strolling in the gardens. He was always accompanied by his closest friends, and several of his spaniels were usually at his heels; and among those people with him I often saw Lady Castlemaine, and she would be walking close to him.

It was a complete defiance of my wishes and brought home to me how little influence I had with him.

Henrietta Maria came to Hampton Court, and during that visit I had opportunities to be alone with her. She comforted me considerably.

In the first place, we were of the same religion, and we worshipped together in my chapel; afterward she told me how glad she was that Charles had married me.

"It was always a matter of sadness to me," she said, "that my husband was not of the faith. My Charles was a good man. Why should good men suffer so in this wicked world while those who commit great sins so often go free! They took him out there at Whitehall and they struck off that noble head. He was the King and they did that to him!"

She wept. I put an arm around her and she embraced me, tenderly. She wept easily; her emotions were very close to the surface. She was different from me. Anger bubbled over when she considered she had been unjustly treated. I wondered how she would have dealt with Lady Castlemaine.

It was easy to confide in her.

She nodded as she listened. "It is not an unusual story, *chérie*. It was a problem I did not have. My Charles was a good husband. He loved me . . . he loved his family dearly. They say he was not a good king. There was that wicked war . . . and they said it need not have been. He believed in the right of kings . . . given by God. The Divine Right. He would have none of the Parliament . . . so they went to war and cut off his head. They say we do not judge him as a man but as a king. Charles, they say, was a good man but a good man does not always make a good king. The two are apart, they say. They made that excuse . . . and they took him out before Whitehall and they cut off his head."

She wept bitterly.

"My son Charles is less like his father than any man I know. They will let him keep his head, I am sure. They love him as they never loved his father. What is it that makes people love? My father was much loved. He was a great king. They say the greatest king the French ever had. But he was not a good man like my Charles."

"Do not talk of it if it distresses you," I said.

"I like to talk to you, my dear. You are of my faith, and you and I understand each other. And now there is this between you and Charles. It does not show. That is Charles for you. I never understood my firstborn. He laughs much. He turns aside one's wrath. He always did. Oh, what an ugly boy he was! When I first saw him after his birth 'This is not my son!' I cried. 'Not the son of my handsome Charles.' Charles my husband was a handsome man, you know. Why did we have such a little monster? And he stayed ugly. Yet somehow he managed to please them all. The nursemaids adored him. They gave him all he wanted, yet he was not what I would call a spoiled child. He loved to be fondled by the nurses. He loved all women . . . and they loved him, for, *ma chérie,* when people love they are inclined to be loved in return. He is his grandfather again. My father, the great Henri, was loved wherever he went. He was merry . . . laughing his way through as Charles does. Sometimes I think Charles is my father born again. Such get their way as they go along. Even great misfortune does not hit them as it does others. While we were wandering on the continent Charles was never really sad . . . as you might have thought he would be. He always hoped, I suppose, and if he did not have his kingdom, well, he was having a very pleasant time while he was waiting.

"My mother was a very clever woman. She was of the Medici family. You have heard of them. A very famous family. She was his second wife. He was a Huguenot at the beginning, but he became a Catholic because it was his only way to the throne. 'Paris is worth a mass,' he said. My son Charles is very like him."

"And Lady Castlemaine, you think . . ."

"Ah, *chérie,* I think you must turn away. You must not look. You say, 'Who is this woman? A mistress! What does such matter to the Queen of England?' My mother had to accept the fact that her husband loved many women. Perhaps he did not love them. Love is rare and there were so many. But they were necessary to his comfort and the King must have his comfort . . . or he will grow unhappy . . . and then he blames those who cause his discomfort." She lifted her shoulders. "It is not wise to be that one."

"And Lady Castlemaine?"

"Ignore her. She is not the Queen. You are the Queen. You are the one who will bear the next King, remember that. The rest is not important . . . an irritation, yes. Let it be no more! It is one I never had to suffer . . . but I saw it with my mother. Oh . . . they are much of a kind . . . my son and his grandfather. Kind at heart . . . they do not cause hurt wantonly . . . only where these needs are strong . . . too strong for them. And that is how it was with my father and your husband."

"So you think I should receive her?"

"No . . . not that. She is at court. Leave it at that. Put her from your mind."

I thought a great deal about what she said. Clearly she thought the storm over Lady Castlemaine was of no great importance.

She was more deeply concerned with religion.

She said to me one day: "It was a great sadness to me that my children did not share my faith. They would not allow that in England. For an irreligious people, I never knew any so set against the Catholic faith as the English. They always hated me because of my religion." She snapped her fingers. "I did not care for that. I know I am right and they are wrong. I did my best to bring the truth to my Charles . . . but he would have none of it. He had to remember that he was King of a Protestant country . . . but I did my best."

I said: "I want so much to bring Charles to the faith."

She put her hand over mine. "God speed to you, my dear," she said, and drew closer to me. "I will tell you something: I believe he has a fancy for it. He would never be a religious man. He would use religion . . . if you understand what I mean. It is difficult to express my feelings when we do not fully understand each other's tongues. Charles would suit the Catholic faith. He would treat it rather as my father did. 'Paris is worth a mass.' Nevertheless, he should come to it. Now James is different."

"Oh yes, James and Charles do not resemble each other."

"Except perhaps in one thing . . . this obsession with women. James was always close to me . . . not as close as my little Minette . . . that is Henrietta, my youngest . . . my beloved one. Now, do not whisper this to any. You see how I trust you. James is taking instruction."

"Instruction?"

"Instruction in the Catholic faith. He is as yet undecided, I am told, but it will come. James will be one of us ere long."

"I did not know."

"It is such a pity that he has made a fool of himself over this marriage. How could he! The girl is a schemer. She must be."

"I think she truly loves James."

"Loves him! She loves the glory. Dear child, he is second in line to the throne. Of course, he will never be King. That is for the son you and Charles will have. But women like that always hope. The upstart daughter of that man Hyde to be Queen of England! That would never be allowed." She was fierce now. She was so governed by her emotions that I was not sure how much of what she had told me I could believe.

"Oh," she went on, "I have great hopes of James. He has seen the Light. Charles perhaps will come to it in time. My little Henrietta—there has never been any question with her. She is truly Catholic, and now she is married into France as well. Of all my children, she is the closest to me. I cannot tell you what a blessing she has been to me all these years. She hardly knew her father. She was only five years old when he was murdered. She escaped to France and has become more French than English. Charles loves her dearly."

"Yes, he has spoken to me of her."

"His dear Minette! She adores Charles and he her. They have always loved each other dearly. She is married now to Philippe, brother of the King of France. It should have been Louis himself. I trust she will be happy."

"It is not often in royal marriages that happiness is found," I said soberly.

"That is true, alas. I was fortunate. I believe you can be, my dear, if you are careful. We all have to pick our way through life. Nothing is easy. Do not ask for too much and you may not be disappointed. Harken to me. When did I ever say I was satisfied? I have made so many mistakes in my life and I greatly regret that I could only see them after I had made them. I often ask myself how much I contributed to the tragedy, how much was due to me that I am a lonely widow and my dear Charles was cruelly murdered. Perhaps I was in some way to blame. Perhaps he might have been here now . . . sitting beside me . . . and I might be Queen of England still and you, my dear, Princess of Wales."

"You must not blame yourself," I said.

"I wonder. When we get old, we look back . . . our lives become overshadowed by memories of the past. But no matter how much one weeps, tears will not wash it out."

"I am making you sad."

"No, *chérie*, you make me happy. You are the wife I would have chosen for Charles. He is fond of you, I know."

"But fonder of Lady Castlemaine."

"No. No. That is a sort of fever, I know. I was brought up at the

court of Henri Quatre. I know how my father felt toward the myriads
of women who surrounded him. They were necessary to him, but it
was not deep love. It is a surrender to the irresistible passion of the
moment. Understand that and you will have nothing to fear. The
crown is yours. You are the King's wife. These women can do you no
harm. Stand firm and remember that . . . and you have won the battle. You will be the Queen when they are forgotten."

"How wonderful it has been for me to be with you."

"For me too, my dear. I came to see you, and I have not been
disappointed."

WE HAD LEFT HAMPTON COURT for Whitehall, that palace
which for Charles must hold some very tragic memories, for it was
there, before the banqueting hall, that his father had been cruelly
murdered.

Whitehall was a fine building. Its gatehouse, made of small square
stones, glazed and tessellated, was most impressive. It had been a royal
palace ever since Cardinal Wolsey had presented it to Henry VIII,
hoping to soften that despotic monarch's heart toward him for a little
longer before he met his inevitable fate. It had been changed since
then and, because some of the buildings which had been added were
in white stone, it was called Whitehall.

I could not be as happy there as I had been at Hampton Court,
where I had gone in blissful ignorance with my romantic dreams.

I had come a long way since then.

I saw a great deal of Lady Castlemaine, who was frequently at
court. I used to watch Charles walking with her or sitting beside her
at the gaming tables. Everyone was aware of his passion for her.

There had been one concession, though. She did not live as close
to me as she might have done. Instead she had her apartments in what
was known as the Cockpit, which was a part of the palace, though not
exactly of it, for coming out of the palace one had to cross the road to
reach it. It was situated next to the tennis courts and bowling green;
and as there was cockfighting there, it took its name from this.

Queen Henrietta Maria was now installed at Somerset House.

The Queen's friendship had cheered me considerably, and I think
Charles was delighted to see us getting on so well together.

It was necessary that I should be present on every occasion of importance, and as there were many such, for numerous entertainments were devised for the pleasure of the Queen Mother, I was constantly in his company. No one would have believed that there was a rift between us, but it was still there, and I supposed would be until I received Lady Castlemaine into my bedchamber.

Both Maria and Elvira had been ill and had absented themselves on many occasions for this reason. Maria was getting feeble; her failing eyesight inconvenienced and disturbed her more than anything else; but she was deeply upset by the manner in which I had been treated.

In spite of the language problems, Maria and Elvira had managed to pick up what was happening in the Castlemaine affair and were incensed by it. Together they talked of the dishonor and insult to their Infanta, and had been on the point of writing to my mother. I had prevented their doing this only by forbidding it. Naturally I did not want my mother to know. She had been adamant about my refusing to receive Lady Castlemaine; and that was exactly what I was doing. I could not return to Portugal, and if I were truthful, I must say I did not want to.

The talk with the Queen Mother had brought me comfort, and I had faced the fact that seeing Charles now and then was at least better than not seeing him at all.

Lady Castlemaine was always prominent at the functions, of course. She was the sort of person who had only to be at a gathering to be the most outstanding person there. She was always sumptuously dressed. She had some valuable jewelry—presents from the King, I imagined—her gowns were always more daringly cut than those of others; her magnificent hair was dressed to advantage on every occasion. She wore the most elegant feathered hats; and, hating her as I did, I had to admit she was splendid and the most handsome woman at court.

One day I noticed a young man in attendance on her. He was scarcely more than a boy. I supposed he was about fifteen . . . perhaps even younger than that. He was exceptionally handsome, tall and dark, with an unmistakable air of assurance. Lady Castlemaine obviously thought highly of him. She was quite coquettish with him; and he seemed to enjoy this.

Several people were with them, and they all seemed to be making much of the boy.

A few days later I saw him again. We were at Somerset House, visiting the Queen Mother, and he was still in the company of Lady Castlemaine. I thought he must be some protégé of hers.

I said to Donna Maria, who had recovered from her illness sufficiently to be with me: "Who is the young man over there?"

She peered ahead, and it was brought home to me how quickly she was losing her sight. Poor Donna Maria, she was trying to hide how blind she was becoming. I turned to one of the women and said: "I should like to speak to the young man who is over there. Do you know who he is?"

"I believe him to be Mr. James Crofts, Your Majesty," said Lettice Ormonde, one of the women who had joined my service. "It is said that he has been long in France and has recently returned to England."

"He seems to be very popular. He has the dignity of a man though he can be little more than a boy."

Lettice Ormonde made her way to the group of which the young man was a part. She spoke to him. I heard Lady Castlemaine laugh and give the boy a little push. He looked slightly embarrassed and immediately walked to me with Lettice.

"Mr. James Crofts, Your Majesty," said Lettice.

He knelt with the utmost grace. I held out my hand and he put his lips to it, and lifted his very attractive dark eyes to my face.

"Please rise," I said. "You may sit beside me. I have seen you here on one or two occasions."

"Yes, Your Majesty."

"Are you with your family?"

"I am with Lord Crofts, Madam."

"He is your father?"

"No, Your Majesty, but I live with him."

"I see." I thought I must be misunderstanding, for though I was improving rapidly, there were occasions when I was baffled.

"And you have recently come to England?"

"Yes, Madam, I came with the household of Queen Henrietta Maria."

"And Lord Crofts . . . your guardian . . . he is here today?"

"Oh yes, Madam."

"You seem to know a number of people."

"Oh yes, Madam."

"And particularly Lady Castlemaine."

"The lady is a friend of mine, Your Majesty."

"Tell me how old you are."

"I am thirteen years old, Your Majesty."

"You have a tutor?"

"Oh yes, Madam, Thomas Ross. He is the King's librarian. Before that it was Stephen Goff. He died, and when I came to England, it was Thomas Ross."

"So great attention has been given to your education."

"Yes, Madam. I want to grow up, though. I want to be done with education."

Thirteen, I thought! At times he seemed much older, and then suddenly he was just a boy. I felt myself to be far more unworldly than he was.

"Is Lord Crofts a friend of the King?" I asked.

"Oh yes, Madam." He went on to tell me that Lord Crofts had been with the King at the Battle of Worcester. "Do you know, Madam," he cried with enthusiasm, "our forces were only thirteen thousand and Cromwell had thirty to forty thousand? It was small wonder we had to retreat."

He spoke as though he had been there.

"You would have been a loyal supporter of the King," I said.

"Of a surety, Madam. I could not have been aught else. Alas, I was not born then. I wish *I* had been with the King . . . riding through the country . . . disguised . . . to Whiteladies . . . to Boscabel. I never tire of hearing of it."

"I, too, like to hear of it. The King has told me the stories . . ."

I was transported to those honeymoon days when, like the simpleton I was, I had thought Charles cared for me as I did for him.

"The King has been good to me," said the boy almost shyly.

"It delights me to hear it."

I looked up and saw that the King himself was coming toward us.

"Well met!" he cried. He smiled from me to James Crofts. "So, sir, you have been entertaining the Queen."

The boy flushed slightly and lowered his eyes.

"I trust you found him amusing," said Charles to me.

"I found him interesting company," I replied.

"Then that pleases me. Well done, James Crofts. I am leaving now," he went on. "Come." He took my arm. "Perhaps you would care to share our coach, James Crofts."

The boy's eyes sparkled.

"Then let us go," said Charles. "I trust, sir, that Thomas Ross will give a good account of your diligence?"

I marvelled that he knew so much about the boy, and I was very pleased that he had suggested I ride with him.

My joy was short-lived, for as I was about to step into the gilded coach which was to take us to Whitehall, I saw Lady Castlemaine sitting in it.

I was taken aback, although I knew that now and then she rode in the royal coach. I hoped the King would ask her to leave, as I was to ride with him, but he did no such thing, and I could not make a scene by refusing to ride with her. I had had my fill of scenes.

Everything that happened to us was noted, and as we passed along the road, I saw surprise in the passersby to see me riding in the royal coach with the King, James Crofts and Lady Castlemaine.

I WAS SOON TO DISCOVER why the sight had aroused such interest. There was something else besides the fact that Lady Castlemaine and I were riding together.

It was Lady Suffolk who, after some pressure, enlightened me. She was my friend, I believed, and in this country I had need of friendship, so I treasured hers.

While she was preparing me to retire for the night, I said to her: "Do you know the boy, James Crofts?"

She paused for a moment with the brush in her hand and said, "Oh yes, Your Majesty."

"I found him interesting."

"Yes, Madam."

"I could not quite understand . . . though he spoke very good English . . . I believe he is English . . . but he has been a good deal in France."

"Yes, Madam."

"He is called Crofts and seems to be related to Lord Crofts, but I gathered Lord Crofts is not his father."

"No, Madam."

"The King seems to know him."

"Oh yes, Madam."

I turned and looked at Lady Suffolk intently. I saw that puzzled look in her face which, knowing her of old, indicated to me that she might be asking herself whether she should tell me something.

I said: "What do you know about James Crofts, Lady Suffolk?"

"Well, Madam, he is well known at court."

"So I gathered. I learned that Lord Crofts was at the Battle of Worcester."

"He has always been a loyal supporter of the monarchy and spent years in exile with the King."

"And the boy is not his son. Who is his father, then?"

Lady Suffolk had turned away. I caught her hand. "You know," I said. "Please tell me."

She said after a pause: "Your Majesty will know in time, and before long, I'll swear. The King is his father."

"The King?"

"Yes. His mother was a certain Lucy Walter. She is dead now. James was put into the care of Lord Crofts. The King has always been interested in his welfare."

I felt the room spinning round me. I clutched the table. I feared I was going to faint again.

Why was it that I was always in the dark when others knew? Those people who had seen me riding in the coach knew; Lady Castlemaine knew; the whole court knew. I was the only one in ignorance.

I had ridden in the royal coach with the King, his mistress and his bastard. It seemed significant in some way.

I was shocked and bewildered.

I COULD NOT SLEEP. I lay on my bed turning from side to side, imagining Charles with Lady Castlemaine. She had been giving birth to a son when I arrived. It was the reason why Charles had given so much time to me. Because she was unavailable.

It was most shameful and humiliating.

Could I endure it? I must. There was no going back. I remembered his voice with a hint of sarcasm. "You should discover first whether your mother would have you." No, there was no turning back. I should have to accept my fate. And the question was in my mind: If I could go back to Portugal and never see him again, should I want to?

The truth was that I wanted to stay. Unhappy, jealous as I was, I would rather be near him than apart. It was hard to set aside my pride and admit this, but it was true.

I had an opportunity of talking to Queen Henrietta Maria about it. She loved to talk to me and give her advice; and, moreover, she was by now very fond of me.

I told her that I had discovered that James Crofts was Charles's son.

"It's true," she said. "Mon Dieu, and who could doubt it! He has a look of the King . . . and the manners at times. Young James cannot forget that he is the son of a king. I like the boy. I advised Charles as to his education and he is being well cared for."

"And his mother?"

"A slut without doubt . . . though not ill-born. Her father had a castle in Wales . . . Roch Castle, I think it was. She was just Charles's age. They must have been about eighteen when they met. She was a beauty . . . though without much wit. But who looks for wit at eighteen? And Charles had enough for the two of them. She was no blushing virgin. Her favors had been somewhat freely dispensed. James once told me that Algernon Sidney had given fifty gold pieces for her, and was very aggrieved because no sooner had he paid the money than he was called away to his regiment and his brother stepped in and took the prize. She had had many lovers before and since Charles. The family's castle had been destroyed by the Roundheads and Lucy had come by stages to the continent. It was at the Hague where they met."

"And he fell in love with her?"

"Well, perhaps. It was something more than a passing fancy. Jemmy—James Crofts—was born in '49 . . . that terrible year when my husband was murdered."

"And did Charles acknowledge James Crofts as his son then?"

"Charles is by nature . . . accommodating. Is that the right word? But it seems certain Jemmy is his. I suppose one can never be absolutely certain . . . even in the most respectable circles." She gave a light laugh. "But there seems little doubt. Jemmy is every inch a Stuart."

"And what happened to his mother? Where is she now?"

"Where sinners go when they leave this earth. She stayed at the Hague while Charles went to Scotland, and when he came back she no longer attracted him. The boy was put with Lord Crofts, and Lucy slipped back into the life which suited her best. She was given a pension and returned to London. But her connection with Charles was known and Cromwell's men soon discovered her whereabouts. She was arrested in some lodgings near Somerset House and spent a time in the Tower, so I heard. But they must have realized she would not have had the wit to spy, so they sent her back to the continent. She died in Paris about two years before the restoration. My son James told me that he has always been uneasy about James Crofts. There was once a rumor that Charles married Lucy Walter. Quite absurd, of course, but it alarmed James. Well, well, until you produce the heir to the throne, James is there . . . next in line . . . and if Jemmy were Charles's *legitimate* son, as he would be if Charles had married Lucy Walter . . . well, you see what I mean. But do not fret. There was no marriage. Charles would not be such a fool . . . and Lucy is long since dead. James Crofts is a delightful boy . . . like his father in many ways. Let us hope that he does not take after his mother."

"I see that I have a great deal to learn."

"*Ma chérie,* we all have much to learn. When I think of the mistakes I have made in my life . . . poof!" She made a gesture as though to blow them away. "I could spend my time saying, 'What if I had not done this, that?' Oh, it is no good. *Sacré bleu,* one must not regret too much . . . concern yourself with what is . . . now. Make up your mind. Is this what I want? you say. Forget all that has gone before. It is now that matters."

"You are so good to me, so understanding."

"Ah, life is so short. Let us live as best we can. It is the life hereafter that is important."

I said: "I was so unprepared. Since I have come here I have had many shocks."

"You mean with Charles?"

"Yes, with Charles."

"I know him well. He is . . . is he not . . . my son? There is much that I would alter if I could. He is a man governed by the love of women . . . or perhaps I must say . . . the need of women. Some are like that. My father was. Charles inherits this . . . through me." She lifted her shoulders and grimaced. "They will have their women, no matter what. For the rest, they are wise and witty, and at heart kindly . . . a little lazy . . . hating trouble. Charles is fond of you. He likes you very much . . . but he will never be faithful to you. It is not in him to be faithful . . . not to any woman. My father was like him. I saw how my mother lived. So I understand. Accept this weakness in him and he will be grateful to you, he will be kind. You will give him the son which is so necessary . . . and that son will be King. But do not try to interfere with those women of his. Remember, they are not important. I tell you before. You are the Queen, and the wife of the King is the mother of the King-to-be. Accept this and all is well. You say you had romantic dreams . . . but, *chérie,* life is not made of dreams. Yet it can be good. I have learned some wisdom in spite of all my follies. Would to God I had learned earlier. Bah . . . but it is always easy when solving the problems of others. It is only one's own that are so difficult."

I took her hand and kissed it.

"My dear, dear child," she said. "It makes me happy that you are here. It is not the King's amours that should concern us. It is his immortal soul. You will persuade him to the true faith in time. Do not whisper this, but I believe James is already there."

"Then," I said, "I must accept these women. I must show friendship to them . . . to Lady Castlemaine?"

"Her time will pass, *chérie.* And there will be another . . . perhaps an easier one. She is an odious creature . . . bold, brazen . . . but, let us face the truth . . . very handsome. She is outrageous and so amuses the King—and he likes to be amused. But never fear. She will be replaced."

I smiled. "What a blessing it is to be able to talk to you! You do me so much good. You are so wise."

She laughed. "I can tell you this: when I look back over my life, I can see that, if there were a palm for the most foolish of queens, that palm would be mine."

"No . . . no!"

"Yes . . . yes! It is so. But never mind it now. It is over and finished. You are young and you are going to bring Charles's soul to God."

"I will do my best."

"And you will succeed."

It was indeed comforting to talk to her. I had gained some advantage. Whatever more I had to learn of Charles's amours, I could no longer be taken by surprise.

HODE AND DISADDOINTMENT

I HAD TAKEN THE QUEEN MOTHER'S ADVICE VERY SERIOUSLY and was trying to do what she suggested. I accepted the fact that I had married a man who was sexually insatiable and that one woman was not enough for him. I must remember that he was the King and, within certain limits, kings could take what they pleased. A certain laxity in the Portuguese court had been referred to. I had never been aware of this because I had been shut away from reality. But I was prepared now, and I must act accordingly.

I no longer averted my eyes when Lady Castlemaine was near. I even talked to her in my faltering English. She seemed delighted at this and responded readily.

I knew that people watched us and raised their eyebrows. Charles was pleased, though. I had been right to take his mother's advice.

We were often quite merry. I remember well that occasion when we were at supper. The King's conversation was always amusing and there was a hushed silence when he spoke. This of course was due to their respect for royalty as well as appreciation of his wit.

He liked to make me speak English on these occasions, and very often my pronunciation, or what I said, caused some mirth.

The Queen Mother was present and I was always comforted by that. She gave me certain courage and Charles always showed his pleasure in our friendship.

James Crofts was also with us, and now I understood why he was so often in close proximity to the King. Charles's eyes often rested on him with pride. This was all clear to me now.

His eyes were on James Crofts when he said to his mother: "There is happy news. Catherine and I shall soon have our son."

Queen Henrietta Maria's expressive face shone with joy.

"But this is *magnifique!*" she cried. "This pleases me much. This is the best news I can hear."

I was astounded. I looked at Charles. I sought for words. I cried: "You lie!"

There was a silence round the table. I had insulted the King. To his face I had accused him of lying. Such a thing had never been heard of.

Unacquainted as I was with the English language, I did not fully realize the impact such an accusation would have.

Lady Castlemaine said jocularly: "But this is treason."

The King was laughing. "My Lady Castlemaine," he said. "What was said might be termed a treasonable outburst in a subject, but surely a wife should be allowed to use a little plain speaking to her husband."

He put his hand over mine. "There, Queen Catherine, you see what a storm you have raised. Treason, they say. And you know the penalty for treason."

"Hanging," said James Crofts.

"And Jemmy," said Charles. "If we were to send this lady to Tyburn, what would you do?"

"I should ride there to rescue her."

"Well done. You are in certain danger, Catherine the Queen. Confess and be hanged." He leaned toward me. "Have no fear. I should be there before Jemmy. I would not allow anyone to harm a hair of my Queen's head."

Then he took my hand and kissed it.

I was bewildered by all this, but the tenderness in his eyes filled me with joy.

Queen Hentietta Maria was watching me, unable as ever to hide her feelings. There was a glitter in her eyes, but I could see that the King's attention to me delighted her.

That night when I was in my bed, Charles came in. He stood at the foot of my bed, smiling at me.

"Tonight," he said, "you were not put out . . . not angry?"

"No. Everyone seemed to be amused. But it was not true . . . what you said."

"One thing that is true is that, if that boy is not on the way, he should be." He came toward me and put his arms around me.

There was within me that which wanted to resist, to talk, to make conditions, but I remembered the Queen Mother's words.

And that night he stayed with me and it was as it had been in the beginning.

I STILL HAD A GREAT DEAL TO LEARN. Charles was so tender and eager, and so did he deceive me with his ardent lovemaking that I began to feel that he wanted to be with me more than any other. I should have remembered that at that particular art he was adept. It all came naturally to him. In the first place he had inherited skills from his grandfather, and practice had made him perfect.

Perhaps I was deliberately blind. However, I was happy for a while.

But almost immediately, another of those shocks to which I was becoming increasingly accustomed was waiting for me.

I found Donna Elvira supervising the packing of her clothes—and not only Elvira. Donna Maria was lying on her bed, too overcome with grief to do anything.

"What has happened?" I asked in dismay.

"We are to leave in two days."

"Leave!"

"All of us. It is the King's orders, they say."

"There was talk of your going, but . . ."

I went to Donna Maria. She said: "All your life I have been beside you. You are as my child . . . this separation will kill me."

"It must not be," I said.

"I am an old woman. My life is nearly over. I would the good God had taken me before this happened to me."

I wept with her. "I cannot let you go," I said.

"I am old and useless now. I can scarcely see you. What use am I?"

"You are dear to me. I cannot imagine my life without you in it. You have always been there."

"Your mother gave me the care of you. I remember well when you were a child . . . so very young . . . at the Villa Viçosa."

"I remember too, for I was only two when we left there and you were with me then."

"Oh—if we had never left . . . if there had not been this fight for a crown . . . this royal marriage."

We wept together.

Then I thought: I cannot let her go. It is true that it will kill her. I am all the life she knows. She has nothing more now. She is old and ill . . . and it is too cruel. I must speak to Charles. Would he come tonight? It would be the only chance of seeing him alone. Surely he would not refuse me this.

I was so agitated that I could not wait. I sent for my secretary Sir Richard Bellings.

"Sir Richard," I said, "I must see the King. It is most urgent. Would you take a message to him."

"I will go at once, Your Majesty."

Charles came to me.

"What ails you?" he asked.

"It is my attendants. They are going to be sent back to Portugal."

"Their departure has been somewhat delayed. They were due to go weeks ago."

"Charles, they are my friends."

"Oh, you have good friends here now."

"These people understand me."

"Attendants always go back to their homeland. It is the custom."

"I do not speak the language here."

"Oh, but you are learning very quickly."

"You used to give me lessons."

"And very good you were. But you are surrounded by the English now and hear the language all the time. You are improving by leaps and bounds."

"Charles, I do not want them to go."

"Alas, my love, we must adhere to the custom. This is what we all have to do."

"You could stop it."

"It would not be good to do so."

"Poor Donna Maria is heartbroken. She is old and feeble. She has been with me all my life and this separation will kill her."

"Oh, come. She will get over it."

"Some people love deeply, Charles. Their emotions are not superficial. I tell you, this will kill Donna Maria."

"Poor old soul. Well, let her stay."

"Thank you. And there are my priests."

"Oh yes . . . some of them too. I have said they should stay, and your cook and some of those servants . . . but the rest, they will have to go."

I could see he was adamant.

I thought of his promising Barbara Castlemaine a place in my household and how he had kept his word to her, no matter what trouble it caused. I told myself then that I had been foolish to think he really cared for me.

I was plunged into melancholy when I said good-bye to my old friends, but at least Donna Maria was still with me.

I HAD A DESIRE TO RIDE OUT—not with the company which usually was with us—but alone. I could not do this, of course, but if I were accompanied by my Master of Horse, that would doubtless be acceptable.

I sent for him.

I said: "Mr. Montague, I wish to ride . . . but not in a party. I have a mood for solitude."

"I will prepare Your Majesty's horse and I shall ride behind you."

"That would give me pleasure, Mr. Montague."

Very soon I was riding away from the palace. I did not have to mention that we should not go onto the open road. Edward Montague was the soul of discretion and would understand that. We took the sylvan paths.

After a while I said: "Please ride beside me, Mr. Montague. I wish to talk to you."

He obeyed with such alacrity that I felt he was both honored and glad to do so.

I had told myself I would sort out my thoughts as I rode, but I found I did not wish to do this. I had already decided on how I must act. I must try to see Charles as he really was, not as I had made him in my dreams. He had so many good qualities, so much that was lovable . . . too much really. But I must face the truth. There was a lasciviousness in his nature which nothing could subdue. I had to accept that, and ask myself whether I would be one of many . . . or simply nothing to him. He could not change, so I must needs do so.

That was clear enough to me. The matter was settled and I would do my best not to torture myself with it further. I would take what I could get, because even though I had discovered this flaw in his nature, I could love him nonetheless.

I tried to interest myself in Edward Montague. I wanted to hear about his life.

He was of that family to which the Earl of Sandwich belonged, and it was the Earl who had been instrumental in getting him his place at court.

I had guessed that Edward Montague was something of a Puritan by the manner of his dress and his way of speaking, and I was sure he was more than a little shocked by some of the frivolity he observed at court.

"The Earl of Sandwich, I believe, commanded the fleet under the Roundheads," I said.

"It is true, Your Majesty. He worked for England, and at one time that meant for Oliver Cromwell."

"I expect he had a respect for the Lord Protector."

"I have always understood, Your Majesty, that the Lord Protector was a man who commanded respect."

"I expect you are right. Life must have been very different under Puritan rule."

"Very different indeed, Madam." I heard the disapproval in his voice. Like everyone else, he would know the kind of life the King and most of his associates lived.

I found it comforting to talk to someone who felt thus. It was in tune with my own thoughts.

How happy I could have been if I had married a man of moral instincts! But, I reminded myself, he would probably not have been as attractive as the one I had married.

I said: "I am sad at this time, Mr. Montague, because I have so recently said good-bye to some of my friends."

"I understand, Madam. But you have good friends here."

"I hope so. But the friends I have lost had been with me for a very long time. They spoke my native language, and it is sometimes difficult for me to talk in English. It is often not easy to find the words, and there can be misunderstandings."

I thought of myself arguing with Charles in Spanish. I wondered if I had sometimes misunderstood him and he me.

"Soon Your Majesty will be speaking the language fluently."

"I hope so, Mr. Montague."

"Madam . . . I should like you to know . . ." He hesitated.

"Yes, Mr. Montague?"

"I am at your service, Your Majesty. Anything you wish . . . anything. It is my urgent desire to serve you with my life."

I was taken aback. He was such a solemn young man. But I liked his earnestness. It was comforting to know that he held me in such esteem. I did not quite understand what he meant, but it was pleasant to hear it said.

I felt better as I rode with him back to the stables.

ALMOST EVERY EVENING I saw Lady Castlemaine. I made a point of being affable to her, which pleased her, and she was inclined to seek every opportunity of speaking to me. I hated her, and I think she despised me; but we both kept our feelings well under a cloak of pretence.

It was a great effort to me and I was often on the point of telling her that I would prefer not to feign this friendship, but I remembered what Queen Henrietta Maria had told me, and I was sure she was right.

Charles and I were on good terms now. He visited me now and then and was always tender and lover-like. I had learned to accept that. It was hard for me, but I had to tell myself that I had to do it, or lose him altogether.

That was why Lord Clarendon's attitude was particularly hurtful to me.

I had noticed several disapproving looks which came my way, not only from him, but from others too; and I wondered what they meant.

Lady Suffolk was my chief informant. Maria had never been that. She was only half aware of what was going on and could not pick up much gossip because of the language difficulty.

Lady Suffolk was a kindly woman and had a fondness for me, I think. She well understood the difficulties of my position, and would have done much to help me if that were possible.

I said to her one day: "I wonder if I have done aught to offend Lord Clarendon. At one time he was quite friendly, full of good advice. Now he scarcely looks my way. Is anything wrong?"

She went into one of her silences, which told me that she was wondering whether she ought to tell me or not.

"If you know what I have done," I said, "you must tell me."

"Your Majesty appears to be very friendly with the Lady." The Lady was of course the name by which Lady Castlemaine was generally known throughout the court.

"I am civil to her, yes."

"Your Majesty is often in her company."

"I could not be otherwise. She is so frequently where I am."

"Lord Clarendon is surprised that you should be so very friendly with her."

I stared at her in amazement. "But it was he who told me that I should accept her . . . if I would keep the King's regard!"

"Your Majesty asked me . . . ," she murmured apologetically.

"I want to know. Pray tell me what else is being said."

"He says that Your Majesty at first protested so vehemently and refused to accept the Lady. You said you would return to Portugal rather than do so. And now it seems you are the greatest friends."

"I am amazed," I cried. "Lord Clarendon told me I should accept Lady Castlemaine, that I was wrong to insist she be banished from court."

"He says that Your Majesty's feelings could not have gone deep, that you deceived us all into believing that the presence of the Lady was obnoxious to you . . . and now it would seem that you are fawning on her."

"Oh . . . this is most cruel! How dare he say such things!"

"The Lord Chancellor will say what he wills . . . even to the King. He says that, in making such a friend of the Lady, you have lost his esteem. Nor has it pleased the King, as you may think. And how can anyone know your real feelings when you are able to feign passion and fury and then turn about so completely."

I felt limp, discouraged and defenseless.

It seemed that whatever I did was wrong.

Lady Suffolk tried to soothe me.

"The Chancellor has many troubles at this time."

"We all have troubles, and it is no excuse for such talk, especially when it was he who advised me to accept Lady Castlemaine."

"Your Majesty should not take it to heart."

"But I do, I do."

"The sale of Dunkirk has upset the Chancellor deeply," said Lady Suffolk.

"I believe it had to be sold to raise money," I said.

"But you see how worried he is. The exchequer should not have been so low that such a sale was necessary."

I had heard much of the sale of Dunkirk. It had been discussed frequently in all quarters. It was that important town which had been taken by Cromwell and now had been sold to the French for five million francs because the money was desperately needed. I could understand Clarendon's anxieties, but that did not excuse him for venting his wrath on me.

I was not popular. A Catholic queen never would be in this country. The King so clearly showed his preference for other women, and for that I was pitied by some, despised by others.

The year was passing, and there was to be a grand ball to mark its end. I did not welcome these occasions. I must be present, of course. I should have to watch Lady Castlemaine flaunting herself, splendidly attired, her jewels more dazzling than any others—the Queen of the Ball, while the Queen of England sat there, looking dejected and ignored . . . smiling bravely, trying to pretend that she was completely unaware of that neglect, not only of the King but of the whole company.

I watched the King dance. He was a graceful dancer, although he performed rarely, but when he did, it was with an effortless skill. Everyone applauded. He shrugged that off with a nonchalance which implied, stripped of my royalty, my performance would only be half as good.

I knew there were some at court who deplored his open liaison with the Lady, but at the same time even they were charmed by him.

I watched Lady Castlemaine dancing with James Crofts.

The young man was looking at her with admiration and she was responding rather coquettishly, I thought. I wondered if the King noticed.

James Crofts is only a boy, I thought. But is she trying to seduce him? Surely even she would not be guilty of such blatant immorality. Yet I had come to believe that the Lady would be guilty of anything.

I danced very little. It was not because I did not enjoy dancing; I did very much. But I did not know the English dances. I sat watching them in the Brantle, which was a kind of cotillion; they pranced round the room, the gentlemen leading their partners. Lady Castlemaine was still with James Crofts.

She was laughing hilariously at something he had said; his eyes were shining with admiration, and she sparkled with all her jewelry . . . given by the King, I imagined. Could he afford it with the exchequer so low that Dunkirk had had to be sold? Perhaps they were royal jewels . . . and gifts which had been presented to him.

I sat there, my smiles hiding my sadness, and I wondered how many people I deceived.

I was thinking of this time last year, when I was so excited because I was going to marry Charles. I remembered my arrival and the belief that my dreams had come true.

So short-lived had been my triumph—how brief my joy! And now here I was . . . one year older in time . . . years older in experience. And wiser, I hoped.

And this was my life. I could only go forward.

I watched Charles. He was surrounded by some of his courtiers, talking to them. He must have been amusing them, for now and then there was a burst of laughter. Lady Castlemaine swept by with James Crofts, laughing, coquetting, bemusing the boy.

This was my life. I had to go on living it . . . forgetting the heartbreak . . . the bitter disillusion.

MY MIND WAS CAKEN FROM my plight by news from my mother and my brother Alfonso.

There was anxiety in Portugal because the Spanish army was stirring itself. It was true that they had set aside their aggression at the time of my marriage, and the sight of the English ships coming to take me to England had prevented their invasion of our land. They had been acting cautiously because of our alliance with England. But England was far away and they must be realizing that it would not be easy for the Portuguese to stand out against them. And now . . . there were signs that they were massing on the borders.

My mother had written that, If only Alfonso could be recognized as the King, there would be more respect for him throughout Europe.

As it was, the Pope would not acknowledge him, and the fact that he was always referred to as the Duke of Braganza was tantamount to an announcement that he was not the rightful king and was an imposter.

If only the Pope would lead in this acknowledgment and Alfonso's sovereignty was not in question, the Spaniards would hesitate before attacking.

I could see that she was right, and I could not bear to think of her anxiety.

I was never sure when I should see Charles. There were times when he came to me, and I was ashamed of how much I looked forward to those occasions. So often he supped with Lady Castlemaine and I knew then that I should not see him. I guessed that he would prefer to be with her; but he did not forget the need to get an heir. If I became pregnant, his visits would cease. I longed for a child. That would compensate me for so much, I believed I could attain a certain contentment then. A new way of life . . . with the child the center of it.

When Charles came in, he would be merry and full of tenderness, and he always behaved as though he wanted to be with me alone. I never learned my lesson well. Again and again I believed him while it lasted. It was a strange, unreal way to live.

On this particular occasion, he noticed my anxiety.

"What ails you?" he asked.

"I have heard from my mother," I replied. "From my brother, too. They are in great fear. The Spaniards are threatening."

"I know this," he said.

"The Spaniards are so strong. My mother, my brother . . . they are afraid they will not be able to withstand them."

"We are aware of what is happening," he told me. "I have sent troops out to help with ammunition and what they will need."

"Oh . . . thank you, Charles. It is so good of you."

"My dear, we are friends. Did they not send us our dear Queen . . . though she is becoming more like an Englishwoman every day! There

is an alliance between us. We shall show those Spaniards that we will
have none of their insolence."

"I am so pleased to hear that. I wish I had known."

"Oh, I did not want to worry you with these state matters."

"I should have been relieved to hear of that one."

He took the pins from my hair and let it fall about my shoulders.
"It is a shame to imprison it," he said.

"There is . . . something else . . . ," I said hesitantly.

"Tell me."

We sat down and he put an arm about me, caressing my neck, and
now and then putting his lips to my hair. He could almost deceive me
into believing he was a faithful husband.

"My mother is very sad. The Spaniards are so close . . . and so
strong."

"We shall hold them off."

"There is one thing I want to do. My mother believes that this
persecution will not cease until my brother is recognized throughout
Europe as the King of Portugal. I want to write to the Pope."

"Write to the Pope! What good do you think that would do?"

"I am the Queen of England."

He took my hand and kissed it. "Which gives me great joy," he
said. "But I would guess that the Pope might be less enchanted."

"I have some position here. You do not hate the Catholics,
Charles."

"On the contrary. Why, have I not an ardent little papist for
wife?"

"Seriously . . ."

He put his hand on his heart. "I speak with the utmost seriousness. I love my papist wife, and shall do so till I die."

I tried to break through this light banter, which hurt me more
than it pleased me, because there was falseness in it. He came to me
as a duty and spent most of his time with Lady Castlemaine. But I
was going to forget that and insist on making my point. My mother
was calling for help and I was going to give it to her if I could.

I said: "My country is a Catholic country. It deserves the support
of the Pope."

"My dear Catherine, Spain is a Catholic country . . . a rich country. It can *afford* the support of the Pope."

"If my brother were acknowledged King, the Pope could not support even a rich country in its aggression."

He looked at me soberly. "What do you want to do?" he asked.

"I want to write to the Pope. I want to tell him that I am a good Catholic. I will work for the Holy Church. I will do everything I can . . . if he will acknowledge my brother."

"You will never bring the Catholic faith to this country. The English would not have it. They had a taste of it with Mary Tudor, and they have said never again. Don't be deluded by them. They are godless in the main, I fear, liking to be merry, thrusting aside what they do not like. I am one of them, Catherine, and you know my failings."

I put out my hand to stop him, and he took it. "They would never have it, my dear." He went on: "But it may be that the Pope is not as sure of that as I am."

"If he would acknowledge my brother as King of Portugal . . ."

"Perhaps you have a point there."

"Spain would hesitate. It is because they insist that he is only a duke that they dare."

He touched my cheek and stroked it.

"It means much to you, little Catherine," he said. "Does it not?"

I nodded.

"My ministers would not be pleased if they knew my wife was corresponding with the Pope."

"It is only one letter."

"That would be enough. They would say you are carrying the Catholic banner into this Protestant land. You are trying to influence your husband to acknowledge that faith. That is so, is it not?"

"Not exactly."

"Not in so many words, but that is the implication."

I was silent.

Then his arms were about me.

"You ask for so little," he said. "And when you do, it is for others. I like that well."

"It means so much," I murmured.

"It is hard for me to refuse you. Bellings would be a good man to send. He is the soul of discretion."

I drew away from him that I might study his face. He was laughing, well pleased. Then, with a joyous gesture, he picked me up and threw me onto the bed.

"There," he said, "you do with me as you will. Such is my desire to please you. You shall write your letter to His Holiness, and Bellings shall convey it to him. It must be done with the utmost secrecy . . . no, let us say discretion. That is a far more diplomatic way of expressing it, and you have become a diplomat, Catherine. In the meantime I think our soldiers will be more effective than your little missive. Now . . . to weightier matters."

If only I could always have believed in his love for me as I let myself do then . . . briefly, how happy I could have been!

THERE MUST ALWAYS be something to disturb me. So often, when I was with Charles, I allowed myself to forget that affection played a small part in his emotional life. This attitude, I think, was partly due to his long exile; he had learned to shrug aside what could not be avoided. I was not by any means unattractive to him; he liked my innocence, I supposed; and connoisseur that he was, he would be completely aware of my feelings for him. Again and again I told myself I must not be deceived by his loving attitude, and the graceful compliments which tripped so lightly from his tongue. But still I was unprepared for this little disturbance.

A new beauty had arrived at court, much to the chagrin of Lady Castlemaine. This was Frances Stuart.

She could not have been much more than sixteen years old, and she really was outstandingly beautiful. Her features were perfectly formed in every way, and in a court where beauty was so admired, she was fêted wherever she went.

She had come over in the Queen Mother's retinue, and Henrietta Maria had talked to me about her.

"Louis was very anxious to keep her at his court. He tried to persuade her mother to let her stay. But I put a stop to that. After all, her mother was my servant, not Louis's. Louis's manners are always perfect, and he would not go against the wishes of his aunt. So I brought the girl with me. I was not going to leave her at the court of France."

I was a little puzzled, since it occurred to me that, if she had wanted to preserve the girl from licentious surroundings, would it have been so different to leave her in France?

"She is a witless creature . . . frivolous. The good God has compensated her with beauty for what she lacks in brains. Poor child. She would be easy prey. So . . . I brought her with me."

Frances was indeed a simple creature. She loved childish games, such as Hunt the Slipper and Blindman's Bluff; and it astonished me that she could induce these sophisticated courtiers to indulge in these infantile activities just for the pleasure of being near her.

One of her favorite games was building up cards to what she called houses, balancing them one on another, to see how high she could make them. She would sit delicately placing the cards on each other, shrieking with delight when her card house was bigger than that of the one with whom she was competing.

I had seen Charles watching her with brooding eyes for he, who so admired beauty, could not be immune to her.

Lady Castlemaine, who was aware of this, was by no means pleased. She was not a woman to hide her feelings. I can imagine the temper that was displayed in her apartments and I pitied her servants.

She sought to discountenance the new beauty, but her efforts fell on stony ground. Frances did not understand the shafts; she greeted them with tinkling laughter.

Sometimes I wondered whether anyone could be so devoid of sense, and being more accustomed to the ways of the court than I had been when I arrived in it, I asked myself whether Frances Stuart's innocence was assumed.

However, in spite of many attempts to seduce her, she remained aloof.

Charles was seeking her out. She might have been flattered to be noticed by the King, but somehow she made it clear to all her admirers that she would become no man's mistress.

She smiled sweetly on those who could amuse her with childish acts. I remember seeing Anthony Hamilton, a connection of the Ormondes, win her approval by putting a lighted taper in his mouth and holding it there. She clapped her hands and told him he was wonderfully brave. Young Hamilton had gone on performing the act for the joy of her approval until someone—I think it was the Duke of

Buckingham—told him not to be such an idiot unless he wanted to kill himself.

Buckingham himself was another of Frances's admirers. He was such a subtle seducer that many thought he would be the one to succeed. But he did not; and Frances remained the simpering, unseducible virgin.

I knew that Charles was deeply interested in her and I marvelled that beauty could mean so much to him that her witless chatter did not deter him any more than it did her other admirers.

When they had first seen her—so pretty and so silly—they had thought she would be an easy conquest. That was why I wondered whether *La Belle Stuarte,* as she was called, was really as stupid as she made out to be.

The King was neglecting Lady Castlemaine. There was no doubt of that. He was spending more and more time with Frances. How could he appear to be so absorbed in those ridiculous card houses!

The Lady herself assumed an air of indifference and gave her attention to James Crofts.

Were they lovers? I could not believe it. He was such a boy. Was she really attracted by him? There had been so many to share her bed that I supposed one more made little difference—and perhaps she would find his youth rather piquant.

I guessed that the King was not pleased by this growing friendship between his mistress and his son.

James Crofts and Charles were often together and Charles clearly showed his affection, as though he wanted everyone to know in what esteem he held the boy. He wanted him to have the respect of everyone and to be treated almost as royalty.

Once when James Crofts was dancing with me, hat in hand, according to the custom of showing respect to royalty, Charles called out that he might put on his hat. James did so with a smile of pleasure. It was tantamount to a public declaration of his royal birth.

James Crofts was in some ways similar to the King. He lacked Charles's wit and wisdom, of course, but then he was very young. though I fancied Charles had been born with his. James Crofts was very handsome, although he had none of Charles's charm, but in looks he resembled the Stuarts and that was enough, for it meant that no one could doubt he was the King's son.

Charles said to me one day, and there was an alert look in his eyes
as he spoke and I, who was beginning to know him well, guessed that
there was something more than the words implied: "It is time I did
something about James Crofts."

I asked what he had in mind.

"He is my son," he said. "There is no doubt of that, and he should
have some standing at court."

"He has already."

"That is so. As my son, he is received by all. But I thought of a
more tangible sign."

"You are going to endow him with titles and estates."

"Exactly so. And I think it is time he married."

"Is he not somewhat young?"

"He is old enough. He is a Stuart. It will keep him out of
mischief."

He was no doubt thinking of James Crofts's involvement with
Lady Castlemaine, I guessed.

"Does marriage do so?" I could not help saying.

"I think it might absorb him . . . for a while . . . until he gets
older . . . wiser . . . more able to conduct his life. So he shall be made
a duke."

"A duke!"

"The titles of the Duke of Orkney are now available."

I felt a sudden shiver of alarm. Did Charles think of giving his
bastard son such honors because there was a possibility of his coming
to the throne? I had been Charles's wife for some months . . . nine or
so . . . and there was no sign that I was to have a child. Perhaps it was
early yet. But was that in his mind?

Charles was saying: "He will be Baron Tyndale, Earl of Doncaster
and Duke of Monmouth."

"That will set him very high, will it not?"

Charles was smiling. "Indeed yes. He will take precedent over all
the dukes who are not of royal blood . . . so my brother James cannot
object. He will still come before Jemmy."

"It will be a great honor for the young man."

"He is a good boy. I have high hopes of him. And when he is the
Duke of Monmouth, he shall be married."

"You have selected the bride?"

"Yes. It is Anne Scott, the Duchess of Buccleuch. She came into the title on the death of her father . . . together with a goodly fortune."

"I see."

"You look doubtful. Do you not think it is a good arrangement?"

"Yes . . . from James's point of view. I wonder what the bride is thinking."

"She will be thinking how lucky she is to get such a handsome young fellow for a bridegroom."

ON A BLEAK FEBRUARY DAY James Crofts became the Duke of Monmouth and less than eight weeks later he was married in the King's Chamber to the Duchess of Buccleuch and took the name of James Scott.

Lady Castlemaine was displeased. She would have to be more careful how she behaved with the Duke of Monmouth than she had been with simple James Crofts. As for myself, I felt a return of melancholy.

Charles was accepting his bastard son. He was giving him great honor; they were often in each other's company. Monmouth could not have been treated with more deference if he had been the King's legitimate son.

True, Charles liked the boy, but his actions I felt showed something more than that.

I was failing. So far I had not produced an heir. The King was saying, see what a handsome boy I can get. It is only the Queen who fails me.

My spirits were lifted by the news from Portugal.

There had been a great victory at Amexial, which was largely due to the efforts of the English whom Charles had sent to fight beside my countrymen.

My mother's letter was ecstatic. She blessed my marriage. She had always known how important it would be, she wrote:

My dearest daughter,
    You cannot know how happy my people are. We shall

always be grateful to our wonderful ally and for you who have done so much to make this possible.

I was proud and happy. I forgot the slights and humiliations then. Charles was my husband. No one could change that . . . not even Lady Castlemaine or *La Belle Stuarte*. I was his wife and it was his soldiers who had saved my country.

I told Charles how delighted I was and would have gone down on my knees to thank him, but he would have none of that.

"It was a small matter," he said. "It is not the first time we have shown these Spaniards that they are not as mighty as they believe themselves to be. And since our little effort has given you so much pleasure, I am happy."

"Oh Charles," I cried. "How can I thank you?"

"By being with me . . . by loving me . . . by giving me so much to be thankful for."

Words of a lover! If only I could have believed them!

"There was one little incident which will amuse you," he said. "It did not amuse our men. But never fear. All is well now."

"What happened?" I asked in alarm.

"Nothing to fear. All is well. But your brother . . . he is an odd fellow."

"Well, my mother usually tells him what to do."

"I'll vow she did not tell him what to do on this occasion. Odds fish! It might have caused a riot."

"Please tell me quickly, what has Alfonso done?"

"He thanked my men for their help and told them that, for their pains, they were to receive a pinch of snuff."

"A pinch of snuff!"

Charles lifted his eyebrows. "These men after all, are not in the business of war because they care for causes. What they look for is some of the spoils, and I do not think these would include a pinch of snuff."

I covered my face with my hands. How could Alfonso have been so stupid! But then he was unfit to govern. I knew that, and none knew it more than my mother. That was why she, to all intents, was the ruler. But Alfonso at that time must have escaped her vigilance. What had they thought of him?

Charles took my hands from my face and kissed them.

"No need for alarm. I have ordered that forty thousand crowns shall be distributed among them to compensate them for their efforts."

"Oh Charles . . . how could he!"

"Let us not think of him. We have beaten the Spaniards. Your country is free of them for now. We should make merry."

I thought then what a lot I owed him. Whatever sadness my life here brought to me, I must accept it. I must remember what my marriage had done for my country. I had to accept Charles's amours. I had to grow up. I had to adopt a new set of morals . . . cast aside my upbringing. I had to act as many a queen before me had had to do.

THERE WAS MORE GOOD NEWS.

I believe my letter to the Pope had had its effect. He had understood the implication that I was going to do all I could to bring Charles to the faith. Perhaps he knew that James was already a secret Catholic. Henrietta Maria knew it and she was scarcely the most discreet of women.

I had heard from Charles that her inability to keep a secret could have been in a measure responsible for his father's downfall. It would have been the last thing she intended; she would have died for her husband, instead she had talked to one of her ladies on that occasion when the five Members of Parliament, headed by John Pym, were to be arrested and taken to the Tower. But, having been warned, the men escaped in time to carry on the war against the King. It seemed to me very likely that somehow, unwittingly, Henrietta Maria would have let out the news of James's conversion. On this occasion, it could have worked for good, because it might be surmised that if one brother had turned, why not the other? And as Charles's wife, I was in a position to influence him, so might the Pope think.

In any event, the Pope had heeded my letter, for to our great joy, he accepted Portugal as a sovereign state and my brother Alfonso as its king.

To add to my happiness, I believed that I was at last pregnant.

I was very excited. Everything would be worthwhile now. A child of my own! Our son and heir! Charles was with me more often now.

We walked together in the Park. People cheered us. Although they were amused by the King's amours, at heart they preferred to see me with him rather than Lady Castlemaine. He was seeing less of her—but I did not think that was because of his preference for my society, so much as his preoccupation with Frances Stuart.

Frances went on in her guileless way, screaming with delight when her opponents' houses of cards toppled to the ground, making them all join in a game of Blindman's Bluff. It was so ridiculous. I could not imagine why they did it—except that she was exquisitely beautiful. I had heard it said that she was the only woman at court who had ever outshone Lady Castlemaine in beauty. And she was so different. Everything the Lady was, Frances was the opposite. Simplicity against sophistication; innocence against experience; purity against blatant sexuality; and one might say stupidity against the utmost guile.

My doctors thought the water of Tunbridge Wells would be good for me, but when I was making arrangements for a journey there, I was informed by my almoner that there were insufficient funds for the journey.

On making inquiries, I learned that, although according to the contract which had been drawn up at the time of my marriage, I had been promised forty thousand pounds for my household expenses, I had received no more than four hundred.

When I mentioned this to Charles he was evasive. He never cared to discuss money with me. He even hinted that I could scarcely complain about the deficiency in my income when I considered what had happened to my dowry. I thought I should never be allowed to forget that spice and sugar which my mother had sent in place of the money.

However, after a great deal of discussion, the expenses for the journey to Tunbridge Wells were raised and I was able to go.

I was delighted when the King announced his intention of coming with me—but perhaps that was because Frances Stuart was a member of my household.

Our journey to Tunbridge Wells was a pleasant one. We were cheered in the towns and villages through which we passed and I felt that the people of England were becoming reconciled to me—doubtless because they had heard of my condition.

I was glad the King's devotion to Lady Castlemaine was waning at last. It was true I had to accept her rival, but I did not feel the same animosity toward Frances Stuart. She was always extremely humble in my presence and was not a very formidable rival; for I firmly believed that when and if she did succumb to the King's passion, he would soon tire of her. Her empty-headedness must surely bore him, for I doubted even beauty such as hers could hold a man of his culture and intelligence for long.

She did not seem to grow up at all. She went on delighting in her games and I never failed to be astonished that her admirers could stand by applauding when her card house was the winner.

Charles was very interested in the chalybeate springs which brought many people to Tunbridge Wells. The spring contained iron salts which were beneficial to the health. Charles had always been intrigued by such cures, and had his own gardens where he cultivated and experimented with herbs. He was very considerate about my health, and I began to feel happier than I had for some time. I was longing for the day when my child should be born. I hoped it would be a boy for the nation's sake, but I knew that, for myself, whatever sex it was, it would delight me. It would be wonderful to have a daughter, but of course, I must pray for the son everyone wanted.

Sometimes Charles and I talked about the child. He would love it, I knew. His affection for James Crofts—the Duke of Monmouth now—showed that.

He had other children too. Lady Castlemaine had several which she swore were his, but in view of the life she led, that was open to doubt: she was the sort of woman who would claim royal parentage for every child she bore.

I tried to stop myself thinking of her. I must be grateful for my good fortune. I was pregnant; Charles was kind and tender; the rapacious Castlemaine was in the shadows and I believed I had little to fear from silly Frances Stuart.

So, if life was not perfect, at least it was good; and I must enjoy it.

So I remember Tunbridge Wells with pleasure.

We could not stay indefinitely, of course; and the court moved to Bath. James, Duke of York, with his Duchess traveled with us; and among the company was the Duke of Buckingham, a man of whom I was very wary. He was never far from the center of events. He was an admirer of Frances Stuart, and I was sure he was hoping to seduce her before the King succeeded in doing so.

I wished him success, but Frances seemed to have a gift for holding these men at bay and at the same time keeping them spellbound.
She did it effortlessly and was consistent in her refusal of them. It
would have to be marriage or nothing for Frances. She did not actually say that, but it was implied—and, of course, neither the King nor
Buckingham could offer that.

Buckingham had in the beginning been an ardent Royalist, yet
oddly enough had married the daughter of one of the Parliamentary
leaders—General Fairfax. It was a most incongruous marriage.

Buckingham was an adventurer by nature; he was reckless in the
extreme and would throw himself into any wild scheme for the excitement of it. A man of poor judgement, I would say. On the other
hand, he was extremely handsome, erudite and charming—the sort
of man who could be outstanding in any company. And . . . he would
be ruthless. That was why I felt I had to be watchful of him.

Charles should have been too. He had some knowledge of Buckingham's methods. The Duke had been one of those who, before the
Restoration, had doubted that it would ever take place; and, weary of
exile, he had secretly returned to England and had a meeting with one
of Cromwell's men as to the possibility of his estates being restored to
him if he came back to England ready to accept Cromwell's rule. He
had previously quarrelled with Charles, when he had contrived to
marry the Princess of Orange, a scheme which had been indignantly
prevented by the royal family. So no doubt he thought he had little
to lose.

Cromwell was too shrewd to accept such a man's word unques-
tioningly, and there again Buckingham showed his recklessness in returning to England without the Protector's consent; so, to consolidate
his position, he married General Fairfax's daughter, Mary, who had
fallen madly in love with him.

It was only Fairfax's influence which saved Buckingham when
eventually his recklessness resulted in a spell in the Tower of London.

When the Restoration came, he managed to win Charles's forgiveness, for Charles found it difficult to bear grudges, and he was amused
by Buckingham, who was the kind of man he liked to have about him.
So Buckingham became a Gentleman of the King's Bedchamber, and
had the honor of carrying the orb at Charles's coronation.

It was odd to see such a man as Buckingham leaning over Frances

Stuart, cheering her on as she built up her card houses with breathless intensity.

Lady Castlemaine, who, before her marriage to Roger Palmer, had been Barbara Villiers, was related to the Duke. The fact made me doubly wary of him.

After we left Tunbridge Wells, we had a pleasant stay in Bath, Bristol and Oxford, and wherever we went there were demonstrations of the people's affection for Charles and their acceptance of me; and I reminded myself that I had a good deal to be thankful for. My country was more secure than it had been for many years; the King's liaison with the evil Castlemaine was coming to an end: and soon I should have my child.

And so we returned to Whitehall.

I WAS DISAPPOINTED that Charles was not with me on the first night of our return to Whitehall. I supposed that he had some business to attend to after the time we had spent away. I saw him during the following day, but briefly, and again that night he was absent.

The next morning I heard the ladies laughing together. Something had evidently happened which was highly amusing.

It was later that afternoon when Lady Ormonde was with me and I said to her: "Something seems to be amusing people today."

"Oh that, Madam." She smiled. "It was the flood at the Lady's lodging."

"I did not know there was a flood."

"The Thames is high just now . . . and, of course, the Cockpit is low lying. The Lady's kitchen was flooded last night."

"Is that such a matter for mirth?"

"Her cook is Mrs. Sarah, Madam, and Mrs. Sarah's husband is cook to Lord Sandwich, who is a neighbor to the Lady. They say that Mrs. Sarah does not care what she says to the Lady and there are some rowdy scenes almost every day between them. People say it is like going to the playhouse to hear the two of them shouting at each other. The Lady is always threatening to throw Mrs. Sarah out . . . but she never will. And Mrs. Sarah is always threatening to go and work for a real lady. They'll never part, though. The fact is they can't do without each other."

"I can see that the difference between Lady Castlemaine and her cook can amuse some, but what was so particularly entertaining about the flood?"

"It was last night. Their shouting could be heard in the palace. Lady Castlemaine was expecting a guest and the kitchen was flooded so Mrs. Sarah could not cook the chine of beef. Well, there was this important supper party. 'Cook that chine of beef,' cried the Lady. 'The only way I can cook that beef will be by setting the kitchen on fire,' replied Mrs. Sarah. 'Then set the kitchen on fire, but cook the beef!' screamed the Lady. The shouting went on and on and in the end Mrs. Sarah took the beef to her husband, who cooked it in Lord Sandwich's kitchen."

I could not understand why this incident should have caused such hilarity.

The King was absent the following night.

Then I learned why they were all so amused. I heard two ladies talking together, and this time I understood what they said.

"He has supped with her these last four nights."

"Does that mean . . . ?"

"She's back. Well, he wasn't the sort to wait forever."

"The Lady saw her chance and, depend upon it, once she's back, she's back for good."

"Well, if Madam Frances . . ."

"Madam Frances won't. And the Lady is back . . . and there she will stay."

"And the whole court knows it . . . thanks to that chine of beef. Everyone's still talking about that. They knew who her guest was that night. She couldn't have the supper spoiled for the King, could she? She'd have the kitchen burned down rather . . ."

They went off into giggles.

So then I understood.

I hated the very sound of the woman's name; and a terrible bitterness enveloped me. I felt I was choking. I could not bear it. I had grown used to her; I had forced myself to accept her, grudgingly it was true. I had almost welcomed Frances Stuart. I had thought I was free of Lady Castlemaine. And now, here she was, back . . . and it was all going to start again . . . her brazen insolence, her patronage of me.

I was tired. I should be resting, but my fury overcame me. I would not endure it all again. I slipped to the ground. I felt the blood on my face. It was like the other occasion when Charles had presented her to me and I discovered who she was.

I FELT VERY WEAK and was not quite sure where I was. For a moment I had thought I was in my cell-like room in the convent. Then I knew that I was in my bed and someone was kneeling at my bedside, holding my hand. It was Charles.

I tried to smile but I felt too tired.

As though from a long way off, I heard him say my name. I wanted to answer him but no words came. Then Donna Maria was saying something, shrilly, disapprovingly.

"She must not be disturbed, Your Majesty."

Charles seemed to drift away.

I thought I was hand in hand with him. We were in Hampton Court. He was explaining the benefits to be derived from certain herbs, and the spaniels were barking. Then I was in the convent. The Mother Superior was saying: "You must work harder. You must remember your place. You must not disappoint your mother."

My mother was there. "When you get to England, you may have to see that woman. Ignore her . . . never let her come near you."

I was thinking of a chine of beef. It had to be cooked for the King, even if the house burned down in the process.

Then I lost all sense of anywhere. I was floating in space and then came . . . oblivion.

I was very ill for days. I did not know what was wrong with me. Vaguely, I remembered falling. I was aware of the blood on my face and then I must have fainted. I confused it with that other occasion. I kept hearing a whisper: "Do you know who that woman is? She is Lady Castlemaine."

It had all happened before . . . and I was too tired to think.

Alas, it was more than an ordinary faint. I had fallen and lost my child.

I did not know this then. I think if I had I should have lost my will to live.

They thought I was dying. I was vaguely aware of Donna Maria, who would not leave my room, I heard later, and was with me night and day. The King was constantly there too. Often I would open my eyes and see him sitting there, but I was too tired to speak to him. When I looked at him, he would press my hand. Sometimes I heard him murmur my name. He looked at me as though imploring me to speak to him. I tried to, but no words came.

There came the day when I learned what had happened . . . I knew that I had lost my child and that the agony I had seen in Donna Maria's face meant that she had thought I was dying.

But at last I knew. I was here in my bed at Whitehall. I was the Queen and I was going to die. I was sure of it, and so were all those about me.

I heard voices.

"She is conscious, Your Majesty."

"Then let me see her."

He was kneeling by the bed. "Catherine . . . my dearest Catherine. You know me . . . now?"

"Yes, I know you, Charles."

"It has seemed so long."

I smiled.

"You must not tire her, Your Majesty." That was Donna Maria.

"I will not, I promise you. I will sit with her . . . quietly."

He had taken my hand. I pressed his to let him know that I was glad he was there.

"My love," he said. "My little love."

I smiled again. "I want . . ." I began.

"Tell me what you want. It shall be yours. Just tell me, dearest."

"I want you to be happy. I am going to leave this world . . . I am going to leave you."

"No," he said. "No."

"It will be best. You will marry." I was going to say Frances . . . but I could not. That would hurt him. It would remind him how he had neglected me while he watched her making her houses of cards. I loved him. I did not want him to reproach himself. I understood him now. He could not curb those violent sexual desires; he had to behave in the way he did. I guessed, of course, that he was reproaching himself for his treatment of me. I had rebelled at first, and then had accepted my fate . . . but I had not done so readily . . . only with bitter resignation. But that was an end of it. The time had come to say good-bye and I did not want the occasion to be marred by reproaches and regrets.

"You will marry again," I said. "Someone better than I."

"There could be none better."

I could almost have believed he meant it. He looked so earnest, so desolate at the prospect of losing me.

"Someone who can give you the healthy son you must have."

"You will, Catherine," he said. "You will get better. I command it."

"Even kings can have no control over life and death," I said. "If my child had lived . . ."

"In your delirium you thought it had," he said. "You talked of him. You said he was an ugly boy, but that he had great charm."

"Did I say that?"

He nodded and I saw that there were tears on his cheeks.

I could not bear that he should weep for me. I suppose that was true love, for I would rather he did not mourn for me than it should make him unhappy to do so.

"Charles . . . ," I murmured. "I am sorry . . . not to have been good enough . . ."

"My dearest," he said, "it is I who have not been good enough. It is I who should ask your pardon."

I smiled at him. I wondered how I could bear to leave him. But perhaps I could because at that moment he really did love me. He meant what he said . . . for that moment. But in my heart I knew that he must be himself. He wished me well. He was fond of me. He loved me in his way. I had my little niche in his life. Perhaps he loved me more than he had ever loved Lady Castlemaine or Frances Stuart. But he did not *desire* me as he did those women. That was something I must understand. And the desire in such a man was so overpowering while it lasted that it overrode a quieter, gentler love.

I said to him: "You have taught me much. You will be happy now. Do not grieve for me. Do not reproach yourself. I did not understand at first. I think I do now."

"I loved you the moment I saw you," he said. "I shall always love you. You must not leave me."

I replied: "I am not afraid to die. There is only one thing I regret and that is leaving you; and now that I understand so much, I would wish to stay. I would be better.

"Please," he begged, "do not talk so. It is not you who must be better; it is I. You must live for my sake. You must give me a chance."

"I love to hear you say that."

"You must get better, Catherine," he said. "You must . . . for me."

He pressed his face against my hands and I felt his tears on them.

"You will forget me," I said, "and marry some princess who will give you sons, and bring much good to the realm. That is what you must do."

He was too moved to speak and Donna Maria was at my bedside.

"The Queen is becoming exhausted," she said. "This must not be."

"I will not talk," said the King, "but I cannot leave her. I shall sit here with you, my love, unless you wish me to go."

"I want you to stay," I said.

So he sat by my bed. My hand was in his, and every now and then I would open my eyes and smile at him.

THE MASTER OF HORSE

I HAD BEGUN TO GET BETTER BUT MY RECOVERY WAS VERY slow. I was desolate to have lost the child, and yet at the same time Charles's grief at the thought of losing me had made me so happy that I was in a measure compensated. I think it was the sight of his sorrowful face, tortured by genuine love and remorse, which gave me the extra willpower I needed.

I saw Charles every day during that time. He would sit by my bed amusing me with tales of what was happening at the court. He told them so wittily that we laughed continuously and I was very happy.

I was also deeply touched, for his hair had gone gray.

"You are to blame for these gray hairs," he told me. "They are the sign of my anxiety over you."

There was a fashion among some of the courtiers, whose hair was not as they would have liked it to be, of wearing periwigs of magnificent curls. When Charles appeared in one I clapped my hands.

"It is splendid," I said.

"I feared you might not like it."

"Oh," I replied. "Since you told me the gray hairs grew out of your concern for me I loved them." On the other hand, I had to admit that the wig was becoming. Whereas on someone of shorter stature it could have seemed overpowering, with his height he could carry it off beautifully.

"Well," he said, "the nation would not want an old grayhead for their King. At least now they will be less aware of it."

As I grew stronger I walked in the park with him. We would, as he said, "saunter." Sauntering was a habit he liked well. We would be surrounded by courtiers, and with Charles at the center of the group the conversation was invariably merry.

When the weather was warm the ladies carried fans. These had be-

come fashionable since my marriage. Most of the fans came from
Bombay and there were all kinds—some most beautifully painted.
The ladies fluttered them coquettishly and they were becoming an es-
sential part of a lady's equipage.

That could have been a happy time for me, but for the fact that
Lady Castlemaine and Frances Stuart were at court and there was
scarcely a day when I did not see them.

The Lady's animosity toward Frances Stuart caused great amusement; and although Charles remained kind and tender toward me, it
was clear that he was deeply infatuated with Frances Stuart.

Donna Maria gave thanks to God every day for my recovery. In
spite of the fact that she exasperated me at times, I was deeply conscious of her devotion to me; and besides, being my only real connection with my native land, she was the best friend I had ever had.

Alas, she was getting more and more feeble every day. It was sad to
see her peering at me, for her eyesight was rapidly fading. She must
have been lonely, for she had little contact with other people; yet
when she had had an opportunity of going home with the other
members of my household, she had refused to take it. In fact she had
fought against it and clung to me.

She knew, of course, how matters stood at court. She understood
that, in spite of his protestations of love for me when he believed I
was on the point of death, Charles was now spending his nights with
Lady Castlemaine and sighing for Frances Stuart.

It was now considered at court that Frances meant that she would
not become any man's mistress; some believed that this was her way of
leading the King on and that he was approaching such desperation
that he would promise her anything in exchange for her surrender.

To console me, Maria often told me how the King had come to sit
with me during my illness, how he had wept, and how his anguish
had been too deep to have been assumed.

"I was surprised that he cared for you so much," she said. "But he
did . . . indeed he did. I often saw his tears. One would not expect a
king to weep. You were light-headed. You rambled on. You were
thinking of the child . . . you thought you had it. You said, 'He is a
fine boy. He is ugly but he has a great charm . . .' And the King cried,
'What do you mean? He is a beautiful boy. He is the most beautiful

boy in the world.' And you talked of the children you believed you had, and the King talked with you and you smiled and listened, and said how wonderful it was to have those children. . . .

"He said afterward that if you talked of the child . . . or the children . . . we must listen to you . . . we must pretend because it made you happy. Above all, he said it was necessary that you should be happy . . . so happy that you would want to live. He said, 'When the Queen is well, she will know the truth, but until then we must keep her happy.' And he would sit there and tell you what the children had done, and you smiled and laughed. And, yes . . . you were happy. And it broke our hearts, it did indeed."

"How wonderful of him!" I cried. "He truly cared."

"One would have thought so." Donna Maria's lips hardened. She would never understand his enthralment to those women.

But he had loved me. He had cared. He had suffered because he had thought he was losing me. I should always remember that. When I saw his gaiety with Lady Castlemaine, his burning gaze fixed on *La Belle Stuarte* . . . I would remember.

CHE DEPCH OF his commitment to Frances Stuart was obvious over the matter of the calash; and all those courtiers who gambled on what the outcome would be began to understand the depth of his feelings for her. It was over a hundred years ago when another King of England had become so enamored of a woman that his kingdom rocked over the matter and he could have lost his crown. England had broken with Rome when Henry VIII decided that he must marry Anne Boleyn, and demanded a divorce from his Queen which the Pope had refused him. There must have been deep speculation in the minds of many as to how far Charles's infatuation with Frances Stuart would carry him.

Then the calash arrived. It was the most magnificent vehicle we had ever seen. It came from France and was a present to Charles to mark the good relations between the two countries.

Everyone was amazed by it and the question arose as to who should be the first to ride in it.

Anne Hyde, Duchess of York, came to me and said: "You should be the one to ride first in it, and if you have a companion, which you should, I should be that one. After all, you are the King's wife. I am the wife of his brother.

I looked at Anne intently. I knew her to be a very shrewd woman; and since my illness, when I had lost the child I was carrying, there was a subtle difference in her manner. I guessed what was in her mind. If I had no children, James would be next in line to the throne . . . and Anne Hyde would be Queen of England.

It was a natural assumption. I had lost one child. There had been hints by the physicians that I might not find it easy to bear children and that, if I attempted to, I might put my life at risk. So, with regard to the calash, I saw her point. It would be fitting that we should ride in the coach to show it to the people—the present Queen and the one who could well one day be the next.

Lady Castlemaine, of course, wanted to be the first to ride in the handsome vehicle. Moreover, she was firmly determined to. She was more aggressive than ever, realizing, I was sure, that she could only cling to the title of *maîtresse-en-titre* because of Frances Stuart's refusal to take her place.

She felt it necessary to show the people that she reigned supreme, and she would do this by riding in the calash, splendidly gowned and glittering with jewels. Perhaps she would take young Monmouth with her.

I had mentioned to the King that I should be pleased to be the first to ride in the calash and I thought Anne Hyde should be beside me.

Charles was evasive, which told me that Lady Castlemaine was already making her demands.

He always took the easy way out, and the Lady's claims would be made in her usual vociferous manner. She was pregnant again, by the King presumably—or that was what she would have everyone believe. What a fruitful woman she was! Why was it that I, who so desperately wanted a child, could not get even one?

She declared that unless the King allowed her to ride in the calash, she would miscarry the child, for it was clear that its father cared nothing for it since he could be so indifferent to its mother.

The court listened amused; and the matter of the calash became quite an issue, with everyone waiting and gambling on the result.

The result came one evening when the court was assembled.

Frances was present, the King hovering near her as usual. She was engaged in her favorite occupation . . . building up the cards. Buckingham was competing with her.

Frances was adept at the silly business. Buckingham's house tottered slightly and when Frances screamed with delight the King applauded.

Those around were taking bets on whose house would stand longest, and Frances was the favorite.

Suddenly Frances said to Charles: "What will you give me if I win?"

There was a certain seriousness in her manner which I had not noticed before. It was almost as though there were some subtle meaning behind her words.

He said: "I will give you anything you ask."

She smiled and turned to her cards.

With a neat little flick of the thumb, which I thought could have been intentional, Buckingham let his house totter and collapse.

Frances squealed with pleasure and everyone applauded.

She turned to the King.

"Well," he said, "what is it you ask?"

"That I be the first to ride in the calash," said Frances guilelessly.

The King hesitated.

"Your Majesty promised," lisped Frances.

"So did I," said Charles. "Then . . ." he lifted his shoulders, "the matter is settled. You must be the first to ride in the calash."

SO FRANCES STUART RODE in the calash; and the people came out to see her and they were amazed by her beauty. She really was a most enchanting-looking creature, and if it were not necessary to listen to her simpering inanities, I could understand why people marvelled at her.

Lady Castlemaine was furious. She went to the Cockpit and stayed there for several days. As for myself, I felt extremely hurt. I tried to think of Charles as he had sat at my bedside, and I said to myself: it was nothing. It was the emotion of the moment, the few pangs of a guilty conscience. How can he care for me if he humiliates me?

Then I remembered the past when I had been so unhappy and I reminded myself that I must accept this if I wanted to stay near him and keep his regard.

There was an alert air in the court. Frances Stuart had made a request which had been granted, much to the chagrin of the Lady, and that must mean something. Frances was tired of playing the innocent game, some believed. She was going to take up her position of reigning mistress at the court. It was an opportunity she had at least realized she could not miss.

The Duke of Buckingham was constantly at Frances's side. I was sure he had some scheme afoot.

I was tired of these amorous intrigues.

Once I found myself alone with Edward Montague and the compassionate look in his eyes made me feel that I wanted to talk to him. He was one of the few people I could trust.

"Your Majesty is grieving over this matter of the calash," he said.

I replied: "I believe Miss Stuart became it well."

Edward's mouth turned down with disapproval.

"Your Majesty and the Duchess of York should have been the first to ride in it."

"Oh . . . it was of no importance."

"Only if Your Majesty found it so."

"There was a great deal of talk throughout the court about the foolish matter."

"Yes, Your Majesty."

"Well, 'tis over and done. Do you think my English is improving, Mr. Montague?"

"Indeed it is, Madam. You have attained fluency."

"You are flattering me. I am still hesitant. The King laughs at me."

Again that look of disapproval.

"Methings he should applaud Your Majesty."

"Oh, he does . . . he does. But as you know, the King laughs at many things."

He nodded again. His eyes were eloquent. He was telling me that he knew of my unhappiness and he would do anything in his power for me.

It was very comforting.

I thought he might be regretting the return of the monarchy. He was very serious-minded, a religious man to whom the foibles of the King seemed very sinful.

I could not doubt his devotion to me. I only had to hint at the smallest service and it was performed with a deep enthusiasm.

THE POSITION AT COURT was still the same. Frances was as aloof as ever. I had a feeling that Buckingham was intriguing in some way. There was an air of secretive amusement about him.

I was right about this, and I learned so from an unexpected quarter; none other than Lady Castlemaine herself.

I was amazed one day when one of her servants arrived with a message for me. Her ladyship begged me to grant her an interview where we might talk alone, for she had something of importance to say to me.

I was filled with apprehension, and my inclination was to refuse to see her. What good had she ever done to me? I had alienated the King by showing my disapproval of her, and had lost his respect by feigning to accept her. I wanted nothing to do with the woman.

Why should she wish to see me? But I knew all the time that I would not refuse. That would be folly. I must know what this meant.

She came, more soberly dressed than usual, yet even so, I was struck by her beauty. It forced itself upon one. There was really no need for the elaborate patches, the feather and the jewels. She was magnificent just in herself.

She looked different, almost pious. That brazen determination to call attention to herself was gone.

"Your Majesty, it is so kind of you to receive me." I could scarcely believe in this humility. There must be a reason.

It came.

"A somewhat dastardly plot has come to my ears. I keep in touch with what is going on around me. I have very good and faithful servants—and my Mrs. Sarah, who cooks for me, has a husband in Lord Sandwich's household. Thus through Mrs. Sarah I heard what is going on there."

"You must be very knowledgeable, Lady Castlemaine."

"I am thankful on this occasion that I am."

"Pray tell me."

"Buckingham is hatching a plot. One can never trust Buckingham. He is a Villiers, as I am . . . of my family. That is why I understand him more than most people can. He is a most ambitious man."

"I quickly became aware of that."

"Of a certainty, Your Majesty would. You have taken his measure.
I doubt not, Madam, we must stop this wicked plot."

"I am waiting to hear what it is."

"Your Majesty must forgive my broaching this matter, but we
must be frank. You and I are not so foolish as to turn our eyes from
what is blatantly true. We face the facts. It is the only way to deal with
them. Your Majesty knows as well as I do that the King is enamored
of that silly little Stuart girl."

I bowed my head in assent.

"And she holds out against his wooing. I know Buckingham. He
has become close to the girl. Oh, I do not mean that he is her lover.
She remains aloof from all her admirers. That much I have proved.
She is quite brainless and as simple as a child of six years. She
has some notion that she must withhold that precious body of hers
until someone comes along who will marry her and give her great
titles."

"There are many who would say that is the moral attitude to
take."

Lady Castlemaine drew a deep breath to suppress her impatience.

"Buckingham believes that he knows how to manipulate her. He
can play that card game better than anyone else, which makes him
something of a genius in silly Frances's eyes. He has a plan that she
shall become the King's mistress and he shall rule through her . . . lead
her to take the King the way he wants him to go. Thus power to
Buckingham and Arlington, and Sandwich, who are in this vile plot."

"How do they propose to bring it about?"

"That is what I have come to tell Your Majesty, for I think they
can be foiled, and after all, much as we despise the silly Stuart, she is
an innocent girl and the plot is monstrous."

"Please go on."

"The Duchess of Buckingham is giving a ball tomorrow night."

"I know of that."

"Poor Mary Fairfax! I do not doubt she wishes she had married a
nice sober gentleman from Cromwell's band. She thought she was

doing so well to get Buckingham . . . and so did Fairfax! What does poor Mary think now? Wife of the Duke? It may have some compensation. Well, Mary is to give a ball. The King will be there . . . and so will Frances . . . and Buckingham, Arlington and Sandwich. They think this game of playing the vestal virgin has gone on too long. It is disturbing the King. He is morose and frustrated and that spoils the fun. So they plan to bring it to an end."

"How?"

"This is what I have come to tell you. Frances will be present. She will call for the cards, of course. And then there will be the usual silly contest. She will sit there and play her game for hours, and while she is doing it, she will be plied with drink. Frances is not accustomed to that. She is by nature abstemious. The drinks will be especially strong—treated in some way—and when she is so absorbed in her game dear Frances will have more than is good for her. In such a mood she will be spirited away. They have a nice little apartment waiting for her and . . . there will be the King."

I felt myself flushing with indignation.

I cried: "And the King . . . does he know of this?"

She lifted her hands. "I believe he knows nothing of it."

I was relieved at that. "It's a dastardly plot," I said. "It is for Miss Stuart to decide what she will do, and to behave toward a young girl in this way is . . . scandalous."

"Your Majesty is of the same opinion as myself. It must not be. We must save this poor girl from this . . . outrage."

"I shall tell the King."

She shook her head emphatically, and I wondered whether she was implying he would be ready to go along with the scheme . . . which he might well be.

"Then Frances Stuart . . ."

Again that shrug. "She would not be able to deal with it. They would swear their innocence . . . and then later try it again. No, we must foil this in a diplomatic way. Your Majesty can do it with the utmost ease."

"How so?"

"You will go to the ball and decide to leave early. Your Majesty is tired and wishes to retire. You need your lady-in-waiting to return with you. You just command Frances to accompany you."

"It seems simple."

"It is," said Lady Castlemaine, "and it is the way to foil this dastardly plot and preserve Miss Stuart's virtue.

"Thank you, Lady Castlemaine," I said. "I will consider what you have told me."

She smiled, bowed and left me. If I had not found the situation so distasteful, I could have been amused to see Lady Castlemaine in the role of defender of virtue.

I WAS CAUTIOUS. I wondered what was behind this. I did not trust the Lady. It might be some scheme of hers to embarrass me.

I was unsure.

I could not exactly like Frances Stuart, but I did think she was genuinely virtuous, and it was not her fault that she had been endowed with so much beauty and so little brain.

In due course I went to the ball accompanied by Charles. I was watchful of both Frances and Buckingham and soon became sure that the Lady had been right. Buckingham was looking amused and secretive. He was a man who betrayed his feelings and was a poor plotter because he could not hide the fact that something was in progress.

I believed the story now. It was natural that the Lady should want to prevent the plot's succeeding, and I knew that Buckingham might well believe that he could rule the King through Frances—absurd as that might seem.

And there was Frances surrounded by her admirers, calling for her beloved cards.

I was watching her. I was aware of Lady Castlemaine, whose eyes met mine conspiratorially.

Buckingham was playing the game with her. Sandwich and Arlington sat one on either side of her. It was true that they were filling her glass.

Frances was flushed and her laughter was louder than usual. Her hands stayed steady, though. She was an adept with her houses of cards.

I said to Lettice Ormonde: "I wish to retire. Please tell Miss Stuart that I shall need her."

Such an order from the Queen could not be ignored.

With a gesture which sent her house of cards tottering to the floor, Frances rose.

She was a little unsteady.

I saw the black faces of the plotters, and Frances's unsteady gait and the vacant smile on her face made me certain that Lady Castlemaine's suspicions had been correct.

What a strange world I lived in when a king's passion for one of the ladies of his court could result in such a conspiracy!

SHORTLY AFTER THAT I was given an unpleasant shock, and I wondered if it was the result of what had happened about Frances Stuart.

Rumors were circulating throughout the court and, as is usually the case, the one most deeply concerned is the last to hear of them.

Buckingham may have realized that his scheme to set up Frances Stuart as Charles's chief mistress, when he, Buckingham, would guide her how to influence the King, had been foiled by me in league with Lady Castlemaine.

I had no desire to be caught up in their intrigues, but it seemed I had in this one.

That Lady Castlemaine should have done everything in her power to prevent Frances Stuart from becoming the King's mistress was clear enough, but why should I care whether it was Lady Castlemaine or Frances Stuart? In fact Frances Stuart woud have been preferable.

In any case, I had spoiled Buckingham's plan and Frances Stuart would be on the alert if he should attempt such a thing again.

I was sure these rumors were set in motion by Buckingham and his friends.

The first clue I had came one evening at supper. We were talking as usual. Charles was in a merry mood and was entertaining the company with his conversation. Buckingham was singing a song—one of the King's own composition about the pleasures of love.

I was following the conversation more easily nowadays and my grasp of the language enabled me to express myself more intelligently, if a little quaintly. Buckingham was talking about a dishonest servant in his household who had been found stealing.

"And our servants . . . they surround us. We have need of them as they have need of us. How fortunate we are when we find those who serve us faithfully and loyally." He was smiling at me. "Your Majesty knows this well. You have at least one good and faithful servant— your noble Master of Horse. I'll warrant he is always ready at hand to give good service to his mistress."

There was a short silence. I distinctly heard someone smother a laugh.

I did not understand what this meant and I forgot it almost at once. It was only later that I realized the implication of these words.

At the time I said: "My Master of Horse has always been a good servant to me . . . from the time I came here."

"But of course," Charles said lightly. "I chose him for you, my dear."

Then the conversation went on as usual.

The next day when I sent for my Master of Horse, I was told that he had gone.

"Gone?" I cried. "Gone where?"

"I do not know, Your Majesty. On the King's orders he was dismissed from his post and told that he was no longer Your Majesty's Master of Horse."

This was a blow to me. My friendship with Edward Montague had been genuine. I had liked his serious conversation and his sympathy, which I sensed though it was not spoken of.

When I saw Charles I said: "They have sent away my Master of Horse. Why?"

Charles looked at me in astonishment. "He could not remain after Buckingham's insinuation."

"I do not understand."

"Buckingham is an insolent fellow. He goes too far. He'll have to be curbed. They have been saying in the court that you had become too friendly with your Master of Horse."

"Too friendly! But he is a good friend."

"My dear Catherine." He laid his hands on my shoulders and smiled gently at me. "I know you would never take a lover. Though . . . God knows . . . could I blame you? It would not be wise though. There is the succession."

"I do not understand what you say."

"Rumors have been going round the court that Montague was your lover."

"How dare they!"

"Oh, they dare a great deal for gossip. They lie . . . they slander . . . it's all a game to them. But Buckingham's insolence made it impossible for Montague to stay in his position."

"It is cruel . . . so untrue."

"The world is cruel sometimes." He looked at me with compassion, and I knew he was telling me how sorry he was that he was not a better husband. He knew I had turned to Edward Montague for a little sympathy and understanding. That was what was so lovable about Charles. He was as worldliwise as his courtiers, but with his cynicism and abandonment to pleasure, there was also kindness and understanding of those who were not like himself.

"Montague had to go," he went on. "I know he was a good fellow . . . a good friend of yours . . . and when I say friend I mean just friend. But there was talk. Malicious talk, as there always is and always will be, and we have to consider the effect of such talk . . . even though we know it to be false. Choose another Master of Horse."

"I will not. I cannot. I should have been consulted."

He shook his head. "It had to be. You must understand that he had to go. You have to walk very carefully because you are the Queen."

"As carefully as you do," I could not help retorting.

"I am a sinner and the world knows it, but you, my dear, must be above reproach."

"And all your friends . . . ?"

He lifted his shoulders.

"You are going to give us the heir to the throne and no one must be allowed by word or look even to imply that his father is other than the King."

"You do not think . . . ," I began.

He shook his head and kissed me tenderly.

"I know you to be good and virtuous . . . far too good for me. But that is life . . . and here we are. Now, you must have a new Master of Horse."

→>-<←

I DID NOT IMMEDIATELY CHOOSE anyone to replace Edward Montague. I was too upset not only by the loss of a good friend but by the wicked interpretation which had been put on our friendship by those who wished me harm.

I knew Charles did not believe this calumny. I wondered whether he would have blamed me if the scandal had been true. He continued in his relationship with Lady Castlemaine, although her lovers were so numerous that I had heard it said she would not remember how many there had been.

Lady Castlemaine had had the temerity to suggest a replacement for my Master of Horse, and I had indignantly rejected her choice. I told Charles that I had no intention of taking a new man yet. I was too upset by the manner in which Edward Montague had been dismissed.

The intrigues of the court were dimmed into insignificance by the trouble with the Dutch. For some time there had been conflict between Dutch and English fishermen and there were several fights at sea during which the vessels of both nationalities were sunk. English merchants were continually complaining that their trade was being damaged by the Dutch.

Caricatures were smuggled into the country. There were many directed against Charles and they caused him considerable annoyance. In one he was depicted with the pockets of his jacket hanging out empty to indicate the poverty of the exchequer, and in another he was led by one woman while another was clinging to his coattails and others were running after him.

They were meant as insults and to show the contempt in which the Dutch held the King of England—and the country, for that matter.

Charles was more serious that I had ever seen him before. He gave up his daily habit of sauntering in the park. He had always loved to walk there, his dogs at his heels and surrounded by his favorites.

But a subtle change had come over him. He had always been interested in ships, an enthusiasm shared by the Duke of York. A new vessel was being built and he paid constant visits to the dockyards and spent a great deal of time there poring over plans and talking with the shipbuilders. Admiral the Earl of Sandwich was constantly in his company.

I realized what was happening. The battles between our sailors and the Dutch, and the insolent comment on the King's activities, were leading somewhere.

On one occasion Charles talked to me.

"I do not like the situation," he said. "I am afraid there may be war. War is senseless. I have had my fill of it. Odds fish, I never want to see a war again as long as I live."

It was inevitable that it should happen. We were at war with Holland. The fleet was to leave with the Duke of York in charge, and Charles was going to Chatham to see it set out. I begged to be allowed to accompany him and was delighted when he agreed that I should.

It was a great occasion, though a solemn one. Queen Henrietta Maria joined us there and I was pleased when she greeted me with the utmost warmth and told me how pleased she was that Lady Castlemaine was not with us on this occasion.

"I cannot understand why Charles keeps that woman about him," she said. "One would have thought he had had enough of her by this time. And that Stuart girl? What of her?"

I could talk easily to my mother-in-law, so I told her that Frances Stuart was still holding back, and that the King remained deeply enamored of her though he still very often supped with Lady Castlemaine.

"It is trying," she said. "It is a pity Charles does not take after his father. He was always such a faithful husband. But I lost him . . . Charles will never go the way he did. Charles has too much respect for his head. He will keep it where it belongs. But I wish his heart was not so susceptible. And there is this war now . . . and England is not very friendly with the French either . . . or the Spaniards. Well, they are the natural enemies.

"I pray this Dutch matter will soon be over and you, my dear, will soon give birth to the heir to the throne."

"I was unfortunate . . ."

"My heart bleeds for you, chérie. And no other in sight? Some breed easily. Others cannot. This is the story of history. It is littered with queens who could not have any children and those who had too many. How perverse life is! But you must have a child, my dear. That will make all the difference."

"I know."

"I pray for it."

It was good to be with her. She stood between Charles and me and shared our pride as the newly launched *Loyal London* sailed away.

THE WINTER WAS BITTERLY COLD—one of the worst people remembered. We were all looking forward to the spring and victory over the Dutch; but with the coming of that beautiful season, tragedy struck.

Earlier in the year, people had been amazed, and not a little alarmed, because a strange spectacle had been seen in the sky. It appeared at certain times and was like a misty star with a bright tail. Charles was very interested in the stars and would watch for it every night. I used to sit with him and look at this strange object. I think he was rather pleased by my interest. It was not the sort of phenomenon which would interest Lady Castlemaine or the fair Stuart.

Some said it was an evil omen and recalled a similar display in the sky in the year 1066—the year of the Norman Conquest.

We heard that in some parts of the country there had been a certain disease which was easily passed from one person to another and few who had the misfortune to fall victim of it survived.

I remember the day well. It was April. The weather was beginning to get warm. A man had collapsed in Cheapside and when people approached him they saw that he was shivering and delirious. He had opened his shirt and there on his chest was the dreaded spot . . . the macula which was a sign that the victim was suffering from the plague.

He was dead. Others were found. They had collapsed in the streets before they could reach shelter.

It soon became clear that the plague had come to London.

It spread with alarming rapidity. There was great consternation and a hasty meeting of Parliament. Everyone in the city was in danger, and drastic measures were needed.

It was decided that the King and the court must leave, for it would be disastrous if the King should become a victim. The country was in a state of uncertainty. We were at war with the Dutch; but the first importance was the health of the citizens.

Charles was no coward. He said he would stay with the people, but the folly of such a sacrifice was pressed upon him. The Duke of York was engaged with the navy; he must of necessity be in a certain danger, so the King must protect himself.

We left London for Salisbury. The Duke of Albermarle remained in London to look after affairs there with Archbishop Sheldon. Both these men proved to be magnificent and I was sure did a great deal to prevent the epidemic becoming more terrible than it was.

Charles was very unhappy at that time. I had never known him to be so serious. He felt deeply disturbed because he was not in London and he had news of what was happening there brought to him every day.

The weather was sweltering hot during that June, July and August and people were dying by the hundreds in the capital.

The Duke of Albermarle had acted quickly and firmly. He reported what he was doing and Charles said he could not have been a better man for the task. The greatest need was to stop the disease spreading. Any house where one of the inmates had contracted the disease must immediately be marked with a red cross and the words "Lord Have Mercy upon us" painted below the cross; and if any of the inmates left that house before a month had elapsed since a victim had died, that would be breaking the law.

Charles and I were closer together during this period. He had little desire to sup with his friends and make merry. He talked seriously of what this would mean.

Firstly we must discover what caused the disease. That it had been brought into England from some other country seemed certain. It was so infectious that it spread with rapidity, which was alarming, and we had to find the cause.

Meanwhile London was like a ghost city. Grass was growing among the cobbles of the streets, for few walked in them now. During the night the death cart roamed through the streets, its dismal bell tinkling in the stillness.

"Bring out your dead," called the crier; and the cart was filled with bodies.

There was no time to bury the corpses ceremonially. Pits had been dug outside the city and into these the bodies were piled.

There were some very noble and selfless men in London at that time. Archbishop Sheldon was one; another was the Reverend

Thomas Vincent. There were others—men of religion who went into stricken houses and gave comfort to the sufferers. It was surprising that they emerged unscathed. I believe their faith preserved them.

There were stories of people who behaved with somewhat less heroism; there were some who deserted wives, husbands and even children to escape infection. Thus many victims were left alone to die.

We were cheered by news of the Duke of York's victory over the Dutch at Harwich.

Charles told me that the English had taken eighteen of the enemy's ships and destroyed fourteen more.

"And what were our losses?" I asked.

"The comparison is trifling. We lost only one ship. Alas, several of our men were lost, but few in comparison with the seven thousand they did. And we lost two admirals; the Earls of Falmouth and Marlborough and Portland have also gone. These things must be."

"Is it going to shorten the war?"

Charles was dubious. "At least," he said, "it is a turn in our fortunes, and people will cease to brood on the evil warnings of the comet."

He looked at me quizzically and went on: "You might be interested to know that your one-time Master of Horse, Edward Montague, has joined the navy . . . under Sandwich."

"The navy?"

"Well, we have need of all the men we can muster."

"But he loved horses."

"Poor Edward. I fear he was deeply hurt by his dismissal."

"Maybe when he returns . . ."

Charles gave me another of those intent looks. "Who can say what will happen when the war is over?"

I THOUGHT OF EDWARD MONTAGUE a good deal. I had not realized before that he really had cared for me. I had been too innocent to recognize the signs. I remembered his concern for me, his compassion and his sympathy. The way his eyes would shine when I appeared. Perhaps those were the signs of love which others had noticed.

He must have been very unhappy when he was dismissed, and

that dismissal was instant so there was no time to tell me what had taken place.

And he had joined the navy. That would have been easy for him as the admiral, the Earl of Sandwich, was related to him.

I missed him more than I had believed possible. I suppose when one's husband so blatantly prefers other women there is great comfort in the attentions of someone else—particularly if he is a serious man, not given to light-hearted flirtations, a man who clearly disapproves of the licentiousness of the court, a man of charm and dignity.

I should never have taken a lover, of course, and I am sure Edward Montague would never have indulged in an illicit affair; but he had been there, he had cared for me, and that had meant a great deal to me.

They were melancholy days. The King was worried about the money which was needed to pursue the war. There was bad news from London where thousands were dying every week.

An attempt had been made at Bergen by the Earl of Sandwich to capture a fleet of Dutch ships which were sheltering in the harbour there. The action had been one of complete disaster for the English and there were many casualties. One of them was Edward Montague.

It was a great shock to hear of his death. I had so many memories of him. I thought how strange fate was. But for those people who had provoked a scandal about him, he would have been with me still.

Edward Montague dead! I was overwhelmed by sadness.

FIRE OVER LONDON

THAT TRAGIC SUMMER WAS PASSING. ALL THROUGH SEPTEM-
ber the heat had persisted. The number of dead during the first week
of the month was over eight thousand; during the second week it was
slightly less; and during the third had risen to ten thousand.

It was difficult to imagine what life was like in a London no
longer a bustling city, the streets deserted, houses painted with the
dreaded red cross, the silence broken only by the ringing of the bell
and the cry: "Bring forth your dead."

The weather changed and with the cooler breezes the plague
abated a little.

We were at Oxford now, and when the King opened Parliament
there he was voted money for the purpose of carrying on the war. The
City of London lent him one hundred thousand pounds, and from
his Privy Purse he contributed one thousand pounds to the relief of
those who were left destitute by the plague.

The very fact that the scourge was losing its virulence gave us great
cause for rejoicing; and then a wonderful thing happened.

I believed I was pregnant.

The King was delighted when I told him.

"All will be well now," he said. "London will be its old self. We
shall defeat that wretched plague together with the Dutch—and
we shall be merry again."

I was happier, for he was very affectionate toward me. I must take
the utmost care, he insisted. This time there was to be a boy.

What a relief it was when the summer was over! If I could have a
child, I told myself, I could be completely happy. Charles was almost
a faithful husband; but I was not so foolish as to think he would not
stray again. But if I had a child I should be content. But that contentment was marred when I was told that Lady Castlemaine was preg-

nant again. She was so fertile and gave birth with such ease that it seemed that no sooner was she delivered of one child that she was to have another. She always insisted that these children were the King's. No one could deny this; nor could they be sure. She was no more faithful to the King than he was to her.

The situation had changed, though. This was because Charles had so many important matters to concern him. There could hardly be carefree balls and banquets when normal life in London was at an end; the war with the Dutch was in bitter progress and the French were becoming estranged. But in spite of this Lady Castlemaine was still close to us, and Frances Stuart remained aloof though still sought after.

I was very careful of my health. Donna Maria cosseted me, as did the Ladies Suffolk and Ormonde. I am not sure what happened, but one afternoon I felt faint and before I could stop myself I fell to the floor.

I was hurried to my bed and the doctors were sent for.

And then it happened. I lost my child.

It was sufficiently developed to show that it would have been a boy.

No one knew why I should have failed to carry it through to the end of the term. I was sunk in depression.

"It is a pity," said Lady Suffolk, "that Lady Castlemaine should seem to be so well."

"When is her child due?" I asked.

"Very shortly now, Your Majesty."

"She has so many. It is unfair."

"Very unfair, Madam."

When her child was born they did not mention it to me but it could not be kept from me for long. I could read Charles's bitter disappointment in his eyes. Did I fancy there was a certain resentment? That would be quite unbearable.

Lady Castlemaine was delivered of a fine boy.

Why . . . oh why . . . could I not have just one? And did not the fertility of the Lady prove that I was the one at fault? It was being asked if the King had married a barren Queen.

→>–<←

THE SPRING HAD COME. People were filtering back to London for the plague had virtually vanished.

Charles went back for periods but he said that I must stay in Oxford as there might be some remains of plague in London and I must remember that I was in a delicate state of health and would be more susceptible to disease.

He did not reproach me as some might have done, but I could not help knowing how bitterly disappointed he was. I could imagine how he felt when he saw Lady Castlemaine's boy in his cradle. At least he could have been sure mine was his, as he never could with hers.

But the fact remained that she was capable of bearing strong and healthy children—one after another—and this was my second attempt which had failed.

There seemed no end to the blows fate was dealing me. I did not hear of this until some days after the news had come to England. Lady Suffolk told me afterward that the King had ordered that I was not to be told until he considered it would be wise to do so.

"He said that Your Majesty would have to know in time but the blow would be too great for you, your health being what it is just now . . ."

He was right. It was a great shock to me. My mother was dead.

It was, of course, some few years since I had seen her, but I had never thought of her dying. She had seemed indestructible . . . immortal.

Charles himself broke the news to me.

He came in looking very sombre, threw his hat aside and, taking my hands in his, led me to a sofa where we sat close together.

He said: "I have sad news for you, Catherine. You are going to find this hard to bear."

I looked at him fearfully.

"It is your mother."

"She is ill?"

He hesitated and I stared at him in horror.

"She has had much to trouble her. She worked too hard. We none of us are here forever, you know."

"But she . . ."

"I know how you cared for her. But she is gone and your home is here now."

I turned to him and he put his arms about me and held me against him.

I felt bereft . . . alone. She had meant so much to me, and although I had not seen her for so long, I had always known that she was there . . . and now she was there no longer.

WHEN I HAD RECOVERED A LITTLE from the initial blow, I began to ask myself what this would mean to Portugal.

True, Alfonso was King—a fact which my younger brother Pedro had always resented, feeling that he himself was more suited to wear the crown—but it was my mother who had ruled, and I knew that Alfonso was incapable of doing so.

The Spaniards would immediately realize the country's vulnerability. England, engaged in war with the Dutch and suffering from the effects of the plague, would be a feeble ally. I feared disaster; and in addition to my overwhelming grief was this added anxiety.

Charles ordered that there should be mourning for my mother throughout the court. The ladies were to wear their hair in plain styles without adornments and they were to stop using patches for the period.

Lady Castlemaine was very put out. Her artificial aids meant a great deal to her. I could not help but be amused and somewhat pleased at her discomfiture. It might have relieved a little of the gloom.

The King had caught a chill. When he had been inspecting the ships at Chatham, he had taken off his coat and wig because of the heat. The temporary relief he had felt had not been good for his health. He caught the cold, which had persisted.

I think everyone was out of humor . . . even Charles. He was usually in such perfect health that he found it more difficult than most to endure the little discomforts; as for myself, I was deeply depressed by the loss of my mother and fears for my country. The only one who could have comforted me then was the child I had lost, and with the calamity came the fears that I might be destined never to have children.

I think people's tempers were a little short at that time. There was quite a scene one day when someone commented that the King was finding it difficult to throw off his cold.

Lady Castlemaine was sitting close to me at the time and her presence intruded on my thoughts which were with Pedro, my brother. I was wondering whether he would try to oust Alfonso from the throne.

Someone remarked on the King's inability to shake off his cold, and, in a sudden burst of irritation, I said with some asperity: "The King's condition does not improve because he stays so late at the lodgings of Lady Castlemaine when he sups with her, and the cold air of the early morning is not good for him."

Lady Castlemaine's eyes glittered. She said: "The King does not stay late at my house, Your Majesty. Methinks he must stay at the house of someone else."

I was taken aback. Was she suggesting he had a new mistress?

I said: "I am of the opinion that it is at your house that he stays so late."

"The King is gracious to so many," retorted Lady Castlemaine, her eyes glinting mischievously. "He bestows his honor on so many ladies that it is not always easy to know which of them is in favor at any moment."

Charles had come in and heard that last remark.

He, too, shared the general dissatisfaction with the court at that time and was less indulgent than he was wont to be.

He stood close to Lady Castlemaine and said quietly, but in a voice which I and those nearby could hear quite clearly: "You are insolent. Please leave the court and do not return until I send for you."

Lady Castlemaine stared at him in amazement.

"What do you mean?" she demanded.

"I have said leave the court. I will send for you if I decide to, but leave now."

She did not lower her voice, but said in such a way that all could hear her: "You dare to talk to me like that?"

"You dare to talk to *me* like that," he repeated. "Go and do not return until I send for you."

She had turned white with rage. I had known for some time that if Frances Stuart responded to his advances, Lady Castlemaine's days would be over.

She said: "I shall go. I do not remain where I am not wanted. But you have not heard the end of this. I shall publish your letters."

I was amazed at her impertinence. She forgot she was talking to the King. Of course, theirs had been a long and intimate relationship and he had always given way to her when she flew into a temper.

She had forgotten that her hold on him depended on the surrender of Frances Stuart; she must have been furious that no woman had impressed him so much as that foolish girl—not even herself, with all the fury of a virago and the magnificence of a mythical goddess.

She suddenly seemed to realize that he meant what he said. She turned from him and flounced out of the room.

Charles was perfectly calm. He behaved as though nothing unusual had happened.

I was exultant. Surely this must mean the end of Lady Castlemaine.

For a few days my hopes were high. Then she came to the Cockpit to collect her belongings. There were many gifts from the King among them and she asked if he would advise her as to the disposal of them.

It was an excuse to see him. He must have known this as well as any. But he went to the Cockpit to see her.

What happened when he was there, one can only guess. I suppose she exercised that overwhelming sensuality, of which she had an abundance to match his own. This must have resulted in an encounter which made them realize that, although the King's affection had been strained to breaking point, the attraction was as potent as ever; and while he failed to receive the satisfaction he craved from Frances Stuart, there was still a place for Barbara Castlemaine in his life.

So she did not leave court after all and she and the King were friends again, though even she must have realized that her hold on him had become somewhat tenuous.

THAT WAS A GLOOMY SUMMER. True, there was no return of the plague, but there was deep anxiety throughout the court. We were at war and the whole of Europe was turning against us. My fears about what might be happening in Portugal were overshadowed by the reality of what was taking place in England. France and Denmark were against us. Charles was particularly depressed by the deterioration of his friendly relationship with Louis XIV. He complained continually of having to beg for money. The effects of the plague had been more devastating than had at first been realized.

It was six years since the Restoration and people might be asking if life had not been better under Cromwell.

There were rumors that certain Roundheads were on the continent conspiring how to oust the monarchy and bring back the protectorate. They were indeed anxious days, and although Charles was outwardly serene, he was a very worried man.

In July I went to Tunbridge Wells, for I had not yet recovered fully from my miscarriage.

Since my earlier visit the place had become fashionable. There was a simplicity about it which I found appealing, and to be there with a few trusted friends was agreeable. We would all gather together round the wells during the morning while we drank the beneficial waters. If the evenings were warm we would sit in the bowling green, and there would be dancing on the smooth turf, which all declared was better than any ballroom. I found great serenity there.

In the afternoons a few ladies would assemble in my rooms, which were not large for there was no grand palace in the town and our lodgings were comparatively humble. We would drink tea, for I had brought this custom with me from Portugal. For a short time people had thought the beverage very strange, but they were soon aware of the pleasure of taking that soothing drink, and my ladies quickly became as ardent tea drinkers as I myself. Indeed the custom was spreading all over the country.

We were passing out of the summer, and after a stay of a few weeks we reluctantly left Tunbridge Wells for London.

I SHALL NEVER FORGET—nor will the rest of England—that night in September.

It began in the early morning of the second day of the month. The wind had been fierce all through the previous night and this played a large part in what happened.

The King's baker—a Mr. Farryner, I believe—lived in Pudding Lane where his kitchen would naturally be stored with wood faggots which would be needed for the baking of his bread. No one was sure how it started, but in a few seconds the house was on fire. It might have been possible to extinguish this, but the house was made of wood and the wind blowing so gustily that in a matter of minutes the fire was out of control to such an extent that, before any action could be taken, the whole of Pudding Lane was ablaze.

We were all awakened, and as we rose from our beds, we saw a strange light in the sky. The wind was sending hot ashes swirling through the air so that they descended on more buildings, causing more fires. People were panic-stricken. There was one aim: to get away from the fire. The river was crowded with crafts of all descriptions and crowds were piling their belongings into these.

Charles was out in the streets. The Duke of York, who was at Whitehall on some navy business, was with him. Everything was forgotten in the need to stamp out the fire.

"The whole of London will be burned down if nothing is done," cried Lady Suffolk. "If only that dreadful wind would drop."

Donna Maria shook her head. She could smell the acrid smell, though she could see very little. She said: "God is showing his anger to this wicked city. First he sent a plague; now he sends a fire. It is Sodom and Gomorrah all over again."

"Wicked things have gone on in all countries, Maria," I reminded her.

She would not accept that; and I think there were others in England who believed that we were suffering from Divine Wrath. It was significant, they said. The plague and then the fire. The licentious manners of the court, following the example set by the King, outstripped even those of that notorious den of iniquity, the court of France.

During that fearful day news kept coming to Whitehall. Houses near London Bridge were on fire; entire streets were ablaze. There was a glow in the sky and the heat from the fire was so fierce that it was dangerous to venture too near.

The Secretary of the Admiralty came to Whitehall to see the King on urgent business. Charles received him at once. Samuel Pepys was clearly overwhelmed to be in the King's company, but at the same time there was a sense of great urgency about him.

The King left at once with Mr. Pepys and the Duke of York. Charles told me afterward what had happened. London was in danger of being completely annihilated. Fires were springing up every-where. It was as though some fire-breathing dragon had taken posses-sion of the city. Fleet Street and the Old Bailey, Newgate, Ludgate Hill and St. Paul's were all ablaze. The cries of the people mingled with crackling burning wood; there were loud explosions as houses collapsed; the flames were stretching up to the sky and the burning heat was almost unbearable.

There was only one way of saving London: to blow up houses so that when the fire reached them there was nothing for it to consume and it could not spread.

Charles was out there directing operations with his brother James. The fact that they were there gave the people hope. Orders, which had been given by the Mayor, had not been obeyed, but when given by the King they could not be ignored.

It was a mercy that this terrible situation lasted only a few days. Indeed, had it lasted longer, the whole city of London would have been destroyed. And how right was the strategy of blowing up the houses, so making gaps which the fire could not bridge.

Charles worked indefatigably, and I am sure that to see their King riding through the streets, wigless, coatless, face blackened by smoke, ordering the blowing up of buildings, working harder than any, changed people's opinions of him. There indeed was truly a king. They were all fighting the battle against the deadly fire and because of the inspiration given by the King they knew they were going to defeat that destructive monster.

Charles talked afterward of the horror and the wonder of it—to see fire, the master, flaring, raging, triumphantly licking the buildings with relish before consuming them . . . the air full of smoke which, when the sun came up, gave a rosy glow to everything, making it the color of blood.

When the fire died down, the doleful task of assessing the damage and giving succor to the homeless began.

It was a great relief to find that only six people had died in the fire. We had feared there would be far more. However, over seven million pounds' worth of damage had been done. But I think the calamities of the plague and the fire—and in particular the latter—had shown the people that Charles could rise to the stature of a great king when the occasion demanded it.

→>-<+

I BEGAN TO UNDERSTAND CHARLES a little better. Beneath that merry insouciance there was a seriousness and when it was touched it could reveal unsuspected strengths of character.

Having put an end to the fire, we learned that the Cathedral of St. Paul's was completely destroyed, with eighty churches; so were the Guild Hall and the Royal Exchange among many other buildings. Over thirty thousand houses and four hundred streets were completely finished. It was reckoned that the damage extended over four hundred and thirty-six acres; and two-thirds of the city was destroyed.

There was a great deal to be done; a quarter of a million people had lost their homes and were camping in the fields around London. There had to be special arrangements to feed them.

Rebuilding must begin at once and Charles called in his best architect, Christopher Wren.

There were ugly rumors in the air. Lady Suffolk reluctantly told me of them.

"They are saying that the fire was started by papists."

"What a wicked lie. It is untrue, I know."

"Yes, Madam. But the people will say anything."

Charles acted promptly. There was an immediate inquiry, which, of course, proved that there was no foundation in the rumor.

It was not a time for false accusations, declared the King. What was important was to house and feed the people . . . to build new homes for them . . . to make a better London . . . a London of wide streets, light houses to replace the old dark ones . . . to make sure that something better arose from the ashes.

THE ELOPEMENT

A NEW YEAR HAD COME. BUILDING WAS GOING ON APACE and London was beginning to look like a prosperous city again. Nearly two million pounds had been voted for the purpose and life was settling down to normal.

The great interest at court was the King's devotion to Frances Stuart.

Charles really seemed to care for her. It amazed me that a man of his intellect could be besotted with such a foolish creature. Her beauty was of course unique: her skin was as smooth as a child's, her eyes clear and innocent, her features perfectly formed; and after the brazen arrogance of Lady Castlemaine one could not help liking her a little. But Charles was becoming really melancholy and the wits around him tried in vain to arouse him. They missed his gaiety. It seemed that nothing could satisfy him but the Fair Stuart.

I had two enemies at court, and they were both powerful; one was the Earl of Bristol and the other the Duke of Buckingham.

The Duke had always promoted Frances Stuart because he had believed he could make her work for him through the King. Charles was fully aware of this but it only seemed to amuse him. The fact remained though that the King could not stop yearning for Frances, and Frances was determined not to give way without marriage.

Such a situation had occurred before in royal circles and I heard the names of Henry VIII and Anne Boleyn often whispered, so it was clear to me what was in the minds of many people.

Henry VIII had been married to Catherine of Aragon who had produced one child—a girl—though there had been a succession of miscarriages. Catherine of Braganza had not produced even one girl.

Clarendon was out of favor; he had been so for some time.

People remembered that it was he who had helped to arrange the Portuguese marriage. Why? asked the people. Because he had known that I was barren. His daughter had married the Duke of York who was in line to the throne, they said, and if the King had no legitimate children who would follow him, the Duke would be king and Clarendon's grandchildren would be heirs to the throne.

They fancied they saw the wily Clarendon's reasoning.

I was inclined to shrug all this aside, but then a great deal of what was happening was kept from me.

It was Anne Hyde who told me, because she thought I should be aware of the direction in which events were moving. She was right, of course.

She said: "Bristol and Buckingham are trying to oust my father from office. They have always been jealous of him." She looked at me shrewdly. "I believe that if all is not well it is better to know it. One can then be prepared to deal with these matters when they are thrust upon one."

I liked Anne. She was forthright. I also liked her daughter Mary, of whom she was so proud. She had a second girl now, Anne, who had been born just before the plague struck London. But the Duchess had suffered the loss of her boys. It seemed perverse of nature to make the girls more hardy when everyone wanted boys. I should have been grateful even for a girl.

I said: "You speak truth. I agree with you that it is not helpful to be in ignorance."

"Buckingham is powerful and an evil influence. I cannot understand why the King tolerates him."

"He is witty and clever, qualities which the King greatly admires."

"And shares, but the King's wit is more kindly. Do you not agree?" I said I did.

She was looking at me intently. "There is this latest lampoon which they have attached to the gate of my father's house."

"And what is this lampoon? And who fixed it on your father's gates?"

"Buckingham's friends doubtless . . . and the lampoon concerns Your Majesty."

"What is it?" I asked faintly.

"You know they blame my father for the sale of Dunkirk . . ."

"But the reason Dunkirk had to be sold was because it was too expensive to hold."

"That's so. But when the people want to blame someone they will do so whatever the facts. Tangiers is proving difficult to hold and they are pretending that it is not worth having."

"And the lampoon?"

"I hesitate to repeat it. But perhaps you should know. It reads:

> *Three sights to be seen*
> *Dunkirk, Tangiers and a barren Queen.*

I flushed hotly.

"Your Majesty must forgive me," said Anne.

"It is better I should be aware. They believe, do they not, that I, with Dunkirk and Tangiers, am a catastrophe which has befallen the nation."

"They are impatient . . ."

"I have been the King's wife long enough . . ."

"It happens sometimes that these things do not come about at once. The important point is that my father's enemies . . . your enemies . . . have dared to write that."

"The King will not be pleased," I said.

She looked at me steadily and said: "I can speak frankly to Your Majesty. You and I both have unfaithful husbands. They are alike in this. We made grand marriages and we have gained a good deal; we must needs accept the disadvantages. I think Your Majesty should not treat this matter lightly."

"You mean to this suggestion that I am barren?"

"They are talking about that other royal marriage."

"Henry VIII's," I said.

She nodded. "I do not know whether this is merely a fabrication but I did hear a rumor that the King was consulting Dr. Seldon."

"The Archbishop of Canterbury!"

I could not believe that I was hearing correctly.

"It may be just a rumor, but sometimes when these things are said there is a little truth in them.

"You are saying that the King wishes to be rid of me so that he may marry Frances Stuart?"

"It is a case similar to that other."

"I do not believe the King would do this. He has always been so kind and considerate to me."

"It is his nature to be kind and considerate. He would regret it, I know. We are all aware of his regard for you. But the King is a man who will go to great lengths for those of whom he is enamoured . . . and if he has talked to the Archbishop of Canterbury . . ."

"What could the Archbishop promise him?"

"There could be talk of the need to get an heir to the throne. It is not unknown in royal circles."

I was feeling faint. I wanted to be alone to think.

Anne was quick to notice this.

She said hastily: "I thought only that you should be aware. Perhaps I have said too much. If I have, it was due to my anxiety for you. You are my sister-in-law. I thought you should be prepared."

"You did right and I thank you. It is better that I should know."

"Of course, one cannot believe all the rumors one hears."

I nodded in agreement. "Thank you, Anne," I said. "I am grateful to you."

I was glad when she left me, for I was stunned by what she had hinted. He wanted to be rid of me. I stood between him and Frances Stuart. If I were no longer his wife, he could offer marriage to her because it was the only way she would succumb.

What should I do? If I agreed to a divorce it would be arranged without doubt. The Pope had not given the sanction which Henry VIII had demanded, but this was different. Catherine of Aragon had been the aunt of the Emperor Charles, one of the most powerful men in Europe whom that Pope dared not offend. It was certain that there would be no one of such importance to defend the rights of Catherine Braganza.

It was foolish to think of that notorious case. All cases were different.

Moreover, there was no need to consider the Church of Rome; and if Charles had in fact consulted the Archbishop of Canterbury, it would mean that the Archbishop would now be considering how best a divorce could be contrived. I supposed a woman could be divorced because she was not fertile.

And Charles! Would he do this to me! I remembered him at my bedside when he had thought I was dying. I recalled his tears . . . the hours he had spent there . . . the genuine grief. Could he do this to me?

I tried not to think what my life would be like without him. There would be no place for me here. I should be sent back to Portugal. My mother was dead, my brothers in conflict with each other. Alfonso would be proving himself useless without my mother to guide him and Pedro, who had always resented not being the elder, would be trying to take what was Alfonso's. I could not bear it. I had to stay here. Charles, I knew, preferred other women physically, but there was friendship between us, and he cared for me in a way; and I had settled for that. I had managed to bring myself to a state when I could accept his infidelities and be moderately happy on those occasions when we were together.

I had believed that our relationship would strengthen in the years to come and that those women would become less important to him; and I would be there—his friend and faithful wife.

I remembered how he had dismissed poor Edward Montague. I had tried to deceive myself into believing it was out of jealousy. But no. Even though I so much wanted it to be, I could not accept that. Edward had gone solely because of the insinuations of Buckingham.

How deep was his passion for Frances Stuart? I asked myself. How strong his regard for me? I knew him well enough to realize that he would be upset to cause me pain; and to divorce me would certainly do that.

And the people? There would be some who would frown at divorce, but I was after all a foreigner and they did not like foreigners. They wanted to see an heir to the throne and they had convinced themselves that I could not provide it. Frances Stuart was beautiful; she would grace all occasions and it would seem that she had an excellent chance of giving the country an heir.

I saw little of Charles then. He was more immersed in state matters than usual. The aftermath of the fire, with the rebuilding, rehabilitation of the people, the progress of the war, the fact that enemies

were taking advantage of the impoverished state of the country, all demanded his constant attention as well as that of his ministers.

It was reasonable enough, but to my tortured imagination it
seemed that he avoided me, which a man of his temperament would
do if he were contemplating getting rid of his wife.

This was one of the most unhappy periods of my life. Each day
the possibility of Charles seeking a divorce seemed more plausible.

And then Edward Hyde, Earl of Clarendon, came to see me.

He was in an uneasy state of mind, for his own future was
precarious.

He was a great statesman and a man of letters. He had written several histories of his times among other things; he was learned and
clever. Charles, who had known him for many years, thought very
highly of his erudition. He was a man of principles and often reproved Charles for his mode of life. Charles did not resent this. He
would say it was true and Clarendon was right and that he should re-
form his ways. But Clarendon was asking more than Charles was prepared to give, so, in characteristic manner, the King shrugged his
shoulders and implied that the people had asked him to come back
and they must accept what they got.

Clarendon, I often thought, was uneasy in this atmosphere of frivolity which surrounded the court; and, being entirely different himself from most of the others, he had many enemies. He had originally
been intended for the Church, which might have suited him very
well, but on the death of his two older brothers, he became his father's
heir; and when he joined the Middle Temple at that time his uncle, Sir
Nicholas Hyde, was the Chief Justice, so he had a good chance of advancement. However, he decided he would not pursue a career in the
law as he wanted to devote himself to writing. This he had done.
Charles had once said it was rare that a man who owed his fame to writing and speaking should have a prominent place in the government.

Well, Clarendon was an unusual man.

At this time he must have been in his late fifties, but, apart from
the gout, he was in good condition.

I sensed as soon as he arrived that he found the matter which had
brought him somewhat delicate and he began by saying that his
daughter had thought that we must talk with the utmost frankness.

I said: "I should prefer that."

The color was high in his habitually ruddy cheeks, and I imagined he was choosing his words carefully.

"I have come to Your Majesty in this matter of the King and Mistress Stuart," he said.

"Yes?" I prompted.

"It seems that the King is greatly taken with the lady and . . . has certain plans for her."

I said: "He has had plans for her for a long time, my Lord Clarendon, but they have come to nothing because of the virtue of the lady."

"Exactly so."

"The Duchess of York has spoken to me of this matter," I said.

I guessed then that Anne had come on her father's advice.

Clarendon went on: "I am sure Your Majesty will agree with me that it would be well for everyone concerned if the lady had a husband." He was looking at me intently, as though assessing me. We had been in a somewhat similar situation when he had warned me about Lady Castlemaine and suggested how I should act. Then he had told me that I should accept her, and had been shocked when I did.

This, of course, was different. Then we had been talking of the King's mistress . . . now we were speaking of one who might become his Queen.

"The King has had a most unhappy time," he said. "The plague . . . the fire . . . this war." He lifted his hands. "He was more disturbed than he would have people know."

I guessed what was in his mind. The King was depressed by all his difficulties; he was frustrated by Frances's refusals; in such circumstances he might be tempted to do something rash.

He cleared his throat. "Your Majesty, Miss Stuart should be married as soon as possible."

I stared at him in horror, and he hastily added: "To one of her admirers, and so prevent this situation from worsening."

"Is she prepared to marry?"

"She seems to be on very good terms with her cousin, that other Charles, the Duke of Richmond and Lennox."

I knew the man. He was of the Stuart family, as Frances herself was. He must have been about ten or eleven years older than she was.

"Is he eager to marry her?" I asked.

Clarendon raised his shoulders to imply who was not eager to marry Frances Stuart?

"He is free to marry," said Clarendon.

"And Frances Stuart?"

He hesitated. "It occurred to me . . . well . . . she is a lady of your bedchamber . . . a word from the Queen. . . . She could be reminded of the pitfalls about her. I am sure she would understand."

"You are suggesting that I should talk to her, that I should tell her she should marry Richmond?"

"She would listen to Your Majesty's advice. She is a very simple girl. She needs advice. She could find herself in a difficult situation which she would not be able to handle."

"Talk to her? I . . . ?"

"Who but the Queen? Perhaps Your Majesty would think about the matter. But I do believe that some prompt action is necessary."

"I understand," I told him.

"I knew Your Majesty would. The girl should be settled. That is most important."

He smiled and took his leave.

When he had gone I felt deeply shocked. He had talked in innuendoes but I knew what was behind it.

It was true that Charles was contemplating divorcing me and marrying Frances Stuart. It might well be that Archbishop Sheldon was already working out a means of getting a divorce for the King on the grounds of my infertility.

I was frightened. Stretching out before me was a dreary future. I should be sent away. I should never see him again. And, strange as it might seem, I would rather be near him enduring jealousy and uncertainty than be away from him.

I thought of going back to Portugal: the emptiness of the palace without my mother, the quarrels between my brothers, myself sitting day after day with my attendants, stitching . . . reading . . . listening to music; perhaps waiting for the Spaniards to attack us.

I could not endure it.

Clarendon was seriously concerned. He would do everything he could to stop the divorce. He had arranged my marriage, and my downfall would be his. He would be making comparisons, as all would be at this time, and thinking of the fate of Cardinal Wolsey. And Thomas Cromwell was another who had arranged an unsatisfactory marriage for his King. Then it might be that Clarendon wanted the King's marriage to be unfruitful to make the way clear for his grandchildren.

For whatever reason, he did not want a divorce for the King, so he and I were allies. He was ready to fight for his position and that of his grandchildren; and I would fight for my future.

I was thinking what I would say to Frances Stuart.

I DID NOT HAVE TO SAY IT. I had forgotten Lady Castlemaine's part in all this. How that woman always seemed to be in the forefront!

I had not given much thought to what she would be feeling about these rumors until then.

She hated Frances. She knew that if Frances Stuart had given way that would have been the end of Barbara Castlemaine; she was lingering on as second best, only holding her position because it was rejected by Frances. The thought of her rival actually sharing the throne must have infuriated her.

She had always made it her affair to know what was going on. She had her spies everywhere. Her Mrs. Sarah would be on good terms with Frances's servants; and if Frances ever turned from her virtuous path, one could be sure that it would reach Barbara's ears before long.

It was the day after Clarendon had spoken to me. There was tension in the air, tittering and sibilant whispers in corners which told me that something had happened.

I learned of it from Lettice, though she was rather reluctant to tell it, for the reason that Charles played a part in it.

Frances was not on duty and I asked where she was. She was not feeling well, I was told.

"What ails her?" I wanted to know.

Lettice looked at Lady Suffolk, then Lettice burst out: "She was somewhat upset last night, Your Majesty."

"Why was that?"

There was silence.

"I know something has happened," I said. "I want to know what. Is there some secret, some conspiracy?"

Lettice decided that I must be told and she said: "It was Lady Castlemaine's doing. She took the King to Miss Stuart's apartments last night." She hesitated, and I said impatiently:

"Yes, yes. What happened?"

"Lady Castlemaine knew the Duke would be with her and wanted the King to see them together."

"The Duke of Richmond and Lennox?" I asked.

"Yes, Your Majesty."

"And in Miss Stuart's apartments?"

"Yes, Your Majesty."

"Alone with her?"

"Yes, Your Majesty. They were just talking, Your Majesty. Lady Castlemaine created a scene. You know, Your Majesty, that she never lowers her voice. Several people heard what she was saying."

"And what was that?"

"That Miss Stuart's modesty was a pose to attract the King, that she was conducting a love affair with the Duke . . . and it was very likely that he was not the only one. It was really rather scandalous. What one would expect from . . ."

"Lady Castlemaine," I finished.

"The King was very angry to see Miss Stuart with the Duke."

"Yes?" I murmured.

"Miss Stuart said that it was a perfectly innocent visit. They were talking together before saying good night . . . nothing more. Lady Castlemaine shouted that that was a likely tale; and she was glad to expose Frances for what she was, and she hoped the King would not be such a fool as to go on believing in all that virginity in future. The King left them . . . but he was clearly hurt and angry."

"And what then?"

"Everyone waits to see. The Duke has gone. He left the court. No one knows where he is . . . except perhaps Miss Stuart. She is staying in her apartments."

"She is there now?"

"Yes, Your Majesty."

"I see. I am glad to be in the secret. Thank you, Lettice."

→>-<←

IT WAS AFTERNOON before I saw Frances. She had not appeared, so I sent for her. I was alone when I received her. She looked frightened.

I said: "Come and sit on the stool, Frances, and tell me what is wrong."

"Your Majesty has doubtless heard what happened last night."

"Yes. The Duke of Richmond and Lennox was in your apartments when Lady Castlemaine burst in with the King. That is so, is it not?"

"Yes. There was nothing wrong. I have never . . . I have always said I wouldn't . . . and I never have."

"I believe you, Frances," I said.

"Oh, thank you, Madam. I fear the King does not. He will be very angry."

"*He* should not be," I said ironically.

"But it was not so. I never have. I've always sworn."

I patted her hand. "I understand the Duke came in for a little chat before saying goodnight. Is that so?"

"Yes . . . yes."

"Perhaps it was a little unwise. I believe he has strong feelings for you."

"He . . . he wants to marry me."

"And you?"

"I should like to be married, Your Majesty."

"Well, Lady Castlemaine brought the King to your apartments because she knew the Duke would be there. I wonder how she knew? Perhaps he made a habit of escorting you to your apartments and coming in to say goodnight."

"He has done it before . . . but that was all. We never . . . ."

I silenced her again. I believed her. If she had been going to be someone's mistress, it would have been the King's, I was sure.

"And now," I said, "what shall you do?"

"I do not know. Perhaps the King will send me away."

"I scarcely think he will do that. I understand the Duke has already gone. Do you know where?"

She looked at me in frightened silence, her lips pressed together. So she did know.

"All right," I said soothingly, as one would to a child. "It is going to be rather uncomfortable for you at court, Frances." She looked at me trustingly. "I should like to help you."

She took my hand and kissed it.

"It is time you were married," I continued. "If you had a husband he would protect you from all these men who are seeking to seduce you."

"Oh yes," she said.

"And you say the Duke wishes to marry you?"

"Yes, Madam. He has asked me."

"And what have you said?"

"I . . . I am not sure."

"You would be a duchess."

She smiled. The prospect was obviously agreeable to her.

I had heard that the King had offered to make her a duchess if she became his mistress. That was before the rumors of divorce had crept in.

She had refused. I believed that she was a virgin. She had no doubt been taught that it was unwise to give in to any man without marriage, and in her rather simple mind that had become an indisputable doctrine to which she clung.

But to be a duchess through marriage would please her.

"You would like to marry the Duke, would you, Frances?"

"Yes," she said.

"If you joined him, you could be married . . . then you would be safe."

"The King . . ."

"The King could do nothing if you were already married."

She was thoughtful.

"There could be an elopement," I suggested.

Her eyes shone with excitement.

"If you knew where the Duke was, you could go to him," I went on. "You could get married without delay. Then you could have a husband to protect you. I am sure the King would soon ask you and your husband to come back to court. Suppose you joined the Duke today? If only you knew where he is . . ."

"I do know. He is taking rooms at The Bear near London Bridge. He has had rooms there before. He is going to stay there until he sees what happens."

"The Bear! That is not far. Why do you not join him there? Why do you not elope? Go back to your apartments. You are not well enough to see anyone and I have told you to go to your bed and stay there until tomorrow. As soon as it's dark, you must leave the palace. Try not to be seen and take a carriage to The Bear near London Bridge. Tell the Duke that you are ready to marry him."

"Oh, Your Majesty!"

"Do as I say. Tell no one. Very soon you will be the Duchess of Richmond and Lennox. I am sure you will be a charming duchess."

"Your Majesty is so kind."

I kissed her and wished her Godspeed, and I meant it from the bottom of my heart.

What good fortune this was! In becoming the Duchess of Richmond and Lennox, Frances could sweep away all my fears of being set aside.

This could not be anything but a fortunate turn of affairs for me.

THE WHOLE COURT WAS TALKING about Frances's elopement. The King was furious and shrouded in melancholy. He was unlike himself. He must have cared deeply for Frances.

At length we heard that she and the Duke were married. I hoped she would be happy. She was such a simpleton, and I should greatly have preferred her to Lady Castlemaine if there had not been this threat of divorce. What I then heard of the Duke led me to believe that Frances might suffer some disillusion. He had already had two wives and he was constantly looking for favors at court; moreover he drank heavily.

I had a few qualms orf conscience when I heard this, even though I had not discovered it all until after the marriage. Perhaps I had been thinking too much of my own advantage. But at least she had married, which was what she had wanted; and it was she who had chosen Richmond.

As the weeks passed, the elopement of Frances Stuart ceased to be the main topic of conversation throughout the court. Lady Castlemaine retained her position and was obviously delighted to be rid of her formidable rival.

The war was going badly and the King was deeply immersed in

the need to rebuild the city. More money was needed. There was never enough.

That June the country suffered one of the most humiliating defeats it had ever known. People were outraged and amazed to see the Dutch fleet right on our shores. It sailed up the Medway as far as Chatham, took possession of Sheerness and burned several of our ships—the *Royal Oak,* the *Great James* and the newly launched *Loyal London* among them. They blew up stores of ammunition worth forty thousand pounds; and they did all this more or less unopposed, having taken the English completely by surprise. During the operation they lost only two of their own ships. Not that these had been taken in battle; they had merely run aground and were set fire to by the Dutch to prevent their falling into English hands.

There was great fear that they would reach London; and ships were sunk at Blackwall and Woolwich to prevent their doing this.

Having wreaked havoc not only on our ships but on our morale, the Dutch sailed triumphantly away.

The English were outraged and, as is customary, they looked for a scapegoat.

They chose Clarendon. He had become increasingly unpopular over the last years. I was deeply sorry for him. I knew he was not guilty of what he was accused. It was no fault of his that we were at war with the Dutch, nor that we had suffered plague and fire and lacked the necessary funds to carry on the war successfully.

Charles was turning away from him even though the Earl had been such a good friend to him during his exile.

Clarendon was a man who lived a very moral life. He believed a husband should be faithful to his wife; he deeply deplored the King's promiscuity and, because of that familiarity rooted in the past, he did not hesitate to say so. Although normally Charles was tolerant, he was under great strain at this time and less inclined to patience. So . . . Clarendon was out of favor . . . not only with the people.

He had powerful enemies at court. Buckingham was one, Lady Castlemaine another; and the King was weary of his continual lectures.

So he was certainly in a lonely position.

While the foreign ships were in the Medway, the mob had gathered outside Clarendon's house. They had uprooted trees, broken windows and set up a gibbet which was an indication of the hatred they had for him.

Charles was deeply anxious. How I wished he would talk more to me of his troubles!

He did on one occasion and I asked him what was happening about Clarendon.

"He will have to go, I fear," he said. "There is nothing I can do to save him. His time has come."

"They are blaming him for the war!"

"That is unfair, of course. He was a good friend to me in the past . . . but now . . ."

"You do not like him as you used to."

"He has frustrated me in so many ways."

I knew what he meant. He blamed Clarendon for Frances Stuart's departure. I never ceased to marvel that physical attraction could be so strong. It could not have been anything beyond that considering Frances's childlike mind. And Charles suspected Clarendon of arranging the elopement. I wondered what he would say if he knew what part I had played in that. I think he might have understood my motives and not judged me too harshly. However, I would not tell him . . . not until we were old and near the end of our lives. Perhaps not even then.

"I do not like these sanctimonious ones," said Charles. "They set themselves up as pillars of virtue and think it is their duty in life to censure those who fall short of their standards. Such men are tiresome."

Previously Charles had been good-humored about criticism. He must certainly be feeling Frances's desertion deeply.

"I have been advised," he went on, "that if I do not rid myself of Clarendon, I might go the way of my father."

"No!"

He looked at me wryly. "The heads of kings are never fixed very securely on their shoulders."

"Please do not talk so."

"Never fear, Catherine. I am deteremined to keep mine where it belongs, and never will I go wandering again. The best thing would be for Clarendon to resign. He could do that gracefully and it might be that we could then avoid unpleasant consequences. James is putting the suggestion to him."

"James?"

"Yes. Perhaps not the most tactful emissary, but he is my brother and Clarendon's son-in-law, and it could scarcely come from me."

Poor Charles! He was very anxious at that time.

The result of James's interview with the Earl was that the latter presented himself at Whitehall and told Charles that he would give up the Great Seal. Which was wise, said Charles, for the only alternative would have been to take it from him.

I was sorry for Clarendon. He, who had once been mighty, was indeed brought low.

The relinquishing of the Great Seal was not enough for his enemies. He must be arraigned for treason. I was glad that his son-in-law the Duke of York stood by him. Alas, in the midst of this James was smitten by smallpox and had to retire. Fortunately he soon recovered, but people said that the smallpox had been a sign of God's displeasure because the Duke had defended Clarendon.

In spite of the feeling against him, the Earl was able to prove that the charges had no foundation and they had to be dropped.

Charles showed me the letter he had received from Clarendon.

He wrote: "I do upon my knees beg Your Majesty's pardon for any over bold or saucy expression I have used to you. It is a natural disease in servants who have received too much countenance . . ."

He went on to ask the King to have the prosecution withdrawn and to allow his old Chancellor to retire overseas where he could spend his last days in peace.

Charles looked at me in consternation. "What can I tell him?" he said. "There will be an uproar if I give him permission to leave."

That did not mean that he did not help Clarendon to get away and put an end to this distressing matter.

Clarendon did leave.

He slipped away quietly to the coast and took a ship for Calais.

JAMES'S CONVERSION

LATE THAT YEAR TWO EVENTS OF SIGNIFICANCE TOOK place. Neither of them attracted much notice. I suppose what was happening in Portugal would not; but they were important to me.

Donna Maria was the only one to whom I could speak of Portuguese affairs. In fact, it was the only subject in which she was really interested. She disliked England and constantly wished that we had never come. In vain did I tell her that I had no desire to return to Portugal, especially now that my mother was dead; and if she yearned so much for her native land I would make sure that she returned to it.

This she firmly thrust aside. Had she not been with me all my life? What did I imagine she would do without me to worry about?

"You could live in peace in the country you love."

"You are the one I love," she said. "Where you are is home to me."

Dear Donna Maria! I am afraid I did not always appreciate her and was impatient with her sometimes. I should have been more grateful for all the devotion she gave me.

So with her I talked of events which were taking place in Portugal.

There has been conflict between my brothers.

"Pedro was always impatient with Alfonso," said Maria. "It is a pity Pedro was not the firstborn."

"Pedro despised Alfonso and was jealous of him because he was the elder," I said. "And now he is known as Regent."

"He was always the one to push himself forward."

"But it was necessary, Maria. Alfonso could not govern without my mother."

"Oh, she was the strong one. She knew at every turn what should be done."

"When she was gone . . . this was inevitable, Maria."

She nodded. "My poor Alfonso. What have they done to the boy?"

"He will be all right. They have sent him into exile. He is to live in the Azores, which I believe is very pleasant."

"As long as he is well looked after."

"There is something else," I said. "His marriage has been annulled."

"What?"

"Alfonso's wife, Maria Françoise Elizabeth . . ."

"I know her name," said Donna Maria impatiently.

"She has been divorced from Alfonso and has married Pedro."

"He has married his brother's wife!"

"That is so."

"So he has not only the crown but the wife as well?"

"It seems so, Maria."

"I wonder what next. Those boys . . . they were so pretty."

"Pedro is making peace with Spain."

"Is that a good thing?"

"It was what my mother would have done. She thought there must always be peace with Spain if possible. It was done with the help of Charles and his government."

Donna Maria grunted. She believed that Charles had treated me badly and she did not forgive him easily for that, however much he had helped Portugal.

She was shaking her head sadly, thinking of two little boys whom she had loved, playing their childish games. They still played games . . . but less childish ones.

I left her dreaming of the old days.

The other important event passed almost unnoticed. No one at that stage could guess what violent repercussions it was to have in the future.

James, Duke of York, no longer made a secret of his religious beliefs. He worshipped publicly as a Catholic.

THERE WAS A NEW MINISTRY after Clarendon had gone. The people called it the Cabal because of the names of the ministers who formed it: Clifford, Arlington, Buckingham, Ashley and Lauderdale.

Charles had high hopes of them.

"They are men of differing opinions," he said, "so between

them they should be able to avoid narrow-minded prejudice. True Clifford is a Catholic—a somewhat fiercely enthusiastic one—and Arlington is also a Catholic, although more moderate in his views. Buckingham . . . well, you know the noble Duke . . . perhaps you could call him independent; Ashley is something of a philosopher and Lauderdale a solid Protestant. So you see, we should be well represented from all sides."

Charles had always been fond of the theater—as it seemed was the whole of London. On his restoration Charles had granted two men of the profession, Sir William D'Avenant and Mr. Thomas Killigrew, a patent to open two theaters.

Charles was on terms of friendship with both these men. They were witty and amusing and Charles found them good companions. Both had been loyal to the royal cause throughout all the troubles and Charles was delighted to be able to reward them by making it possible for them to come back to a profession which they loved; and he naturally honored them with his patronage.

D'Avenant's theater was called the Duke's—actually the Duke of York's. D'Avenant was a playwright and a poet. He had been knighted for valor in the battlefield during the Civil War and had lived in France in exile where he had became a favorite of Queen Henrietta Maria. He claimed to be related to William Shakespeare and he had frequented the court of Charles I, for whom he had written plays and poetry, and made quite a name for himself.

I occasionally went to the theater. I enjoyed the plays and meeting some of the players. We were always on show and the people liked to see us there. Sometimes I felt the people came to see us as much as the play. Charles agreed. "We must not disappoint them," he said.

During the time of the plague the theaters had naturally been closed; and when the great fire followed, people seemed to have lost their zest for playgoing. It was coming back at this time and the playhouses were beginning to flourish again.

It was Lettice who said to me one day how pleased the people were that the King was going more frequently to the playhouse nowadays.

She said: "He seems to have a preference for Sir William D'Avenant's players."

I said: "He always found pleasure in the theater. The reason he has not been there so much of late is because he has had weightier matters on his mind."

"Well, he is certainly finding D'Avenant's *The Rivals* good entertainment."

I might have known there was some insinuation behind her words. There was one name which I heard mentioned frequently. It was that of a certain Moll Davis.

I asked Lady Suffolk who Moll Davis was.

"Oh, Madam, she is an actress of Sir William D'Avenant's company."

"She seems to be attracting a good deal of attention. Is she very good?"

"They say she is very good indeed."

"Perhaps I should go to see her."

"It may be, Madam, that you would not care for the play."

"But since everyone is talking about her . . ."

"She is a pretty girl . . . and some people like that."

She was telling me something.

She went on: "It is her dancing perhaps. She dances a very merry jig."

Suddenly the truth dawned on me. I heard one of the maids singing a song which sounded like "My lodging is on the cold ground . . ."

"You don't sing it like Moll Davis," said another.

"I'll swear she doesn't have to sleep on the cold ground now."

There was laughter and giggles. "Changed the cold ground for a royal bed, eh?"

So then I knew. I flushed with shame. Why was I always the last to hear?

He was tired of Lady Castlemaine. He would have finished with her altogether, I believed, but for the fact that she would not allow herself to be set aside without making a great noise about it, so I supposed it was easier to let her go on clinging.

I gradually learned that Moll Davis had left the Duke's Theatre and was set up in a house of her own. She possessed a handsome ring worth six hundred pounds.

Lady Castlemaine was heard to say that the King's taste had gone from simpering idiots who played making card houses to vulgar actresses who danced jigs.

I was very sad. I thought he had changed a little, grown more serious. But no, nothing had changed. There would always be women . . . ladies of the court . . . actresses . . . it would always be thus.

On reflection, though, it was easier to accept the actresses than the ladies of the court, and when I contemplated what I had suffered through Lady Castlemaine and Frances Stuart, I told myself that I had little to fear from Moll Davis.

THE COUNTRY WAS in a very precarious position and there was a recklessness in the air. We were on the verge of bankruptcy. Rarely could so many misfortunes have occurred in such a short time.

Charles was worried. There were two sides to his nature. People might think him selfish and self-indulgent, but beneath all that insouciance there was a shrewd and clever mind backed by a determination never to go the way his father had gone. People declared that Clarendon had been the author of our ills. They refused to accept the absurdity of this and waited for the Cabal to produce a miracle.

There was an uneasy situation between James, Duke of York, and the Duke of Monmouth. It was obvious that Charles doted on his son. As for myself, I could never look at that handsome young man's face without being filled with foreboding. He was a constant reminder of what Charles might have had from the right woman.

Monmouth resembled his father in some ways. He was sought after by women because of his looks and position. He was already known as a rake. He was full of high spirits and liked to roam the streets with his rowdy companions causing trouble. Charles was constantly making excuses for him and smoothing over difficulties made by the young man's conduct.

There was no doubt that Monmouth was attractive and could be charming. I said that he was like the King . . . not in looks though, except that he was dark. I think he must have inherited his mother's beauty. He liked to call attention to himself and remind people that he was the King's son. It was natural, I suppose, particularly as he was not legitimate, but he did want everyone to remember that he was the King's *eldest* son.

James, Duke of York, was very wary of him. I liked James because he had been pleasant to me from the first moment of my arrival in England. He was quite unlike Charles except in one respect: he shared the King's obsession with women and was as unfaithful to Anne as Charles was to me. But there the resemblance ended. James had none of Charles's grace, though he was a good naval commander. He had proved that, but he had no subtlety and every enterprise of his—apart from naval operations—seemed to go wrong.

There was something alarming in the attitude of James and Monmouth toward each other. I guessed what it was and that I was concerned in this. Monmouth was the King's beloved son. It was Monmouth who accompanied the King to Newmarket for the races and to Bagshot for the shooting. What if the King, despairing of ever having a child through me, legitimized Monmouth? Then what of James? James must have an eye on the throne, for Charles was no longer very young and was still without legitimate offspring.

Monmouth yearned to be made legitimate and James feared that it might happen. Therefore they were very watchful of each other . . . and of me, for if I produced a child the matter could no longer concern them so deeply.

When I had discovered that Charles contemplated divorcing me, that he might marry Frances Stuart, I had been deeply shocked and, even though Frances had now married, I had not yet recovered from it.

What was so hard to endure was that Charles had numerous children. Barbara Castlemaine alone had, I believed, six—healthy boys among them. There were others scattered around, so there was no doubt as to whose fault it was that the marriage was unproductive. I felt wretchedly inadequate and never quite sure when Charles might attempt to get rid of me . . . not only for his own satisfaction but for that of the state.

When James committed some inanity which set the people laughing behind their hands, Charles said to me: "The people are wondering whether they did right to call me back. Cromwell gave them drab lives, telling them that pleasure was sin—and they did not like that. Is it possible though that they might prefer even that to what they are getting now?"

And when I protested that the people loved him, he went on:

"They might just tolerate me for my time . . . but if it is James who comes after . . ." He shook his head gravely. "I fear for James." I could see speculation in his eyes. Was he thinking of that other James . . . Monmouth?

It seemed at that time that manners became even more licentious. Courtiers were blatant in their promiscuity. I supposed they would say they were following the King's example. Lady Castlemaine's affairs were the talk of the town. The King was involved with a play actress, Moll Davis. He was turning more and more away from Lady Castlemaine, who retaliated by conducting love affairs with people in all stations of life. She would go to the theater and afterward summon actors to visit her. She made no secret of her amours.

"I always follow the royal example," she said flippantly.

She was insatiable, it was said. I supposed that had been the reason for the attraction between her and Charles.

Yet he still visited her.

In the streets bawdy songs were sung about the various personalities of the court. Lampoons were passed round and Barbara Castlemaine could not be expected to be left out.

I was shocked to hear someone in the palace singing: "Full forty men a day provided for the whore, Yet like a bitch she wags her tail for more."

These lines on Barbara were attributed to the Earl of Rochester, who was a great favorite with the King. He was a wild rake, noted for his wit, and he and Charles were often together. He was related to Barbara Castlemaine, and he spared no one in his verses . . . not even the King.

Buckingham, of course, was in the center of the scene, more outrageous, impulsive and wilder than any. He behaved very badly to his long-suffering wife. I often wondered what Mary Fairfax thought of marriage to a grand duke; I imagined she longed for the dignity of her father's Puritan home. Buckingham, whose morals could be compared with those of Lady Castlemaine, was quite shamelessly carrying on an amorous intrigue with the Countess of Shrewsbury. He had brought her into his house and expected his wife to accept the presence of his mistress.

It was reported that Mary Fairfax had confronted the Countess, saying there was not room for both of them in the house and she must therefore ask the Countess to leave at once. At which time Buckingham had come upon the scene and declared that she was right. There was not room for the three of them, therefore he had ordered his carriage to conduct Mary to her father's house.

Such stories, even in the immoral climate of London at that time, were considered by most people to be outrageous.

The Earl of Rochester had abducted the heiress Elizabeth Malet, married her and taken possession of her fortune.

There was a great scandal when the Duke of Buckingham fought a duel with the Earl of Shrewsbury and one of Buckingham's seconds was killed on the spot and Shrewsbury died from his wounds a few weeks later. Lady Shrewsbury, the cause of the dispute, stood by dressed as a page holding Buckingham's horse while the duel was in progress.

Buckingham continued to live in blatant adultery with Lady Shrewsbury.

It seemed that however outrageously people behaved, it was acceptable. What could be expected, some of the more serious-minded asked, when the King showed such contempt for moral standards?

"There is a new actress at the Theatre Royal," said Lettice, "who, they say, can outshine Moll Davis. She should be seen in this Beaumont and Fletcher piece. *Pilaster,* I think it is called."

I said I should be interested to go one evening.

When I went to the theater, it was considered fitting that I should be in the company of the King, so we went together. The people liked to see us there. Charles was affable to everyone, even the humblest orange girls.

Tom Killigrew, the manager, to whom Charles had given the grant to open the theater, was on terms of familiarity with the King, who had lately been frequenting the Duke's Theatre because Moll Davis had been there.

I settled down to enjoy the play, and as soon as I saw the actress I realized that she had some special quality. She was small yet dainty with abundant reddish hair, rather wild and curly, framing a piquant face. There was saucy mischief in that expression and an unmistakable vitality.

She played the part of Bellario, a girl so much in love that she goes off to follow her lover, disguising herself as a pageboy. I might say that it was no disguise at all. She was completely feminine and could never be mistaken for anything else, and she had the kind of face which would be recognizable anywhere.

But it was an appealing piece. The King laughed and clapped his hands with pleasure. He was very intent on the stage and the actress was obviously aware of it. She gave the impression that she was playing for him.

All the young men in the house—and they were prominent among the audience—appreciated her, and when the play was over they demanded that she dance a jig, which she obligingly did with great animation.

The audience began to chant verses which some poet must have written about her. There were always verses, for many of the young men who haunted the theater believed themselves to be young Shakespeares waiting to be recognized.

> *She is pretty and she knows it*
> *She is witty and she shows it*
> *And besides that she's so witty*
> *And so little and so pretty*
> *She's a hundred other parts*
> *For to take and conquer hearts*
> *But for that suffice to tell ye*
> *She's the little pretty Nelly.*

Lady Suffolk was beside me, so I said, "Who is this actress?"

"Her name is Nell Gwynne, Your Majesty. She is a great favorite, as you see."

"The audience seems to like her," I replied.

I turned to the King. His eyes were still on the girl. He seemed to like her too.

I WAS NOT SURPRISED when I heard that the King had invited Mistress Eleanor Gwynne to sup with him.

It was impossible to keep secret the fact that the King was sending for pretty little Nelly, but she did not replace Moll Davis immediately. Charles liked variety and apparently Moll Davis was a pretty little creature also. So Moll lived in her fine house and continued to flaunt her six-hundred-pound ring and Nell Gwynne was just the King's casual playmate.

There were times when I felt dejected. The whole of London—and perhaps beyond—would be talking about the King's latest mistresses—and the rivalry between Nelly and Moll.

Nell was a madcap who did wild things. A story was in circulation that one day Moll was boasting that the King had sent for her and she would be with him that night. Poor Nelly, she said, when had she last seen the King? Moll could sympathize. It must be maddening for her dear friend to be sent for so rarely.

Nell said that there was no ill feeling, and to show this, she would like to drink to her friend's success. Moll agreed to this and Nell laced her rival's drink with a strong purge so that Moll was unable to visit the King that night. Nell coolly presented herself to take Moll's place.

It was said that when the King heard what had happened, he was greatly amused and soon after that Nell began to gain ascendancy over her rival.

I thought often of the romantic love which I had believed in before I came to England. What an innocent I had been! But perhaps not. Perhaps it did exist. Queen Henrietta Maria had found it when she came to England. But she had come in fear, most reluctantly and had discovered a faithful husband who had grown to love her as she had him. And I had come in joy and expectation and even for a short time believed I had found perfection. At least I had had that. And in this London of the Restoration, faithful husbands were rare indeed. Promiscuity, infidelity, adultery . . . that was the custom of the day.

So . . . I must not brood on my misfortune. I must hide my jealousy. I must adjust myself to this careless cynical age; I must be part of court life . . . enjoy the wit of those who crowded round the King, and try to be one of them.

I could not do that, but at least I had little to fear from actresses such as Moll and Nell and could forget the humiliation I had suffered through Barbara Castlemaine and the fear when I thought Charles would set me aside for the sake of Frances Stuart.

I must be grateful that that had passed.

→>-<←

IT WAS EARLY SEPTEMBER when the news came.

I was at Hampton Court. Charles, with his brother James, had gone off to hunt in the New Forest when a courier arrived from France. He came in great haste and said he would speak only to the King.

Messengers were immediately dispatched and Charles and James very soon arrived at Hampton.

I was with them when the courier told them the news.

"Your Majesty and my Lord Duke," he began, "I have sad tidings. Queen Henrietta Maria expired on the last day of August."

Charles was shaken. "How, how? She was well . . ."

"Your Majesty, she suffered frequently from sleeplessness. She had to take pills each night in order to sleep. On that morning . . . she did not wake up."

Charles fired questions at the messenger. James stood by dazed.

All we could discover was that the Queen had suffered from various ailments since her return from England.

"She took the baths at Bourbon, Your Majesty. They helped but could not cure her. She was very brave and always said she did not wish to be like those ladies who lamented when they had an aching finger. King Louis sent his first physician, Monsieur Valot, to her."

"Louis was fond of her, I know," said Charles. "He would have done anything to help her."

"He was very sad when he learned of her death, Your Majesty. He said a courier must be sent to England immediately."

"It was good of him," said Charles.

"Monsieur Valot is now a very unhappy man, for it was he who prescribed the grains to make Her Majesty sleep."

"She was always averse to taking such things," commented Charles. "And Dr. Mayerne, who attended her when she was here, agreed with her that such aids to sleep could be dangerous. Tell me, how was she before she died?"

"She suffered a cough, Sire."

"Had she taken to her bed?"

"Oh no, Your Majesty. She was at supper as usual. She talked and laughed. She took her grains and went to sleep at once, her ladies said. When one of them went in to awaken her she could not do so and the doctor came. They said she was not dead but some vapor had touched her brain and prevented her from speaking. However, the priest had the ceremony of extreme unction performed. They said she revived a little but only for a few moments, and then she expired. There is great sadness at the court of France, Your Majesty. The King deeply mourns his beloved aunt, and the Princess Henriette is prostrate with grief."

"My poor Henriette . . . she would be," murmured Charles. "The Queen loved her more than any of us . . . even James."

I felt as though I had lost a friend. I had not seen a great deal of her but there had sprung up a warm relationship between us.

I could grieve with them.

THE COURT WENT INTO MOURNING and Charles seemed a little closer to me then. I think he wanted to talk about his mother and he could do that with me more easily than with Lady Castlemaine or one of his actresses.

"Dear Mam," he said. "I was never a favorite with her. She was disappointed in me from the day I was born. 'What an ugly child!' she said. 'Can it belong to me and my handsome Charles?' "

"They say you were very like her father and she admired him greatly, I believe."

"Like him in my ways . . . at least in the worst of them." He looked at me with that half-amused, half-apologetic smile. "He was a great king, that Henri—one of the best the French have had. I should do well to emulate him in that respect . . . instead of others. I think of my dearest sister, Henriette. I would I could be with her. She was the closest to Mam. She is more French than English. She was only a child when she ran away from this country, and Mam . . . she was all French . . . she would never be anything else. That is why the English did not like her. They blame her for my father's death."

"The people must always blame someone."

"Oh yes, it is comforting to pick a scapegoat. But I fear my dear Mam may not have helped matters. In the first place they did not like her religion."

I flinched and he put a hand over mine.

"You are not like her. Mam made her opinions known and she believed she was always right. I think that was where she went wrong.

She was indiscreet; she talked when she should have been silent. She went marching through life . . . blundering, you might say . . . taking action when she should have been passive . . . bringing disaster to her husband whom she wanted to help more than anything on earth. That was Mam, quick to rage . . . effusive in her affections . . . everything she did was done with the utmost enthusiasm. Perhaps that was why we loved her. I wish I could see my little sister."

"You love her best of all your family, I think," I said.

"Little Minette. Yes, she was my favorite. It is sad that we never meet. I do not think she is happy over there. The French court is different from ours. Perhaps what people here resent about our court is that it is too like the French, but, as I say, the difference is there. It is as free as ours . . . but shall I say less blatant. Our characters differ. I am half French, Catherine, so I know. Perhaps that is my misfortune."

"Your misfortune! The people love you. They will forgive you anything."

He smiled at me. "There is a strong puritanical influence in the country. You do not see it at court, but it is there. The stern rules of Cromwell and his followers are not easily forgotten. The country must become prosperous. There must be an end to these wars. We have to be friendly with our neighbors. It is not enough to give people pageants and playhouses. There has to be security too."

"I know that you have your anxieties and that when people hear scandals they believe that you are more interested in pleasure than in duty."

He took my hand and pressed it. I thought he was trying to explain to me, to ask forgiveness for his weakness. Then he shrugged his shoulders. "Poor Mam," he said. "She could not help what she was, any more than the rest of us can. And now she is gone . . ."

QUEEN HENRIETTA MARIA was buried on the twelfth of September, nearly two weeks after her death; and she was laid to rest beside her ancestors in the Abbey of Saint Denis.

There were a great many rumors about her death, as there usually are about royal people who die before they are expected to.

Dr. Valot, I believe, had an uncomfortable time defending the

"grains" he had subscribed. He declared he had given her these because she could not sleep, and so effective had they been that she had
failed to wake up.

In England we mourned her. People ceased to talk of the part she
had played in the Civil War and remembered the good things about
her: her stoical attitude toward physical pain; her goodness; her care
for her servants. I knew how warm-hearted she could be and I believed there had been much that was good in Henrietta Maria.

And then Frances Stuart, now Duchess of Richmond and Lennox,
returned to court and I was deeply concerned as to what effect this
would have on Charles.

She had changed. She was still beautiful, but she had lost just a little of that innocence . . . that childish outlook on life; but she was not
subtle enough to hide the fact that the marriage was not a success.

Charles received her in a friendly but somewhat aloof manner. I
was relieved by this, although it was no longer of vital importance to
me; the Duchess of Richmond and Lennox could not be the threat
that plain Miss Stuart had been.

Moreover, he was becoming more involved with the play actress
Nell Gwynne who, I had heard, was expecting his child.

Poor Frances, she was not a happy woman.

I sent for her one day and dismissed everyone else, so that we
could be alone together.

"Frances," I said, "are you happy?"

She raised those beautiful eyes to my face and there was a mournful expression in them.

"It is not what I expected it would be, Your Majesty."

"Oh," I replied. "You thought there was something divine about
marriage . . . did you, Frances? And now you find . . ."

"I was happier before," she said.

I saw the regret in her eyes. It was natural that she should have
been fascinated by the King, for, apart from that aura, he was attractive to men and women alike. His very ugliness—if it could be called
that—was appealing; his tall lean figure moved with exceptional
grace, but it was in his expression and smile that one recognized that
easy tolerance, that sympathy, that acceptance of life and the determination to make it a pleasure for others as well as himself. He had a
rare kindliness which drew people to him. So naturally Frances would

have been attracted by him and would doubtless have preferred him to her drunken duke.

She had had the choice—as someone in my position would never have had. If Charles had been free to marry, most certainly she would have married him. But she had selected the way of morality and insisted on marriage, and she was regretting that.

Now she was back at court. I guessed it was the Duke who had insisted on their return, knowing that the King would forgive the woman on whom he had once so clearly set his heart.

He was right. Charles did not bear grudges for long. He had forgiven many who had trespassed against him; so he would forgive the Duke and Duchess of Richmond and Lennox.

He obviously did.

He was contented with the women he had. I began to believe that Nell Gwynne was responsible for this satisfaction. It was strange that an uneducated girl—though I believe she had a lively mind—could be so important to Charles. But then, when I considered Frances Stuart, was it so surprising?

He was still seeing Lady Castlemaine. She seemed to have some hold on him. I had heard her threaten to publish his letters to her. I think he could easily have prevented that, but perhaps he was fascinated by her insolence. She was notoriously unfaithful to him; her lovers were numerous and there were hints that many of them had to be paid for their services. Unpleasant scandals about her abounded. I could not understand why he continued to see her—but he did. This new serenity seemed certain to come from his association with Nell Gwynne.

I tried to discover something about her. I imagined for Charles she would provide a complete escape from formality, for Nell would be no respecter of persons. She was undemanding and asked for nothing. She was in love with the King in a way, as he was with her.

So perhaps it was due to Nell Gwynne that Charles did not dash to the side of Frances Stuart.

I said to her: "Frances, you wanted to be married, and you are. You are a duchess. You wanted a title, did you not?"

She agreed. "I thought it was right to be married. I did not want to be like so many at court."

"Poor Frances. Life does not always turn out as we plan, you know."

"No, Madam."

"But you are the Duchess now . . . a married woman. Always remember, Frances, that is what you wanted. I am sorry you are disappointed. You used to be so happy in the old days."

"But they could not go on, Madam."

"No. You had to make a choice. Well, Frances, you made it, and now you are back at court. There is no turning back. So is it with us all."

She was easy to read. I could see in her eyes that she was asking herself, what did I do? I chose the right thing and found unhappiness . . . when I might have been happy, doing what was wrong.

What a dilemma! It was one which I had not had to face.

I WAS WATCHFUL OF CHARLES, wondering what he was feeling about Frances. I guessed that if he wanted her to be his mistress there would be no obstacles this time.

The Duke would be complaisant enough, seeing advantages through such an arrangement. And Frances? What of her morals? I was not sure, but I believed she would succumb with ease. There was a great stir throughout the court when Frances contracted smallpox.

This was the most dreaded disease for, even if it did not kill, there must almost certainly be the inevitable disfigurement. Beauty could be destroyed in a few days by the hideous pits in the skin left after the sores had healed. And Frances Stuart, whose sole claim to fame had been her outstanding beauty, now stood at risk.

Charles was quite distressed when he heard. He could not bear to think of that incomparable beauty being destroyed. Frances was very ill. We heard that she had been badly smitten.

I thought the court would soon be in mourning for her. She had few enemies—only those who had been jealous of her good looks; she had never willingly done anything to harm anyone. I, who had suffered through her more than most, could only feel friendly toward her.

Then we heard that she was going to recover.

I was surprised when Charles went to see her. People did not visit smallpox sufferers. He was putting himself in danger.

That was characteristic of him. He must have truly loved her. I remembered his long pursuit of her, his contemplating divorcing me that he might marry her. Oh yes, indeed, he had cared deeply for her, for he would have hated to hurt me. Yet he had been ready to do it for her.

And now there she was, isolated because of the terrible affliction which had struck her. No one wanted to go near her; but he went.

When he returned I confronted him. I said: "Is it true that you have been to see Frances?"

He nodded, looking inifinitely sad.

"It was dangerous. What if you . . . ?"

He shook his head. "She is past the illness."

"But . . ."

He lifted a hand. "I went to see . . . an old friend."

"And how was she?"

He turned away, unable to speak, and I knew then that the worst had happened.

"Poor Frances," I murmured. "Poor, poor Frances."

THE MEETING AT DOVER

THERE WAS TROUBLE BREWING AND TO MY DISMAY I LEARNED that I was at the heart of it.

James, Duke of York, had made the mistake of not keeping his change of religion a secret. If Charles and I had had a child, the fact that James had turned to the Catholic faith, though it might have caused a little resentment in some quarters, would not have been of vital importance. But James was the heir to the throne and the English were against accepting a Catholic monarch.

So far there had been the hope that Charles would have a son who would be brought up in the Protestant faith, but he had not made his appearance and time was passing. Charles did have a son, however, but alas he was not legitimate. This was Monmouth. Monmouth was attractive and merry, as would be expected of a son of Charles. That he lacked Charles's wit and shrewdness was of no great moment. Monmouth was young; he could learn wisdom.

Alas, he had been born on the wrong side of the blanket, as they said; he could not come to the throne—and so the country was left with James.

I am sure that at this time ambition was growing in Monmouth's mind; as for James, dislike for the boy was only natural since it was possible that he could be a menace to him.

The King's evident love for his illegitimate son was another factor to be considered. They were constantly in each other's company and Monmouth took liberties which others would have hesitated to take; he behaved as the King's legitimate son and was gathering about him a circle of friends who were looking to the future.

In the other camp was James, the heir presumptive to the throne, until I produced that longed-for child.

I knew that Charles was concerned about what was happening.

He said to me: "James is a fool. Why does he have to do all that worshipping in public?"

"He feels that he would be betraying God by being ashamed of the way he worships."

"It's the fact that he is betraying himself that I am afraid of," said Charles. "God help James if he ever comes to the throne . . . and for that matter, God help England."

It was Lady Castlemaine who told me the significance of this to myself. She had reasons for it. She always had her reasons.

I had listened to her before, and if her interests coincided with mine, I might do well to follow her advice.

She asked to see me. I hesitated, for I loathed the sight of the woman; and now that I knew of the depth to which she had sunk, I did not want her near me. But I decided I must at least hear what she had to say.

She came. She looked older and was showing signs of dissipation. She was overweight; her magnificent hair was piled up on her head and she wore a diamond ornament in it. Her gown revealed too much of her ample flesh; but she managed to look splendid still.

I bade her be seated, which she was already doing without waiting for my permission. She came straight to the point.

"Your Majesty, there is a conspiracy of which I am sure you are ignorant."

I replied: "Pray inform me of it, Lady Castlemaine."

"Once before there was a plot," she went on. "Now there is another." Her next words sent a shiver through my body. "They are trying to arrange a divorce so that the King may marry a woman who can give him children."

"But now . . . ," I stammered.

"Your Majesty must forgive my frankness. It is not Frances Stuart now." Her lips curled with a certain satisfaction. "She is a poor creature now with her pitted face. There is no one in mind. That is to come. Some foreign princess . . . French possibly. But this is a threat to you and we must prevent its happening."

"How can you know this?"

"I mingle. I talk to these men. I have my faithful friends . . . my servants serve me well. I know."

"Before there was . . ."

"Yes, and we foiled them, did we not? This is more serious. There is no one in view. They cannot say it is the King's desire for a new wife. The Cabal will choose her when the time comes."

"The Cabal!"

"Oh yes. They are for it . . . most of them. My friend Buckingham . . . Arlington . . . it is because of James."

"You mean the Duke of York, or . . ."

"Or Monmouth? Both of them. They will not have the Duke of York. They will not have a Catholic on the throne. On the other hand there is Monmouth. Now if he were not a bastard, there would be no question of James. But Monmouth *is* a bastard, in spite of all his efforts to be the Prince of Wales."

"Is this true . . . ?"

"Madam, it is for you to believe or disbelieve. I only come to warn you."

"Why?" I asked.

She smiled at me conspiratorially. "Your Majesty, I have always had a great respect for you, ever since you came to our shores. It would grieve me greatly to see you . . . replaced."

I understood. She visualized a new queen . . . someone young and possibly beautiful . . . someone who insisted on clearing the harem . . . reigning supreme.

When I came, she had had a great hold on the King. That was not very strong now. She was unsure of her position. That was why she wanted my help. She felt it was easier for her to maintain her position if I held mine.

I had to listen to her with all attention. The Cabal was urging this, trying to persuade the King. There must be an heir, they were saying. The country will not accept the Duke of York. There was young Monmouth . . . a Protestant . . . a bastard, but preferable to York.

"They cannot have Monmouth," I said. "That would be unacceptable."

"No . . . unless he . . . But there you are. They are saying that the King must have a divorce and marry a woman who will give him a son."

I sat back, feeling faint.

She was smiling at me. "There is one other thing. The King might announce that he was married to Lucy Walter."

"Married Lucy Walter?"

"Monmouth's mother. If the King had married her, Monmouth would be the legitimate heir. It's one way out."

"But the King was not married to Lucy Walter."

"They were on the continent. It would not be difficult to find evidence."

"False evidence?"

She smiled and shrugged her shoulders.

"Why are you telling me this, Lady Castlemaine?" I asked.

"So that you may take action."

"What action?"

"The King has a great regard for you. I am suggesting that you speak to him. He wavers. . . . He knows that York will be a disaster. He knows of Monmouth's ambitions. He realizes how all this could be set aside if only he had a son. He can beget handsome children." She preened herself a little, no doubt thinking of those she had produced. "You see his predicament. You must make up his mind for him."

"How?"

"I believe that if you pleaded with him . . . made him understand how much this means to you . . . if he knew how much you cared for him . . . which you do, I know . . . if he knew how desolate you would be . . . I think he would turn away from the persuasion of his ministers. I know the King well. This is a chance. . . ."

"It is good of you to be concerned for me."

She smiled at me. She did not say that she was thinking of her own advantage. She did not want to lose the King entirely, and she knew she could do so if there were a new wife.

I thanked her and she left. I sat down in desolation to contemplate the situation.

I knew that what she had told me was the truth.

WHEN I WAS ALONE WITH CHARLES, I came straight to the point.

"I have heard disquieting news," I said.

"There is nothing unusual in that," he replied. "The news is always disquieting now."

"About this proposed divorce," I went on.

His face was serious suddenly. "What have you heard?" he asked sharply.

"That—as you did once before—you are considering divorcing me so that you can marry a new wife . . . younger, I presume, and one who can give you and the country an heir."

He was silent for a moment, then he said: "This has been a suggestion which was presented to me."

"And what are you going to do about it?"

"Do you want to be divorced?"

I felt my face crumpling. He put his arms about me and held me close to him.

"You see," he said. "It is this devilish business of James and his religion. This is what has set all this trouble about our ears. They do not want James. I don't blame them. Poor James. He stumbles around . . . tripping headlong into trouble. Why did he want to do this? Why couldn't he have kept his religion secret? And then there is Jemmy. He is an ambitious boy. You see, Catherine, I am beset on all sides."

"And you think that by ridding yourself of me you will settle these difficulties?"

"I should be heart-broken if you were taken from me."

"Please, Charles," I said, "this is a time for plain speaking."

"I am speaking plain. I am speaking from my heart."

"But this is a matter for heads, not hearts. They want a son . . . your son . . . and they think I cannot get one. It may be they are right. And you are a lusty begetter of sons. I do not know how many. Do you?"

"Let me tell you this, Catherine. I never want you to leave me."

"But you will have so many consolations."

"I am myself, I fear, and that is not a very noble thing to be. I know that. I am what I have always been and was born to be. That does not mean I do not love you."

"It is a theme I have often heard. It is a pleasure to hear it, but it is a fiction . . . a romantic story. It is not real."

"It is real," he said. "They are talking about it incessantly. To listen to them is like being at the playhouse."

"It is the Cabal."

He nodded. "They do not want James. That's the heart of the matter. They'd rather have Jemmy. He's a bastard, but a popular bastard."

"How could that possibly be?"

"If he were legitimate."

"But he is not."

"They plan to make him so."

"How could that be?"

"Oh . . . a little box suddenly found . . . somewhere far away . . . on the continent, of course. In this box would be a document showing that I married Lucy Walter, Jemmy's mother, and therefore he is the rightful heir to the throne."

"But there is no box and you were not married to Lucy Walter."

"A trifling detail in the minds of these schemers. If I give my permission they will find the box with the appropriate documents."

"And you would allow this?"

He shook his head. "Never," he said emphatically.

"So then the alternative . . . you will agree to this divorce."

He took my face in his hands. "Do you want to go away from me, Catherine? God knows I would not blame you if you did. I deserve to lose you."

All my defenses had gone. I could only stand there with the tears on my cheeks. I had to tell the truth. I had to jettison my pride.

"I never want to leave you, Charles," I said. "I love you."

"You must regret . . ."

"Never. Never. I would rather be here with you . . . whatever you did . . . than anywhere else on earth."

He kissed me with tenderness. "Do you think I would ever agree to part from you?" he said. "I know it is difficult to understand. I know my weaknesses, but whatever I am, Catherine, I love you . . . with all my heart and while you want to stay with me you shall."

I was happy. He did love me, I knew . . . in his way.

I HAD REASON to be grateful to Lady Castlemaine, because I believed that, had I not spoken to Charles and made him aware of the deep affection I had for him—and perhaps reminded him of his for me—he might have been persuaded to divorce me for the sake of the country.

Lady Castlemaine had naturally been thinking of her own interests. She could not have believed that the end was in sight for her.

She was growing old; her reputation had become scandalous, even for this era; and she had ceased to be amusing.

One of the prime movers in the plot to persuade Charles to divorce me was my old enemy Buckingham.

He was a strange man; there were so many contrasts in his nature. He was clever, erudite, witty and brilliant. At the same time he could be foolishly impulsive, reckless beyond belief and could conceive hare-brained schemes which most people would have seen from the moment of their inception were doomed to failure.

He was fierce in anger and if he thought anyone was working against him he would go to any lengths to destroy that person. He had shown this in the case of Shrewsbury, whom he had murdered . . . for it was murder, even though Shrewsbury had agreed to face him in the duel which had resulted in his death. Buckingham was quite outrageous—not unlike his kinswoman, Lady Castlemaine. It was said that after the duel, Lady Shrewsbury's page-boy's garments were splashed with her husband's blood and the pair made love while she was wearing them.

Of course, there were many stories about Buckingham, but I believed some of them were true.

Ashley and Lauderdale were his special allies in the Cabal. In fact, people said that the Cabal was split and there were two factions. These three had schemed for the divorce. The main reason was not their antipathy to me, for to them I was of little importance, just a pawn in the game. The real enemy was James, Duke of York, and they were determined at all costs to prevent his coming to the throne. The best way of doing this was of course for Charles to have an heir. That was why they planned my exit from the scene, for it seemed unlikely that I should have a healthy child.

After that scene with me, the King had firmly said that he had no intention of divorcing me; and Buckingham was furious.

It was impossible to keep secrets from him, for he had his spies everywhere. He had discovered that Lady Castlemaine had visited me, and that after her visit I had spoken to the King.

Buckingham immediately understood Lady Castlemaine's reasons for not wanting a change. Or it may have been that he had taxed her with interfering. I am sure she would have quickly lost her temper and told him of her interview with me. She would see no reason to keep up a pretence with Buckingham, and would doubtless have told him to keep out of her affairs. So . . . Buckingham was intent on revenge.

He knew that Barbara entertained handsome young men in her lodgings and, as Barbara had once in the case of Frances Stuart, he had the idea of taking the King to visit her, catching her in a compromising situation.

He therefore suggested that it would be amusing to call on Barbara unexpectedly, and Charles allowed himself to go along.

I heard the story of what happened. It was passed on by the servants and there were several versions, but they all agreed on the salient points.

When the King and Buckingham arrived, Mrs. Sarah was in a state of great dismay. She knew, of course, that Barbara was entertaining that evening and it was no time to let visitors in, particularly the King. According to the stories, Mrs. Sarah blustered and insisted that Lady Castlemaine was ill and could see nobody. I could imagine Buckingham's response to that. He pushed Mrs. Sarah aside and bounded into Barbara's bedroom.

At the door of the room Buckingham stood, the King beside him. On the bed, in the most compromising position, was Barbara with a young ensign.

The young man was known to the King because his sister Arabella Churchill was the mistress of the Duke of York. He was John Churchill, who had been a page of the Duke of York while his sister had been lady-in-waiting to Anne Hyde. The Churchills had been loyal during the Civil War, hence the favor shown to them.

Arabella had caused quite a stir, for she was the most unlikely girl to have been noticed by the Duke. But then everyone knew the Duke's strange tastes. I had never seen her, but I had heard she was tall and thin, all skin and bone, someone had remarked, and not in the least beautiful. But she had apparently pleased the Duke, for she had had a child by him and was still in favor. Charles was always amused by James's poor taste in women. However, this was the girl's young brother, and he was destined for promotion and he would get it, people said, as long as his sister continued to please the Duke.

I could imagine the young man's terror when he saw the King, his hope of advancement doubtless evaporating.

He did not know what to do. Half naked as he was, he leaped from the bed and jumped out of the window.

Charles and Buckingham burst into laughter. Charles shouted: "Don't worry, Churchill, I know you only do it for the money!"

From the bed Barbara let out a stream of abuse. She was furious with Buckingham, for she suspected immediately that he had arranged this for her discomfiture, because she had meddled in the matter of the King's divorce.

Buckingham had had his revenge; and that event seemed to have its effect on the King, for after it Barbara lost the King's favor. She had had years of power, but that had been coming to a close for some time and this really seemed to be the end.

I HAD RARELY SEEN Charles in such good spirits, and the reason was that his sister was coming to England.

He had talked now and then of Henriette—Minette was his name for her. She was the youngest of the family and when she was born the Civil War had already started.

"Poor Minette," said Charles. "She never knew peace in England. When she was about two years old, the situation had become dangerous and she had escaped to France with her governess, Lady Dalkeith, she who became the Countess of Morton later. She was a wonderful woman of great courage. Had they stayed in England, they would have become Cromwell's prisoners."

"I suppose she would not remember much as she was so young."

"Oh yes, she does. Or it may be that she has heard the story so vividly told that she thinks she remembers, but Minette always says that what she recalls so clearly is the tattered gown she was forced to wear." He smiled. "Minette is beautiful and always aware of her appearance, so that was natural. It must have seemed strange to a child accustomed to living in a palace to find herself tramping along the road to Dover. Lady Dalkeith was pretending to be the wife of a valet and one of the grooms was posing as her husband. Minette was supposed to be their child. Minette, of course, knew that she was a princess and expected to be addressed as such. Poor Lady Dalkeith must have been sorely tried to pass off this haughty little creature as the daughter of a valet. They decided that she must be called Peter, which was as near 'Princess' as she could get."

"And the journey, of course, was safely made."

"Yes. And what joy there was when they joined my mother, who was already in Paris. Minette said she thought the best thing that happened then was getting out of that horrible dress."

"And then she was brought up in France?"

Charles nodded. "She is more French than English. Louis has been very good to us. So he should be, to his own family! I should have liked to see Minette married to Louis and Queen of France, as she might have been if I had been restored to the throne a little earlier. That would have suited her very well. She and Louis are fond of each other. He talks to her a great deal and she is in his confidence. Well, it was not to be, and she was paired off with Louis's brother, Philippe . . . a poor consolation, I fear."

"How sad for her!"

"Poor Minette. She is clever, though. She can take care of herself, but it would have been very good for us all if she had married Louis instead of Philippe."

"I can see that you anticipate her visit with the utmost pleasure."

He agreed that this was so.

Charles and James went to Dover to meet her, where the castle there had been made ready for her, and the court followed.

When I was presented to her, I was immediately charmed by her. She had that indefinable quality which she shared with Charles. She was perhaps not quite as beautiful as I had expected her to be, but there was an inner radiance about her which was fascinating.

She was graceful and she spoke English rather haltingly, with a decided French accent; and it was difficult to remember that she was a member of the English royal family. She seemed to be so entirely French—well, she was the Duchess of Orléans and a leading figure in the court of Louis XIV.

One of her attendants immediately caught the eyes of everyone at court. This was a young and beautiful Breton girl named Louise de Keroualle. I was particularly interested in her because I saw that Charles was watching her closely.

Henriette's stay in England was brief. Most of the time she was with Charles. I would often see the two of them alone, walking arm in arm, their attendants some little way behind, and I had the impression that there was some important purpose behind Henriette's visit and that possibly she came as the confidential emissary of the King of France.

There was a good deal of gossip about her and some of it came to my ears.

She was unhappily married to Philippe of Orléans, who was by no means a satisfactory husband. Some said she should have married Louis as there was a very friendly relationship between them; others implied that the King used his friendship with her as a cloak to the visits he made to a certain Louise de la Vallière, who was a maid of honor to Henriette. There must always be rumors—half truths, I supposed—so that one was never quite sure what to believe.

Philippe, they said, was annoyed by the friendship between his brother and his wife.

There was another reason why the marriage was not satisfactory. Philippe had a great friend in the Chevalier de Lorraine, who was constantly trying to make trouble between Henriette and Philippe. I imagined this escape from the intrigues of the court of France must have been very welcome to Henriette—particularly as it gave her an opportunity to be with her beloved brother.

But the trip was not meant to be entirely devoted to pleasure. Henriette had work to do; and I believe that during that short time she spent in England she did it very well.

What she had to say to Charles was for his ears alone; it was for Charles to make a decision, and he would do this without the advice of his ministers.

There was something mysterious about that treaty Charles made with Louis. I think the details were known only to Charles himself. There was, however, a treaty which a few of his ministers signed with him; but there remained this one with which only he was concerned.

Henriette must return to France as soon as the mission was accomplished. She was most eager to please the King of France, and knowing Charles, I guessed that he would do all he could to make his sister happy.

But from what I later heard of that treaty, I believed that Charles had acted in a very shrewd and clever way.

The exchequer was as usual unable to meet the demands made upon it and Louis had offered a great deal of money if England would assist him in the war against Holland. Louis was anxious to quell Dutch ambitions and Holland was, of course, a great rival of England in trade. They were old adversaries and it seemed that if Louis's rewards were great enough, there would be few who would want to hold out against that clause. Another clause was that England should assist France in placing a Bourbon on the Spanish throne.

All this was in the future, and Charles was to receive a large sum of money in advance. The last and most secret part of the treaty concerned religion.

Charles did talk to me about this, for he knew he could trust me on this point entirely.

He said: "James has already publicly announced his conversion to the Catholic faith, and see what harm he has done."

"It is brave of him to have made an acknowledgment of his faith," I insisted.

"It is foolhardy," muttered Charles. "Depend upon it, I shall not indulge in such folly. If I did, more than likely I should soon be wandering again."

"Charles," I said earnestly, "I believe you are a Catholic at heart."

"At heart," he mused. "Well, was I not brought up in it . . . halfway perhaps. My mother was one of the most fervent Catholics I ever knew. And you . . . my dear, almost equal her."

"It would give me the greatest pleasure if you . . ."

He looked at me ruefully. "I fear it would not have the same effect on my subjects. They are set on one thing. If they thought I was even interested in the Catholic faith, they would be planning to send me the way of my father."

"No!" I said fiercely.

"Fear not. I shall do nothing to offend them in that quarter. Louis has strange ideas of the English. He suggests that I offer concessions to the Puritans. Let them go the way they will . . . and then . . . suddenly we turn Catholic. We purge the land of all those who do not believe as we command. Do you think the English would accept that?"

"If it were the law . . ."

He laughed. "You don't know the English, Catherine. They are lazy, careless, you think. But when they decide to take a stand, they are the most stubborn people in the world. When Mary died, that was the end of Catholicism for them. Never again, they said. Elizabeth was a wise woman. She would have gone the way they wanted. They would have none but a Protestant to rule them, so Elizabeth was a Protestant. She would have been equally at home in the Catholic faith. She was a shrewd one, Catherine. I intend to be as shrewd."

"But Louis is paying you . . ."

"Louis is paying me to take this country into the Catholic faith."

"And this you have agreed to do!"

"Yes . . . when the time is ripe. That is the clause. He will give me my pension, because I have given my word on this."

"Then how . . . ?

"Catherine, I have said 'when the time is ripe.' That is the heart of the matter. When the time is ripe I take my country into the Catholic faith." He was smiling at me in that quizzical way of his. "It may well be that during my lifetime the time will never be ripe."

Then I understood. Charles would never admit to Catholicism because he knew the English would never accept it.

He had promised to take the country into the Catholic faith when the time was ripe. But he knew that while he was King the time would never be ripe.

CHARLES WAS ANXIOUS for Henriette to prolong her visit. There were reasons for this. One was, of course, his desire to keep his sister with him, and the other was his interest in Louise de Keroualle.

I believed that he did not visit Barbara at all now. The Churchill incident had been his excuse, but for some time he had been tired of her. In his easy-going way, though, he had found it easier not to tell her so but to drift along avoiding seeing her as much as possible.

It seemed that there must always be one of his mistresses who reigned supreme. Moll Davis was fading out and Nell Gwynne was still in favor. I was sure he liked her sharp cockney wit, but what he needed was an elegant mistress who was accustomed to court life.

And here was this delectable girl—fresh from the court of France, undeniably beautiful, someone who could replace poor Frances Stuart.

Henriette greatly wished to stay longer in England but she appeared to be afraid of her husband, who had not wished her to come at all and had only given way because his brother Louis insisted on it.

I was unsure of Louise de Keroualle. She had an appearance of innocence but I detected something calculating about her. I was sure she must find Charles attractive. Most women did. But the choice was not theirs. Henriette decided that she could not allow her lady-in-waiting to stay in England until she had consulted with the girl's parents or some authority in France.

I knew Charles was very disappointed. He had made his wishes clear. I heard that Henriette wished to give him a jewel as a parting gift. She sent for her jewel box, opened it and asked her brother to take anything that pleased him.

Louise was standing beside Henriette at the time and the King lifted his eyes to the girl's face and said: "There is the jewel I covet above all other." Then he took Louise's hand and looked appealingly at Henriette.

But Henriette was firm. That particular jewel was going back to France with her.

Charles was very sorrowful when they left.

He had the treaty which he thought would bring great good to England—and himself—but he had to say good-bye to his beloved sister and Louise de Keroualle.

WHEN THE SAD NEWS CAME we were completely amazed and horrified.

I could not believe what the messenger was telling us.

Henriette was dead.

It was less than three weeks after her arrival in France that she had died in mysterious circumstances.

When Charles recovered from the first shock he was very angry, for he could not believe she had died from natural causes.

He made the messenger repeat what had happened. He was completely distraught. He paced up and down the apartment, his eyes wild; now and then he stopped to clench his fists and wring his hands.

"This is my sister, Catherine," he said. "The one I loved best. We were always good friends. She should have stayed here with me. Then this would never have happened."

He seemed to find comfort in going over it and told me what he had heard.

"It was soon after she returned. Someone has done this. It is Philippe . . . that creature. She should never have married him. He is unworthy. My sister . . . given to that . . . dandy! He put the Chevalier de Lorraine before her. They have killed her. And Louis . . . what has he done? Why does he not find the murderers? Because he knows his own brother is involved! He pretends to accept this stupid doctor's verdict."

I pieced the story together. Henriette had returned to France. She had been at Versailles . . . with Louis. Of course, Louis would want her to tell in every detail what had happened in England. She had come here in his service, but against Philippe's wishes. Philippe could not bear to think that the King placed more confidence in his brother's wife than in his brother.

At Versailles, Philippe had come upon his wife and the King in deep conversation. He had stamped his foot and flounced away in a state of pique.

Shortly afterward—it was the afternoon of the twenty-ninth of June, and Henriette had left England only on the twelfth of that month—she had asked for a cup of chicory water. She drank this and was immediately sick.

She said: "I have been poisoned."

There was great concern, the doctors were summoned and ten hours later she was dead.

There was a postmortem. The doctor who conducted it was young and unpracticed. Charles swore that he had been procured by Philippe. His verdict was that death was due to natural causes.

There were the inevitable whisperings and rumors throughout the court of France, for there had been every indication that Henriette had been poisoned. What was in the chicory water? people asked. A servant had brought it but that servant could not be the one who had put the poison in the cup. There was no reason for a servant to do so. But there were others.

Charles was certain that the Chevalier de Lorraine had killed

Henriette with Philippe's connivance. The Chevalier de Lorraine was jealous of her; Philippe greatly resented her friendship with the King and the fact that she could be trusted with special missions. Philippe could have been in the plot to kill Henriette, and almost certainly was. Philippe's squire D'Effiat and the Count de Bevron, the captain of Philippe's guard, could easily have poisoned the chicory water. They had been on the spot at the time. Charles wanted them brought to trial with Philippe.

But Louis would not interfere. He thought he could compensate by giving Henriette a grand funeral at St. Denis.

Charles was consumed by grief and anger. He shut himself in his apartments and refused to see anyone. When he did emerge he was pale and subdued.

"I shall never feel the same toward Louis," he said. "He has allowed my sister's murderers to go free because they are in high places."

Louis would know what effect his sister's death would have on Charles. He tried to make amends in a special way. I could wish he had chosen some other method.

Charles told me he was giving a place in my household to a lady who, he was sure, would be useful to me. Louis had heard that Mademoiselle Louise de Keroualle was much liked at our court and he was sending her over to join us.

I must have shown my dismay.

Charles put his hand on my shoulder. "She is very young, and I am sure will be most eager to please," he said.

I guessed whom she would be eager to please. I was no longer the innocent girl I had been.

This was how it would always be.

Barbara Castlemaine was no longer in the ascendant; Frances Stuart, poor girl, had lost her appeal; Nell Gwynne was not cultivated enough to hold him; so now there would be a new one: a lady from the court of France—Louise de Keroualle.

CHARLES SENT one of the royal yachts to meet Louise de Keroualle when she came to England. He was considerably cheered by the prospect of a new mistress.

Louise undoubtedly had a social appeal. There was a childishness about her. She reminded me in some ways of Frances Stuart. But Frances's innocence was not assumed, as I was sure was that of Mademoiselle de Keroualle. I sensed those demure looks covered a certain shrewdness and self-interest. I guessed that Louis had sent her over for a purpose other than to present Charles with a new toy as consolation for his grief over his sister's death. Louise would be watchful of the situation in England and, if she were as close to the King as Louis would expect her to be, she would be well qualified to pass on vital information to Louis.

Moreover, I guessed that Louise would make sure that she, besides Louis, profited from the arrangement.

She did not take up her apartments in Whitehall immediately. She had met the Arlingtons and had accepted an invitation to stay with them for a while until she "became accustomed to England, improved her knowledge of the language and was able to converse with ease."

Arlington was suspected of being a Catholic, or at least of having sympathy with the faith. Louis had at one time tried to bribe him but Arlington—as a member of the Cabal—was too wise to accept bribes from a foreign king. He was married to Isabella von Beverweert, daughter of Louis of Nassau; and Isabella had accepted a gift of ten thousand crowns from the French King. It seemed possible that Arlington had formed a friendship with Louise de Keroualle and offered her hospitality because he was aware of the work she would be expected to do for France.

I must admit that this did not occur to me at the time, but it emerged later.

Louise de Keroualle was Louis's spy. He and Charles had become wary of each other since Henriette's death. Louis was well aware that Charles resented his lack of energy in unmasking his sister's killers. All the same, I knew that Louise would consider her own good before that of anyone else. What plans she had for her relationship with Charles, I could only guess. But she would have heard of the King's obsession with Frances Stuart and might have thought there was a chance of becoming Queen of England.

CAPTAIN BLOOD

IT WAS ABOUT THIS TIME WHEN CAPTAIN BLOOD CAME INTO prominence and seemed to arouse many of the young gallants to a spirit of adventure. One of these was the Duke of Monmouth.

Jemmy, as he was invariably called, was very much aware of his position, and the more unpopular the Duke of York became, the more Jemmy flaunted himself, not only at court but throughout the capital.

He was determined that no one should forget that he was the King's eldest son. He was disappointed that Charles would not go along with the plan to pretend he had married his mother. At the same time, Monmouth behaved as though he were indeed the Prince of Wales.

There was great antagonism between him and the Duke. Anne, the Duchess, was very worried about it. Every time I saw her I grew more concerned for her health, and the anxiety she was feeling was not helpful to her.

The Duke of York was, of course, without subtlety and completely devoid of diplomacy. I knew Charles constantly despaired of him, but Charles had a habit of shrugging aside unpleasant possibilities and while he was on the throne Monmouth and York could be kept in check. It was only after he had gone that trouble might arise. That was why he could shrug his shoulders and thrust the matter aside.

Meanwhile, the Duke of York was somewhat ostentatiously making sure that everyone knew he was a Catholic and would like to see the whole of the country of the same persuasion. Monmouth was a constant reminder to us all that he was a Protestant and that I, the Queen, seemed unlikely to produce a legitimate heir.

It was then that Captain Blood, the dashing adventurer, made the city aware of him.

He must have been quite fifty years of age. He was of humble origins—and Irish—an adventurer without doubt; he lived for excitement. He was a leader who had a talent for taking people along with him to support him in his various exploits.

One of his associates, a Captain Mason, had been arrested and sent to Doncaster. A guard of eight soldiers had been chosen by the Duke of York to guard the man, and Blood, with only three helpers, rescued Mason, killing several soldiers during the process.

Captain Blood was discussed everywhere and with a certain awe and admiration.

His latest escapade had been to attack the house of the Duke of Ormonde, for when Ormonde had been in command in Ireland, he had arrested several of Blood's friends. They were brought in for trial and several of them had been hanged. Now, Captain Blood decided to avenge the death of his friends.

He and some of his accomplices waylaid Ormonde's coach and, after disabling the coachman, were planning to take the Duke to Tyburn and hang him there. Fortunately for Ormonde, his coachman was able to give the alarm and guards arrived in time. Consequently Blood and his men were forced to flee for their lives.

The adventure was much talked of.

Shortly afterward Sir John Coventry was badly injured when his nose was slit in a street brawl.

Sir John had made some remarks derogatory to the King and his mistresses, Nell Gwynne and Moll Davis.

It had all begun when some members of Parliament wished to levy a tax on playhouses. The King and many of his friends were against this, being ardent supporters of the playhouses. During the debate Sir John Coventry asked whether the King's interest was in the playhouses or the women who played in them.

This was considered to be an insult to the King and there was an uproar. The following day when Sir John's carriage was taking him to his home in Suffolk Street, it was set upon by a band of young men and his nose was slit for his insolence.

There was a great deal of indignation over the affair, and it seeped out that the Duke of Monmouth had been a member of the gang which had attacked Sir John.

Because of this, Charles was anxious that the matter should be hushed up. He himself would talk to Jemmy.

I could imagine that interview, with Charles gently admonishing Monmouth and Monmouth vehemently declaring that he would allow no one to insult his father.

However, an act was passed that the slitting of noses and any other mutilation was a felony. The act was called Coventry's Act.

Before long, there was another incident in the streets. Monmouth and the young Duke of Albermarle, who had recently succeeded to the title on the death of his father, were involved in a drunken brawl in which a beadle, who had tried to restrain them, was killed.

This was serious because it was a case of murder. Charles was outraged by the incident until he learned that Monmouth was one of the group concerned.

I said: "That young man is becoming notorious. It is not long since he attacked Sir John Coventry."

"I must speak to him," said Charles.

I could not help replying: "Do you think the people will be satisfied with that? A man has committed murder and he is merely given a talking to?"

"I shall speak to him very severely. This has to be stopped."

"The people will expect him to be punished."

"I can hardly punish Albermarle without punishing Jemmy."

"Well then . . ."

He did not answer. But later he pardoned all the young men involved with the excuse that there was insufficient evidence against them.

After that Monmouth was a little quieter, so I supposed he had been "spoken to very severely." But it was just another example of the King's indulgence toward him.

And Jemmy was behaving more royally every day.

IT HAD BEEN A COLD WINTER, and during it Anne's health had declined. I had always liked her. She lacked certain courtly graces, but I was always aware of her sincerity. She had been hurt by James's infidelities, as I had been by those of Charles, and that had made a bond between us.

Anne had suffered her husband's neglect with less stoicism than I had, and James was completely lacking in Charles's charm. She had

had a hard time from the beginning when she had had to face so much disapproval.

For some time she had suffered from a pain in her breast. She had a growth there and it could be excruciatingly painful. I used to visit her often and she liked to talk to me of her early days.

She knew she could not live long. One day she said to me: "What I regret leaving so much are my two girls. Mary is nine years old. It is young to be left without a mother; and Anne is two years younger. It is ironical, Catherine. My little boys died. James wanted boys. They always want boys. There were eight children . . . and only two left. I often wonder what will become of Mary and Anne. They are in line to the throne. Of course, you may yet . . ."

"It is so long now," I interrupted. "I have come to believe I shall never have children. How I envy you! Mary and Anne are such fine girls."

"I pray all will go well with them. If only one could see into the future!"

"Methinks at times it would be better not to."

"I have not long left to me now."

"You will recover in the spring."

"No. That will not be. I am not sorry to go . . . except for my girls. Catherine, will you watch over them? Life is full of dangers for children in their position. I hope beyond all things that they will make good marriages . . . I mean that they will be happy ones."

"I will do all I can," I promised. "But for people such as myself, Mary and Anne, marriages are made for us."

"That is true. But Catherine . . . remember . . ."

"I will. I will do all that is possible."

That satisfied her.

The next time I saw her she had grown worse. They had given her drugs to help the pain. Poor Anne, her mind wandered.

I learned then a little about what she had suffered in those early days when there was so much opposition to her marriage, and she had even wondered whether James himself would stand by her. James was uncertain by nature. I was often surprised that he should be Charles's brother. They were so dissimilar.

In her ramblings, Anne was back at the court of Orange where she had first met James. People had been surprised that she had attracted him, for Anne had never been a beauty. But then James's countless mistresses had always been on the plain side. The outstanding exam ple was that one who had had his attention longer than any of them—Arabella Churchill. She could never be called beautiful, though she did have a very fine pair of legs. The story was that she had fallen from her horse and, being close by at the time, James had had an opportunity to see them. They had presumably enchanted him and made up for her lack of facial perfection. One of his mistresses remarked that they were all ugly and if they had had any brains James would have lacked the necessary wit to recognize them.

However, James had been taken with Anne Hyde and had actually gone through a form of marriage with her at his sister Mary's court.

At that time, of course, Charles was in exile and the fate of the royal family was very insecure. Whether James would have taken that step if he had known that Charles would soon be King, I could not know. But he was impulsive. However, it had been an uneasy time for Anne, and as she lay dying she thought she was back in those troublous days.

"Catherine," she murmured, "are you there?"

I leaned forward and said: "I am here, Anne. I will stay while you want me."

She put her fevered hand into mine and held it firmly.

She said: "Maurits Beverweert would have married me. It would have been a good match . . . with the Orange family. But . . . it was James. They blamed me . . . my father even. They tried . . . they all worked against it. They tried to stop it. They pretended it was no marriage . . . and James . . . James . . ."

I bent over her. "Try to rest," I said.

She smiled and was quiet for a few moments, then she said: "I am going to have a child. I am married . . . I am . . ."

I knew she was in the past again.

"It is all right now," I soothed her. "You are in your bed. You should rest. You will feel better then."

"Catherine . . ."

"Yes, Anne?"

"Where am I?"

"You are in your bed in your apartments."

"They will try to stop the marriage. They will say it was no marriage. And I am with child . . ."

"I said: "Everyone knows you are married. You are the Duchess of York."

She smiled.

"We were married, were we not? It was in Worcester House in the Strand."

"Yes," I said. "Your father's house."

"He is not there now. He is away . . . in disgrace. It was no fault of mine. It was all secret . . . but a true marriage. The baby died . . ." Her face was tragic suddenly. "My little boy . . ."

"But you have two fine girls now."

"Mary," she whispered. "Anne. All those deaths . . . all those little ones . . . mostly boys. Catherine . . . James has turned to your faith."

She had returned to the present.

I said: "Yes, I know."

"The people do not like it . . . but he must be true to his conscience."

"It shows his strength."

She smiled a little sadly. "James . . . he does not always think clearly. He is not clever like Charles."

"No," I said.

"The people are not pleased. They seek to destroy him. But James has his conscience. James is weak. He always was. He does not see how necessary it is for him to act with caution, because he is the King's brother. What will he do without me to help him?"

"Do you guide him?"

"More than you know. I think Charles knows. He talks to me sometimes. He is anxious about James . . . as anxious as he could be about anything. He thinks of what will come when he is no longer there. As I do . . . Catherine."

"So much can happen before that. Charles is strong . . . stronger than most men at court. He will live for a long time yet."

"But the time will come . . ."

"Let us not worry about something which is so far off."

"James had to worship openly. James has a conscience." She

smiled ruefully. "That is why we were remarried. He knew that I was with child and he owed it to me. Perhaps he was not so eager for the second marriage ceremony as he was for the first."

"Anne, he relies on you. He wanted to marry you or he would not have done so."

"Heaven knows, he would have had enough support if he had decided to discard me. But it was his conscience. It is one of the finest things about him, Catherine. He owed it to me then . . . as he owes it to God to worship Him openly as he believes is right. Catherine, I have not communicated as a member of the Church of England for some time."

"I have heard that. Are you a Catholic, Anne?"

She was silent for a while and then said: "I do not know. There are so many questions to be answered. I have been studying. You have been brought up in the Catholic faith. You accept it without question. I find it difficult to do that. But now the end is near . . . I desperately wish I could feel sure."

"James would be pleased if you shared his faith."

"I want to, but it is not easy. I keep saying to myself: What is the truth? If only I could have some revelation before I die."

I held her hand and once more she went into a reverie. She talked of her children. What a lot of suffering there had been in her life. She had lost so many of her children. I thought of the months of waiting, the exultation when the child was in her arms, the overwhelming grief when it was taken from her.

"James, Edward, Charles," she murmured their names. Born into this world for a very short time . . . and out of eight only Mary and Anne left.

I was with her when she died. It was the last day of March. The Duke of York was at her bedside. He looked very sad. Anne had spoken of his conscience and I wondered what he was thinking. Was it of all the unhappiness he had caused her? I believed it was. He was very gentle with her in those last moments, and very anxious that she should receive the viaticum of the Church of Rome.

The Bishop of Worcester had been sent for. I knew that Anne was still unsure. How I wished I could have talked to her, have explained to her why she must turn to Rome. Anne had a clever mind; she was the sort of person who must reason. She could not believe without logical understanding. It was hard for her; she was greatly perplexed.

I was praying that at the end she would have some divine inspiration . . . some understanding. But I believe it did not come.

The Bishop gave an exhortation, but he was not really successful in convincing her, for she said quite clearly when he had finished, "What is the truth?"

I was beside the Duke of York as we watched life ebb away.

Her lips moved at the end and I leaned forward to hear what she said. It was: "Truth . . ." And I knew that she died undecided.

The Duke was very moved. He covered his face with his hands and was silent for a while; and when he dropped them, I saw that his features were distorted with grief.

Yes, I thought, whatever his weakness, the Duke of York has a conscience.

Anne was buried in Henry VII's chapel in Westminster.

I had lost a friend.

THAT EXTRAORDINARY MAN, Captain Blood, came into prominence again.

His exploits were well known and there were many who admired his daring panache, and his tendency to involve himself in wild situations from which he seemed to escape unscathed.

The latest episode was the most outrageous of them all. It was criminal in the extreme and the result for most would have been the hangman's rope. But not for Captain Blood.

Charles himself told me about it. He thought it was an amusing tale.

"You must admire that man Blood," he said. "He plans the most daring adventures. He lost his estates in Ireland at the time of my restoration, and that set him off on his adventurous life. His plans are so ingenious. You must be impressed by this. He tried to steal the Crown Jewels. Have you ever heard of anything so preposterous?"

"How could he possibly do that? Is not the regalia well guarded?"

"Indeed it is. That is what makes it such a feat—even to get as far as he did. He is a clever fellow. There is no doubt of that." Charles began to laugh. "There should be a place at court for him. I find him more amusing than some of those around me."

"What has he done to amuse you so much?"

"The Crown Jewels, my love. As I told you, he tried to steal them. He had worked out a most devious plan. I'll tell you all about it. Three weeks before the attempted robbery he came to the Tower of London, dressed as a parson in cloak and cassock. With him was a woman whom he called his wife. She was not, of course. Probably the wife of one of his accomplices. The guardian of the jewels was a man called Edwards and, while looking at them, Parson Blood made himself very affable. Odds fish! How I should have loved to see him playing the part."

"A parson! Hardly fitting, I should think."

"Oh, but Blood could handle it. However, the 'wife' expressed a great desire to see the crown. There was no harm in showing her this, and Edwards did so, and while this was going on she pretended to faint. There was consternation, and Mrs. Edwards appeared and took the lady to her apartments that she might rest. Blood thanked the Edwards profusely and a few days later returned with a present for Mrs. Edwards. Blood and his 'wife' stopped awhile to talk and before they left they had formed a friendship, and Blood asked permission to call again."

"And Edwards suspected nothing?"

"My dear, Blood is a superb actor. He could join the players at any time."

"He would find stealing the crown jewels more profitable, if he could succeed, that is."

"There you speak truth, but what a conceit the man has! And but for ill luck, he would have succeeded."

"Pray tell me more."

"It seemed that the Edwards were much impressed and after a few visits Blood asked if he might bring his nephew to visit them. The nephew, they were told, was a young man with a few hundred a year. You can imagine what effect this had on the Edwards, because they had a marriageable daughter. Blood and the 'wife' were immediately asked to dine and bring the nephew along with them."

"The poor daughter. How dreadful for her!"

"The nephew and she were immediately friendly. Meanwhile,

Blood was able to make a thorough examination of the premises. He discovered a fine case of pistols which he offered to buy as a present for a nobleman who, he said, was his neighbor."

"Even then the Edwards did not suspect anything?"

"Indeed no. I can tell you, Blood is a supreme actor . . . and no doubt he had coached his fellow players well. The Edwardses were delighted at the prospect of their daughter's union with a man who owned a small fortune. Now it was time for the deed to take place. Blood and the nephew came early to the Tower and, as the ladies were not ready, Blood suggested that Edwards show the nephew the Crown Jewels while they were waiting for them. When they went into the room where the jewels were, Edwards closed the door, then Blood went into action. He threw a cloak over Edwards's head and put a gag in his mouth. They would not harm him, Blood said, as long as he remained silent. Realizing how thoroughly he had been duped, Edwards struggled and tried to remove the gag from his mouth. Blood had to silence him; he knocked him down and momentarily stunned him."

"Poor man," I said. "How can you admire this Blood?"

Charles shrugged his shoulders. "It was a clever plan, and Edwards was a fool to be so duped. They would have escaped with the jewels, but a strange thing happened. Edwards's son, who had been in Flanders with Sir John Talbot's army, had come home unexpectedly, and by that time Mrs. Edwards and her daughter had realized that something unusual had happened. Young Edwards dashed into the room in time to see the conspirators escaping, and found his father lying on the floor. The old man had sufficiently recovered to cry: 'Treason! They have taken the Crown Jewels!'

"The young man dashed after them. One of the guards, hearing the commotion, had come out of his quarters, and went off with young Edwards in pursuit. The jewels were heavy and, knowing every inch of the Tower, the pursuers had the advantage. Blood and his accomplice were caught with the jewels in their possession. There has never been such an attempt and it could so easily have succeeded but for the fortuitous return of that young soldier . . . which, you have to admit, was a chance in a million. Poor Blood! His scheme failed."

"You can say 'Poor Blood! His scheme failed'? He would have murdered that old man."

"But to attempt to steal the Crown Jewels is not an ordinary theft, is it?"

"Indeed it is not! It is a very serious one."

Charles laughed. "He is a saucy fellow. He was caught with the crown under his cloak. Yet he would make no confession unless it were to me."

"And you have seen him! You allowed him to come to you?"

"I had a wish to see him. I always knew he was no ordinary man. He said to me, 'Your Majesty will understand my temptation. You once had a great fancy for a crown. It was denied you for a long time, and you risked a great deal to attain it. So . . . we understand each other, you and I. We had the same motive. It was a bold attempt . . . yes. But remember, it was for a crown.'

"I could not resist the temptation to talk to him, and made him tell me of his adventures. He amused me mightily. He had not a care for what would happen to him. It was impossible not to like the man."

"So . . . he was pardoned!"

"Such men are an asset to the country. They should be forgiven their little misdemeanors. To attempt to steal the Crown Jewels! What a proposition! I could not allow a man who had amused me so much to be punished. He would give no account of his fellow con-spirators. He said the scheme was entirely his. He alone had con-ceived it. Who else, he asked, would have had the wit to do so? It would have worked admirably but for the return of that zealous young man. So . . . the jewels are safe. What harm is done?"

"What of Edwards?"

"He is not badly hurt. He will recover. It will teach him to be more careful in future. I offered Blood a place at court. He prefers, however, the return of his estates. But I doubt not that we shall be vis-ited by him . . . occasionally."

That was the strange affair of Captain Blood's attempt to steal the Crown Jewels. People marvelled that a man who had committed such a felony should not only go free but be rewarded for it.

THE ORANGE MARRIAGE

THEY WERE TROUBLOUS TIMES. WE HAD DECLARED WAR ON the Dutch with our French allies. It had to be. It was a clause in the Dover Treaty which we had pledged and must therefore be honored. Charles had received great benefits from the treaty and must keep on good terms with his powerful kinsman across the water.

The perpetual need was money . . . and men. Mothers and wives tried to keep their men at home for fear of their falling into the hands of the pressgangs who would send them to fight on land or sea.

Charles made speeches in Parliament. The Dutch war was necessary, he declared. The Dutch were our natural enemies: they filched our trade; they attacked our ships; we must drive them from the seas.

There was growing concern about religion. Charles, it was said, had been too lenient with the Catholics. The fact that the Duke of York openly professed his faith was causing greater anxiety as time passed and it seemed certain that he would follow his brother to the throne.

This, of course, brought home to me afresh my own deficiencies. I was clearly to blame. Barbara Castlemaine had given ample proof of the King's virility; Nell Gwynne now had two sons; and Louise de Keroualle, who after her initial reticence had become the acknowledged mistress of the King, had just given birth to a son.

So there could be no doubt. I was always on the watch for the suggestion which might arise again, since it had twice before. Many would continue to ask: should not the King free himself from this barren wife?

I had had Charles's assurance that he would never divorce me, but could one rely on Charles? There was a rhyme, written by the irrepressible Earl of Rochester, which was being circulated throughout the court. Rochester had had the effrontery to pin it on the door of the King's bedroom. It was:

Here lies our Sovereign Lord the King
Whose word no man relies on
He never said a foolish thing
And never did a wise one.

Charles was the first to appreciate the rhyme. It was amusing, witty and there was some truth in it.

His retort was typical of him. " 'Tis true, Rochester," he said. "But remember my words are my own, my actions my ministers.' "

I quickly learned that Louise de Keroualle was more clever than any of her predecessors, and therefore more dangerous. She was indeed Louis's spy.

She was possessed of all the graces she had learned at the French court; she was elegant and dignified; I imagined Charles enjoyed mental as well as physical stimulation with her. She was without doubt *maîtresse en titre.* Nell Gwynne was her great rival, but Nell, of course, was a child of the streets of London: she could amuse; she had wit; and she was very pretty. But Charles was a cultured man and there were times when he wished to be with people of his own kind. Yet I imagined there were occasions when he wanted to escape from Louise to Nell.

From what I knew of the little playactress, she was of a tolerant nature. It must have been a great adventure for her to have attracted the King. She was, I believe, less demanding than any of his mistresses had ever been, and asked only for privileges for her sons. She had two of them now—fine boys and a further reproach to me. And because she did not ask, she did not receive.

She had, though, demanded a title for her eldest son, who was now the Earl of Burford. How she must have laughed to think of herself . . . little Nelly . . . fighting for a living, selling her oranges, getting her chance on the stage . . . and then becoming a favorite mistress of the King, side by side with such as Lady Castlemaine and the Duchess of Portsmouth, as Louise de Keroualle had now become.

There was a story that in the King's presence she referred to their little son Charles—named after his father—as the "little bastard."

Charles protested and she flashed back "I call him so because that is what he is. I might as well drop him from this window for who cares for him? Certainly not his father. So I say, poor little bastard."

It was playacting, of course. They were in the town of Burford at the time and Charles called out dramatically, "Save the Earl of Burford!"

That was good enough for Nell. Her son had a title. He could stand beside the offspring of Barbara Castlemaine and Louise de Keroualle.

There was an undercurrent of unease everywhere. The conversion of the Duke of York was at the root of it. The country was divided. I knew that many prayed that I would have an heir—the King's legitimate son to be brought up in the Protestant faith. There would be trouble if James came to the throne.

And then . . . there was Monmouth; and the deeper the resentment against the Duke of York became, the more blatantly Monmouth displayed his Protestantism. It was clear what was in his mind. What he longed for was that the King should declare he had married Lucy Walter. The fact that she would have been completely unsuitable to marry the King was of no importance. Charles had been merely an exile at the time. How simple everything could have been! But much as Charles doted on his son, he was not prepared to lie to that extent for him. Monmouth had his followers and he was very wary of Louise—a Catholic who would surely work against him.

The young Duke sought every way of showing people that the King regarded him as his beloved son, and the rumor about the box containing documents proving Charles's marriage to Lucy Walter was revived.

"There never was a marriage, so there never were these documents," Charles declared emphatically, "and therefore they cannot be discovered."

Monmouth wanted to command the forces which were being sent to Flanders.

Charles told me of this, for he was perplexed.

He said: "How can he? He lacks experience. I know he is popular. He is so good-looking, but that is not enough. He came to me, begging me on his knees to give him the command."

"You have not done so!" I cried in dismay, knowing his weakness where Monmouth was concerned.

He shook his head. "No . . . but he was so appealing. He really is a handsome boy . . . and affectionate. I know that much of his love and devotion is for my crown, but perhaps without that useful ornament, there might be just a little for my plain self. Poor Jemmy. It is not an easy position for him. There is adulation wherever he goes, and he is ambitious, as most of the young are. I sometimes think he might have been happier if he had been a son of one of Lucy's other lovers."

"Are you sure he is your son?"

"There is little doubt of it. He is pure Stuart. I see ourselves reflected in him."

"And what have you decided?"

"I've sent for Arlington. He will take care of it. Monmouth will be known as commander, but there will be others to take care of the troops."

I marvelled at his tolerance toward Monmouth. I often thought of the affair of Sir John Coventry and that poor beadle who had lost his life. Surely those two events should have shown Charles the nature of his beloved son and how dangerous his ambition could become.

Louise was very unpopular with the people. In the first place she was a foreigner and, even more detrimental, a Catholic. I had always been under suspicion because of my religion. It was strange that the English, who were lackadaisical in their attitude toward religion, should have felt this passionate determination not to tolerate a Catholic on the throne.

There were times when it was quite dangerous for Louise to ride out in her carriage, for the mob could be fierce against her.

"Go home, papist," they shouted at her. "Go back to where you came from."

It was different with Nell Gwynne. She had a way of charming the people. After all, she was one of them. They would surround her carriage, shouting good wishes, and she sometimes gave a performance of mock-royalty, which amused them and made them cheer her the more.

"Long live Nelly," they cried. "God bless pretty, witty Nell."

There was one occasion when she was in a closed carriage and people mistook her for Louise. They gathered round, shouting abuse, and someone threw a stone. Nell let down the window and looked out.

"You are mistaken, good people," she cried. "This is not the Catholic whore but the Protestant one."

There was much laughter and cheering, and shouts of "God bless Nelly."

Nell bowed and smiled and waved her hand in imitation of a languid royal personage, which amused them the more; and, instead of a dangerous situation, it turned out to be a very merry one.

IT OFTEN AMAZED ME, when I looked back on that innocent girl I had been on my arrival in England, that I had been able to accept Charles's mistress as a matter of course. There could have been only a few faithful husbands at court, or wives for that matter. Licentiousness was the way of life here. I deplored it and sometimes thought how happy I could have been if Charles had loved me as I loved him; but that was not to be and I had had to come to terms with it.

I was grateful to him because he had refused to set me aside. I must be relieved because he had a great deal of kindness in his nature and the rare ability of putting himself in the place of others. He understood my love for him and appreciated it; he understood that Monmouth's arrogance grew out of his insecurity. There was so much love in Charles and I had long before decided that I would rather accept his mistresses than be without him.

The war with the Dutch gave cause for anxiety. We had our victories but, like many such, they were hollow ones.

There was news that a battle had taken place under the Duke of York at Southwold Bay. Ineffectual as James could be in so many ways, the navy was an obsession with him and he had become a good commander. Against him on that occasion was De Ruyter, the Dutch commander of some renown. It had been a fierce battle and the struggle a desperate one. Many ships were lost and among the casualties was the Earl of Sandwich.

I was saddened, remembering the day he had come to bring me to England, and felt how pointless were those hard-won victories which turned out to be so indecisive.

Charles too was distressed by the death of Sandwich. He sailed to the Nore to meet James who was returning with the fleet. Many of the ships had been severely damaged and the number of wounded appalled him. He was particularly depressed by the latter and gave orders that care for them must be the primary concern.

About a month later he took me down to inspect the ships. Then all signs of battle had been removed and I enjoyed the expedition with him. It was on such occasions that I felt that I truly was the Queen.

And so the time was passing. Charles showed little sign of age. He was as vigorous as ever; when he removed his wigs one did see that his black hair was liberally streaked with gray, but when the wig of luxurious curls was on his head he seemed as young as ever.

James was looking for a wife and when Mary Beatrice of Modena was found for him, there was dissatisfaction throughout the country. The English, as ever, were wary of Catholics. I was one—but I think that by this time they had come to realize I was a docile one. But Catholicism allied with barrenness could make a queen very unpopular.

However, the marriage went ahead. Mary Beatrice, a young girl of fifteen, could not have much influence, and in any case James was already too steeped in his religion to be weaned from it even if he did have a Protestant wife.

I was also sad when I heard that the Earl of Clarendon had died abroad. I remembered him so well and wondered if he had felt a twinge of conscience when his daughter Anne died. He had not been very kind to her at a time when she needed kindness. But he had been a good husband . . . if that meant a faithful one. He was a man of high moral standing, but lacking in kindliness, so different from Charles who would never have turned against his own daughter in her time of need. Clarendon had not always been a friend to me—still I could be saddened by his death.

A certain interest was aroused when workmen, doing repairs in the Tower of London, found the skeletons of two young boys buried under the stairs. These, it seemed without doubt, were the remains of the young princes who had disappeared some two hundred years before—little Edward V and his brother the Duke of York. It was during the reign of Richard III that they disappeared, and it was said that they had been murdered on the orders of King Richard. People talked of the unfortunate boys for a while and then forgot them.

Life went on much as usual. Louise de Keroualle and Nell

Gwynne still reigned in Charles's seraglio, but I had my place and if Charles often preferred the society of his mistresses, there was a growing affection between us. There were times when he came to me, I believe, for quietness and peace.

I began to feel a certain satisfaction in my role. At least I had some place in his life.

But behind the serenity the storm was growing. It was still what many people in England thought of as the Catholic menace. It was the old story: the Queen was Catholic and barren; James, the heir to the throne, was openly Catholic, and now he had married a Catholic wife.

Something was certain to erupt.

I HAD PROMISED ANNE HYDE that I would keep an eye on her daughters, and I was a frequent visitor to Richmond Palace where they were being brought up.

The Duke of York was an indulgent father, as Anne had been another. There was, I have to say, little discipline in the household. Anne, the younger, had taken very little advantage of the tuition which was provided. It was a matter of study if you want to—and Anne clearly did not want to.

Her handwriting was indecipherable and if she were reproved she would say that writing made her eyes tired. She did have an affliction of the eyes which seemed to contract her lids, and it was true that she was short-sighted. So this excuse was accepted, for the Duke had made it clear that above all things he wanted his daughters to be happy. It may be that he remembered his own childhood when, like most of the family, he had been a homeless exile; and I imagined that Henrietta Maria might have been an exacting parent even with James, one of her favorites.

It was always interesting to go to Richmond and on this occasion I wanted to see them, particularly Mary, because I knew of the secret negotiations which were in progress, now we were at peace with Holland, for a marriage between her and Prince William of Orange. Mary was only fifteen, and I could guess how disturbed she would be at the prospect of leaving her comfortable home.

Moreover, from what I knew, William was not the most attractive of young men. He was a Protestant, though, and the country would approve; and it was very necessary to have that approval.

I remembered, some years ago, William had paid a visit to our court. He had probably been about twenty then, for he was twelve years older than Mary. His mother was Charles's sister Mary, who had been the Princess Royal of England, and his father, the Prince of Orange, had died at the time of young William's birth, so in his cradle the boy became Prince of Orange.

He must have been amazed by what he discovered at his uncle's court. Young, inexperienced as he was, he attracted the interest of the courtiers and they decided to amuse themselves at his expense.

I remember the occasion well, for I felt sorry for the young man.

They had made him drunk—a condition which was new to him. They had caroused with him . . . leading him on to such mischief that he tried to force his way into the quarters of the ladies-in-waiting, and when he met resistance, broke a window and attempted to climb in. The jokers then thought that was enough and took him away. I recall how Charles laughed about his sober nephew's drunken attempts at depravity.

And this was the young man whom it would be expedient for Mary to marry.

I came to Richmond with some trepidation, for I was sure I should find Mary very apprehensive.

As soon as I arrived I realized that she had heard the rumors.

Everything was much as usual in their apartments. Mary and Anne had always been together, Mary being the more dominant of the two, and they were surrounded by their close friends and attendants.

Their governess was Frances Villiers, daughter of the Earl of Suffolk. I had heard from her how difficult it was to teach Anne.

"Mary is different," she said. "She is quite interested in learning. Of course, the Duke adores her, and she does not want him to think she is ignorant like her sister. Anne does not care. The only one who can tell her what to do is Sarah Jennings. They are very close friends and you would sometimes think Sarah was the mistress. It is pleasant to see the friendship between all the girls."

I joined them. Anne was sitting next to Sarah Jennings, a very bright-looking young woman, the kind who would stand out among others . . . not necessarily because of her looks . . . but perhaps because of her somewhat imperious manner. I could well believe in her mastery over her lazy mistress.

They rose when I entered and came to do homage to the Queen—Mary first. I felt a pang of anxiety. She was so young and rather pretty with her dark hair and almond-shaped eyes. She had the Stuart look, and she was a sensible girl. I knew that the Duke was passionately devoted to her and indulged her greatly. She could have been spoiled but, to her credit, she was not, and was a very pleasant girl.

"Your Majesty," she began.

I smiled and took her into my arms.

"Dear Mary," I said. "You are well, are you?"

"Yes, thank you, Your Majesty, and you?"

"I am well, thank you. And here is Anne."

Anne looked at me with that rather vague expression which was due to her short-sightedness.

"Anne, my dear, you are well?"

"I thank Your Majesty, yes."

I smiled at the attendants: Anne Trelawny, Mary's special friend, and Elizabeth Villiers, Frances's daughter, and, of course, Sarah Jennings.

They rose and curtsied, then retired so that I was apart with Mary and Anne.

I wished there need not be this ceremony. I would have liked to talk naturally to all the girls. I was particularly interested in Sarah Jennings and Elizabeth Villiers.

"Madam, has the new baby come yet?" asked Mary.

She was referring to the expected child of her stepmother, the new Duchess. Birth was always a rather depressing topic for me. Mary of Modena had already borne three children in the short time since her marriage. The first, a girl, had been named Catherine after me, but had died almost as soon as she was born. There was a son who had died and a daughter Isabel . . . and now the prospect of another.

"Not yet," I told them.

"It would be nice to have a little stepbrother," said Mary. "Though it is not the same as if it were our mother."

Both she and Anne looked mournful. They had loved their mother and I fancied they both resented their father's remarriage.

Anne took a sweetmeat from a bowl beside her.

"Oh, Anne," said Mary with a little laugh. "You should not eat so many of those."

"I like them," said Anne.

"She eats them all the time," Mary told me.

"Do they not spoil your appetite?" I asked.

Anne said they did not. Nibbling sweets was a habit she had acquired from her mother. Anne had become very fat in the last months of her life. I could not forget her lying on her deathbed . . . searching for the truth . . . worrying about the future of her girls.

"Sarah will be getting married soon," said Anne. "John Churchill is always coming here to court her. His family think she is not good enough for him."

"Sarah will certainly not agree with that, I am sure," I remarked.

"Sarah is wondering if she is too good for him," said Mary.

"I am not surprised at that," I said. "Well, is she going to marry him?"

Anne nodded. "She really wants to. But she is saying . . . not yet. She thinks they ought to wait."

I wonder," said Mary, "what it is like to be married?" There was a faint note of fear in her voice.

"In time you will know," I told her.

"Yes . . . a husband will be found for each of us."

"That is certain to be so."

"Sarah must not go when she marries," went on Anne. "I could not do without Sarah."

"You are very fond of her," I said.

"So is my stepmother. She knows that John Churchill wants to marry Sarah. She likes to help them. She thinks it is romantic."

"In my opinion," I commented, "from what I know of Sarah, if *she* wants a marriage, a marriage there will be."

Anne smiled and nodded.

"My stepmother was not very happy when she was told she must marry," said Mary.

"She was very young. It was a shock. It can be a shock when you are very young."

"When you married the King you were old."

"In comparison, yes. I was nearly twenty-four."

"That is very old. My stepmother was fifteen."

"That is very young."

"I am fifteen," said Mary, almost pleadingly.

I thought, she wants to talk to me, alone. I decided I must arrange this.

"When my stepmother heard she was to marry my father," went on Mary, "she wept all day. She screamed and kicked and refused to leave her bed."

"Did she tell you this?"

"Yes. She is not very much older than I am. Four years only."

"Then she is like one of you girls."

"She is happier now," put in Anne.

"I think she does not mind our father so much. I think she quite likes him. She loves the King. She says he has been kind to her . . . always."

"The King is always kind," I said warmly.

"Yes," agreed Mary. "And when you came to England, were you frightened?"

"A little. But I wanted to come. I had heard of the King."

"Oh yes, my uncle is a very nice man. The nicest man in the world . . . next to my father."

She looked at me steadily and I wondered how much a fifteen-year-old girl knew of what happened in a court like this one.

"And now she has one baby," said Mary. "That must be nice."

"Nice! I thought what a mild way of describing the experience! What joy it must be! If only it had happened to me.

I felt sorry for Mary groping in the dark, aware that it was going to be her turn very soon.

When I was taking my leave, I kissed Anne but I held Mary close. I said quietly: "I would speak with you, Mary."

We looked at Anne who was peering at the box of sweetmeats, and Mary followed me out of the room into the small antechamber.

"What is it, Mary?" I asked.

"They are talking about my cousin, the Prince of Orange."

"Do you know him?"

"No, not well."

"And there is often talk . . ."

"Are they arranging a marriage?"

"People in places like ours will always have plans made for them. Sometimes . . . quite often . . . they come to nothing."

"I do not want to go away. I want to stay here always . . . with us all together. My friend Anne Trelawny, and Elizabeth Villiers and Sarah Jennings . . . and most of all my sister. I want it to go on like this."

"There is always change, my dear."

"But if this Prince of Orange . . ."

"You will probably like him. Your stepmother did not want to come here but she is happy now."

"The Prince of Orange is old."

"Oh no . . . he is a young man."

"He is twelve years older than I."

"That is not so very much for princes. Think of your stepmother and how much older your father is than she."

She looked at me, her eyes brimming with tears.

I took her in my arms and comforted her. But what could I say? Mary would be sacrificed as thousands like her had been before.

POOR MARY! I was so sorry for her.

The Prince of Orange had arrived in England. From what I heard from Charles, he was not a very attractive young man.

"Plain spoken, as you would expect," said Charles. "Not given to courtly manners."

"Perhaps he has other qualities."

"I have no doubt he has. He is a very serious young man. He has informed me that, before he proceeds with the marriage, he wishes to see the Princess. Ah well, it is one of the terms of the peace treaty between us. To my mind, he is an ambitious young man. Mary has a chance . . . a faint one . . . of reaching the throne."

I winced and Charles, realizing why, laid a reassurign hand on my arm. He was reconciled to the position and he wanted me to be. I must drop this habit of mine of reproaching myself every time this matter was hinted at.

He went on: "We shall see what the Duchess of York gives us this time. It is likely that the infant may entirely spoil Mary's chances. But

who is to say? I was telling you that young Orange is a very serious
young man."

"I am thinking of Mary."

"I also. Poor child! James dotes on her, and I think she will not be
happy to leave her home."

"I know she is frightened."

"They are all frightened when they have to go away to a strange
man and a strange court. You know that, Catherine."

"I was not frightened. I wanted to come."

He looked melancholy. "Your disillusion came after."

"Oh no . . . no."

"I understand, my dear. We were not so unfortunate, you and I.
Certainly not I. But the ordeal now lies before my poor little niece.
She has confided in you?"

"A little."

"And her stepmother too, I'll swear. 'Tis a pity she has had such a
good home, as it gives her the more grief to leave it. Well, the young
man wishes to make his inspection. He is quite blunt about it. He
does not get his manners from the Stuarts. It's the stolid Dutch influence coming out."

When Mary heard the news, she was smitten with grief and she
was in a state of fright when she was presented to her prospective
bridegroom. I did not know what happened at that interview, and I
believe for Mary it was mercifully brief. He appeared to be satisfied
with her; she was less pleased with him.

She took to her bed and gave herself up to futile tears. In vain did
Anne and the other girls try to pacify her. Nothing could turn her
from her melancholy.

I went to see her. There was a note of cheerfulness then because
negotiations were lagging a little and Mary's eyes shone with the hope
that the marriage might come to nothing.

William was insisting that it take place immediately, but Charles
wished the peace terms to be dealt with first.

He said: "The young man behaves like an impatient lover. I can
scarcely believe that of him. He is an astute fellow. He wants to make
sure of the marriage. There will be a close bond between our countries
if it is settled, which it would not be easy to break. Well, he is my sis-

ter's son and soon now he will be my brother's son-in-law. He is clever, you know. I wish I could like him as much as I respect him."

He certainly does not resemble the friends you like to have around you."

"There you have it. There is no wit in him. He is all sound common sense and honesty. A stern Protestant. That is why the people like this marriage. It really is a desirable match from all sides."

"Except poor Mary's," I said.

"Mary will get used to him. After all, she has to marry one day. Why not Orange?"

"She is so very young."

"James was hoping to get the Dauphin for her, but she'll do better with Orange than at the court of France."

"Let us hope so."

Mary's tears availed nothing. On the Sunday of the fourth of November she was married. I could have wept for her. She looked such a child.

An altar had been set up in her bedchamber. The King was beside me; the Duke of York and his Duchess Mary Beatrice, so heavily pregnant that she looked as though she would give birth at any moment, and the Bishop of London who was to perform the ceremony.

Mary looked dejected and I longed to comfort her.

Charles took her to the altar. He smiled at the pregnant Duchess and said: "We must make haste, lest my sister the Duchess gives us a boy." Smiling roguishly at William, he added: "And the marriage should be disappointing."

There was no smile on the face of the Prince of Orange, but he must be hoping that the child would not be of that sought-after sex.

Charles was in a light-hearted mood that day. I could see that he was amused by the Prince of Orange; he had a certain admiration for his astuteness and amazement at his inability to see a joke. He could not help calling attention to William's foibles, and during the service, when William must say he would endow his wife with all his worldly goods, he placed some gold coins on the book which was open before the pair.

"Gather it quickly," Charles whispered to Mary. "Put it in your pocket, for it is all clear gain."

William did not appreciate such frivolity; but he had achieved what he wanted: alliance with England.

There was great rejoicing throughout London because Mary had made a Protestant marriage. Poor little Mary! If only she had been as satisfied! It was sad to see her woebegone face, which was an indication of what she thought of the marriage.

I wondered what was in William's mind when, two days after the wedding, the Duchess of York gave birth to a boy who seemed likely to survive.

With somewhat malicious intent, Charles decided that the Prince of Orange should stand as sponsor at the baptism of the child, who had disappointed him in his hopes of the crown of England. It was implied that this was a great honor for the Prince. William was not of a nature to respond with the charm Charles would expect from one of his own courtiers in a similar situation, and he did so with a bad grace, knowing full well why the offer had been made.

He made no secret of this disappointment and looked so glum that people wondered whether he was already regretting his marriage.

As for Mary, she was the picture of wretchedness, and every now and then burst into tears.

Then there was consternation throughout the court, for Anne had been smitten with the smallpox. The Duke of York was frantic with anxiety. He gave orders that Mary must not on any account go near her sister—nor must any who had been in contact with Anne approach Mary.

Mary was more unhappy than ever. Besides her miserable situation, she had to endure separation from her beloved sister. She wanted to be alone and it seemed that her bridegroom was quite content to let her be so. The ladies-in-waiting whispered together about his uncouth behavior. They called him the Dutch Monster until someone thought of Caliban and that became the favorite.

Meanwhile the mournful bride kept mainly to her own apartment, praying that the wind would be too strong for her to leave England.

When I saw her she burst into tears.

I said: "My dear Mary, it will not be so bad."

"He doesn't like me," she answered.

"He does. He wanted to marry you. Remember, he insisted on the marriage taking place at once."

That was because he wanted the alliance. And now my half-brother is here, and he wishes he hadn't married me. Oh, how I wish he had not!"

"You'll feel better in time. One always does. It seems difficult at first. We most of us have to leave our homes and families . . . just as you are doing. I had to."

"But you were *coming* to England . . . I am going away from it."

"But England was not my home."

"You came to my uncle the King. I have to go with . . . Caliban."

"You must not call him that. You will find him a loving husband when you get to know him."

"I have to leave it all . . . my dear, dear father . . . Anne. What of Anne? She will get better, will she not?"

"Of course she will get better. She is already improving."

"But I shall not see her . . . and we have always been together."

"Dear Mary, you have to accept your fate."

"How I wish I could see Anne . . . say good-bye to her."

"Your father has given instructions that this must not be. It is for your sake."

"But to go right away . . . without saying good-bye."

"You will come back on a visit."

"It is not the same." She threw herself into my arms. "Oh . . . I want to stay. I want it to be like it used to be."

What was the use of trying to comfort her? She would not be comforted.

We heard that Frances Villiers, who was to have accompanied Mary, had caught the smallpox. That was a further blow for Mary. She looked so young and lonely, and fervently she prayed that the wind would not change.

But it did and the time for departure had come.

Mary was weeping profusely. She threw herself into her father's arms. She took a tender farewell of the King. She and I embraced, and she gave me two letters which she asked me to give to her sister Anne as soon as I was able to see her.

"Tell her I love her and pray every night for her recovery."

"I will," I assured her.

"Tell her that I wish more than anything on earth that I could be with her."

"I will tell her that."

Frances Villiers was to die a few days later, and I was glad that Mary did not know this. Three of Frances's daughters were in the suite going with Mary to Holland. They were Mary Villiers, who was now Lady Inchiquin, Anne Villiers, and that other sister Elizabeth who had been Mary's companion at Richmond.

At least Mary would have some familiar faces around her. Fortunately she did not know then what trouble Elizabeth Villiers would cause her.

My heart was smitten with pity when I looked at the poor child's blotched face, and I was sure it could not have given much pleasure to her surly husband.

The Duke of York was greatly distressed. I thought at one stage he was going to refuse to allow her to go.

But that, of course, was out of the question. She was now William's wife.

The last farewells were said. The time had come for Mary to embark on her new life as Princess of Orange.

TITUS OATES

I WAS OFTEN AT SOMERSET HOUSE NOW. I DID NOT CARE TO be at Whitehall where it seemed that Louise de Keroualle was Queen rather than I. She was so much cleverer than Barbara Castlemaine had been. She had the dignity of a queen and I was more sure than ever that she was a spy for Louis. Charles must have known that and still he kept her at his side, which was evidence of the strength of her attraction.

Of course, she was not the only one. It amazed me that Nell Gwynne had kept her place so long. I realized, of course, that these two women had special qualities, and in a way I was glad of the King's fidelity to Nell, and heartily wished he would dispense with Louise altogether.

She had become quite a personage at court, playing a part in state affairs. Ministers knew they must tread warily with her. She worked secretly; she never interfered in the King's amatory adventures, and did not make scenes as Barbara had done. Decorously she held her place. There was some powerful and sinister quality about Louise which I was always aware of—and because of her presence at Whitehall, I found the seclusion of Somerset House very desirable.

Soon after Mary had left, Anne recovered. Her father had visited her every day. He knew how sad she would be at the loss of her sister. While she was very ill he would not allow her to be told that Mary had left; and when he considered she was well enough he told her himself.

I think she took the news in her usual placid manner.

I saw Charles now and then. He was always affectionate, and I had learned never to reproach him for his neglect. When he came, I received him with a mild show of pleasure and never referred to his absence. He appreciated that.

It was some months after the Orange marriage—a lovely August day, I remember—when those events which were to place me in the utmost danger were set in motion.

Charles loved to walk in St. James's Park . . . sauntering, as it was called. He would go there to exercise his spaniels and it was one of the sights of the town to see him strolling along with the dogs at his heels, chatting with one or two of his friends.

On this day he called in to see me at Somerset House, and I noticed at once that he was looking a little perplexed.

"A strange thing happened in the park this morning," he said.

He was staring ahead, and I waited expectantly until he went on: "A fellow came up and told me that there was a plot afoot to kill me."

I caught my breath in alarm.

"I am still here, as you see," he said. "And I think likely to remain for a while. But this was the wildest thing I ever heard."

"Tell me about it."

"Well, there was I, sauntering beside the lake, watching the water fowl. Rochester was with me and one or two others . . . suddenly this fellow was beside me. 'Sire,' he said, 'I crave the honor of speaking to Your Majesty.' I replied that it appeared to me that that was exactly what he was doing. He said 'Alone.' "

"You did not allow it," I cried.

He looked at me, smiling indulgently. "We were in the park. It's true he was an ill-kempt-looking rogue. I told Rochester and the others to stand back and leave us."

"Was that wise?"

"You are too fearful, Catherine. There was something about the man. I thought I had seen him before."

"And had you?"

"Yes. He had worked in one of my laboratories. When he told me his name was Kirby, I remembered him vaguely."

"And what did he have to tell you?"

"It was a wild story of a plot to abolish the Church of England, murder all the Protestants . . . a sort of St. Bartholomew's Eve . . . then murder me and set up a Catholic monarch in my place."

"James?" I said.

"Who else? The government was to be replaced by the Jesuits. The plot was already in progress and at any moment I might be shot."

I could not hide my alarm.

"They had planned it to the last detail . . . according to Kirby. They knew of my sauntering habits. Perhaps someone was hiding in the bushes at this moment ready to set all in motion by my instant demise."

"Charles, this is not a joking matter!"

"Ah, as soon as a man puts a crown on his head, there will be some seeking to remove it. This is just another tale. The man Kirby has fallen on hard times. That much was obvious. He wanted a reward for saving me from murderers who existed only in his own mind."

"Are you sure?"

"They already had the silver bullet which was to send me into oblivion. You see how aware they were of protocol. Silver out of respect for royalty. You cannot accuse them of *lèse-majesté.*"

"Charles . . . I am afraid."

"Poor Catherine. What anxieties I have caused you, and now I add this to them. I should never have mentioned this madman's diatribe to you."

"I believe it has disconcerted you more than you would have me believe."

He was serious just for a few seconds. "I suppose a threat to one's life is bound to give one pause for thought," he said slowly. "Particularly if there is much to be repented in it."

"Charles, what will you do?"

He lifted his shoulders. "According to Kirby, the French were involved. They have their spies here, he says. He mentioned names. It is all nonsense, but I have agreed to look at what he calls 'the evidence.' But . . . it is nothing."

"I trust so."

When he left me I could see that he was vaguely puzzled.

I was always alarmed when I heard of plots. It was a fact that kings were in danger and Charles must be aware of this more than most. Had not his father been murdered by his own people?

However, he thrust the matter aside. He treated it lightly and for the time I tried to see it in the same way.

I did not know that it was the beginning of the most dangerous period of my life.

+>-<+

IT WAS UNFORTUNATE, I often thought afterward, that Charles should have passed over the unravelling of what was to be known as the Popish Plot to Thomas Osborne, Earl of Danby.

Charles had been right when he said that the plot was the fabrication of mischievous men. Danby must have been aware of this, but he was in such dire straits himself that he seized the opportunity to turn attention to another quarter.

Danby was a very ambitious man who at this time saw his dreams of greatness crumbling away. His administration of the country's finances had been somewhat questionable and it had been discovered that on occasion he had taken bribes. He had been involved with Charles in some of the secret negotiations with Louis and this had been revealed to his old enemy Ralph Montague. Montague had shown his enmity to Danby by exposing these revelations to the House of Commons; as a consequence of this—in addition to his questionable financial dealings—Danby had been put in danger of being impeached.

Another who had scores to settle was the Earl of Shaftesbury. He was one of those who had tried hard to persuade Charles to divorce me and he was obsessed by the idea of bringing in a Protestant queen to take my place. He had made many miscalculations. He had, however, succeeded in introducing an Act to exclude Catholics from holding high office; but in his great desire to rid the King of his Catholic wife he had failed.

I did not know Shaftesbury well but from what I gathered he was a vindictive man. He was a fanatical Protestant and as such there were two people he wished to destroy: first the Duke of York, and second, myself.

I often wondered how much credence would have been attached to the Popish Plot if these two had not been there to fan the sparks which had been ignited by unscrupulous men.

Certain men sprang into prominence then. I am a little confused about it even now and I think it is best to set out the plot as it unfolded, that it may be seen how I was drawn into it and how it so easily could have led to my downfall.

At the heart of the plot was Titus Oates, who in a short time was being talked of everywhere as the country's savior.

He was a scoundrel and any who looked into his background

could have discovered this. But he was plausible and had his friends; and there were stern Protestants in the country who dreaded a return to Catholicism and desired Catholics to be discredited at all costs.

Titus Oates was the son of a ribbon weaver who had been involved with anabaptists. The ribbon wearer became an army chaplain and was expelled for trying to rouse rebellion in the ranks. He found a living in Hastings from which he was again expelled for misconduct. Titus seemed to have followed in his father's footsteps.

They were in continual trouble, from which they invariably seemed to extricate themselves, and by some means Titus found a place in the University of Cambridge. There he disgraced himself by falling deeply in debt and failing to get his degree, but with his customary dexterity he managed to slip into Holy Orders and returned to his father as a curate.

There was soon trouble, however. Both father and son seemed to have a mischievous compulsion to seek it; and a few months after Titus joined his father, the two of them brought a charge against a local schoolmaster. This was proved to be absurd and Titus and his father found themselves faced with damages which they were quite unable to meet. Titus was sent to prison and his father lost his living.

It was not long, however, before Titus escaped from jail. He joined the navy, from which he was soon expelled. I was never able to understand how he could extricate himself from these situations and establish himself afresh.

He then spent some time in Spain, where he decided to join the Jesuits. After a few months, once more he was expelled and he returned to England, styling himself D.D. of Salamanca, a title to which, of course, he had no right.

In spite of everything, he managed to find a place in the household of the Duke of Norfolk where he encountered many papists. It was probably there that the idea of the Popish Plot began to grow in his mind.

He was not welcome there for long and soon found himself in London. Without the means to support himself, he turned to a man he had met some years before when he had been vicar of a Kentish parish.

Israel Tonge was not the villain Oates was. He was a scholar who had emerged from the university with his degree, but in spite of his scholarship he had found it hard to make a living. He had been rector of a London church at the time of the great fire and his was one of the many churches which had been burned to the ground. After that he had translated some holy works, but this brought him little money. Then Sir Richard Barker, who had admired his work, offered him a place in his house in the Barbican.

At that time he had come into contact with Titus Oates. He believed that the Catholics in England were trying to get into power, and they would have a chance of doing this when James came to the throne. But this might not be for some time, and the Protestants should refuse to have him.

Tonge was convinced that the plot which the Catholics had devised must be prevented from being carried out, and those concerned in it must be brought to trial.

This was a project close to the heart of Titus Oates. Intrigue was life to him; also it was a means of getting a roof over his head.

The two conspirators worked in unison and with Oates's imagination and love of plotting, Tonge's original suspicions were greatly increased. Enthusiasm grew and it was agreed that the King should be warned without delay. Kirby had joined them and, because he had once worked in a royal laboratory, he was considered to be the one most suited to approach the King.

Tonge's statement was set out with great care and some erudition. Oates's sojourn with the Jesuits and the information he had collected about them gave him the chance to add to Tonge's statement and the plot became mainly Titus's own.

It was presented to Danby and, faced with what he deemed might be a good diversion from his own affairs, he gave it more consideration than he would otherwise have done.

I heard rumors of this and it filled me with anxiety. In the first place, I was disturbed to learn of designs on the King's life; and I was deeply concerned that the Catholics should be blamed.

Charles knew this and came to tell me what was happening, so that I should not be worried by all the wild rumors which were circulating.

"You will have heard of this Popish Plot which is being talked about," he said.

"I want to hear about it," I replied. "I want to know the truth."

"It is the wildest fabrication. This man Oates seems to be behind it . . . with Israel Tonge."

"What does it mean?"

"That certain people want to make themselves appear more important than they are."

"Do you really think that is all?"

Charles was thoughtful. "Danby thinks it should be investigated," he said.

"What exactly are these people supposed to be plotting?"

"That is easy to answer. They want the removal of the Black Bastard—that is myself, as you know. Pope Innocent XI is to be the Supreme Head of the Church of England. The French are involved in this. Père La Chaise has lodged ten thousand pounds in London for anyone who will kill me, and there is another ten thousand promised by the Jesuits when the deed is done . . . and yet another six thousand from Savoy. So you see how valuable I am."

"Please do not speak of it so flippantly. These scoundrels could harm you."

He smiled at me tenderly. "The King is dead. Long live the King." He shrugged his shoulders. "It is James who concerns me. I have often thought I was safe because they would never want to kill me, for if they did they would have to have James."

"It seems that these people *want* James."

"To be the papist puppet. The idea is that my death will be followed by those of my ministers. The French will invade Ireland . . ."

"Do you believe that?"

"I am inclined to believe that these two . . . Oates and Tonge . . . have put their heads together and invented the whole thing."

"But this is criminal."

"A natural way of life to such as they are. Poor Danby! His enemies are at his heels, you know. This gives them something else to think about. There is one thing, Catherine, you must not think for one moment . . . but perhaps I should not tell you."

"Please tell me, I must know what it is."

"They say that a sum of money has already been paid to a doctor in the household. It is to be his reward for poisoning me."

"One of the doctors in the household! Do they say which one?"

He was silent for a moment. He looked at me apologetically.

"Well, it is nonsense, of course."

"Who is it? Please tell me."

"Sir George Wakeman."

I felt faint. Sir George Wakeman was my physician.

I began to see that they were going to implicate me in this plot. Charles caught me as I swayed.

"You must not take it to heart," he said. "It is a package of nonsense. These men are trying to call attention to themselves. It is clear what they are up to."

"Sir George Wakeman is an honorable man."

"Of course he is."

"Does he know . . . ?"

Charles shook his head. "We are going to prove it is nonsense. These men should be sent to the Tower for causing such a stir. I know this, but as I tell you, Danby wants to make an issue of it. You know his reasons. He is not going to let it drop easily. We do not know what they will come up with next."

I could guess. They were going to implicate me in their schemes.

Charles made me sit down and he sat beside me and put an arm about me.

"You must not fret," he said. "There will be these rumors. They are nonsense. We'll prove them to be nonsense. I no more suspect Wakeman than you do. I am sure we shall be able to prove that this Oates is nothing more than a troublemaker."

I felt better when I listened to him, but after he had left me my anxieties returned.

THERE WAS A FEVER OF EXCITEMENT in the streets. Titus Oates was the country's savior. He had discovered the plot in time and we were saved from the wicked papists—or at least we knew what they were planning and would be able to foil them.

Danby was all for setting the findings before the Privy Council. Charles was against it.

"It would only put the idea of murdering me into someone's head," he said. "As for these tales about the papists, I simply do not believe them."

I was not sure that Danby did either, but it made the diversion he needed. With the whole country worrying about the papists, there was little interest in the misdemeanors of one of the ministers.

I could imagine the disappointment of Titus Oates and his fellow conspirators when they realized the King refused to take them seriously. Oates told Tonge that he must make their declaration before a Justice of the Peace, since the King had not wished to go before the Privy Council. This was the duty of a good citizen, insisted Oates. So, accordingly, this was done. He and Tongue went to the offices of Sir Edmund Berry Godfrey and set their "discoveries" before him. They gave their oath on this, and, realizing the nature of their revelations, Sir Edmund decided that he must bring the matter to the notice of the Council.

This made it impossible for even the King to thrust it aside, and as a result Oates and Tonge were summoned to appear and substantiate their accusations.

I think this might have put an end to the matter, but for two events which favored Oates.

There had been a number of arrests after Sir Edmund Berry Godfrey had received the declaration, and among them was a certain Coleman, who had been a secretary to the Duchess of York.

However, Oates was not clever enough to deceive Charles, although the Council was inclined to be swayed by him.

The man had a certain eloquence, but he allowed himself to be carried away by his own rhetoric, and this led him into pitfalls.

After the meeting Charles came to see me. It was one of his most lovable traits that, knowing my fears—not only for myself but for my servants such as Sir George Wakeman—his aim at that time was to assure me that, unfaithful husband though he might be, he could be a loyal friend.

He was quite gleeful on this occasion.

"That fellow is a fraud," he said. "I'll grant him this much. He knows how to tell a good story, but he gets carried away by the drama of his own invention, and that is where he goes awry. He should join the players. I'll warrant he could give them some rousing plays."

"Tell me . . . what did he say?" I asked.

"Well, he began by telling us that the Jesuits had decided they would kill me and, unless James agreed to put himself in their hands, he would go the same way. Père La Chaise has paid over ten thousand pounds already to be given to the assassin when the deed was done. I asked him if he had been told this. 'No, Sire,' he answered. 'I was attending a meeting in your service, Sire, in the disguise of one of them. I overheard the discussion and saw Père La Chaise hand over the money to the messenger who was to bring it to England.'

"I said to him, 'Mr. Oates, you were most assiduous on my behalf and I thank you. Tell me, where was this transaction made?' He replied, 'In the house of the Jesuits.' 'And which one was that?' I asked. 'It was the one close to the Louvre, Sire.' 'That is odd,' I replied, 'I had a long sojourn in Paris, so I know that the Jesuits do not have a house within a mile of the Louvre.' "

"He was lying," I said.

"Of course he was lying. One would have thought that was obvious. But how people love a good conspiracy. It was clear that they did not want to stop this ingenious Mr. Oates in his flow. He would have us believe now that, on our behalf, he had labored long and faced many difficulties, for he implied what his fate would have been if those fanatical Jesuits had learned that he was a spy for His Protestant Majesty of England. When he was in Spain, he went on to tell us, he had been received by Don John of Austria. Mind you, it had needed a great deal of cunning planning to reach that gentleman. 'Do describe him to me,' I said. 'Oh, Your Majesty, he is a tall and lean man, and swarthy.' 'You surprise me,' I replied, 'for when I met him he was short, fat and fair.' All this confirmed what I had suspected. Our Mr. Oates is a fraud . . . a man who is determined to call attention to himself . . . to earn notoriety . . . and fortune . . . no matter whom he destroys on the way to it."

I was relieved.

"Then this will be an end to this tiresome matter," I said.

"I pray so. Though Danby will be reluctant to let it go. At the moment people have turned their attention from him. After all, what is a defaulting minister compared with a plot to murder the King?"

IN SPITE OF DANBY'S EFFORTS to keep the Popish Plot the issue of the day, the appearance of Titus Oates before the Council and the errors into which he had fallen discredited him to a certain extent and the conclusion that he was a cheat began to be expressed.

Then there was a change. It came about through Coleman, who had been one of those men whom Titus Oates had accused and who, on Oates's evidence, had been arrested. Coleman was indeed a spy; he had received a pension from France; he was in the service of Père La Chaise and letters from the French priest were found in his possession. The sum of twenty thousand pounds had been offered to him for his continued services to France and for working to bring the Catholic faith to England.

This was one of those unfortunate coincidences. I had no doubt that Coleman had been in the pay of France for many years, for they had their spies everywhere. He was a Catholic, of course, and that was known and was the reason why Titus Oates had named him as one of the suspects.

What luck this was for Titus Oates! In the eyes of the people he was vindicated. He had brought a dangerous spy to justice.

There was something else—and I believe this was less fortuitous— in fact a part of the plot.

It concerned the Justice of the Peace Sir Edmund Berry Godfrey.

It appeared that on Saturday morning he left his home at nine o'clock to go to Marylebone to see one of the church wardens at St. Martin's in the Fields on parochial business. Later he went to St. Clement Danes, calling at Somerset House. After that no one knew where he had gone, but when he did not return, his servants became alarmed, for he was a man of regular habits.

It was Lady Suffolk who told me what had happened. I think my friends were all growing a little uneasy since Titus Oates had sprung into prominence, for the very fact that the so-called plot was directed against Catholics would mean that I could not escape suspicion. I had had my enemies before, but this was a particularly dangerous one.

It was Friday, I remember, six days after Sir Edmund had last been seen.

Lady Suffolk could not hide her consternation, and I demanded to know what was wrong.

She said: "Your Majesty, they have found Sir Edmund Berry Godfrey."

"I am glad of that," I said. "What had happened to him?"

"He is dead, Madam. He had been run through with his own sword."

"Killed himself?"

She shook her head. "It is believed that the wound was not self-inflicted."

"But why . . . ?"

"There is great excitement. There are crowds in the streets. They are saying . . ."

"What are they saying?"

"That he was the one who laid the information before the Privy Council. They are saying it is the papists' revenge."

I held onto a table for support. I felt dizzy. It was not enough that Coleman had been proved to be a spy. Now this would be further evidence.

Catholics in this country were in acute danger—not least myself.

THERE WAS TENSION EVERYWHERE. People wanted to know how the Justice of the Peace had been murdered and by whom. I knew a great deal hung on the answer. He it was who had brought the plot to the notice of the Privy Council, which had resulted in the arrest of certain spies—one of whom was Coleman who had been caught red-handed.

And now . . . what?

Charles himself told me what had happened at the inquest which had been held at White House on Primrose Hill in Hampstead, as it was in that neighborhood that Sir Edmund's body had been found. The doctors declared that he had not died through the stabbing but had died of suffocation. He had not been murdered on Primrose Hill, but his body had been taken there after the deed was done . . . several days after, probably five. There was money on him so it had not been a crime of robbery.

It was clear that Fate was working in Oates's favor. First Coleman and now Sir Edmund Berry Godfrey.

For some days I lived in a state of trepidation, wondering what the outcome would be. I knew what rumors were going round the city. People were saying that the murder had clearly been the work of Catholics. It was their revenge on Sir Edmund for putting the case before the Council. Titus Oates was once more the hero of the day. They said that it was now quite clear that in our midst were those who would stop at nothing to bring the country back to the faith it had rejected.

There followed attacks on the houses of well-known Catholics. Everywhere there were cheers for Titus Oates.

I dreaded the day of Sir Edmund's funeral. People crowded into the streets to pay homage to the martyr, as they called him. They shouted anti-Catholic slogans. "No Popery!" "Down with the devils of Rome!" I knew that among these they included the Duke of York and myself.

Charles came to see me. He was assiduous in his care for me during that time. I cannot imagine how I could ever have lived through those days without him. I tried to forget his preoccupation with Nell Gwynne and Louise de Keroualle. I saw him as my best friend . . . unfaithful husband though he might be.

But I understood him now. He had been born with those sexual needs and they were insatiable. No woman would be enough for him. But what a loyal friend he was!

He said: "There is chaos in the streets."

"It is the funeral," I said.

"Why did this have to happen now? This . . . and Coleman. There could have been an end of it."

"And was Godfrey really murdered?"

"There does not seem a doubt of it."

"By whom?"

He hesitated. "Oates is a fraud. It may be that he and his friends have done this. He has some knowledge but he cannot resist the impulse to embellish. Remember how I caught him out. He is brimming over with eagerness to present his case . . . and this is for his own glory. I would dearly love to be rid of the fellow." He lifted his shoulders. "But what can I do? The people love him . . . at the moment. They see him as the savior. They could as easily turn against him, though." He was melancholy for a moment. "None knows more than I how quickly the people can turn. At the moment Oates is exalted. He is the exposer of plotters. This is how the people see him and, for the time being . . . we must needs go along with them . . . up to a point."

"What shall you do?"

"Our first duty is to discover who murdered this man. If it could be proved that he was a robber . . ."

"But whoever killed him did not take his money."

"That's true. If we could prove he was murdered by friends of Oates, that would finish the matter once and for all. I am offering a reward of five hundred pounds for the discovery of the murderer of Sir Edmund Berry Godfrey." He turned to me. "Be of good cheer. These villains shall not harm you while I am here to defend you."

I was filled with apprehension, but I could not express how happy those words made me.

THE KING'S OFFER of five hundred pounds brought a new figure into the drama. This was William Bedloe, an ex-convict, adventurer and a man practiced in dishonest business.

He came forward and announced that he had been aware of a plot which was brewing among Catholics. He had made many discoveries and would have put them before the Council himself if Titus Oates had not been just a little ahead of him.

He knew who had murdered Sir Edmund Berry Godfrey. The deed had been done at Somerset House.

As soon as I heard this I knew these people had decided that I should be more deeply incriminated.

What followed confirmed this, and made me even more aware of the danger in which I stood and into which I was sinking deeper every day.

Bedloe declared that he had seen the body of Sir Edmund Berry Godfrey lying on the back stairs of my apartments in Somerset House. According to him, it had been there for two days before it had been removed. My servants had then taken it to the ditch on Primrose Hill to be discovered far away from where the murder had been committed. He had heard the talk of my popish servants, he said, those who had assisted in the murder. The Justice of the Peace had been suffocated between two pillows because he had assisted in bringing to light the details of the Popish Plot.

This was of course a scheme to involve me, and I was now convinced that these people were intent on my destruction.

Bedloe even mentioned the names of two of my servants, who he alleged had committed the murder.

I was thrown into deep distress when they were arrested.

Bedloe said that he was shown the body by a certain member of my household and offered a thousand pounds if he would remove it. This, so he said, he had declined to do.

It was such a wild accusation that I could not believe anyone would give it credence. But it was what the people wanted to hear, and they were ready to accept it.

It was Charles who saved me again.

"The story is clearly nonsense," he said to me. He himself had been at Somerset House on the day in question and, because of his presence, his guards would have been there. They would have been posted at all exits and entrances and it would have been quite impossible for anyone not of the household to slip in unnoticed.

But the people wanted to believe it . . . so they did.

Moreover, Danby was still eager to keep public interest in the plot.

Bedloe received his reward; Titus Oates was being paid expenses for his work; and those villains who had been unknown and rejected by society were now heroes. They were continually trying to enhance their importance in the eyes of the people.

I OFTEN WONDERED where it would end. I had realized by this time that it was the aim of Titus Oates and his friends to attack me and perhaps bring me to the block.

There was a certain furtiveness among those about me. I wondered if they knew more than I did. There were constant references to Henry VIII and Anne Boleyn. The King was devoted to Louise de Keroualle. Would he marry her if he could? She had proved herself capable of bearing children. She already had a son by the King. But no. She was another Catholic, so this would be nonsense. A Protestant queen would be found for him.

It was true that the King stood beside me and had proved the evidence of Oates and Bedloe to be false when they had sought to move against me; but such men would believe that in his heart the King must want to be rid of me.

He was still young enough to get a son . . . an heir to the

throne . . . a Protestant heir, of course. So they set out to trap me. I was now the main target of these wicked men. It was not enough for them that many people—innocent, I was sure—were now in prison awaiting possible death for treason they had never committed.

I would be the big prize. If I were discarded the people would be pleased. They had never wanted me. I was a foreigner, and, most heinous of all at this time, a Catholic.

With the almost hysterical acclamation which greeted him everywhere he went, Oates grew bolder.

The King so far had protected me, but Oates obviously felt he must increase his efforts if he were not to be defeated in bringing me—as he would say—to justice.

There seemed no end to the man's machinations.

He now said that he had seen a letter in which the Queen's physician Sir George Wakeman had stated that Her Majesty the Queen had given her assent to the murder of the King. Having seen this letter, in his great determination to save the King's life and the continuance of a Protestant England, he, Titus Oates, had gone to Somerset House. He did not state on what business, which would have made quite clear the fact that he was lying. But, as I said, people believe what they want to, and there is no doubt that they wanted to believe every shred of "evidence" against me. He was aware, he went on, that several Jesuits were visiting me, which was the reason why he was there. He crept into an audience chamber and hid there. He had seen the Jesuits enter my chamber and, as they had left the door open, he was able to hear what was said.

He had heard me say I was weary of the humiliations I had to suffer through the King's infidelities and would no longer endure such a state of affairs. I would help Sir George Wakeman to poison my husband and set up the Catholic faith in England.

Charles was very angry. His inclination was to send Titus Oates to the Tower. I could imagine what would have happened if he had. The people would have been in revolt. They had made up their minds that they were going to believe Titus Oates. They had had enough of Catholics and would not suffer another Catholic king on the throne.

Charles sent for Oates. He told me afterward what had taken place.

"I challenged him," he said. "I suggested that he was lying. He had not been to Somerset House any more than William Bedloe had been when he said he had seen Sir Edmund Berry Godfrey's body there. I asked him to describe the Queen's apartments. The confidence of the man is amazing. He has no shame. He blatantly lies with an air of truth. He could not describe your apartments for the simple reason that he has never seen them. He built up a picture of one of the rooms—an audience chamber which could have been in any of the palaces. I told him he was a liar. He just bowed obsequiously, but I saw his evil smile. He knew that if I ordered his arrest the whole of London would be crying out for revenge on any who touched his sacred person. I can tell you, it is a damnable situation. But never fear. I shall make him rue what he has done . . . one day."

I knew Charles was right. To have stood out against him now would have resulted in riots . . . discord throughout the country. Monmouth was waiting somewhere in the shadows . . . ready for the opportunity when it came.

Who would have believed that so much could have arisen out of the lies of an unscrupulous adventurer?

COUNT CASTELMELHOR CALLED to see me. The Count was a man on whom I could completely rely. He had left Portugal when my brother Alfonso had been deposed and had remained loyal to him—so he was not welcome at Pedro's court.

I said to him: "My dear Count, I can see you are very anxious."

"It is a situation which arouses the utmost anxiety. I am indeed afraid for Your Majesty."

"These wicked men are telling such terrible lies about me."

He nodded. "My dear lady, perhaps we should write to your brother."

"What could Pedro do to help me?"

The Count looked melancholy. "He might protest."

"To the King? The King hates what is going on as much as I do."

"But for the King, my lady, I fear they would have had you in the Tower."

"I know what I owe him. I can only pray that this nightmare will soon end."

"It is time Oates was recognized for what he is, but he has the people with him. They hate those of our religion. All the resentment created during the reign of Queen Mary is being revived. It is because they fear that Charles will die without an heir and James will be King . . . a Catholic. That is the only reason why this man Oates has been able to do what he has. They are arresting people everywhere . . . on this man's evidence . . . and it is false . . . false."

"I know. Many of them are my friends. Dr. Wakeman is in the Tower accused of attempting to poison the King . . . and they say that he was to do this with my help. I verily believe that I should be in the Tower at this moment if it were not for the King."

"It is true. The King stands between you and these villains. Thank God for that. But you are in great danger, and it may be that even the King cannot save you. You must take great care. I think you should write to your brother. It would be better for you to leave the country . . . perhaps . . ."

I shook my head. "I would never do that, Count. I shall remain here. I have great faith in my husband."

"There is something else. I must tell you, for I think it is important that you should understand all and miss nothing. The fact that Oates has been proved to be lying . . . although the people do not accept this . . . is forgotten, for Bedloe is now supporting these accusations against you."

"Bedloe?"

"Yes, my lady. He, also, is now saying that he overheard a conversation between you and two French priests. Coleman was there at the time, he says, and some Jesuits. It was in the gallery of the chapel at Somerset House. He says you were told of the plot to murder the King. At first you wept and said you would have nothing to do with such a plan, and when you were reminded of the King's infidelities you at length consented to take part in it."

"What lies!"

"Your Majesty, these people have achieved notoriety through lies."

"How can people believe their wild tales?"

"Because they want to believe. There are so many who fear a Catholic king on the throne of this country. But they will have to take James . . . when the time comes."

"They will not have James."

"They will . . . and with God's help England will in time be brought back to the true faith . . . but I know there are many who are set against it."

They do not like me. There are many who would like to see me in the Tower. They think they will overcome the King's scruples because he is eager to be rid of me. They see him with the Duchess of Portsmouth. He is so often in her company. He is devoted to the playactress Nell Gwynne. And I am a Catholic and barren. Quite unsuitable, you see. They think it will be safe to tempt him to be rid of me. Sometimes it seems like a miracle that he is determined to stand beside me."

"Your Majesty, I am convinced that you should write to your brother."

"What could he do?"

"He is the King of Portugal. They have been whispering about King Henry VIII. Remember, Catherine of Aragon might have lost her head if she had not been the aunt of the Emperor Charles."

"And so she lived through years of unhappiness and humiliation."

"This is different. This King shows his concern for you and the other showed none for his wife. Write to King Pedro. It can do no harm. I would do so, but I am out of favor. If it were Alfonso it would be different."

"I feel very uneasy. . . ."

"It is understandable that you should be."

"Come and see me soon," I said. "You are one of the few I can trust."

When he had gone I wrote to Pedro, though I could not believe there was anything he could do to save me. I could rely only on Charles.

QUEEN IN DANGER

I AM SURE TITUS OATES WAS DETERMINED TO INCRIMINATE me after Charles had disconcerted him over his false descriptions of my apartments.

It is difficult now to see myself as I was at that time. How does one feel when one is more or less under sentence of death? There were times when I felt that the axe was poised over my head, and I would become numb with fear. At others I would feel a certain exultation. One swift sharp blow and my troubles would be over. There was even a moment when I felt a sublime indifference. I was innocent of what they accused me. As if I would plot to kill the one I loved beyond all others! There was one thought which was always with me during those days. It was that he believed in my innocence and it was he who had stood between me and my enemies. There were times when I said to myself, they will have to destroy him before he allows them to destroy me.

Perhaps it was that thought which enabled me to meet the days with a serenity which amazed those about me.

Poor Donna Maria was too old and infirm to know what was happening. I was glad of that. I was relieved that my mother was no longer here, for she would have learned of my danger and it would have wounded her deeply to know that all her plans for me had led to this.

I often thought of those first days in England at Hampton, where I had known the supreme joy of loving and believing myself to be loved; and I tried not to remember that cruel awakening when Lady Castlemaine came to shatter my happiness.

It was over . . . and Charles was now here beside me, my protector.

The Count had been right when he had said that Bedloe had told of how he had heard me plotting with the Jesuits in the chapel at

Somerset House. Bedloe, no doubt urged on by Titus Oates, had written his accusation and delivered it to the House of Commons.

I heard what had happened when his words were read out, how Titus Oates approached the Bar and declared in ringing tones: "I, Titus Oates, accuse Catherine Queen of England of High Treason."

I was told of the astonishment of the House and how, for some seconds after the announcement, there was a deep silence.

Titus Oates had his supporters, Shaftesbury at the head of them, and it was proposed that an address should be sent to the King without delay and that I, with all my household, should be committed to the Tower on a charge of High Treason.

I had never come nearer death. They had accused me, and they would find means of proving me guilty. The truth was of no consequence to them.

It was fortunate for me that such action could not be taken without the consent of the Lords and their verdict was that they would not treat me as guilty until it was proved that I was, and they would need more than the accusation of men like Oates before they did.

Shaftesbury was infuriated by the rejection of the Commons decision, but there was nothing he could do.

It was Charles's reaction which put heart into me.

He was very angry. He ordered that Oates should be arrested and put under guard. He declared that he would not suffer an innocent lady to be wronged as these men were trying to wrong the Queen.

I wept with joy at his response, but I soon realized that, in spite of his power, even he could not completely withstand the demands of the people.

There was an outcry about the incarceration of Titus Oates, and the people demanded that he be freed.

It was only then that Charles realized what a hold that man had on the people, how they revered him, how they waited for every word he uttered.

And my fate seemed to be in the hands of such a creature.

Count Castelmelhor came to me in great dismay.

"Oh, my lady," he cried, "I have lived in such fear. When I heard of Oates's declamation at the Bar I thought it was the end."

"I, too," I said.

I touched my neck with my fingers. I could almost feel the axe there.

"But," went on the Count, "it did not happen."

"No. The Peers saved me . . . and then the King."

"The Peers just wanted more evidence . . . and do you doubt Oates would not have invented that? It was the King who saved Your Majesty. If he had given way in the slightest degree . . ."

"It would have been the end of me."

"Thank God and all the saints for His Majesty the King."

What strange feelings possessed me! I had come within a few steps of the axe. No one who has not experienced that can understand what it is like . . . and at the same time I was exultant because I owed my life to Charles.

Charles himself came to see me.

He looked at me, smiling that rather careless smile, as though there was nothing to disturb our serenity.

I said: "I have heard what you did . . ."

"Oh, you mean that villain and his familiar, Bedloe, do you?"

"The Commons . . . and the Lords . . . ," I began.

He shrugged his shoulders. Then he came to me and put his arms about me, holding me tightly, protectively.

I said: "Thank you . . . thank you . . . for what you have done for me."

"What have I done?" He laughed and raised his eyes to the ceiling. "Very little that is good, I fear. Now I want you to come back to Whitehall with me. I like not this long sojourn at Somerset House."

I forgot that I was in danger. I forgot all that I had suffered through his preoccupation with other women. He was taking me back to Whitehall . . . to be close to him. I knew why he wanted this. It was to show them all that I was his Queen and he was there to protect me against all those who wished me ill. They should not succeed because he was there to care for me.

WE WERE TOGETHER NOW. I sauntered with him; we rode together; and I was happier than I had been for a long time. It was because he was afraid for me. I was fully aware of that, though he shrugged his shoulders and spoke contemptuously of the plotters.

I was overcome with joy when I overheard someone whisper mockingly: "The King has a new mistress. It is his Queen."

It was wonderful that his aim should now be to protect me, to show the court that any who attacked me must first deal with him.

I had my fearful moments. There were cries of, "No Popery!" in the streets; and I knew that Charles would like to keep Oates and his associates in the Tower. But even he dared not do that. When he talked of what he called his wandering years, I often saw the determination in his eyes. He would never go wandering again.

I knew the mood of the people. They would not have a Catholic king. Charles himself leaned toward the Catholic faith, but he was never going to admit it . . . for none knew better than he that it would be the first step toward that fate which he had determined should never be his again.

He often said that James was a fool. Why could he not do his worshipping in secret? Why did he have to proclaim his faith to the world?

During that time he and I grew close together and there were occasions when he implied that if he were free to make a choice it would be for my faith. It appealed to him. It had been his mother's faith, and he had French blood in his veins. His grandfather had begun life as a Huguenot and his well-known assertion that Paris was worth a Mass would never be forgotten.

"My grandfather was a wise man," Charles once said. "He wanted the crown, so blithely he changed his religion to keep it. I have the same respect for my crown as he had for his."

He told me that we were in a precarious situation. These men would stop at nothing. They were adventurers. If one looked into their history one saw clearly that they would do anything for gain. Why could not the people see this? It was the old story. They would not because they did not want to. They wanted to believe in Oates because they wanted a Protestant country.

"We must be watchful," he said. "This man Oates will strike again."

How right he was! A few days later I heard that one of the silversmiths in my household had been arrested.

This was Miles Prance—a meek and inoffensive man who, I was sure, was far more interested in his silver work, cleaning it and generally keeping it in good order, then becoming involved in any state plot.

Poor Miles! How could be withstand the torture Oates insisted should be applied to extricate his "confession." What they did to him exactly I never heard, but they reduced him to a gibbering wretch ready to say anything they demanded of him.

Had he been involved in a plot to poison the King? they asked.

Poor Miles! How could he endure the pain?

"Yes, yes," he cried.

"At the Queen's command?"

"Yes, yes," if that was what they wanted to leave him alone.

He must name other accomplices. He called out all the names he could think of.

More arrests. More executions.

Miles had confessed and was freed; and no sooner was he at liberty than he repented so earnestly of what he had done that he proclaimed to everyone that he had lied and lied and knew of no attempt to poison the King. He would never rest again if he did not put right what he had done. He had spoken against the Queen which was false . . . all false. They had tortured him so fiercely that he did not know what he was saying.

He disappeared and we heard that he was back in Newgate. It was not enough to let him disappear. He had done enough harm to Oates, so he was chained to the floor in a cell where he was tormented. He did not admit to more misdeeds; he simply went mad. He was no use to them—so they hanged him with those whom he had accused.

In the streets people went on shouting, "No Popery!" Shaftesbury was "discovering" several people who declared they had witnessed the marriage of the King to Lucy Walter. In the taverns Monmouth's health was drunk. People were calling him the Prince of Wales. This was done so frequently that Charles publicly made a declaration stating that he had never been married to Lucy Walter. He had been married only once in his lifetime and that was to Queen Catherine. It was not what the people wanted, but it was amazing how popular Charles remained. He had the gift of making people love him. I sometimes thought that if he decided to become a Catholic they would still have wanted him to rule them.

His grace and charm won their hearts, and always had. His

infidelities were laughed at and looked upon as the waywardness of a charming boy. He was everybody's darling.

It this had not been so, events might have turned out very differently. Even so, the people were determined, and even Charles had to be watchful.

I heard that Sir George Wakeman was about to be tried, and I knew that this could be of the utmost importance to me. If the court found my physician guilty of trying to poison the King, that would be tantamount to condemning me.

The trial, I guessed, would not be fair. Many people had been executed on the evidence of Oates and Bedloe . . . innocent people. Why should Sir George Wakeman be different from those?

And if he were declared guilty, in the minds of the people so should I be.

I knew that Oates would do everything in his power to bring about Sir George's downfall; and if he were successful, could even the King save me?

THOSE ABOUT ME WERE in a state of tension . . . but none more so than I. I felt light-headed. I wondered how much longer I could endure this persecution. It was only my innocence—and Charles's support—which kept me from collapsing, I believed. I tried to tell myself that they could not prove anything against me because there was nothing to prove. But what of others equally innocent? When had these people cared for the truth?"

I often wondered how a man with such a record as Titus Oates behind him could so delude the people. But, as Charles always said, they believed because they wanted to. Oates was the enemy of Catholics and that was at the heart of the matter. If I had had a child, if James had not publicly acclaimed his conversion, all this would not have arisen. But these were the facts, and out of them had come Titus Oates and his criminal associates who were destroying so many, including myself.

So Sir George Wakeman was indicted for High Treason and was to appear at the Old Bailey to be tried by Lord Chief Justice Sproggs, and never was the outcome of a trial awaited with such excitement and interest as this one. So much hung upon it . . . and especially for me.

I felt that Titus Oates was rubbing his hands with glee. I guessed that in his imagination I was already imprisoned in the Tower awaiting execution, for once my physician Sir George Wakeman was found guilty, the implication must be that I was too. Members of my household had already been found guilty because of the insistence of Oates . . . poor innocent people . . . but this was my physician, a friend, one who would be in my confidence.

Sir George had never made any secret of the fact that he was a Catholic. He and his brother had, during the war, raised a troop of horse for the Royalist cause. He had fought against the Parliament and had been in prison at the time of the Restoration. He was a man of charm and intellect; he was well liked. There must surely have been many who marvelled that a man like Titus Oates could set himself against such as Sir George and have the weight of public opinion supporting him.

Accused with Sir George were three Benedictine monks who, Oates asserted, were working with the physician in these dastardly schemes.

The chief witnesses for the prosecution were, of course, Oates and his crony Bedloe.

I was glad in a way that I was not present, although I knew that everything that was said would be of the utmost importance to me.

I heard an account of the trial from an eyewitness, so I could well imagine the tension in that court room. Everything depended on Lord Chief Justice Sproggs. I had heard of him. He was the one who had condemned Coleman to death.

Oates, I was told, gave his evidence with the assurance that he must be believed. He was a little sanctimonious, trying to create the impression that he was God's advocate, throwing off his lies as though they were inspired by heaven. It was so difficult to understand why people could not see through him. He said that Wakeman had been offered ten thousand pounds to kill the King, which he could do with the Queen's help, but at first he had folded his hands and refused.

"The court was so still," said my informant, "that you could hear the sharp intake of people's breath." Was Oates going to admit that he had lied? But of course not. He went on to say that Wakeman had protested that it was a daring operation they were asking him to undertake and ten thousand pounds was not enough. "Moreover, what of his post in Your Majesty's household? He would lose that. There would be a new queen. No, ten thousand pounds was not enough. 'Then,' said Oates, 'came the offer.' When the deed was done, Sir George was to be offered the post of Physician General to the Army, and five thousand would be added to the reward. 'That was an offer,' said Oates, 'which he could not refuse.' Sir George declared that there was not a shred of truth in this. Then Bedloe was called to corroborate Oates's story."

I heard how outside the Old Bailey the mob was calling for a verdict of guilty. I could imagine the satisfaction of Oates and Bedloe. They were confident of success. However, the Lord Chief Justice was not afraid of the mob, and the comparison between the evil countenances and the wild accusations of the witnesses for the prosecution and a man of Sir George's reputation and obvious integrity had its effect on him.

Sir George was shrewd in his evidence. He proved that some of the papers produced by Oates were forgeries. Bedloe professed that he himself had had several interviews with Sir George.

"Does Your Honor think that I would consort with a man such as that?" Sir George demanded.

Most people would admit that it was unlikely.

Oates grew very excited. He could not endure opposition. He went a little too far, even for him. He declared that he had seen Sir George sign the receipt for the first thousand pounds. In his zeal he said that he had been present—hidden as usual—and had actually seen another receipt which Sir George had signed accepting the five thousand pounds and the appointment as Physician General to the Army.

The Lord Chief Justice asked him how he knew that the document was not a false one. Anyone could produce such a piece of paper.

"Oh, it was Sir George's signature, my lord."

"You know his signature well?"

"Oh yes, my lord. I have seen it many times. There was no mistaking it."

"And how did it come into your possession?"

Oates looked sly. "My lord, in my zealous pursuit of those who would seek to destroy our country, I have engaged people . . . those whom I can trust and who have the same ideals that I have . . . to work for me. It is dangerous work for which I must pay them."

"So you tell me, Mr. Oates," said Lord Chief Justice Sproggs, "that you were sure this document was not false because you knew the signature of Sir George Wakeman so well."

"That is so, my lord."

It was then that Oates was greatly discomfited, for the Lord Chief Justice brought out several specimens of handwriting in the name of George Wakeman.

"Now, Mr. Oates," said Sproggs, "will you be good enough to tell me which of these is the signature of Sir George Wakeman?"

With an air of confidence Oates made his selection.

The Lord Chief Justice smiled slowly. "Mr. Oates," he said, "you clearly could not recognize Sir George's signature, for it was among those shown to you, and you have selected one which is quite unlike his."

Oates was furious. He would soon be discovering that Sproggs was plotting treachery.

The Lord Chief Justice summed up the case decisively. He addressed the jury with eloquence. Could they in the light of what they had heard in the court find Sir George Wakeman guilty? Of course they could not.

Charles came to me in great delight. He swept me into his arms.

"Odds fish!" he cried. "This must be the beginning of the end. Wakeman is acquitted."

SHORTLY AFTERWARD Sir George was asking the King to receive him. Charles did so with the utmost pleasure, and I was with him when Sir George arrived.

He came and knelt before the King. He looked pale and drawn, which was not surprising after his ordeal.

Charles congratulated him. "I cannot express my joy," he said with emotion.

"Your Majesty is gracious."

I took his hand. "I have prayed for you," I said. "I thank God my prayers were answered.

"That villain got a trouncing," said Charles. "Thank God Sproggs had the courage to do it."

"It takes courage, Sire, at this time."

"Are you going to return to my household?" I asked.

He hesitated. Then he said: "There is something I would say to your Majesties. Oates will not let this matter rest."

Charles nodded in agreement.

"He will find some other charge," went on Sir George. "He will not be content to let me go. He will hate me the more for this."

"It would appear to me," said Charles, "that he will be less confident now. I am of the opinion that even the people who shout for him in the streets may be asking themselves whether they should not look at his actions more closely."

"That may be so, Sire, but the man is dangerous still. I would not feel confident to remain where he could wreak his vengeance on me."

"I understand your feelings," said Charles ruefully.

"Your Majesty, I am asking your permission to leave the country."

I was dismayed, but I saw his reasoning, and recognized the wisdom of it.

"What do you propose to do?" I asked.

"To cross the Channel tomorrow, Your Majesty."

"I see," said Charles. "Of course, you must go and you are right. You want no more of these ordeals. I trust that soon we shall be free of this obnoxious fellow. Godspeed. I shall write letters for you to take, and one day perhaps you will come back to us."

Sir George fell onto his knees in a state of great relief.

I wished him well and he left us.

I was very sorry to see him go, but I knew he was wise to do so. He was free and yet with a lesser man than Lord Chief Justice Sproggs, he might have been in a cell at this moment awaiting execution.

And if that had been the case, I might very well soon have been sharing his fate.

-+->-<-+-

I DO BELIEVE that the trial of Sir George Wakeman was a turning point for Titus Oates and his confederates, though this was not immediately apparent.

Oates was, of course, incensed by the acquittal. It was an absolute rebuff by Lord Chief Justice Sproggs, who had hitherto been a zealous Protestant and far from lenient to Oates's victims.

I did not like much what I heard of Sproggs. He was rather a crude man with a not very good reputation. He was brash, but his asset was a certain power with words. He could be outstandingly eloquent, both with speech and pen. This set him apart, and the fact that he had used his skills on the side of good against evil and had secured the release of Sir George Wakeman aroused the King's interest in him.

As was expected, Oates was not going to accept the rebuttal meekly.

He immediately began stirring up trouble for Sproggs. He incited the people against him, and defamatory libels were set in motion; broadsheets were circulated and rhymes were set to tunes to be sung in the streets. These implied that Sproggs had been bribed with gold from Portugal. Sproggs knew that Wakeman was guilty and with him the Queen. In the ordinary course of justice that would have been the verdict . . . but Sproggs had diverted the course of justice for Portuguese gold.

Sproggs, however, was a man able to defend himself. At the King's Bench, he answered his critics in a brilliant speech. He said that at the trial of Sir George Wakeman he had acted "without fear, favor or reward, without the gift of one shilling or promise of expectation."

I believed that even Oates realized that there was little to be hoped for from attacks on such a man.

The King sent for Sproggs and he came to Windsor. I was present at the interview.

I was a little repulsed by the man. There was something unpleasant about him, but Charles received him warmly, for he said to me in private that the man had saved us from God alone knew what. I knew that he was thinking that, had Wakeman been judged guilty, there would have been demands to question me; and moreover, those who did so would have been determined to prove me guilty. So we owed a good deal to Sproggs.

Charles congratulated him on his actions in Sir George's trial.

"I did my duty, Your Majesty," said Sproggs.

"Knowing that it was not what the people wanted."

"Knowing that, Sire. The accusation was aimed beyond Sir George Wakeman . . . that much was clear."

The King laid his hand on my arm and nodded gravely.

I said: "Thank you, Lord Chief Justice."

"The people are using you ill," added Charles.

"Your Majesty, the mob is easily led . . . and very changeable."

"And these have some strong leaders. They have used you ill. They have used me worse." He smiled at me. "We stand or fall together."

Sproggs bowed. He was obviously delighted, and I believed counted the King's favor as worth more than the approval of the mob.

When he had gone, Charles said: "I don't much like the fellow, but he has a way with words . . . and that is a very powerful thing to have. He will stand for us . . . and it may well be that Mr. Titus Oates will not maintain his glory much longer."

IT WAS TRUE that Oates was deflated by the Wakeman trial and his inability to take adequate revenge on the Lord Chief Justice. There was another case in which Oates met a similar fate.

There was a certain notoriety about this one, because the accused was Roger Palmer, Earl of Castlemaine, husband of the infamous Barbara. He was a well-known Catholic, and therefore a target for Titus Oates.

On Oates's accusation he was sent to the Tower, and while there he wrote a pamphlet on those who had been falsely arrested and charged with being concerned in a plot which had no reality outside the imagination of Titus Oates.

This was a further insult to Oates and he could not allow it to pass. Fresh evidence against Castlemaine was procured and in time the case was brought before Lord Chief Justice Sproggs.

The Earl of Castlemaine was a great friend of the Duke of York. I sometimes wondered when Oates would have the temerity to attempt to bring James himself to trial. After all, he had tried hard enough to involve me. But then, of course, because Charles spent so much time with other women they had not expected so much opposition from

him. Yet when he had protected me, they had not stopped their prosecution. But I supposed that even they would hesitate to attack the
King's brother and heir to the throne.

Castlemaine faced the court with courage and determination. He
shrugged aside the insults of the prosecution and defended himself
with dignity, restraint and a sincerity which could not be ignored.
And, like Sir George Wakeman, he was acquitted.

Oates's power was considerably subdued, but I had another
enemy in Shaftesbury. His was the cause of Protestantism, and I was a
Catholic. He did not accuse me of attempting to poison the King. He
merely wanted to remove me so that the King might marry a Protestant queen and have children who would ensure a Protestant heir to
the throne.

He knew that he could rely on considerable support throughout
the country, and he brought in a Bill for the exclusion of the Duke of
York and a divorce for the King that he might marry a Protestant and
leave the crown to legitimate issue.

If Charles had wished to divorce me then, it would have been easy
for him to have done so. He could have shrugged his shoulders in his
nonchalant way and declared that it was his duty to do so.

I shall never forget how he stood by me in that time of danger. I
knew how he hated trouble, how his great desire was to live a life of
comfort and pleasure. His sauntering, his interest in the stars, his
herbs, his dogs, the navy, planning buildings with the architects . . .
that was the life he wanted to live. He had been so long in exile that
these pleasures were of particular importance to him. He had had
enough of conflict.

Yet with great vigor, he became my champion, and because of this
I was ready to fight beside him. Indeed, what else could I do? To be
parted from him was something I could not contemplate. It would be
the end of everything I wanted. Anything, even this persecution, was
better than that.

Charles made a point of going to the Peers to stress his abhorrence
of the Bill, and to tell them that it was against his wishes that it
should proceed. He would not see an innocent woman wronged. He
was married to me and so he would remain. As for the Duke of York,
he was the legitimate heir to the throne and only if he, the King, had
legitimate heirs could that be changed.

Charles won the day. His wishes were respected and the Bill did not proceed.

Then William Bedloe died. This was quite unexpected, and it was another blow for Oates, for on his deathbed, Bedloe decided that he could not meet his Maker with so much on his conscience. So he repented and confessed that he had told many lies, that he knew nothing against me, except that I had given money to some Catholic institutions and was a Catholic myself. He admitted that accounts he had given of my attempts to poison the King were all lies.

Titus Oates must have been infuriated. Already he had lost some of his credibility by the acquittals of Sir George Wakeman and the Earl of Castlemaine. He might strut round in his episcopal robes—silk gown, cassock and long scarf—calling himself the nation's savior, and enjoying his pension from the privy purse, but he must be suffering some qualms of fear and asking himself how long his glory would last.

I heard he had three servants to wait on him and dress him, as though he were royal; they vied for the honor of holding the basin in which he washed his hands. Everywhere people fawned on him, fearing that if they did not he might name them as conspirators and they find themselves under arrest.

He had so much to lose and Bedloe's deathbed confession must have given him great concern.

His spirits were no doubt uplifted by the trial of William Howard, Viscount Stafford. There was as much interest in this as there had been in that of Sir George Wakeman; and there was a certain desperation about Oates and his followers now. There must be no more acquittals. Stafford was a noble lord . . . a man of integrity, son of the Earl of Arundel . . . and a Catholic.

He had been accused by Titus Oates, with several other Catholic lords, but Stafford was the one they decided to send for trial. I was of the opinion that this was because he was old, in frail health and perhaps less able to defend himself.

He was to be tried in Westminster Hall and I had a great urge to be there. I knew that, even if I were not mentioned as one of the conspirators, my complicity would be hinted at and I felt I must hear what was said.

A box was provided for me in the Hall and in this I sat, with some of my ladies.

It was a heart-rending experience to see that old man so perse-cuted. He was innocent, of course, and people in that hall knew it, but were afraid to say so.

Oates and his men gave evidence. There were two I had not heard of before—Dugdale and Tuberville. They swore that Stafford had tried to persuade them to murder the King. Oates affirmed that he had seen a document sent from the Pope to Stafford in which it was clear that Stafford was promoting Catholic interests.

The trial lasted for seven days. It was the same as before—lies, in-nuendoes and the continual suggestions that I was concerned in the plot to kill Charles.

Surely, I said to myself, everyone must see how false these people are. They are so obviously liars. Again and again they are proved wrong over details.

But there was fear in the hall. I could sense it. Titus Oates had a satanic power to terrify people. They did not seem to realize that if they all stood together against him they need not fear him.

Lord Chief Justice Sproggs had been persecuted after the acquittal of Sir George Wakeman. He had succeeded because of his powerfully ex-pressed arguments. But for that, Sir George would have been con-demned. It was pitiable. There was no such help for Stafford, and the verdict was what Oates demanded: Stafford was found guilty of treason. And the sentence for such a crime was hanging, drawing and quartering.

When I looked at that noble old man I felt sick with horror. When would all this end?

Why had I thought the power of Oates was waning? He was still an evil influence in the land.

I HAD RARELY SEEN Charles so distressed. Before him was the war-rant for Stafford's execution and it was to be signed by him.

There was anguish in his eyes.

"You cannot sign it," I said.

"It is the law. He has been judged."

"It is all so false," I cried. "He is not guilty of treason. He would never join in a plot to kill you. You cannot believe it."

Charles said. "He has had his trial and they have judged him guilty."

"But he is *not* guilty."

"They have judged him so."

"If you refuse to sign . . ."

He shook his head. I understood. Even the King could not defy the law. His father had stood against the Parliament and what had happened to him must be a never-forgotten lesson to all the kings of England.

"I shall have to do my duty," he said.

"That old man! But not to hang, draw and quarter. That is barbaric."

"It is the law."

He was still staring at the paper before him, reluctant to take up his pen.

He said: "Catherine, I must sign . . ."

I looked at him sadly, for he was so deeply disturbed.

To hang, to draw and quarter. I knew what that fearful sentence meant.

"I shall change that," he said. "It shall be the axe. It is the least . . . and the most . . . I can do."

Then he took up his pen and signed.

I believe that was something he regretted for the rest of his life.

SO THEY TOOK STAFFORD out to Tower Hill. Oates and his friends had been angered because the King had changed the sentence and they had some of their supporters on the scene, but their voices were silenced by the many who had gathered there and who did not think the verdict was just.

That should have been a further warning to Oates that his popularity was waning, for someone was heard to shout: "May God bless you, my Lord Stafford."

Stafford made a declaration before he died. He persisted that he was entirely innocent. And a voice in the crowd was distinctly heard to say: "We believe you, my lord. You are innocent. This is a crime against justice."

I was told that for a few moments the executioner looked perplexed, but like others, he would be afraid of what might happen to him if he did not do what was expected of him.

He lifted the axe and struck.

They buried Lord Stafford in the Chapel of St. Peter ad Vincula; and Charles was melancholy for some days and kept to his apartments.

→►◄◄

WITH THE COMING OF SPRING there was more trouble.

Shaftesbury and his supporters had been so angry that their Bill to exclude the Duke of York and bring about my divorce had not been given a hearing that they were determined to bring it up again and force it through Parliament.

Then Edward Fitzharris appeared on the scene. He wanted to be another Titus Oates, which was not surprising, since Titus had done so well for himself.

The interesting point about Edward Fitzharris was that he had been associated with Louise de Keroualle, from whom doubtless he would have learned something of the art of spying.

His plan was to produce a document advocating the exclusion of the Duke of York from the succession because he was a foolish man unfit to rule, and that I should be removed because I had been suspected of being involved in a plot to poison the King.

It might have been that Louise de Keroualle was behind him in this. Being a Catholic, she could not hope to take my place and become Queen, but she was very ambitious for her son—who was also the King's.

It was a slightly different version of the Popish Plot.

A document in the form of a letter, which was called "The True Englishman speaking Plain English in a letter from a friend to a friend," was to be discovered in the house of some prominent member of the government and through it Fitzharris was to be a savior of his country, such as Titus Oates, the man on whom he was modelling himself.

Unfortunately for Fitzharris, one of his accomplices betrayed him before he was able to put his plot into action. He was arrested and sent to the Tower.

This was the state of affairs when we heard that Shaftesbury was going to present his Bill to Parliament and this time intended to force it through.

Charles came to me. He was very disturbed. I knew that he was still thinking of Stafford and blaming himself for signing the death warrant.

On this occasion there was a light of determination in his eyes.

He said: "I have been a coward. Ever since my restoration I have been clinging to my crown at all costs. I have never forgotten what happened to my father, and it has made a weakling of me in this respect. But better to go wandering again than live in fear. I should have refused to sign Stafford's death warrant. What would they have done then?"

"I think they would have killed him in any case."

"And there were complaints because I gave him a little relief at the end. They wanted that barbarous sentence carried out on that frail innocent old man."

I shivered. "At least you saved him from that," I comforted.

"True, and I must not look back. I am not going to allow Shaftesbury the satisfaction of making his Bill law."

"Sometimes," I said, "I think they are so determined to be rid of me that they will succeed in the end."

"Never while I am here."

I put out my hand and, with that courtly gesture which charmed so many, he kissed it.

"You are so good to me," I said. "You have made me very happy."

"You . . . shame me," he replied, not meeting my eyes. After a pause he went on: "Do you know, my dear, I think the people here like me. Or perhaps they want to keep me alive in order to defer the coming of James. Well, I am not going to let that villain Oates and that fanatical Shaftesbury have it all their own way."

"What shall you do?"

"You will see. Prepare to leave for Windsor on Monday."

"Will not Parliament then be in session?"

He nodded. "I shall expect you to be ready to leave."

I SOON LEARNED what he was going to do.

It was a Saturday when the Bill was introduced to the Parliament. On the following Monday, the King left Whitehall in a sedan chair in which the curtains were drawn so that none was aware of who was in it. He wore his state robes and carried his crown in his hands.

Without any preamble he went into the House and took his place on the throne. His crown was then on his head.

Then he ordered Black Rod to summon the Commons to the chamber, and when they were assembled, he said in ringing tones: "The substance of this session has begun in so ill a way as can bring no good to any; therefore it is better to end it." He turned to his Chancellor. "I pray you, declare this Parliament dissolved."

With that he rose and in silence left the astonished members.

He came to Whitehall where I was waiting for him.

"Now," he said, "we leave for Windsor. It will be a short stay. There is work to be done."

CHE VERY NEXT DAY we left Windsor and returned to Whitehall together. The people cheered us in the streets of the capital. Charles was as smiling and affable as ever. He was right when he said they loved him.

The court was subdued. I guessed everyone would have been talking about the manner in which the King had dissolved Parliament, so dismissing Shaftesbury's Bill. This was the King's prerogative, and in a few days it became clear that what Charles had done was acceptable to most people. But I could imagine Shaftesbury's fuming; and surely now Oates must be feeling anxious.

The people were with the King, though. That much was obvious. They would not want him to "go wandering" again. They would not be eager to accept James—but I hoped I would never see that day— and Charles might say that they kept him on the throne because they preferred him to his brother, but I knew they loved him, as so many of us did.

He said to me at that time: "There can be no doubt that on this occasion I took the right turning. Odds fish! I should have done this before. If one is a king, one must act like one."

People were waiting for what could come next.

They were saying that Fitzharris would go free because to try him might be an inconvenience to Louise de Keroualle, Duchess of Portsmouth, since he had been a servant of hers and might involve her.

I wondered, too. Even those of us who loved Charles had to admit his weakness over women.

But no. He gave orders that Fitzharris should stand for trial, and, although the Duchess and one of her women were witnesses for the defence, Fitzharris was found guilty and hanged.

Then there was Monmouth. I knew how fond Charles was of that young man. Charles was proud of him, but during this period Monmouth had played a disturbing role. He was ambitious in the extreme. He could not help casting covetous eyes on the throne, and the faction which had wanted to prove there had been a marriage with Lucy Walter had raised his hopes high.

Charles said to me: "I cannot receive Jemmy knowing what part he has played in this."

"He is young . . . and ambitious," I reminded him.

Charles looked at me steadily. "You are forgetting that he is in league with these men who would seek to destroy you."

"I do know that."

"I cannot believe that he could plot to poison me."

"No, he does love you."

"But he loves my crown more."

"He must know in his heart that it can never be his."

"Does he? He was involved in that plan to produce the famous box in which was the evidence to prove I married his mother."

"Well, that would be a temptation, would it not?"

"Knowing it to be lies . . ."

"How could he be sure? I daresay they would convince him that there was such a box."

"He would need little convincing, I'll swear."

"He is young. Naturally he is ambitious. He will be very unhappy if you turn from him."

"Catherine, these people do not love me. They are bemused by the glitter of the crown. I know this well. But I think my brother James is a little fond of me."

"He is very fond of you. Your subjects love you. Many people love you, Charles."

"I know one who does, though I often ask God why." He looked at me whimsically.

I was too moved for speech. Such moments were very precious to me and I should remember and cherish them throughout my life.

I said: "And Monmouth . . . you will forgive him?"

"You are asking me to, and if it is your wish . . . but remember, he has not been such a good friend to you."

"I have one friend here whose goodness throughout these troubles has given me great happiness."

"Thank you, Catherine," he said. "Because you ask it, I will receive him."

"And kindly?" I asked.

"Since it is your wish. But I shall insist that Jemmy is my *illegitimate* son. His mother and I were *never* married. And I will not allow it to be said otherwise."

I said: "I think it will be enough if you receive him."

SO MONMOUTH WAS back in favor . . . a little subdued for a while, but he quickly regained his confidence as the weeks passed.

The Duchess of Portsmouth was there too. I wondered how she felt about the execution of Edward Fitzharris, which was something of a reflection on herself.

She was as arrogant as ever, as certain of herself, still showing outward respect for me which concealed an almost imperceptible veiled insolence.

I found her presence disturbing.

Charles had made it impossible for Shaftesbury's Bill to get a hearing; he had commanded that Fitzharris should be tried; and he had said he was behaving like a King, which he should have done before. But the Duchess of Portsmouth was still there. It was true that he spent less time with her and more with me, but she remained close to the King.

One evening when the court was assembled, she had taken her place beside him . . . a place which should have been mine. She did this with an assumption of unconcern, as though it were the most natural place for her to be.

Charles looked at her suddenly with a certain coldness rare in him.

He said: "You are looking pale, Duchess. May I suggest you try the Bourbon waters? They are said to be most beneficial."

She looked at him in surprise tinged with dismay. I felt my heart bound in pleasure. This was diplomatic dismissal.

"I thank Your Majesty for your concern," she said lightly. "Yes . . . I have heard they are very health giving."

"You must try them, Duchess, I insist."

She bowed her head.

Her eyes then met mine briefly. I hoped I did not betray my triumph.

WHAT A JOY IT WAS to be without Louise de Keroualle. The King and I were together frequently and it was almost like those first days at Hampton Court.

Monmouth was affable to me and I fancied Charles must have told him that he owed his reception to my good graces.

Charles was slipping into a routine which he enjoyed. He had ceased to concern himself with the calumnies of Titus Oates. The man had been discredited so many times, but even now his reign of terror persisted and people were afraid to offend him. But events were turning against him. When he accused a priest of complicity in his plot, the priest was tried and found guilty, but Charles intervened and the priest was reprieved. Oates was foolish. He did not seem to be aware that people were turning against him.

A certain Isaac Backhouse, a schoolmaster by profession, had, according to Oates, called after him: "There goes that perjured rogue." Oates immediately took action against the schoolmaster, but the case was dismissed. Some months later he brought an action against a writer named Adam Elliot whom he accused of being a Jesuit priest. The case was disproved and Oates was forced to pay damages. Indeed, the tide was running against him. His pension was reduced and he was forbidden to come to court.

It was remembered that thirty-five people had been executed on account of the charges he had brought against them.

It was gratifying that Oates was being recognized for what he was.

These were happier times. Charles had for some years devoted himself to the rebuilding of London, so much of which had been destroyed during the great fire. One of his passions was a love of architecture, and he spent hours with his architect, Christopher Wren, whose work was now transforming London. Instead of the overhanging gables, which had almost met across the narrow streets, we now had wide thoroughfares, and the wooden houses, which had been so easily burned, were replaced by brick and stone. Fifty-three churches had already been built, as well as many houses. The building of the great cathedral had begun and Charles was interested in the construction of a Royal Observatory at Greenwich.

London was growing into a fine city. We heard that all over Europe people were talking of the beauty of its buildings and the speed with which the old city was being transformed.

Charles said we were fortunate to have such a fine architect as Wren; and I think we were lucky to have a king who cared so much about the grace and beauty of buildings, so that he could work in close cooperation with such a man.

Charles took his saunters in the park and was as merry as he had ever been. There was laughter about him and people walking past saluted and cheered him.

It was more than twenty years since he had returned, and they loved him as much as they had on the May day when he had come home after his long exile.

I began to feel happy, with a serenity I had not known since before that day when Barbara Castlemaine had been presented to me.

The power of Titus Oates was waning fast and Charles had stood by me through my troubles. He had learned that he had a strong enough hold on the affections of his subjects to stand out against tyranny. He was their King and they wanted his benevolent rule to continue.

It would have been wonderful to record that I had attained perfect happiness, but the Duchess of Portsmouth had returned to court, radiant after the Bourbon waters. Charles found her irresistible; and, of course, through all our troubles, there had been Nell Gwynne.

DEATH IN WHITEHALL

THE PRINCESS ANNE, DAUGHTER OF THE DUKE OF YORK AND Anne Hyde, was now eighteen years old and a possible bridegroom had been found for her.

Anne had been very sad at the departure of her sister, Mary, but that was some five years ago, and during that time her friendship with Sarah Jennings had grown even stronger. Sarah had now married John Churchill but had remained in attendance on Anne. Indeed, Anne would not hear of her going and had created such a scene when it was suggested, that it was decided that Sarah must stay.

Sarah herself was not averse to this. I was sure she enjoyed her position. I had seen right from the first that she was one of those people who enjoyed dominating others—particularly when they were in a position higher than her own.

There had been talk of a union between Anne and Prince George of Hanover, a proposition which did not greatly delight Anne. She had heard rumors that he was a boorish young man who spoke no English. Moreover, she would have to leave England and, as Sarah was married to John Churchill, how could she accompany her?

This she confided to me, for I was on good terms with her. She was delighted when George of Hanover married Sophia Dorothea of Celle, so that she need concern herself with him no longer.

"They have now found Prince George of Denmark for me," she told me. "I think I shall like him better. Besides, he will have to stay in England and so I shall not have to go away. Sarah could scarcely go to Denmark."

Her conversation was filled with comments about Sarah.

I was glad for Anne. She was a pleasant girl . . . comfortable . . . homely in a way. There was nothing haughty about her. I found her easier to get on with than her sister Mary had been. There had been rumors of some sort of romance between her and John Sheffield, Earl of Mulgrave. Charles had not approved and Mulgrave had been exiled from the court for some time. However, Anne seemed quite ready now to accept Prince George.

It appeared that he was something of a hero, having distinguished himself in battle during the troubles between his country and Sweden. His brother, King Christian, had been taken prisoner by the Swedes and George, with his cavalry, had broken through the Swedish lines and rescued him.

But what made him most acceptable in Anne's eyes was that he had very little income—not much more than five thousand crowns—and only a few possessions in Denmark, so it would be necessary for him to stay in England, and she would be able to keep Sarah Churchill with her.

He was quite handsome and of a mild disposition, all of which recommended him to her further. He was given the Order of the Garter and the marriage was celebrated in St. James's Chapel. Charles gave Anne away, and I was there with the Duke and Duchess of York.

I could not help remembering poor Mary, who had been bathed in tears during her wedding to William of Orange.

By contrast this was a very merry occasion; everybody seemed happy. Anne appeared completely to have recovered from her flutter with the Earl of Mulgrave; the bridegroom was obviously very happy to be so welcome in his new country; in the streets the bells rang out; the people made bonfires and there was rejoicing everywhere. A Protestant marriage was very desirable—not that there seemed any chance that Anne would ever come to the throne. But she was the daughter of the Duke of York, and it seemed certain that he would be the next king.

Oates was in decline and the King had clearly shown that he would never consent to a divorce.

AT THIS TIME, there was consternation first over Shaftesbury and then the discovery of a plot to murder the King and the Duke of York. We had heard so much of plots over the last years through the machinations of Titus Oates that at first we had thought this was just another version of the old story. But this proved not to be the case.

Shaftesbury was not the man to give up. Charles had frustrated him over the Exclusion Bill and he was determined on action. For some time he had been urging Monmouth to start a rebellion. Since the scheme for the discovery of the box containing details of a marriage between Lucy Walter and the King had failed, it must have seemed to Shaftesbury that the only chance was to take the crown by force.

He was playing a very dangerous game, and, as Monmouth was showing great reluctance to take part in such a risky adventure, Shaftesbury decided to leave the country and work from abroad.

I cannot imagine what this would have led to, but soon after he left the country Shaftesbury had suddenly died. So that was the end of that dangerous enemy.

Then came the discovery of the plot. It was only after the danger had passed that it came to light, when one of the conspirators betrayed what had happened.

I was filled with horror when I heard, for I saw it might so easily have succeeded, and failed only by chance. There happened to have been a fire at the house in Newmarket where the King and Duke were staying for the races, which meant that they left the town earlier than they intended to.

The conspirators were determined on the exclusion of the Duke of York from the throne; the King would not agree to this; therefore both King and Duke were to die.

On their way back to London from Newmarket, they would pass along the high road near Hoddeston in Hertfordshire. On that lonely road was a dwelling known as the Rye House. It was owned by a malt-ster named Rumbold, who was in the plot, and there at the Rye House the conspirators would lie in wait.

What distressed the King more than anything was that the Duke of Monmouth's name was mentioned in connection with the plot. Moreover, the leading figures in this conspiracy were not men such as Titus Oates, but important people headed by William, Lord Russell, the Earl of Essex and Algernon Sidney.

They were arrested and found guilty.

Essex died rather mysteriously in his cell, and it was believed that he had killed himself. Sidney and Russell were executed.

There remained Monmouth.

When he came and begged an audience with the King, I asked Charles if I could be present, and he said I might be there.

Charles was clearly perplexed. This was his own son. He had loved Monmouth, though it was not the first time he had suspected him of treachery; but that could not completely change his affection.

Monmouth threw himself at his feet.

"My son," said Charles. "Your yearning for the crown is even greater than I thought."

"Sire, Your Majesty . . . father . . . it is not so."

"Do you think you would be wearing it now but for that tiresome fire at Newmarket which drove me out of the town before my time? I'll say your looks would become it well . . . but there is more to being a king, Jemmy, than a handsome face under a golden crown."

"Sire . . . I swear . . ."

The King had turned to me. "He swears," he said. Then to Monmouth: "You look foolish sprawling there. Tell me the truth. Do you want my crown so much?"

"I swear I would never be involved in a plot to kill you. You are my father."

"And you, Jemmy, remember, are my bastard. It is a simple fact. It is not pleasing to you, I know full well, but one which it is very dangerous for you to forget."

"I know. I listened to them. Yes, I was there one time when they plotted. But I had to know. I had to stop them from harming you. I had to find out what they were going to do . . . to make sure they were not going to harm you."

"Fate was kind to me on that occasion, Jemmy . . . taking me from Newmarket before the appointed time. Bad luck for those who were working against me, but we must understand that Fate cannot please everyone all the time."

"You must believe me . . ."

"Should the King be told by his bastard what he must do?"

Monmouth winced every time the King used the term. But I knew why Charles repeated it. It was to impress on this young man who he was and that he, the King, insisted that he should be known as such.

"If you will not believe me," said Monmouth pathetically, "I must ask your leave to retire from court."

"A sojourn abroad would be preferable to one in the Tower, I doubt not. And there is one other with whom you should intercede— your uncle, the Duke of York."

"I will go to him if he will receive me, but it was to you I came first."

The King was smiling at me. "He is a pretty boy, is he not?" he said. "He pleads well . . . so well, that he has an air of truth about him."

"It is because I speak the truth," said Monmouth. "Father, I beg of you. I have been foolish. I have been reckless. But never . . . never . . . I swear, in my life would I have harmed you."

Charles was silent.

He said: "You should see the Duke of York. He is as concerned in this as I am. See if you can make your peace with him."

"I will," said Monmouth earnestly.

"And then," said the King, "bring him here to me. As we were both to be the victims, it is only fitting that we should decide this matter between us."

Monmouth knelt and kissed the King's hand and, after doing the same to me, he went off to seek an audience with the Duke of York.

I knew of course that he would be forgiven.

Charles saw him again when the Duke of York was present. As I had predicted, Monmouth was forgiven, but as it was clear that he had been aware of the plot and had remained silent about it, it seemed desirable that he should stay away from the court for some time.

No charges were brought against him and after a while he set sail for the continent.

THERE WAS A MESSAGE from Portugal. My brother Alfonso had died at Sintra. Although it was many years since I had seen him, and he had been living in a kind of shadow land for so long, I was sad, remembering our childhood when he and Pedro had been little boys playing happily together; and I was sad thinking of my mother and what she would have thought of one of her sons taking the other's throne . . . and his wife.

I believed Pedro must be remorseful now that his brother was dead, but at least Alfonso would be at peace.

The court went into mourning for my brother; and when it was over we slipped back into the old way of life.

Charles was as enamored as he had ever been of Louise de Keroualle. The fascination she exerted over him amazed me. The playactress Nell Gwynne was still important to him; and now that I was no longer in danger, I saw less of him.

The winter at that time was one of the harshest any living person remembered. The cold was intense. Never before had the Thames been frozen so hard. An ox was roasted on it and people crowded onto the hard ice to watch the spectacle.

Of course, the weather brought great hardship to the poor. Transport was impossible and ships could not get into the ports. There were prayers for relief in the churches, but it seemed that the frost continued for a very long time.

But spring was with us at last. Charles had not been very well for some time. He had always been so strong that he had been able to shrug off minor troubles, and so accustomed to perfect health that he was impatient with ailments. He hated to admit that he was feeling less than well and it seemed an affront to him that he should be so.

I could see that he had lost some of his vigor during that cruel winter.

Charles had not seemed well during the day. However, he supped as he often did with the Duchess of Portsmouth.

The following morning Lord Aylesbury, one of the Gentlemen of his Bedchamber, called on me in agitation.

"Your Majesty," he said, "the King is unwell."

I stood up in alarm, for Aylesbury looked very grave.

"What is wrong?" I asked.

"Dr. King is with him now. He has bled him."

"Bled him?" I repeated blankly. "But . . . why?"

"The King was up early, as was his wont, Your Majesty. He went to his closet and was there longer than usual, and we became uneasy. When he came out he seemed to stagger . . . and then fell."

"What was it? A fit?"

"I cannot say, Your Majesty. Dr. King seemed upset and said that bleeding was necessary without delay."

"I must go to him at once," I said.

When I reached his bedchamber I saw Charles sitting in a chair. He looked unlike himself . . . and when I came near I saw that his features were distorted.

"Oh . . . Charles," I murmured.

He attempted to smile reassuringly.

Dr. King ordered that a warm iron should be put on his head. I thought he was dying. He could not be. He had always been so strong. He looked at me helplessly . . . as though he were apologizing for his weakness.

The Duke and Duchess of York appeared. James fell on his knees beside Charles's chair and I saw real anguish in his face. I had always known of his affection for his brother. Poor James, he must be feeling many a qualm. He knew what Charles's death would mean to him; he would be thrust into a position of danger, for many were opposed to him.

As the news spread through the street there was melancholy throughout the city. It was more than a rejection of James; it was a sign of the people's love for the King. He was their Merry Monarch; he had come back and saved them from years of repression under Puritan rule. No matter what he had done, he had amused them with his amorous affairs; he had enchanted them with his smiles and his affable ways with all had won their hearts. There was never a king more loved by his subjects than Charles.

During the day he recovered a little.

The news seeped out and bells were rang. "He is recovered," said the people. "He is going to live. Long may he reign."

He was put into his bed and rested there, sitting up in bed, looking tired, but his features were no longer distorted and his speech was clear.

I sat by the bed and he held my hand, smiling at me. I was overcome with emotion.

"You are better," I said. "You are going to recover."

He lifted his shoulders characteristically.

"Life would be so empty without you," I said.

"No," he replied. "You will fill it."

I said: "I have been foolish at times. I beg your pardon, Charles, I wish I had been better."

His lips twisted into a wry smile. "You beg my pardon," he said. "My poor dear Catherine. It is I who should beg yours . . . and I do . . . with all my heart."

That night he had another seizure . . . more violent than the first . . . and we knew then that the end was near.

The Archbishop of Canterbury with the Bishops of London, Bath and Wells, and Durham were sent for.

There could be no hope now. Services were held in all the churches, and there was a hushed scene in the streets; people stood about and talked in whispers.

I asked the Duchess of York to come to me. We had always been good friends and I wanted her advice.

I said to her: "I know that the King was at heart a Catholic. He had contracted with Louis to be one and turn the country to Catholicism when the opportunity arose."

"Louis paid him well for that," said the Duchess, "and Charles accepted the payments knowing full well that the opportunity would never arise in his lifetime."

"It has now," I said.

"What do you mean? The King is dying."

"I know that. He would want to receive the rites of the Catholic Church."

She stared at me. "You are sure?"

I nodded. "I want you to explain to James."

"I will," she said.

I felt relieved. It was what he would have wished. It would be a secret, of course. What would the people's reaction be if they knew their beloved King had died in the Catholic faith?

I saw James. He was haggard with anxiety. He said to me: "He shall have a priest. If they kill me for it, I will do this for his sake."

I thanked him with deep gratitude.

→>-<←

TIME WAS PASSING. It was five days since Charles had had the first seizure. He was in great pain and all the remedies that had been heard of had been tried on him.

He retained his humor and asked the pardon of all those about him for being an unconscionable long time a-dying.

"Oh God," I prayed, "how shall I live without him?"

The sixth day dawned—that black sixth of February—and the first seizure had taken place on the first of the month.

There was no hope now. I myself had been ill. I had fainted and my nose had bled profusely. Dr. King said that I must keep to my bed. That was impossible. I must be ready, lest he should call for me.

The King's bedchamber was crowded with people . . . churchmen, peers, doctors, ambassadors . . . they must all be there to see the end of the King.

He needed to rest . . . to sleep . . . but a king cannot die like an ordinary man. They tried more remedies . . . and he lay there, dead pigeons at his feet, a warm iron on his head.

"Please let them leave him in peace," I prayed.

The time was near and the Duke of York, assuming authority because he was almost King by this time, cleared the room. Father Huddleston was brought to Charles. He had had the forethought to dress himself as a clergyman of the Church of England and was taken up by a secret staircase, and Charles was given the sacrament in the rites of the Catholic Church.

I rejoiced in this. I had always hoped that one day he would come to the true faith in his lifetime. He had, however, come to it on the point of death.

He seemed greatly comforted. I was close to him and I saw the peace settle on his face.

"Catherine," he said gently, and I knew in my heart that he was thinking of me as I had been when I first came to England almost twenty-three years ago . . . innocent, inexperienced, already in love with the mythical prince who had lived only in my imagination.

I said, as I had on that other occasion: "Forgive me for my faults, my stupidity, my foolishness."

He shook his head and there were tears in his eyes.

"You did no wrong," he said. "And I am guilty of many offences against you. I beg of you, sweet Catherine, forgive me."

I was choked with emotion.

I whispered: "I cannot bear to lose you."

He smiled at me sadly.

James was kneeling at the bedside.

"Farewell, brother," said Charles. "I wish you well. You have been a good brother to me."

James was openly weeping.

"I would it were I," he said. "You know, brother, I would willingly die for you."

"James . . . James . . . my time has come . . . yours is far away. May God go with you, James. If I have ever seemed harsh, it was for your own sake."

"I know, I know."

"James, have a care . . . of yourself . . . and those I love. Be good to the Queen . . . the Duchess of Portsmouth . . . see that she is well-treated. And my children . . . James. They need your care. Let not poor Nelly starve . . ."

He lived through the night and the next morning he awoke at six. Two hours later he ceased to breathe.

The King was dead and on that day the Privy Council proclaimed his successor: James II.

REBELLION

I HAVE LOST COUNT OF THE DAYS THAT FOLLOWED. FOR SO long he had been the center of my life, and now that he was taken from me I felt bereft, drifting, vaguely wondering what life held for me. I did not greatly care at that time.

The new King and Queen were kind to me. James had truly loved his brother. He was a good man at heart. He had many weaknesses, of course, but there was a fundamental kindness in him of which I had always been aware. Charles had thought he lacked the power to govern and had been very apprehensive for him; but let me say he was kind to me—and kindness, I have always held to be the greatest of the virtues.

He visited me almost immediately, which was good of him, because he was beset by many anxieties. It was not that he was unprepared for the position in which he found himself; but no one had expected Charles to die for many years, and although he had said he had been an unconscionable long time a-dying, it had been barely a week between his first unexpected attack and his death. We had, of course, lived through the troublous time of the Popish and Rye House Plots and there had been a constant possibility of death . . . but it had been unexpected when it came.

Yet, in spite of everything, James had time to spare for me.

"Dear sister," he said. "I know you loved him well. I loved him too. He was the best brother a man ever had. I cannot hope to be like him."

We wept together and James went on: "You must stay here in your apartments at Whitehall until you feel well enough to move."

I remembered then that I was no longer Queen of England. The Duchess of York bore the title now, and I was occupying those apartments set aside for the Queen. I had become the Queen Dowager.

"I had forgotten," I said apologetically. "I must leave them."

"No . . . no, not until you are prepared to do so. The Queen joins me in saying that she hopes you will act on your inclination and not feel there is any need for haste."

"That is gracious," I said. "How is the Queen?"

"She is well enough," he said. "As well as any of us can be at this sad time. She hopes that when you have recovered a little you and she will meet."

I thanked him and forgot a little of my own sorrow in my deep pity for him. He was so overwhelmed with cares; and I wondered how he would fare . . . a proclaimed Catholic king of a Protestant country.

I tried to arouse myself. Life must go on. I must make up my mind what I should do without Charles. What place had I here? I had lost my poor Donna Maria, but for a long time she had been ailing and she had never made any attempt to adjust herself to the English way of life. She had been very critical of Charles's infidelities. Poor Maria. But at least she had been a link with my native land.

I wondered if I ought to return there. What should I do? There had been so many changes. My mother dead, Alfonso too. There was only Pedro and his wife . . . who had been Alfonso's wife. Would there be a place for me?

I discussed the matter with Lord Feversham, who controlled my household affairs. He was a handsome man, dignified and sympathetic.

"It is perhaps a little early to make plans, Your Majesty," he said. "You are not well enough to think of traveling, and His Majesty, King James has given you permission to use these apartments until you wish to move. May I suggest that you go to Somerset House? It has always been a favorite residence of Your Majesty."

"You may be right, Lord Feversham," I said.

"Then, of course, if Your Majesty wished to retire for a while from the court, there is the convent at Hammersmith."

"Oh yes," I said, thinking of the convent with which I had been connected for some time. A sojourn with the nuns would be very desirable. There could be complete peace. I could pray and ask for guidance. I could perhaps reshape my life.

"Thank you, Lord Feversham," I said. "You understand so well."

"Madam," he said earnestly, "I would give my life to serve you."

He looked at me with great affection, and in that moment he reminded me of Edward Montague who had shown a similar care for me . . . and perhaps because of it had lost his life, for if people had not noticed it and commented on it, he would have remained my Master of Horse and never been present at the battle during which he had been killed.

For two months I remained undecided at Whitehall, and then I moved my household to Somerset House.

I WAS RELYING more and more on Lord Feversham. He would talk to me of state affairs and was very frank, knowing that he could safely be so with me.

"There is a certain uneasiness," he said. "The Whigs remain quiet . . . which could be ominous. In my opinion, they will be watching very carefully for any sign of Catholic influence in the country. That is something they will try hard to prevent."

"How can they?"

"There are means."

"They will be loyal to the King."

"Let us pray for that, Your Majesty."

"But he has given his support to the Church of England," I said. "Did he not announce this in his speech to the Privy Council?"

"He did. But on Easter Sunday he attended the Catholic Church openly."

"But he has long made clear his support of it."

"That is so, Your Majesty. But he is now the King, and the ceremony of that visit to the church was noted. It was an official occasion."

"You sound apprehensive, Lord Feversham."

"I fear conflict, Your Majesty. The last is not long behind us, and we know the effects of that one."

"The late King often spoke of it. He was determined the like should never happen again."

"He was wise. I pray God that . . ."

He did not finish, but I knew he feared for James.

I wanted to know what was happening, which showed I was being taken out of the lethargy which had been with me since Charles's death. I was no less unhappy, but at least I was interested in what was going on about me. My own future was hazy and bleak. For so long Charles had dominated my life . . . even before I had met him. I could not believe that those days were over forever.

I was very grateful to my Lord Chamberlain, who was doing so much to draw me out of my melancholy.

IC WAS ONLY LOGICAL CHAC, now we had a Catholic monarch on the throne, the position of Titus Oates must be a little uncertain. He had been very quiet of late and had indeed lost a great deal of his popularity over the last few years.

Yet I was entirely surprised when one day Lord Feversham came to me and said: "Oates has been arrested."

"On what charge?" I asked.

"On that of perjury, Your Majesty."

"There must be a wealth of evidence to support that," I said.

"Your Majesty speaks truth."

"Who *is* prosecuting him?"

"Judge George Jeffreys."

"I have heard of him, I think."

"That does not surprise me, Your Majesty. He has dealt with several cases in which Oates has appeared, and always seemed to favor him. He is a clever judge—amusing, witty . . . but a hard drinker, often seeming to relish the punishments he has to inflict. I think he is open to seek advantages for himself and has little sympathy for those who can be of no use to him. He likes, it is said, to 'give a lick with the rough of his tongue' to those he has to sentence."

"He sounds most unpleasant."

"I am in agreement with Your Majesty, but it is said that he can show a certain charm to those with whom it would be an advantage to do so."

"And he is to try Oates?"

"It would appear so."

"I shall be most interested to hear the verdict."

"I will report to Your Majesty if I discover anything."

As a compliment to the new King, Judge Jeffreys found Titus Oates guilty. Not that that needed any great effort.

Oates was fined, stripped of his ecclesiastical robes and sentenced to stand in the pillory; he was whipped through the streets, starting at Aldgate and finishing at Newgate. That was not all. Two days later there was to be a further whipping from Newgate to Tyburn. For the rest of his life he was to be a prisoner.

It was harsh, but it had to be remembered that he had caused the deaths of thirty-five innocent people.

I felt almost sorry for the man when Lord Feversham told me how Jack Ketch, the notorious executioner, known for his delight in prolonging the suffering of his victims, together with his men, laid a whip of six thongs on the bare back of Titus Oates, and the people flocked into the streets to see this once proud man brought low.

He must have been almost dead when they brought him to his cell; but James had refused to stop the second flogging, although it was said that at the first Oates had been almost flayed alive.

A just reward perhaps for all the misery he had caused to countless people, besides those who had lost their lives because of him.

IT WAS JUNE. Charles had been dead four months. I was wondering whether James, who had since his accession shown great moderation, might have learned wisdom from his brother, and while he remained a Catholic, be able to maintain peace in the realm.

He had shown no desire so far to force his religion on his subjects, but I guessed the Whigs were alert and at the first sign of James's favour toward the Catholics, there would be trouble.

I was alarmed when Lord Feversham told me that Archibald Campbell, the Earl of Argyll, had been arrested in Scotland.

Argyll had come from Amsterdam, where he had been in the company of the Duke of Monmouth, in three ships in which were three hundred men. His plan was to collect more on his arrival. He was displaying banners on which were written the words "For God and Religion against Popery, Tyranny, Arbitrary Government and Erastianism."

In Scotland he gathered more men, but unfortunately for him, one of them had been captured and confessed that he had come with Argyll to turn the King off the throne and give the crown to the Duke of Monmouth.

The plot was therefore prematurely disclosed and those who were involved took fright and deserted.

"They would have had no chance against the King's forces," said Lord Feversham. "Poor Argyll! His venture did not last, and he found himself alone, and was captured and brought to Edinburgh Castle."

"How could he have hoped to succeed?" I asked.

" 'Tis my belief that he had no thought of attacking until Monmouth arrived."

"Surely Monmouth cannot be so foolish as to think he can overthrow the King?"

"He will insist that his father was married to Lucy Walter."

"But the King denied it so often."

"The King is dead."

"You cannot think that such a venture would succeed?"

"I am not sure. It depends on how many will support him."

"But Charles always swore that he was illegitimate."

"He is a Protestant."

"But if he has no right . . ."

"So much depends on what the people want."

"Do you think King James will give up lightly because the people want it?"

"Do not the people always have their choice . . . in time?"

"Did they want Cromwell . . . and the Parliament to govern them?"

"Cromwell was strong. He had many supporters."

"And you think if he had not died, the King would not have been recalled?"

"That may have been, but at the time he came to power, the majority of the people wanted Cromwell."

"And if they want the Duke of Monmouth as their King . . . ?"

"Your Majesty, I should tremble if that came to pass." He looked at me anxiously.

I said, "Please, always be frank with me. I shall know, Lord Feversham, that what you have to say to me is between us two."

"Thank you, Your Majesty. I shall always tell you what is in my mind."

Later he told me that the Earl of Argyll had been beheaded in Edinburgh. His head was placed on a spike at the west end of the

Tolbooth, but, before that, came the news that the Duke of Monmouth had landed at Lyme Regis.

THE DRAMA HAD BEGUN. Jemmy had come for that which all his life he had coveted. Poor Jemmy, I feared for him. I had so often felt that he was far from the valiant ruler he had imagined himself to be. He had mistaken his charm and good looks for kingly qualities. He had not inherited his father's wisdom.

I waited eagerly for news. I was fond of Jemmy. There was something lovable about him and, in some ways, he reminded me of his father. How often had I wished that he had been my son! How much easier my life would have been. Now I feared deeply for him. He would have to learn that charm of manner does not make up for a lack of wisdom.

I understood what his plan was. Argyll, as a Scot, was to capture Scotland for him, while he took England, and as the West Country was strongly Protestant, that seemed an ideal spot for him to begin his campaign.

Lord Feversham kept me in touch with the news. These tête-à-têtes had become a custom with us, and from him I learned much more than I could from the gossip of the ladies or the scraps of news which came to me from other sources.

"Monmouth has had a proclamation read in the market place," Lord Feversham told me. "He announces that he now heads the Protestant forces in the kingdom and is the legitimate heir to the throne."

"What will become of him?" I asked.

"I fear the impulsive young man will lose his head ere long."

"King Charles would have been greatly distressed. He loved him devotedly. I knew there was discord at times, but that was all due to the Duke's recklessness and ambition."

"As is the present situation, Your Majesty. Oh, what a tragedy for this country when the King passed on."

"You are right. It is a tragedy for us all."

The next news I heard was that a Bill of Attainder had been issued against Monmouth and there was a price of five thousand pounds on his head.

Monmouth retaliated by marching to Taunton, where he was proclaimed King. He had gathered an army of seven thousand men and declared the Westminster Parliament was traitorous, and he had the effrontery to put a price on King James's head. He swore he was the rightful heir to the throne, for his mother had been married to King Charles, and in time he would prove this. I am sure he believed this would be so, for there would be no hesitation in producing the little box with its documents once he had defeated James.

At Bridgwater he was proclaimed King. Then he went to Glastonbury and Shepton Mallet. The West Country was with him.

I could imagine his bitter disappointment—for I knew him so well—when Bath refused to surrender to him and when the troops he was expecting did not arrive. By that time he would have heard of Argyll's capture. Poor Jemmy! He had no great stamina for the tremendous task which he had set himself.

His men, fearing retaliation, were deserting in hundreds. There was one great hope. The peasantry was gathering round him shouting "No Popery! King Monmouth for us!" He marched back to Bridgwater to meet his new army: unskilled men, brandishing their scythes and pitchforks.

I hoped that he would escape to Amsterdam. What his reception would be there, I could not imagine.

Churchill marched westwards with two thousand regular soldiers, and fifteen hundred more joined him from Wiltshire. They encamped on Sedgemoor.

The battle was swift, as was inevitable. Monmouth's west country yokels were unfit to stand up to trained soldiers. Monmouth was no Churchill, and very soon more than half of his army were lying dead on the field. The enterprise had failed.

I tried to make excuses for Jemmy. He was only a boy, playing at being a king.

He made his excuses for flight from the field. Lord Grey had urged him to leave, for he must save his life to fight again for the cause. Whatever happened, he left his poor sad army and fled with Grey.

I heard later how they had ridden hard toward the Bristol Channel, how they had to leave their exhausted horses and travel on foot, how they disguised themselves as farm laborers.

About a month after his arrival in England, Monmouth was captured in a ditch in which he had hidden himself under bracken.

King Monmouth's reign was over.

He was brought to the Tower to await his trial.

I COULD NOT STOP THINKING how saddened Charles would have
been. He would have forgiven his son, as he had so often in the past.
But Jemmy had never attempted any prank of such magnitude before. The slitting of Sir John Coventry's nose, the murder of the beadle, suspicion of being involved in the Rye House Plot . . . that had all
been forgiven. But this was an attempt on his uncle's crown, and his
father was no longer there to shield him.

How I wished he had not acted in his way! If he had been wiser he
would have known the enterprise could not but fail. There would be
so many who would never accept him as Charles's legitimate son—for
he himself knew, as well as any of us, that that was false.

His courage failed him. He had believed in success and had never
considered what failure would mean. Now he was faced with reality
and he was a very frightened young man.

I was surprised to receive a letter from him. He had written from
the Tower. He knew of my regard for him, he wrote, and, being so
close to his father, I had been aware of the love between them.

I smiled a little sadly. Indeed, I knew of the King's love for his son.
I could almost hear Charles's voice: "Jemmy has some regard for me,
but a greater fondness for my crown."

James had always been my friend, Monmouth wrote. He would
listen to me. He, Monmouth, believed that if he could speak to
James . . . he might be able to explain and let him see how contrite
he was.

I let the letter fall from my hand.

It was true James had always been a friend to me, but what Monmouth had done was beyond forgiveness. Did he think James would
forgive him, and give him a chance to try again?

I did not think so.

I spent a sleepless night, and when I did doze, I fancied that
Charles was close. "He was my son," I seemed to hear him say. "He
was a foolish, impulsive boy."

And when I arose I decided I would attempt to see James.

I was surprised that, in view of all the state matters which must be occupying him at this time, he granted me an interview.

He greeted me warmly and asked how I was faring.

I told him I was living peacefully at Somerset House and occasionally spent a few days at Hammersmith. Then I came straight to the point.

"I have had a letter from the Duke of Monmouth."

I saw the surprise in his face.

"He is asking me to beg you to see him."

"He has been a traitor. He was to his father . . . and now to me."

I said: "He could never harm you. He has not the power."

"He could surround himself with those who have more sense."

"That is true. He will lose his head, I suppose."

"What else? He deserves it. Perhaps he should have lost it before . . . and would have if Charles had not been so soft with him. He was implicated in the Rye House Plot. He would have murdered his own father."

"He swore that he would not have done that."

"As now doubtless he will swear that he came over for a friendly visit."

"You have always been so good to me, James. I shall never forget the time I arrived, when you made me feel so welcome. Thank you, James."

"My dear Catherine, I have done little for you."

"If Charles were here, he would ask you to see Jemmy."

"Charles is not here. If he had been, this would not have happened."

"If you listened to him . . . you know he is only a foolish boy . . . not to be feared."

"He came to invade. He brought men and ammunition. He is a featherweight . . . but those behind him are not."

"He is your nephew."

"Charles had some odd bedfellows."

I looked at him and he flushed slightly. He had perhaps some equally odd ones. Charles would have laughed and made some witty remark, but it was not in James to do so. Yet I thought I had touched a tender chord in him. His mistresses had been almost as numerous as Charles's, and some of them had been undoubtedly unusual.

He said suddenly: "He has to die, Catherine. There is no help for it. I will send for him, but it will do nothing for him."

"But at least he will know that you have answered his plea. Thank you, James. You are good to me."

He said with emotion: "Charles asked me to care for you. I will, Catherine, I want you to know that, if I can help you at any time . . ."

"I do know it, and I thank you from the bottom of my heart."

I knew he was thinking of Charles, as I was, and it was because of him that James would see his son.

HE DID SEE MONMOUTH, but I knew that the interview would not save him. James was right when he implied that the young man would always be a menace. There was only one way for a wise monarch to deal with such as Monmouth, for he could never be trusted not to rouse rebellion again.

Monmouth was not of the stuff of which leaders are made. James told me what had taken place.

It had been pathetic. Charles had said God help England when James became King. What would he have said of Monmouth?

James told me that Monmouth had begged for his life. He declared he had been led astray. If his life were spared he would become a Catholic. That was the ultimate betrayal of all those men who had fought with him . . . those poor peasants who had picked up their scythes to fight for him and what they believed was the true faith.

How could he?

I could hear Charles making excuses. "He is a poor frightened boy. He is fighting for his life. He will jettison everything for it . . . his faith, his hopes of the crown, his charity toward those poor ignorant souls who came to fight with him."

Alas, poor Jemmy!

James had granted the interview but refused to save his life.

They took him from his prison to the Tower and before he laid his head upon the block he told the watching crowd that he was a member of the Church of England.

Jack Ketch, whether by accident or design, did not make a clean job of the execution. He struck five blows at Monmouth's head before it was severed from his body.

And so . . . the end of Jemmy's dreams.

IMMEDIACELY AFCER the battle of Sedgemoor, the judges, led by George Jeffreys, set out on the circuit of the West Country.

I believe that those trials, which became known as the Bloody Assizes, will never be forgotten.

Jeffreys was at his most brutal and I was overcome with pity for those simple young men who, with their scythes and pitchforks, had joined Monmouth's cause in an excess of religious fervor. Little could they have thought when they boldly went into action what their end would be.

Jeffreys delighted in torment and never before had he shown such cruelty as he did toward those people. Blithely he sentenced them to death, and, what seemed to me even worse, more than eight hundred were either sold into slavery or whipped and imprisoned.

The lamentation throughout those small towns of the West Country was great; and it was said that those with wealthy relations and friends, who could pay Jeffreys for the favor of saving their lives, were the only ones who escaped.

The rumor was that Jeffreys emerged from the Bloody Assizes a much richer man than he went in.

Was this the manner in which people were to be treated under the new reign? King Charles would never have allowed it. And when Jeffreys came to London he was greeted warmly by the King who thanked him for his services and awarded him the post of Chancellor.

When I looked back over those years, I came to the conclusion that that may have hastened the King's downfall.

THE WARMING-PAN BABY

THE DAYS SEEMED LONG. DURING EVERY ONE OF THEM I thought of Charles and wished that I were back in the past, even those times when I had had to watch his dalliances with his mistresses. I would rather endure that jealous resentment, that heart-break, than be without him.

I tried hard to find compensations. I was thankful for the kindness of the King and Queen. I could sympathize with the Queen, who had had several children, all of whom had died. An heir was desperately needed. Why was it that queens were so tormented in this way? How well I understood the feelings of Mary Beatrice.

James had made it clear that I was the second lady of the court, preceded only by the Queen. He was eager to let me know he remembered his promise to Charles. He was at heart a sentimental, kindly man—but alas for him, not meant to be a king.

I was fond of music and found solace in it. I gave concerts at Somerset House. I had always liked to dance, although I was not graceful enough to excel at it, so we often danced. I was passionately fond of card games and I indulged in all those pastimes more frequently than I had during Charles's lifetime.

Lord Feversham was in constant attendance, and was a great comfort to me, until I suddenly realized what malicious interpretation could be put on an innocent friendship.

I discovered this when I heard two of the lower servants below my window—out of sight of me, as I was of them.

They were discussing some incident which had happened among my ladies.

"And where was the Dowager Queen?" asked one.

"With the Dowager King, of course. Could you not guess?"

They giggled.

"The Dowager King?" I was bewildered.

Then I understood. They meant Lord Feversham. So that was what they called him. I was horrified. Memories of Edward Montague and the vicious gossip about my friendship with him came back to me.

Of course, I did see Lord Feversham often; his company was agreeable to me. And they had noticed.

I felt sick and angry. What lies were they building up? To how many in my household was Lord Feversham known as the "Dowager King"?

I thought then: What is there for me here? They were going to spoil my friendship with Lord Feversham now. They were going to whisper all sorts of slander about me.

Charles had dismissed Montague, not because he believed in the insinuations, but because of the harm they could do to me.

I made up my mind in that moment. I was going home. I could no longer endure it here.

But could I find peace in my native land? The King of Portugal was my brother. It would be a sorrowful homecoming, because of memories of my mother . . . and poor Alfonso. But Pedro *was* my brother. Indeed I often thought of him as my *little* brother, and there was a family bond between us.

On impulse I sat down and wrote to him.

I told him I wanted to come home.

PEDRO'S RESPONSE was immediate.

He wrote that Count Castelmelhor would be coming to England to arrange my departure.

On the death of Alfonso, Castelmelhor had returned to Portugal, made his peace with Pedro and was now in his service. I looked forward to seeing my old friend; but I had written to Pedro on impulse and was beginning to regret it.

For so long this country had been my home. The King and Queen were kind to me. I looked forward to my concerts . . . and my card games.

Manners and customs were easygoing here. I remembered the formality of life in Portugal. Did I want to leave familiar surroundings for somewhere which after all these years would be a strange place to me?

When the Count arrived in England, I was still very uncertain. I had come to the conclusion that I had taken the remark I had overheard about the "Dowager King" too seriously. It was merely the idle chatter of servants.

How understanding the Count was! I was able to open my heart to him, and he knew so much of what had happened to me. He reminded me that Portugal was not a rich country; one might say it was impoverished. As Queen of England, I should have certain revenues, he presumed. I told him that I had, although the marriage settlement, which had been promised to me, had never been paid in full or punctually. A great deal was owing to me. The Count said this should be paid in full before I left the country.

I had not thought about the money before, and I think I was so uncertain about leaving that I grasped every excuse to delay my departure.

This opened up a certain controversy. The Earl of Halifax, who was looking after my financial affairs, approached the Earl of Clarendon—who was the son of the first Earl whom I had known on my arrival. There was a suggestion from Halifax that Clarendon had been guilty of falsifying the accounts.

Clarendon, who was, of course, the King's brother-in-law, immediately put the matter before James. The result was that the King summoned me to his presence.

As soon as I saw him I noticed a coldness in his manner toward me.

"It surprises me," he said, "that you should have decided to leave the country without consulting me."

"Your Majesty, I thought the matter would have been of little concern to you, so weighed down by state matters as you are at this time."

"Of a certainty it is of concern to me. So you wish to leave us."

"I am not sure," I said.

"Yet you have written to your brother and he has sent Count Castelmelhor."

"I wrote to him in a moment of despondency. They come to me now and then, and I felt I had to get away . . . to start anew."

He looked at me with some compassion and I think he understood, for he said, more gently: "And now you are unsure?"

"Yes."

"And this case . . . against my brother-in-law, is it wise?"

"They seem to have taken it out of my hands."

"Clarendon has been accused of misappropriation of funds."

"I did not wish to accuse him."

"You will be ill advised to proceed with this case. But it is the law that you may do so, and I have no right to interfere with the law."

"I understand," I said.

"And, Catherine," he went on, "it is for you to decide whether you wish to return to Portugal or stay. For my part, you will be welcome here for as long as you want to remain."

ALCHOUGH CLARENDON had been found guity of misappropriation of funds, the lawsuit was a mistake. It branded me as a greedy, grasping woman—although I had only asked for what was legally mine.

People's attitude changed toward me. I was no longer regarded as the meek woman who had taken a complacent attitude toward her husband's infidelities, and sought to be on good terms with those about her. However, to be truthful, I did need the money which was due to me.

I had begun to realize that I must make provision for myself, for if I did decide to go to Portugal, I must be in a position to do so in some sort of comfort. Charles had been careless about money and consequently he had been in perpetual need of it.

I determined I should not be like that. I had to go back to Portugal and I did not want to throw myself on the charity of my brother.

If that was being hard and grasping—then I was. But in my own defense, I must say that I did not want to be a burden to others.

But the King, sadly, remained a little cooler than he had been toward me. And I think the people were only too ready to criticize me.

So . . . I would say that the court case was a mistake and I should not have been carried along by my advisors.

IN JUNE OF CHAT YEAR 1688, three years after the death of Charles, the Queen was about to give birth to a child.

There was an air of excitement everywhere. This child was of the greatest importance. We were fast moving toward that situation which bedevilled so many kings and queens—the inability to produce an heir. Therefore there were great expectations and fears of disappointment.

It was very important that the birth of the child should be witnessed, for the country was at this time in a state of unrest.

James's rule was giving cause for dissasdsfaction and uneasiness. There was too much favor shown to Catholics and people were constantly referring to the golden days when King Charles was on the throne.

It seemed that Charles's prophecies about James were coming true.

Accompanied by one or two of the married ladies of my household, I came to the place and was taken to the bedchamber where the birth was to take place.

What an ordeal for Mary Beatrice, to have her agonies witnessed by so many. But it was the royal custom, and in this case certainly proved to be a necessity.

How glad I was when at last I heard the cry of the child, and to my great joy, and that of everyone, it was a boy and looked likely to survive.

He was named James Francis Edward; and seven days after his birth he was christened and I was appointed his godmother.

IT WAS SOON AFTER the birth that the wicked rumors started.

There were many who were planning that the King should go, and, now that he had a son to follow him, there could be difficulties, for if the father were deposed, the son would be there to take the crown.

I believe that to be the reason for the rumors, because they certainly were absurd and without foundation.

Who first put the story about, I did not know, but very soon it was talked of throughout the court and in the streets. I was sure that the whole of country would soon be discussing it.

It was said that while the attendants crowded round the Queen's bed, one of the King's trusted servants had been standing by with a warming-pan in which was a live and healthy baby boy.

The Queen, they said, had given birth to a stillborn child; the warming-pan had been thrust into the bed and under cover of the bedclothes the infants had been changed and the healthy one brought out as the Queen's child, while the stillborn child was hastily put into the warming-pan and taken away.

It was a preposterous story but, as Charles often said, people believe what they want to. Such a foolish rumor should have been dismissed immediately, but such was the unpopularity of the King and Queen that it persisted.

It was surprising that so much credence should have been given to it that it was necessary to call a meeting of the Privy Council, that all those who had been present at the birth could give evidence of having witnessed it.

I was one of these.

What an extraordinary occasion it was!

The King was present and I was given a chair beside him. The ladies who had been in the lying-in chamber were also present.

The King spoke to us and the Council listened attentively. "It grieves me," he said, "that there has been this necessity of bringing you here. There has been much malicious gossip concerning my son, the Prince of Wales. There are those who maintain that the child which bears that title is not mine. Your Majesty, my lords and ladies here today, I am asking you who were present at the birth to declare what you know of it."

I spoke first. "I was sent for when the Queen began her labor. I was in the bedchamber with her when the Prince of Wales was born." And I went on to say that I had seen the Prince of Wales born and that the story of the warming-pan was an utter lie.

The others gave evidence in the same vein and what we said was written down and afterward we all signed the document.

That should have been enough, for we all declared that there had been only one baby and he was certainly the Prince of Wales. But the rumor persisted and people continued to whisper about the warming-pan baby.

AS THAT YEAR PASSED a certain menace crept into the atmosphere. If James was aware of it, he did not change his ways. He heard Mass in a manner which could only be called ostentatious. He prosecuted the convenanters in Scotland; he was at odds with the Church and seven bishops were prosecuted for seditious libel.

When they were declared "not guilty" there were loud cheers

throughout the court; and when the people waiting in the streets heard the verdict there was loud singing and cheering and the entire city was in uproar.

This should have shown James how unpopular his policies were, and he should have known the English would never accept Catholicism, and that if he persisted in trying to promote it, his days would be numbered.

Oh James, I thought, why cannot you understand? Why do you do this foolish, dangerous thing? He was like his father, who had defied Parliament by his insistence on the Divine Right of Kings.

And as the year progressed, it was becoming more and more clear that the people were deciding they would not have James.

The next in line of succession, if one did not count the little Prince of Wales, was James's elder daughter Mary, and she was married to Protestant William of Orange.

It had to come. The country demanded it.

A deputation was sent to Holland inviting William of Orange, with his wife Mary, to depose James and take the throne.

LORD FEVERSHAM CAME TO ME.

He said: "Your Majesty, you know this means war."

"War!" I repeated blankly.

"Most likely. The King will never relinquish the throne without a struggle."

"The people will not have him."

"He is the King," said Lord Feversham. "I have given my oath to serve him. I must say good-bye to you and join King James."

"This is tragic," I cried.

"It has been coming for some time."

"Do you think the Prince of Orange will accept?"

Lord Feversham smiled. "It is what he has been waiting for since the death of Charles."

"I trust the King will come safely out of this."

"I promise Your Majesty that I shall do my best to assist him in that."

November was with us when news came that William of Orange had landed at Torbay.

WILLIAM AND MARY

THERE FOLLOWED A TIME OF UNCERTAINTY WHEN THERE was chaos in the streets of London, and mobs were always eager to find an excuse to attack the homes of rich and well-known Catholics. I wondered if they would turn on me.

I think James must have realized from the first that he was going to lose his throne. It was typical of him that, after the first shock, he would accept this in an almost resigned manner as the inevitable sacrifice he had had to make for his faith.

I was filled with pity for him and his Queen, so recently proud of their little son.

James would have been desolate by the news of the desertion of those on whom he had relied. John Churchill was the first, and he had most of the army with him; others followed. James's son-in-law, the Prince of Denmark, had declared for William.

The most cruel desertion was by his daughter Anne. He had called on her for comfort, only to find that, in the company of Sarah Churchill, she had left, which meant that she too was not on his side.

I remembered well his love for his daughters. I had often seen him playing with them when they were little more than babies. Now Mary, who had been his favorite, was the wife of the man who had come against him. He would expect her to stand with her husband. But Anne . . . his little Anne . . . influenced no doubt by Sarah Churchill, had left him and gone over to the enemy.

It may have been that after that he had little heart for the fight. How could he, with only a few friends to help him?

Perhaps even then, if he had given up his faith, he might have reinstated himself; but that was something he would never do. Knowing how precarious his position was, he had sent the Queen and her little baby to France.

I wondered what would become of me. Charles's niece Mary would now be Queen. I remembered her as she had been on her wedding day—a tearful bride, dreading marriage, particularly marriage to William, Prince of Orange. I knew a little about him now, for he had made himself an important figure on the continent and had become a man of some significance. I wondered if Mary was reconciled to her marriage.

Then I began to question the wisdom of staying here. Perhaps I should have left when I had first planned to do so. I knew that William was a Protestant, a Calvinist, and I believed somewhat puritanical, though there had been rumors that he had not been entirely faithful to his wife. Not in the blatant manner of Charles, of course, but secretly, which suggested that he liked to keep his vices hidden. Elizabeth Villiers, who had gone to Holland with Mary at the time of her marriage, had been his mistress for years, according to rumor, while outwardly he maintained a strict moral attitude. I wondered whether Charles's way was more acceptable.

Perhaps I was prepared to judge William harshly. For some time he had had his eyes on the English crown. He had a claim, of course. His wife, Mary, had been in line for the succession before the birth of the new baby; William himself was the son of another Mary, daughter of the first King Charles. At the birth of James's son, William must have heartily approved of the story of the baby in the warming-pan. In any case, it was clear that he had long decided that the throne of England should be his.

I had been fond of James . . . as Charles had, but how much wiser Charles had been! He had always known that he must never admit the religion he would have preferred to follow . . . at least not until he was on his deathbed. He had made that agreement with Louis that he would change his religion when the time was ripe, knowing that it never would be. If only James had had his brother's foresight. People would say that James deserved his fate, but being fond of him, I could not bear to see him brought so low, deserted by his own daughters. And I must dislike those who had brought him to this state.

It was December. James had fled from the capital and I heard that Lord Feversham had been captured by William's men. I was horrified by the circumstances in which this had taken place, for he had come to William with a message from James, and they had made him a prisoner.

It was evening when one of my ladies came to me in dismay.

"Your Majesty, King William is here. He has come to see you."

I was astonished. "He . . . he must not be kept waiting," I stammered. "Bring him in at once."

There he was. He had changed little from the young man who had come to marry Mary. That must have been ten years ago. He was a small man with little grace, yet I sensed in him great strength.

He bowed rather stiffly. I inclined my head, trying to assume a coolness I did not feel. I was not going to accept him as King yet. If he succeeded in taking the crown, I should have to leave.

He was somewhat tight-lipped and pale; there was a certain fragility in his body which belied the determination of the firm jaw and the piercing alertness of the eyes.

Charles's nephew! I thought. There is no resemblance between them whatsoever.

"Your Majesty," he said, "I have no doubt that you are disturbed by events, and I have come to tell you that my wife and I feel nothing but kindness for you."

"That is gracious of you," I said, with perhaps a touch of asperity.

He feigned not to notice my tone and went on: "I trust you are comfortable here."

"Thank you. I am."

He waved his hand. "I have heard that you like to listen to music and play the cards."

"I do."

"I myself like a game. 'Tis a pleasant pastime, is it not? I see no tables here."

I replied: "My Chamberlain, Lord Feversham, looks after the tables. Since he departed I have not had the heart for cards."

"That must not be. I would not care to think that you are missing so much of what you enjoy. Your Majesty's diversions must continue."

I stared at him in astonishment, and his face twisted into a smile almost reluctantly, as though it were a position in which it rarely found itself.

"Thank you," I said.

He bowed and took his leave. I could not understand why he had come to see me. He was a man who would always have motives. In this case it was the matter of Lord Feversham. It must have been others who had detained him, and it was not ethical to arrest an emissary. William was precise, very much aware of the orderly conduct of diplomacy and he would not tolerate any departure from the rules.

It must have been the reason for his visit, for he was incapable of sentimental feelings. Lord Feversham should never have been detained; therefore he was released, the excuse being that I needed him to organize my card games.

It was a pleasure to see Lord Feversham again. I learned from him something of what was happening throughout the country, and it was far from reassuring.

CHOSE WERE UNEASY DAYS. I was never sure what was going to happen next. It seemed certain that James would leave the country. It would be the best thing he could do, but it was hardly likely that he would not make some effort to return.

Louis would receive him as he had received Mary Beatrice and the Prince of Wales. Once over there, perhaps James would gather a force together and come back to challenge William. I hoped he would not do so, for I was sure such an action could only result in disaster for him. I knew nothing of warfare but instinct told me that in a conflict between them, William must be the victor. Moreover, for years the people had been indicating that they would not accept a Catholic king. Throughout the country they were welcoming William and Mary.

I came to the conclusion that I must delay my departure no longer when a Bill was introduced into the Commons to limit my household, and many of my servants were sent away because they were Catholics. I was angry, but I had to obey. It was distressing to part with so many of my old friends.

James landed in Ireland where he had some support.

I feared for him. I feared for myself, because two or three days before William was due to leave for Ireland, there to do battle with James, I had a visit from Lord Nottingham, Queen Mary's Chamberlain.

He came to Somerset House and asked for an interview . . . perhaps not so much asked as demanded.

He did not treat me with the respect to which I had become

accustomed, and when I asked him what his business was he said I was to move from Somerset House to Windsor or Audley End, as it was understood that at Somerset House there were meetings where certain Catholics were "caballing" in a manner opposed to the King's government.

I pointed out to him that Somerset House was my residence. It had been given to me as part of my marriage settlement and, although I had not received all that was due to me, at least I intended to keep this.

"It is His Majesty's wish that you leave here," said Nottingham.

I refused to be intimidated. I knew that I was unpopular in the country and people did not care what happened to me. I was of no use to William and Mary. I was, in fact, an encumbrance. I supposed that since it was William's policy to remove all privileges from Catholics, I, being one of them, must expect such treatment.

But I would not give in easily.

I said: "Will you please return to King William and tell him that I desire to leave his dominions. If he would provide ships for the voyage, I should be ready to leave without delay. If he does not do this, I intend to stay in this house, which is undoubtedly mine by treaty."

Nottingham was astounded, but not more so than I when I received William's reply.

Here again he showed his respect for law. He knew that, by right, Somerset House belonged to me.

He was apologetic. There had been a mistake. If I wished to stay at my residence of Somerest House I must do so and not think of leaving.

It was a triumph—though a small one.

I had expected Mary to remember me with affection. We had, as I thought, been fond of each other in the past, but she was beginning to show a certain animosity toward me.

Although she had gone into her marriage with great reluctance, she now seemed devoted to her husband, and was urging the nation to pray for his success in Ireland, and caused a prayer to be circulated throughout the country which she ordered to be said in all churches.

I could not pray against James. I regarded him as my brother and he had always been a good friend to me.

"I will not have it said in my chapel," I said to Lord Feversham.

"Then," he replied, "it shall be excluded."

All might have been well but for the gossip. There were a number of Protestants in my household since the expulsion of my Catholic servants, and it was not long before Mary heard that prayers for her husband's success had not been said in my chapel.

Questions were asked and the priest in charge was arrested.

He confessed that he had acted on the orders of Queen Catherine's Chamberlain.

As a result of this Lord Feversham was summoned to an audience with the Queen.

How I wished she had asked me to visit her instead of Lord Feversham. I was very anxious that he should not be blamed for what was entirely my decision.

Lord Feversham returned in a state of some concern.

"Queen Mary is very angry," he said. "Alas, she blames you. She says a closer watch should be kept on you because she doubts your loyalty to King William and herself."

"Why does she behave so?" I cried. "She used to be so different. She sounds as though she hates me."

"She stands beside her husband now," said Lord Feversham. "Everyone who is not his friend is her enemy. Your Majesty will have to act with care."

How right he was.

I must get into touch with my brother. I knew most definitely now that there was no place for me here.

IT WAS THREE YEARS before I was able to leave.

During that time William was victorious in the famous battle of the Boyne and James retired to France. His defeat was final. William and Mary were the acknowledged King and Queen of England. The country settled down. The people had determined they would not be ruled by James and they had had their way.

Indeed, there was no place for me in England, and I knew I must leave as soon as possible.

But it was not until the March of that year 1692—thirty years after I had first set foot in England—that I was able to leave.

PORTUGAL

IT WAS WITH MIXED EMOTIONS THAT I WENT. I WAS TOR-
tured with memories of my arrival all those years ago, and Charles
was often in my thoughts.

It was hard to accept that I wanted to leave—but England was a
new country under William and Mary. It was no longer Merry England. Morals had changed. If the King did have a mistress this was
discreetly hidden. He was never seen dallying with her in the apartments or sauntering in the park. That behavior belonged to another
age. There were many who said the change was good for the country,
and they may have been right.

Yet how I longed for those earlier days—but I had to look ahead.

I was taking a few of my household with me, among them the
Countess of Fingall. It showed the depth of their affection for me that
they wanted to come. They could not be sure what would happen in
my native land—and I was not able to tell them.

On landing in France, I was received with honor at Louis's command. He invited me to break my journey with a stay at his court.

I sent a grateful message back to him, but I told him I could not
stay with him, as I must not disappoint my brother who was expecting me. I knew Louis's methods. He would want to control me in
matters of state.

I must be free of that. I wanted peace. I often thought of the Villa
Viçosa and how my father had longed to return to it. I understood his
feelings well—more now than I ever did. I, too, just wanted to live
quietly.

Moreover, I had not been in the best of health. During the journey I suffered from an attack of erysipelas—a most distressing, disfig-
uring disease which made me feel that I wanted to shut myself away
and see no one.

My brother had sent a party to meet me and accompany me across Spain, so when I felt so ill I had help at hand. Pedro had had news of my indisposition and sent Dr. Antonio Medes, his chief physician, to me. That was a great relief, for I soon recovered under his care, and by the time I reached Lisbon I was entirely well.

I was greeted with great acclaim by the people of my homeland. I was deeply moved. It was wonderful to know that they wanted me here. The people of England had never really liked me. How different this was! Here they still remembered that it was my marriage to England which helped free Portugal from the grip of the tyrant Spain.

And there was Pedro. He had changed . . . naturally he would, in thirty years. He had become a man with cares and responsibilities, and this had left its mark. There was a new dignity about him, though.

We gazed at each other in silence for a few moments before we embraced.

"Catherine," he said. "I am so happy to see you. At last you have come home."

"And you, little brother, you have become a king."

He lifted his shoulders . . . and a look of regret crossed his face. I guessed he was thinking of Alfonso—as I was.

He said: "There is much to talk of. First I must present you to the Queen."

This was not the wife of Alfonso, whom he had married when Alfonso was sent to the Azores, leaving his kingdom and his wife to Pedro. She had died some years before, and he was now married to Maria Sophia of the Palatinate of Neuburg.

We exchanged greetings. She was very pleasant and I felt that I could be her friend.

Then Pedro insisted that I must sit in his coach with him and his Queen so that we might ride into the capital together.

What a triumph that entry was! I knew then that I had been right to come.

Later my brother and his Queen took me to the palace they had prepared for me. I was delighted with the Quinta de Alcantara, and when I saw how eager my brother and his wife were that I should have every comfort there, I believed I could be at peace.

→>-<←

AND SO I CAME HOME.

The years are passing, as they do quickly as one grows old.

I am surrounded by good friends. My dear Countess of Fingall left me at the turn of the century. She was longing for her home but she wept at our parting. I shared her sadness, but I understood her need to return. In her place there came my dear Donna Inez Antonia de Tavora, who has become very close to me.

My brother's wife, Maria Sophia, has become a dear friend, and we spend much time together. Pedro is determined that I shall have every comfort and be treated with honor wherever I go. He need have no concern about this. The affection shown me by my country-men and women is spontaneous and comes from the heart. They have known the horrors of war and they can never be grateful enough to me, for they always consider that it was due to my marriage that we emerged from the yoke of oppression.

I am happy now . . . in my way. Frequently I think of Charles. It is almost as though he is with me. I often say to myself: "What would he have said to that?" And I try to conjure up some witty remark. But of course, I could never match his wit.

I try not to think of him, laughing with Barbara Castlemaine, jok-ing with Nell Gwynne, gazing longingly at Frances Stuart, in deep conversation with Louise de Keroualle. Instead I remember him by my bedside when he thought I lay dying. I remember his tenderness when my enemies sought to destroy me. I would think of the song he once wrote, and I felt that the last verse was meant for me:

> But when I consider the truth of her heart
> Such an innocent passion, so kind, without art
> I fear I have wronged her, and hope she may be
> So full of true love to be jealous of me
> O then 'tis I think no joys are above
> The pleasures of love.

I was the innocent one. He wanted my love. He could never be faithful to any one woman, but that did not mean he did not love.

I heard news from England. Mary died a few years after I left and William remained to reign alone.

I was sad to hear of Mary's death and I regretted that we had not been good friends at the end. I believed she realized that I cared too much for her father to like what she and William had done in robbing him of his throne. I reminded myself that she had stood beside her husband. I wondered whether she was haunted by what she had done to the father who had loved her and her sister so devotedly.

I was even more saddened by the death of James himself in the year 1701.

I thought of his life . . . his romance with Anne Hyde, mother of Queen Mary and possibly another Queen, for since William and Mary had had no offspring, Anne would be next. Clarendon's daughter—the mother of Queens. And there was poor Mary Beatrice. What of her son? He must have been thirteen years old at that time.

And what was Princess Anne thinking? I feared she must have felt some remorse at her father's death.

So many deaths . . . so many changes. And there could not be many more years left to me.

I suffered from bouts of ill health. Maria Sophia had felt that the Quinta de Alcantara might not be healthy and I moved for a while to Santa Martha; and after that, as she liked to have me close at hand, I went to Belem near Lisbon.

One day I had a message from my brother. He asked me to come and see him.

I went in some trepidation, for the messenger appeared grave, and I had been worried about Pedro's health for some time.

Before I went to him I saw Maria Sophia. She told me how anxious Pedro was. His responsibilities weighed heavily upon him. She feared he needed rest and he must leave the country in capable hands while he took it.

"He wishes to talk with you about this."

I wondered what advice he expected me to give him.

I sat by his bed. He looked strained and very pale.

"Catherine," he said. "I wish to speak to you most seriously. I am not strong enough to continue. My son is young yet. He could not take over the government . . . I want you to do that . . . for the time being."

"I? You cannot mean that!"

"I do. Remember our mother. What would Portugal have done without her? You remind me of her."

"*I* . . . remind you of her! Pedro, you cannot mean that. She was a great woman."

"Catherine, you are too."

This seemed preposterous, and if I had not been so anxious about him I should have laughed.

"Always you have been too modest," he said. "Listen to me. The people love you. They admire you. They call you their savior."

"It was the English who saved the country, not I."

"Without you there could have been no alliance. They do not forget. If you will not do this, I shall have to rouse myself and . . . I know I cannot last long without rest."

"I cannot believe this."

"You must."

Maria Sophia was watching me. "You do not realize how the people regard you," she said. "They will say you saved them once and they will believe you can do it again."

"Then they endow me with qualities I do not possess."

"It is what they believe," she said. And I remembered a remark of Charles's. "If the people believe it, then it is the truth . . . at least to them."

I had been living in comfortable peace . . . serenely quiet. How could I . . . innocent and without art—the words of Charles's song came back to me—how could I take on this tremendous task?

"You must," said Maria Sophia. "If you do not, what will become of us? What will become of our country?"

"You will have your advisors."

"You mean I shall be a sort of figurehead?"

"You have wisdom, Catherine," said Pedro. "You are our mother again. Remember her. God will help you and with His help you will do it."

HOW SCRANGE IC WAS.

I, Catherine, Regent of Portugal. On every occasion the people cheered me in the streets. They proclaimed their belief in me.

History repeated itself. When my mother had been Regent, the Spaniards attacked; and now here again was a woman, and they attacked once more.

Those days were filled with activity. I gave myself entirely to the task. I felt as though my mother were beside me, applauding. She had believed once that I would save Portugal by my marriage . . . and Portugal had been saved. Now I was to save my country through my government.

I swear that God was on my side. He gave me the wisdom. I could not believe this was myself . . . that Catherine who had made so little impression on the English court. But at least that Catherine had won the love of the most amorous man in the world—a special love—a tender love which I allowed myself to believe he never gave to any other.

Our armies were victorious. When I rode through the streets, I was treated with something like idolatry.

I wished that Charles could have lived to see this. How he would have delighted in my achievement.

Pedro recovered his health and came out of retirement. He and Maria Sophia showed their gratitude and love in every way.

How fortunate I was at the end of my life to come to glory!

That can happen to few.

I AM NOW IN BELEM and well into my sixties. It has been a long life, and when, through my pen, I recall it all . . . the dreams . . . the disillusion . . . the humiliations of the past . . . the triumphs of the present . . . I long to be back in Charles's court, the most licentious of Europe—dominated as it was, and I shall ever be, by the King and the pleasures of love.

Bibliography

Aubrey, William Hickman Smith *The National and Domestic History of England*

Bryant, Arthur *King Charles II*

Burnet, Bishop *History of His Own Time*

Clark, Sir George *The Later Stuarts 1660–1714*

Cunningham, Peter *The Story of Nell Gwyn*

Dasent, Arthur Irin *The Private Life of Charles II*

Evelyn, John *Diaries of Evelyn Pepys, Clarendon and Other Contemporary Writers*

Green, Mary Anne Everett *Lives of the Princesses of England*

Guizot, M. (translated by Robert Black) *History of France*

Hume, David *History of England*

Loth, David *Royal Charles, Ruler and Rake*

Lyon, Rev. C.J. *Personal History of Charles II*

Macaulay, Lord *The History of England*

Montague, F.C. *Political History of England*

Nicoll, Allardyce *A History of English Drama* (1660–1700)

Pepys, Samuel *Diary and Correspondence* Edited by Wheatley, Henry B.

Senior, Dorothy *The Gay King*

Stevens, Sir Leslie and Lee, Sir Sidney *The Dictionary of National Biography*

Strickland, Agnes *Lives of the Queens of England*

Wade, John *British History*

Reader's Group Guide

ABOUT THIS BOOK

CATHERINE OF BRAGANZA was raised during a tumultuous time in Portugal. Although her father was called King Juan IV, the Pope (due to pressure from Spain) refused to recognize him as anything other than a duke. Looking for an advantageous political alliance, Catherine's mother, Donna Luiza, sets her sights on the English throne. Even when Oliver Cromwell takes power in England, Donna Luiza does not lose hope in marrying Catherine to the young Prince Charles, and when Charles is restored to England's throne, marriage negotiations begin immediately.

Catherine's marriage, like so many royal marriages, is arranged out of strategy, yet Catherine and Charles begin their lives happily together. As a Catholic, she is not trusted by the people—they believe she will convert Charles, just as his brother James had been converted by their mother. Catherine spends her marriage as Queen in name, yet is sadly unable to keep her merry husband King in her bed. Her inability to produce an heir, despite the fact that all of Charles's mistresses have healthy boys, sets the people of England and the court strongly against her. Charles, however, remains faithful to Catherine by never divorcing her, not even to legitimize at least one of his "bastard" sons.

Outliving her husband and witnessing the brief reign of James II before the co-regents, William and Mary, overthrow the Catholic king, Catherine returns to Portugal as her life comes full circle.

The questions in this guide are intended as a framework for your group's discussion of *The Merry Monarch's Wife*.

QUESTIONS FOR DISCUSSION

1. Religion plays an important part in this novel. There is very little tension between Charles and Catherine over religion, yet Catherine's Catholicism matters deeply to the people of England. Why was religion so important?

2. Charles has many children out of wedlock, the most famous being James Crofts, the Duke of Monmouth. Why is Charles so indulgent of Jemmy? Do you believe that he was behind any of the plots to murder Charles? Why does Charles never legitimize him?

3. While still in Portugal, Donna Maria tells Catherine on p. 28 "The King cannot come here and you cannot go into a strange country as an unmarried woman." If this was the case, how was it that Catherine went to England unmarried?

4. Charles says to Catherine at the beginning of their marriage, "You are completely unworldly. You reason like a child." (p. 78) Is this true? How does Catherine change by the end of the novel?

5. Charles famously dislikes conflict. On p. 267 Catherine states, "I knew how he hated trouble, how his great desire was to live a life of comfort and pleasure." Do you believe that this is the reason he stayed married to Catherine, or did he really love her?

6. Donna Luiza's advice to Catherine regarding Lady Castlemaine is simple: "You should treat her as though she does not exist." Does Catherine follow her mother's advice? What would you do in that situation?

7. Buckingham says to Catherine: "You have at least one good and faithful servant—your noble Master of Horse. I'll warrant he is always ready at hand to give good service to his mistress." (p. 140) After this statement, Edward Montague is dismissed from his service as Master

of Horse. Were you surprised by this, as Catherine was? Does it seem fair that Charles is allowed his mistresses yet Catherine cannot have a male friend?

8. Frances Stuart was a chaste and innocent girl who loved to play the house of cards game. What, if anything, do you think this game signifies?

9. Charles is referred to as "merry" throughout the novel. What does that word mean to you? Do you think Plaidy portrays him as a "merry monarch"?

10. Charles had two mistresses who were both important at the same time in his life, Louise de Keroualle and Nell Gwynne. Discuss their differences and similarities.

11. Who was Captain Blood? Discuss his plot to steal the Crown Jewels. Why did Charles find this so amusing?

12. Discuss the importance of having an heir. Catherine was dismayed when she was unable to have a healthy child, and it further tarnished her reputation with the people of England. Lady Castlemaine, Nell Gwynne, Louise de Keroualle, and Lucy Walter all had sons. How would you feel if you were Catherine? What would you do in her situation?

13. Why was James unable to keep the throne? Do you believe he would have had the people's love, support, and protection had he been Protestant?

14. After the kindness that Catherine shows Mary as a young girl, how did you feel about the way Mary treated Catherine when she and William take the throne? Lord Feversham says, "Queen Mary is very angry. . . . She says a closer watch should be kept on you because she doubts your loyalty to King William and herself." (p. 312)

15. There is a quote from Charles that begins the book and then appears in the last chapter:

> *But when I consider the truth of her heart*
> *Such an innocent passion, so kind, without art*
> *I fear I have wronged her, and hope she may be*
> *So full of true love to be jealous of me*
> *O then 'tis I think no joys are above*
> *The pleasures of love.*

Do you think this was written for Catherine? Discuss.

An Excerpt from

CHE QUEEN'S DEVOTION

EARLY DAYS

THERE HAVE BEEN TWO PEOPLE IN MY LIFE WHOM I HAVE loved beyond all others, and it has always weighed heavily upon me that I was called upon to decide between them and, in choosing one, I betrayed the other. I did what my heart, my faith, my sense of duty dictated, and ever since I have suffered from the torment of knowing of the pain I inflicted and from which I myself will suffer to the end of my days.

I want to go right back to the beginning, to project myself into the past, to see it more clearly than I could when it was happening. I want to ask myself: what should I have done?

I was born in St. James's Palace at a time when my birth was of little interest to any except my parents, for a most significant event was taking place. My uncle, King Charles, recently restored to his throne after more than ten years' exile, was about to marry the Infanta of Portugal—an event which generated great excitement and expectation throughout the country. In any case, I was only a girl, and fifteen months after my birth, a boy was born to my parents, a fact which robbed my birth of any importance it might have had.

In the beginning the world was a wonderful place; the days were full of sunshine; I was surrounded by people who loved me and, being cherished by all, I was led to believe that the world had been created for my pleasure.

The best times of all were when my parents visited us. Everyone was so respectful to them that I quickly realized how important they were. My mother would take me up into her arms. She was like a big soft cushion into which I could sink with a feeling of cozy security. She would caress me, murmur words of love to me, and pop a sweetmeat into my mouth and show me in a hundred ways how much she loved me. But the most important of all was my father. When he came into the nursery crying: "Where is my little daughter? Where is the Lady Mary?" I would stagger or toddle and later run to him, and he would pick me up and set me on his shoulder so that I could look down on everything from my lofty perch. I loved all those around me but no one so much as I loved my father.

Once I heard someone say: "The Duke loves the little Mary beyond all others."

I never forgot that and I used to say it to myself when I was in my bed alone. I would listen for his coming; and often in later years, when I was haunted by memories of the fate which had overtaken him, I would recall those days and, sickened with doubts and self-reproaches, I would contemplate the part I had played in his tragedy.

How often then did I sigh for those days of my youthful innocence, when I thought the world a beautiful place in which I should be happy forever.

When he visited us he would not let me out of his sight. I remember an occasion when he even received some of his officers to discuss some naval matter and he kept me there with him. He was Lord High Admiral of England then and I remember his seating me on the table while he talked to them; and, to please him, I know now, the men commented on the extraordinary intelligence, vitality and charm of his daughter—and how delighted he was.

Sometimes it is difficult to know whether I really remember certain incidents from those days or whether they were talked of so frequently that I convince myself I do.

There is a miniature of me painted by Nechscher, a Flemish artist of whom my father thought highly. I am holding a black rabbit. They told me how my father used to join us at the sittings and watch me fondly while the artist was working. In my mind's eye I can see him clearly, but was I really aware of him at the time?

There are some days which I do remember and I can be certain of this. I was nearly three years old. It was cold, for it was the month of February. I knew something important was taking place. Snatches of overheard conversations came to me.

"I hope the Duke and Duchess will get what they want this time."

"Well, I don't know. The boys are sickly and I reckon he wouldn't change the Lady Mary for all the boys in Christendom."

When my father came to see me, after the usual rapturous greeting, he said: "You will be happy to hear, my daughter, that you have a little sister."

I remember my bewilderment. A little sister? I already had a little brother. There were always nurses around him and he did not mean a great deal to me.

"She will join you here," went on my father, "and you will love her, dearly."

"You love her?" I asked.

I must have shown my father that I feared she might supplant me in his affections, for he gave me a smile of immediate understanding.

"I love her," he said. "But whoever came, it would always be the Lady Mary who had first place in my heart."

Excitement followed. Young as I was, I was to stand as sponsor for my sister; and Anne Scot, the Duchess of Buccleugh, was to be the other. Later I learned that this honor had been bestowed on her because she had recently married my cousin Jemmy, who had become the Duke of Monmouth.

I certainly remember that occasion well. It was presided over by Gilbert Sheldon, who was the Archbishop of Canterbury at the time, a very stern and formidable man of whom I should have been very much in awe but for the presence of my powerful father who would never be stern with me, or allow anyone else to be.

The new baby was christened Anne, after our mother, and in due course she joined the nursery at Twickenham.

THE HOUSE IN TWICKENHAM belonged to my grandfather—my mother's father, the Earl of Clarendon. He was a very important man, I realized, though I saw him rarely. There was another grandfather, whose name was always spoken in hushed whispers because he was dead, and when I was very young indeed I knew there had been something very shocking about his death.

Some people called him The Martyr. Later I learned that he had been king and that wicked men had cut off his head. I shivered every time I rode past that spot in Whitehall where they had performed this dreadful deed.

I was growing very fond of the new baby. My sister Anne was a placid child. She rarely cried and smiled readily. She was always eager for her food and everyone was delighted because of this. I was with her a great deal, and thought of her as my baby. She seemed to like me to sit near her cradle. She gripped my finger in her dimpled hand so tightly when I held it out to her and I found that endearing.

And then suddenly the peace of Twickenham was shattered. There was commotion everywhere; people were running back and forth, all talking at once. I had to find out what was wrong.

Then I heard that one of the maids had been found dead in her bed. There was no mystery as to how this had happened. It seemed they had thought we were safe at Twickenham, but the dreaded plague which had been sweeping through London had reached us here.

"The Plague!" Those words were on everybody's lips.

My parents arrived. I was caught up in my father's arms. Anne and my brother were examined by our mother. My father did the same to me.

"Praise be to God!" he cried. "Mary is well. And Anne and the boy?"

"All is well," said my mother.

"There is no time to be lost. We must leave at once."

The next thing I remember is riding away from Twickenham and on to York.

I WAS HAPPY IN YORK. The time sped by. We saw our parents more often there, although my father was absent now and then for long spells which seemed intolerable. The Fleet was at that time stationed on the East Coast and he was often with it.

There was war as well as plague. We knew little of that in York until we heard of the glorious victories not only off the coast of Lowestoft but also at Solebay.

These names sent a glow of pride in me for years after because my father was always mentioned in connection with them. He had been in charge of the Fleet which had beaten our wicked enemies, the Dutch. I loved to hear of his successes. I only regretted that he had to go so far away from us to do these wonderful deeds.

I heard one of the attendants say: "These victories will bring a little comfort, and the Lord knows, we need it in these terrible times."

I had heard only a little of the scourge which was sweeping through the country and devastating the capital. All it meant to me was that we had had to leave in a hurry for York, where I saw more of my parents than I had in Twickenham. It was only after that I heard accounts of the red crosses on the doors with the words "God have Mercy on us," which meant that there was plague in the house. I did not hear until much later of the macabre death carts which roamed the streets, and the dismal cry of "Bring out your dead," and how the bodies which were piled into those carts were taken to pits outside the city walls where they were hastily buried.

It was much later when I heard of the terrible tragedy which had followed the plague year, when London faced another monumental catastrophe and was almost completely destroyed by fire.

And when I did hear in lurid detail of the horrors of those burning buildings, of weeping, homeless people, of the crafts on the river into which they crowded with as many of their belongings as they could hope to save, my thoughts were dominated by two men, the brothers who had gone out unceremoniously into the streets, wigless, short sleeves rolled up, sweat streaming from their faces while they gave instructions and supervised the blowing up of buildings to make gaps and so stop the fire spreading further. For those two men were the King and my father, his brother, the Duke of York.

He was a hero, my clever, wonderful father. He had saved the country from the Dutch at Lowestoft and Solebay as he had helped to save London from that all-consuming fire.

Of course, I learned all this later. In the meantime I was kept in my cocoon of safety.

The memories of York were of days of great happiness, broken only by occasional clouds when my father disappeared for a while. Then I heard that his absences would be even longer, because the King had summoned him to attend Parliament, which was now held in Oxford, because of the state of the capital.

Then my dismay was great, but he consoled me by saying he would come to see me whenever he could.

"When you are older, I will tell you all about it," he said. "Now all you have to do is wait and as soon as I am free I shall be here to see my little Lady Mary."

"I will come with you to Oxford," I said hopefully.

"Ah! What a pleasure that would be!" he replied, smiling. "But, alas, there is no place for little girls in the King's Parliament. But one day . . . soon . . . we shall all be together . . . your little brother, your little sister, your mother . . . the whole family of York."

It was a long time before we were.

And so I was growing up. There were times when I was vaguely aware of trouble. My grandfather Clarendon suddenly disappeared from the scene. We had never seen a great deal of him, but it seemed strange when his name ceased to be mentioned. I knew he had been very important and Lord Chancellor and a friend of the King and my father, having been with them when they were in exile. He was my mother's father, so it seemed strange that we should stop speaking of him.

I did hear someone say that he was lucky to have escaped to exile before he lost his head. There was enough against him to bring about his downfall, and his continual carping at the King's way of life meant that even that long-suffering monarch was eager to be rid of him.

I was bemused by these scraps of gossip which I tried hard to understand. I had one grandfather who had lost his head; and here was another who, it appeared, had escaped in time before being deprived of his.

I knew my mother was deeply affected by his departure and I believed my father was, too.

But when they were with us, they were always their affectionate selves. I think my sister Anne was my mother's favorite, though Anne did not resemble her at all except in looks. I had heard it said: "The Lady Mary is Stuart from head to toe. The Lady Anne is a Hyde." I was tall and at that age slender, dark-haired with rather long almond-shaped eyes. Anne was always plump; her hair was light brown with a reddish tinge in it. I was pale; she was rosy. She would have been very pretty but for a slight deformity of the eyes. Her lids were contracted a little which gave her a rather vague look. It had affected her sight in some way.

Anne was very good-natured, rarely cross and fundamentally lazy.

She did not like trouble of any sort and, in her sunny, good-natured way, she made a very good job of avoiding it. When she was tired of doing something, and as we grew older that particularly meant lessons, she made the excuse that her eyes hurt.

We were very happy together in those days. She laughed at me for wanting to learn about everything.

"You do it, sister," she would say, "and then you can tell me all about it."

I quickly realized that my mother was reckoned to be clever. It was true that she often decided what was to be done. My father used to say: "You are right, of course, my dear." She was very friendly with a great number of the serious people at court. I had heard the King refer to her as "my serious-minded, clever sister-in-law." I was rather surprised that she should have doted so fondly on Anne, who had little to say and refused to learn. Their only common interest seemed to be their love of sweet foods. Many times I had seen them sitting close, a dish of sweetmeats between them, and they would be eating all the time.

There was an occasion when the physicians pointed out that my sister was growing unhealthily fat and could damage her health if she did not give up the habit of consuming sweetmeats at every opportunity.

My mother was frightened. Perhaps she blamed herself for allowing her daughter to share her own weakness. In any case, Anne was sent away for a while with one of my mother's ladies. She was to be watchful of what Anne ate and my mother could trust her friends to keep a sharper eye on my sister in a different house than in her own, for there she suspected that her friends would give way to her pleadings for more of the sweetmeats she loved so much.

I was very sad to lose my sister. Life was not the same without her good-natured smiles. I pictured her on a strict diet, deprived of her sweetmeats. Perhaps she was taking it all in her good-tempered manner.

It was a happy day when she returned, good-natured as ever and, if not exactly thin, less rotund than she had been.

Everyone declared that the cure had been a miraculous one, but it soon became clear that the temptation presented by a dish of

sweetmeats was still irresistible. However, we were all so delighted to
have her back that we could only smile at her indulgences.

During Anne's absence I missed her so much that my parents decided I must have a companion to compensate me for the loss of my
sister and, to my great joy, Anne Trelawny joined the household. She
was a few years older than I and we were firm friends from the beginning. It was wonderful to have someone to confide in; and Anne was
sympathetic, understanding and all that I could ask for in a friend.

My sister Anne must always have what I had and when she came
home and saw that I had a friend, she must have one too.

She made this desire known to our mother who immediately set
about looking for someone suitable.

She had been particularly interested in one of the maids of honor,
a certain Frances Jennings who came from a family of somewhat ob-
scure origins. It was something of a mystery that she should be received at court, but Frances herself was very engaging—not exactly
beautiful, but attractive and quick-witted. My mother, herself of a
lively mind, liked to have people of her own sort about her, and she
was more attracted to intelligence than ancient lineage. Hence she
took a special interest in Frances and when a connection of the noble
house of Hamilton was attracted by her, my mother helped to advance the match.

Frances had a younger sister, Sarah, whom she was anxious to
bring to court and when the young girl was introduced to my mother,
she found her very bright indeed. She was about five years older than
my sister Anne, which seemed no drawback, and she would, my
mother was sure, be a lively, entertaining companion for our somewhat lethargic Anne.

A position in our household was naturally accepted with alacrity
by the ambitious Frances for her sister, and I am sure now that from
the moment Sarah entered our household, she was fully aware of the
advantages which had opened up for her.

She knew exactly how to behave with Anne and, almost from
the day of her arrival, they were the closest friends. We were a happy
quartet: Anne Trelawny and myself, my sister Anne and Sarah
Jennings.

Then a certain anxiety crept into my mind. I felt something was
not quite right. My mother had changed. She seemed a little absent-

minded at times. She would smile and nod but her thoughts seemed elsewhere. In spite of her plumpness, there was a drawn look about her face. I noticed that its color had changed. Her skin had a strange yellowish tinge and now and then she would put her hand to her breast and wince.

I thought at first that she was anxious because her father had gone away, and when I thought of what I should feel if I lost mine, I could understand her sorrow. But there was only one Duke of York and Lady Mary; and no father and daughter loved each other as we did. My mother had lost her father, who had run away to save his head. But there was something else. Once I saw her walking in the gardens with Father Hunt, a Franciscan; and they were talking earnestly together.

I knew that Father Hunt was a Catholic and I was sure that Gilbert Sheldon, Archbishop of Canterbury, would not be very pleased to see my mother in close conversation with him. Then I saw my father join them and the three of them walked off talking closely together.

I did not think very much about that at the time, until I heard that the people did not like my uncle's marriage to Catherine of Braganza, because she was a Catholic, and the English did not like Catholics.

This and the change in my mother's looks were like vague shadows, but so slight that they did not linger long in the warm sunshine of those happy days.

MY MOTHER WAS GOING to have a baby. That was the reason for her being ill, I supposed. She was so plump and her figure so round that her pregnancy was scarcely noticeable.

Anne and I eagerly waited to hear whether we should have a little brother or sister. We hoped for a sister. Brothers were a disappointment. They were always ill.

To our delight it was a little girl. They named her Catherine, in honor of the Queen.

We talked a great deal about her—or rather, I talked and Anne listened. Anne preferred to listen. Sometimes I thought she was getting more and more lazy.

My father came to see us. It was a cold day in March and the year was 1671. I was at that time nearly nine years old and Anne already six. I was greatly alarmed because I saw the pain and suffering in my father's face.

He sat down and, putting an arm round each of us, drew us to him and held us closely. Sobs shook his body. I was filled with horror as well as sadness to see my invincible hero so broken with grief.

"My dearest daughters," he said. "The most terrible of calamities has befallen us. How can I tell you? Your mother . . . your mother . . ."

I kissed him tenderly, which only made him weep the more.

He said: "Children, you have no mother now."

"Where has she gone?" asked Anne.

"To heaven, my child."

"Dead . . . ?" I whispered.

He nodded.

"But she was here . . ."

"She was so brave. She knew it could not be long. She was very ill indeed. There was nothing that could be done to save her. My children, you have only your father now."

I clung to him: so did Anne.

He told us that he had been with her at the end. She had died in his arms. She had died happy . . . in the way she wished. We must try not to grieve. We must think of her happy with the angels in the true faith of the Lord.

We were bewildered. We could not believe that we should never see our mother again. Neither of us could visualize what our lives would be like without her. There would be changes.

We were soon to discover that.

We had lost her, yes. But there was something more than that. What we did not know then was that, on her deathbed, she had received the *viaticum* of the Church of Rome and that my father was also wavering toward the Catholic faith.

Unfortunately, my father was not keeping this a secret. He was too honest. He believed he would be false to his faith if he tried to disguise it. I was to learn that he was a man of very little judgment. Already he had taken the first step which was to lead to disaster. And we children, because he was after all his brother's heir, were not without importance to the State.

So there were changes. In view of his religious leanings, which were becoming public knowledge, the Duke of York could no longer be allowed to supervise his children's upbringing, and because of their position in the country, it was necessary for the King to take the matter in hand.

About the Author

JEAN PLAIDY is the pen name of the prolific English author Eleanor Hibbert, also known as Victoria Holt. More than 14 million copies of her books have been sold worldwide.
Visit www.CrownHistorical.com to learn of other Jean Plaidy titles available from Three Rivers Press.

Read Jean Plaidy's
Queens of England series
in historical order:

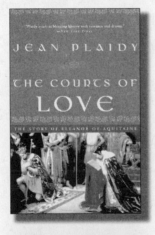

The Courts of Love
The Story of Eleanor of Aquitaine

AVAILABLE NOW FROM
THREE RIVERS PRESS

1

The Queen's Secret
The Story of Queen Katherine

AVAILABLE NOW FROM
THREE RIVERS PRESS

2

The Reluctant Queen
The Story of Anne of York

AVAILABLE NOW FROM
THREE RIVERS PRESS

The Lady in the Tower
The Story of Anne Boleyn

AVAILABLE NOW FROM
THREE RIVERS PRESS

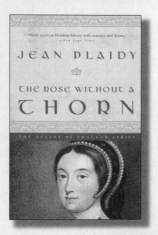

The Rose Without a Thorn
The Story of Katherine Howard

AVAILABLE NOW FROM
THREE RIVERS PRESS

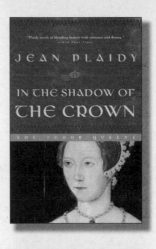

In the Shadow of the Crown
The Story of Mary Tudor

AVAILABLE NOW FROM
THREE RIVERS PRESS

6

Queen of This Realm
Memoir of Elizabeth I

AVAILABLE NOW FROM
THREE RIVERS PRESS

7

Loyal in Love
Henrietta Maria, Queen of Charles I

previously published as
Myself My Enemy
AVAILABLE NOW FROM
THREE RIVERS PRESS

8

The Merry Monarch's Wife
The Story of Catherine
of Bragnaza

previously published as
The Pleasures of Love
AVAILABLE NOW FROM
THREE RIVERS PRESS

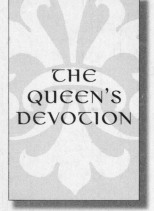

The Queen's Devotion
Princess Mary of York,
Daughter of James II,
Wife of William of Orange

previously published as
William's Wife
AVAILABLE FROM
THREE RIVERS PRESS
IN SUMMER '08

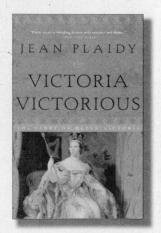

Victoria Victorious
Memoir of Queen Victoria
AVAILABLE NOW FROM
THREE RIVERS PRESS